Clay Country

Rowena Summers
Clay Country

CANELO

First published in Great Britain in 1987 by Severn House Publishers Ltd by arrangement with Sphere Books Ltd

This edition published in the United Kingdom in 2020 by

Canelo Digital Publishing Limited
Third Floor, 20 Mortimer Street
London W1T 3JW
United Kingdom

Print ISBN 978 1 78863 849 4
Ebook ISBN 978 1 78863 468 7

Look for more great books at www.canelo.co

Printed and bound in Great Britain by Clays Ltd, Elcograf S.p.A.

'As we entered St Austell we were met by several carts loaded with barrels containing a white earthy substance, which on enquiry we understood to be the porcelain earth.'

Reverend Richard Warner, 1809

Chapter One

Fielding's Tea Room was as crowded as ever on the mellow spring afternoon. The Misses Fielding who owned and managed it, welcomed their newest customer with a small twist of envy. The young woman with the beautiful black hair and deep blue eyes and the innocent air of being someone special epitomised everything they had vainly envied in their youth.

Like most people in the town, they knew that Morwen Killigrew had humble beginnings. A bal maiden at a clay works was hardly the expected background for the wife of the young owner of Killigrew Clay... but few who knew her begrudged her the status.

Miss Fielding moved quickly to hold a chair for Mrs Killigrew, and Morwen sat down gracefully, with none of the elaborate fuss of some of the good dames of St Austell town. She gave Miss Fielding a smile as warm as the day, as she ordered hot tea and fruit buns.

'Will 'ee be wanting them now, Mrs Killigrew, or will your mother be joining 'ee today?' Miss Fielding asked.

'Yes she will, so I'll wait for her to arrive, thank you.' Morwen answered carefully, as though she had behaved as graciously every day of her life.

She glanced around the Tea Room, nodding to the other ladies, and resisting the laughter that bubbled inside at the absurdity of being so elegant. She was serene and poised, but inwardly burned all the fire and vitality that had made Ben

Killigrew want her so badly. Four years of marriage had only strengthened their love, however mis-matched the town had once thought them, and Morwen was fiercely proud of him.

It was Ben who had relieved the town of the dangers of the heavy clay waggons thundering through the narrow cobbled streets, and built the fine new rail tracks that carried Killigrew's clay blocks to Charlestown port.

Because of his efforts the streets of the town were no longer white with clouds of clay dust from Killigrew's Clay Works. Several smaller works still used the old method of transporting the clay to the port, but Killigrew's had prospered and expanded, thanks to Ben's keen eye for business.

Morwen's mouth watered as the aroma of hot fruit buns spiced the air in the Tea Room. It was odd that fruit buns were the Misses Fielding's speciality. On this very site the terrible accident had happened... it had been Nott's bakery then, and he had baked delicious fruit buns too. Those who remembered, all referred to him now as poor old Nott...

Morwen shivered faintly. Yet the Tea Room had long since become a friendly meeting-place, on one of St Austell's steeply winding cobbled hills. It was clinically clean, transformed from the old steamy bakery, and betraying none of the terror that had struck the building on that horrific night... Morwen was one who would never forget.

She had seen the carnage left by the clay waggon, driven by the drunken, desperate clayworkers trying to make a few shillings by the illegal transport of clay blocks during the clay strike. The badly-loaded waggon had torn through Nott's bakery, killing men and horses and poor old Nott too. She and Ben had been among those who had scrabbled through the wreckage trying to help, and she had been sickened at seeing what remained of clay men that she knew...

2

The bell above the Tea Room door tinkled, and Morwen blinked quickly, away from old memories that still haunted her at times, her eyes gladdening as she saw the familiar figure of her mother.

Bess Tremayne was a little stouter now than when she too had worked as a bal maiden at Killigrew Clay Works, but she said cheerfully that if that was the result of life in the snug house rented to them by Ben's father, and her adored sedentary occupation of seamstress, then it was a small price to pay.

'I thought you were never coming, Mammie!' Morwen exclaimed. She spoke in the soft lilting voice that had refused to lose its accent despite her advancement in the world, and which had charmed Ben so effortlessly.

Her mother smiled, seeing Morwen's poised mask slip, and her natural impatience show through. 'I've been wrangling with Freddie. He's still pestering to be sent away to this posh school he's heard about. The schoolteacher came to see us, and says Freddie's too bright to stay at school here, and he thinks he could get a scholarship place in London. Can you imagine Freddie wanting to go away to school? Your Daddy's dead against it, and 'twill still cost us money for clothes and books—'

'It would be a fine chance for him, Mammie, and if it's money you're worrying over, I'm sure Ben would help. He's a strong believer in schooling—'

'We don't want no more of Ben's money, lamb. If 'tis decided that Freddie goes away to school, then your Daddy and me will see to it, and I know our Sam will help if necessary,' Bess said tartly.

'With a wife and babbies of his own to support?' Morwen felt the twist in her heart as she spoke the words. Her brother Sam had married his Dora a few months before she and Ben

3

had been wed in Penwithick church. In four years Dora had produced two lusty boys, and a new baby girl had arrived not three months ago, while Morwen herself was still childless, to her searing disappointment.

But that wasn't what she had been so impatient to see her mother about today. Miss Fielding brought their order, and Morwen drew a deep breath as Bess took a drink of tea and cut through the fruit bun like the towns ladies did.

'Who do you think I saw on the way here, Mammie?'

Bess looked quizzical, glad to see that empty look disappear from Morwen's lovely brow. Morwen and Ben were so much in love, so passionate a pair of love-birds... it was inexplicable to Bess that they hadn't conceived a child yet. But it did no good to dwell on it, and she spoke lightly.

'You know I'm no good at guessing games, so you'd best tell me and put me out of my misery!'

'Hannah Pascoe!'

Bess stared at her daughter. There could be nothing wonderful about that meeting! There was no love lost between Morwen and Ben's waspish aunt, who had once been house-keeper at Killigrew House, and undoubtedly still resented the fact that Morwen was now its mistress.

'I fail to see how that could charm 'ee, Morwen! Did the old biddy even give 'ee the time of day?' Bess chuckled quietly as she lapsed into the old country dialect, so the elegant townsladies at the other tables couldn't hear.

'She gave me more than that! She sniffed and snorted as usual, looked me up and down as though I was an insect, and then asked if I'd had any news of that pale brother of mine who'd gone off with her son—'

Bess's eyes flashed dangerously, as blue as her daughter's and all the Tremaynes at that moment. Morwen put a calming hand over her mother's needle-pricked fingers.

''Tis only her way, Mammie, and she can't hurt me any more. Anyway, I was more curious to know why she was asking after our Matt. I thought you would be too—'

'Of course I am! But I doubt she'd have more news than we do, and that's precious little.'

She couldn't quite keep the bitterness out of her voice. In more than four years, they had heard very little from Matt, the second Tremayne son. Bess loved her close-knit family dearly, and mourned him privately as though he were dead. He might as well be, to be across the sea in America with Jude Pascoe, the son of the awful woman Morwen spoke about. Jude Pascoe was the bad influence in Matt's life, and Bess stubbornly refused to see that it was Matt's own weakness that had been his downfall. God knew how they fared now…

'Hannah Pascoe said she'd had a long letter from – her son.' Morwen still couldn't bring herself to speak his name with ease, though not solely for the same reason as her mother. She had more grievances against Jude Pascoe than his merely luring her brother away from home and family, but they were known only to herself and Ben.

'Did he mention our Matt, then?' Bess looked eager now, and Morwen smiled crookedly on reflecting that, according to his mother, Jude Pascoe had been sorely aggrieved.

It sometimes shocked Morwen to know how much she still hated Jude Pascoe… if she allowed her Cornish fancies to intrude she could even begin wondering if it was a punishment on her to be barren because of Jude Pascoe… but those thoughts were quickly squashed because that was the way madness lay. And strictly speaking, he had not physically harmed Morwen herself… though the girl he had harmed had been closer to Morwen than a twin…

'Well, are you going to tell me or not?' Bess demanded. Morwen might be all of twenty-one years and a young matron, but sometimes she could tease with a secret as capriciously as young Freddie, nine years her junior. And if there was news of Matthew, then Bess wanted to know it.

'Hannah Pascoe says the two boys didn't stay together very long after they started working at the docks in New York,' Morwen said quickly, feeling a vast relief in the knowledge. 'Matt heard about some gold diggings in a place in the west of America called California. He left New York with a waggon-train to go there and make his fortune!'

Bess's mouth dropped open in astonishment at these glib words. The names meant nothing to either of them, but Morwen meant to find them on Ben's atlas the minute she got home that afternoon.

Ben himself spent a lot of time poring over the atlas in his father's old study, following the progress of the war in the Crimea, and sometimes exclaiming over names of old college friends whose exploits were reported in the London newspapers sent to him every week. Old friends who were now army Captains, and clearly important. It all seemed so far away to Morwen, and nothing to do with them… but now she too had a reason for studying the atlas.

Bess was impatient to know more. 'What's this waggon-train? Like the clay waggons, d'you mean? Or a train like the little one on Ben's rail tracks?'

'I don't know! I'm just telling you what Mrs Pascoe told me. Her son thinks our Matt's deserted him by going off to California—'

'And a good thing too,' Bess said keenly. 'I feel a mite happier knowing our Matt's not with that roughneck any longer. So perhaps when he's settled we'll be getting a letter from un soon. I'll look out for it.'

Morwen covered her mother's hand with her own again, and gave it a squeeze.

'Don't be too hopeful, Mammie,' she said gently. 'Our Matt made his choice. He knows he could come home any time—'

She left the sentence unfinished. If Matt had wanted to come back, or to get in touch with them more frequently, there had been nothing to stop him. It was something Bess could never accept. Morwen changed the conversation.

'How goes everything with you and Daddy?'

'Fair to middlin' as ever.' Bess spoke in an understatement. She and Hal were sometimes as lovey-dovey as the young uns, now they had space to breathe, and solid walls between them and the children after the cramped cottage on the moors where Sam and his family now lived. Morwen smiled, seeing the cloud lift from her mother's brow.

She loved this weekly meeting with her mother, gossiping in the little Tea Room the way the townsladies did. Old Charles Killigrew had known a thing or two when he'd told her how much she would enjoy it, once her parents moved to the small house he'd put at their disposal all those years ago. This small lull in the weekly routine of their lives was a genteel pleasure she and Bess relished, the more so because it was a way of life neither had foreseen in the old days.

From bal maiden to owner's wife was spectacular enough for Morwen herself. But for her family too, life had changed. Her father was now Works Manager of Killigrew Clay; her oldest brother Sam was pit captain of Clay One works, stepping into her Daddy's shoes as smoothly as though they were made

7

on the same last; her Mammie was happy with the new house and the sewing, acknowledged as an expert seamstress; young Freddie was a bright lad who must surely get his chance at the schooling… and Jack…

'You haven't mentioned our Jack, Mammie. Is he still hanging on to Sam's coat-tails and being his shadow?' she said mischievously. To her surprise she saw her mother's smile fade, and she frowned.

'Truth to tell, I'm a bit worried about our Jack,' Bess said. 'Your Daddy says there's been friction between him and Sam at the works, and that's unusual for a start. Our Jack's allus taken his grub at the cottage when he's been on the day shift, but Hal says he's been eating it with the other young clayworkers lately—'

'That's nothing to worry about! The boys always took their grub on to the moors in fine weather—'

As she spoke the words, a swift image of the moorland hill swept through Morwen's mind, bringing with it a sharp nostalgia that surprised her. It was a while since she had been to the works or to Sam's cottage. A while since she had seen the moors in all their spring glory, the short turf fragrant with the wild flowers and bright yellow furze; the whispering of the bracken; the gaunt granite oddity of the Larnie Stone, through whose hole could be seen the distant sea beyond St Austell town…

The scars of the clay works in the hillside had their own strange beauty, with the milky-green pools and the spoil heaps surrounding them, glinting like diamonds in the sunlight with all the waste materials tipped there. Charles Killigrew used to call them his sky-tips, a name that had once charmed Morwen.

The name still lingered, though the townsfolk had begun calling them the white hills of late, which had incensed some of the clayworkers, seeing the snobbery in it. Sky-tips or white hills… Morwen and her friend, Celia Penry, had shared their secrets there… she swallowed the sudden lump in her throat.

''Tis more than that,' Bess went on slowly. 'I fear our Jack's moving away from us, like our Matt did. 'Twould break your daddy's heart if Jack left us too.'

'Jack's no sailor, Mammie!' Morwen tried to cheer her. 'You wouldn't get him on a ship that went all the way to America. And I can't believe he's lost his feelings for our Sam! He always wanted to be like Sam. It was his only ambition!'

She began to laugh, for they had all teased Jack so over the years. But her mother wasn't laughing back.

'I don't know what's wrong with un, Morwen, and that's a fact. He's seventeen now, and a man, but to your daddy and me he's still our Jack, and I hate to see un so tetchy at times. He was tickled pink wi' Sam's babbies at first, but now all that's worn off.'

'Well, I don't know what to say about it,' Morwen said. 'I'll see for myself when we all come to the church for the babby's baptising next Sunday, and perhaps Ben can find out something when we get back to the cottage afterwards.'

'Perhaps so,' Bess agreed. She looked thoughtfully at her daughter. 'Sometimes I think we all rely on your Ben too much. He can't solve all our problems, and Lord knows he has enough of his own wi' the clay works. He's got a good head on his shoulders, Morwen. I only wish—'

Her voice trailed away as she saw the tight look come over Morwen's face. They all wished there was a son to ensure the future of Killigrew Clay, the way Ben had secured it when the strike had threatened its very existence. But wishing didn't make it happen, and Bess knew better than to pursue the subject with her daughter. Morwen was as strong-willed as her handsome husband, and if a perverse mood took her, just as likely to snub her mother as confide in her whole-heartedly.

–

For once Morwen was quite glad when the hour at the Tea Room was over. For all that she had been eager to see her mother, now she was just as anxious to see Ben, and it frustrated her that he wasn't at home when she arrived there in the trap. He had left a message for her with the housekeeper.

'He's gone to the clay works, Ma'am,' Mrs Tilley informed her. 'And didn't rightly know when he'd be back.'

'Thank you, Mrs Tilley,' Morwen tried not to sigh as she spoke. Ben took his responsibilities as clay owner seriously. So had his father, but while Charles Killigrew had made irregular visits to the works on the moors, Ben believed his presence should be felt more often. It was a rare week that didn't see him at the works at least three times. It was to his credit, but sometimes the days seemed long to Morwen.

If only she had a child to care for, the hours would pass more quickly... she tried to push the thought aside, but somehow there was no escaping it. And knowing that on Sunday the whole family would be at Penwithick church during the Sunday-school hour to witness the baptism of Sam's newest child, seemed to sharpen the longing inside her.

She had never kept secrets from Ben, but even he was unaware of just how unfulfilled Morwen felt, how inadequate at being unable to do what even the cows in the field did with ease. She had hesitated from asking Doctor Pender if there might be anything wrong... Ben would hate the idea, but maybe she would do so without telling him, and that would be another secret he wouldn't share...

'Mr Charles has been asking for you, Ma'am,' Mrs Tilley said as an afterthought. 'I fear this fine weather hasn't improved his temper at all. He wants to go into the garden, but Doctor Pender has forbidden it until April's out.'

She spoke with the candour of one who had been in the same family's service for some years, and Morwen nodded sympathetically.

'I'll go and sit with him awhile. He'll have seen me come home and will be impatient to hear my family news.'

Charles Killigrew was practically bedridden now, having cruelly suffered a second stroke a year after the first one. He'd seemed to improve dramatically, then was struck down again, and this time there had been no visible improvement for three years. They all knew it was unlikely that it would happen now.

Ben had done everything to make his father's life as comfortable as possible. A nurse was a permanent resident at Killigrew House. Her presence took much of the weight from Morwen's slender shoulders, but Charles still infinitely preferred his daughter-in-law's calming influence in his bedroom.

It was Morwen's hand he sought in his despairing moments, and for Morwen's step on the stairs that he listened. Ben had arranged large mirrors at either side of Charles's long bedroom window, so that he could see the world outside his room.

Ben had done all he could, but it was a poor substitute to a man who had been used to lording it in the town and at his clay works, and whose voice had been heard bellowing like a bull when he was roused. That voice was no more than a pathetic whine at best now, and a dribbling gurgle at worst.

Morwen quickened her step as she went into Charles's room. She smiled at the angular nurse, who went away discreetly at Morwen's approach, no doubt glad of a much-needed rest. Charles was scowling, his face lopsided and twisted. He had grown much thinner of late and bore little resemblance to the lion he had always felt himself to be. He was still large-framed, but for all that he was a frail old man now.

'How are you, Father?' Morwen asked brightly. 'You're looking much better—'

'Nonsense!' Charles spoke with painful slowness, but at least his speech wasn't totally impaired, even if it sounded as though he held a plum in his mouth when he formed the words.

'All right, then. You don't look much better.' Morwen shrugged, knowing it was best to agree with him rather than bully him with false cheerfulness as the nurse did.

'Would you like me to read to you, or do you want to hear about what I did today?'

'About you first. Then read.' He leaned back against the pillow exhausted. From the tidy look of his bed, Morwen guessed that Nurse had been fussing him again. Why didn't she just leave him, instead of having this obsessive need to straighten and smooth as though he were a little boy?

'I saw your sister today. She's well, and she says that her – her son is working in New York.' That should please Charles, who had never had a good word for his lazy nephew; and yet, for all that he had turned Hannah Pascoe out of his house, he still paid her an allowance so that she could be independent. Family duty was inherent in the Killigrews.

Charles gave an apology for a snort. 'And your brother?'

'Mrs Pascoe says he's gone to California to work in some gold mining. I don't know how true it is. I hope our Matt will find his feet at last. I want him to be a success.'

Her voice was wistful, but suddenly she didn't want to talk about her family any more. 'There's nothing else to tell you, except a lot of womens' gossip between Mammie and me, and you won't want to hear all that. I'll read to you for a while and then you can have your sleep before dinner.'

She picked up the current book they were sharing, and Charles's eyes never left her face as her soft voice took him into yet another world. As she read to him of pirates on the high seas, Morwen was filled with a rush of pity for the man lying so still and listening so intently. If her days were tedious, then how much more were his!

She read quietly, until at last she glanced up and saw that Charles was already sleeping, lulled by the music of the words. Morwen looked down at him, touched his twisted cheek with her lips, and tip-toed out.

There were voices coming from the drawing-room, and her step quickened at once as she heard Ben speaking with Mrs Tilley. Her heart beat a little faster, and she marvelled that after four years of marriage the mere sound of his voice still had the power to stir her. Without Ben she was only half alive.

As she entered the room he turned at once, a tall masculine figure whose looks had matured with the responsibility of ownership since taking over the clay works from his father. He was still only twenty-five years old, but maturity suited Ben Killigrew, and there was many a young bal maiden at the works who sighed after him. They wasted their dreams for Ben was too much in love with his beautiful wife to look at anyone else, even for dalliance.

Morwen ran straight into his arms. He held her captive there, his hands spanning her small waist and curving her towards him. His mouth sought hers and she could taste the freshness of outdoors on his lips. The tang of the moorland was on his skin. Her fingers dug into the dark hair at his nape and she could feel the hard maleness of him against her soft pliant body.

'I missed you, Ben,' she murmured against his mouth when he released her a little. 'I didn't know you were going out this afternoon.'

'Did you expect me to be waiting here like an obliging pet while my wife goes out for a gossip in the town?' he teased.

'I never gossip!' She took the bait at once, and then laughed, for it was exactly what she and Bess had been doing – and enjoying it. Her blue eyes glowed into his at his teasing, as she ran her hands down the length of his arms. And then she became instantly aware of the tension there.

He had held her and kissed her because it was natural to them, and every reunion was another avowal of love, however briefly they had been apart. But she knew him too well. She knew the heart and soul of him, and something was wrong. Something that had taken him unexpectedly to the clay works that day.

Even as the intuitive thoughts sped through her mind and she looked sharply into Ben's face, she saw his expression change from teasing to frowning. A flicker of fear ran over her. There had been peace and harmony at Killigrew Clay for four years now, the same length of time as their marriage had existed. If one should begin to crumble, then so could the other...

Morwen wished the thought away. There was no reason for it, but the Cornish didn't always look for reasons. Feelings were often enough, and the feeling she was experiencing now was enough to churn her stomach. Making her want to cling to Ben, and add her strength to his, if strength were needed. Her fingers curled around his arms and he looked into her delicately-featured face, unable to hide his unease.

'Ben, what's wrong?' Morwen said quietly. She was almost afraid to ask, but more afraid not to know.

Chapter Two

Ben released her from his embrace, and the small action made the chill run through Morwen again. She knew it was ridiculous, but for a moment she still wanted him to hold her, to feel that closeness, that shared empathy…

'You'd think we were ill-wished at times,' Ben said abruptly. 'Just when things are going smoothly, trouble rears its head again. And all because of some nervous matron who swears she felt the earth shudder beneath the rail tracks on this morning's excursion trip from the town to the works. The first trip of the season, and now we have to put people's minds at rest. If the rail tracks are safe enough to transport the heavy clay, there can hardly be any risk to a load of passengers—'

'Ben, stop!' Morwen clutched at his arm as his voice rose angrily and his handsome face darkened. 'This is Morwen, remember? I'm on your side! You don't have to explain your safety precautions to me! How did all this come about?'

His eyes softened as he looked down at her, though he was still too wrapped up in the altercations of the afternoon to relax immediately. There had been bitter words and demands for a public declaration of safety… and the presence of the legal representative of the Honourable Mrs Stanforth and the county officials had alarmed many of the clayworkers.

'The driver stopped the train when it neared Clay One works as usual, to give the engine and passengers a breather from the steep climb, and to point out the various pits. Apparently it was then that the Honourable Mrs Stanforth was sure she could feel the earth move a little, and hear a cracking sound. It was enough to cause a near-panic among the other passengers, and they wanted no more tours of the clay works but to get back to St Austell and safety as quickly as possible!'

'Ben, that's terrible!' Morwen's eyes were saucer-round at hearing this. It was a new innovation, to carry the paying townsfolk from St Austell high on to the moors for a round trip during late spring and summer, to view the clay works from the safety of the little rail carriages, scrubbed clean after the twice-yearly despatch of the clay blocks to Charlestown port.

The clayworkers themselves were divided about the idea, some saying they felt on display to these fine folk who had dubbed the clay spoil heaps the white hills, and said it in a quaint, patronising tone. Others didn't care, as long as it helped Killigrew Clay to prosper, for the more shillings in Ben Killigrew's coffers, the more pennies in their own wage-packets.

Ben had other plans in mind too. The rail tracks were idle for much of the year, which seemed a total waste to him. So as well as the townsfolk visiting the clay works on the moors, this year he also planned free excursions to the sea for the clayworkers' children, and to make the railway line available for Sunday-school outings during the summer months.

The scheme had been welcomed, and Ben Killigrew's generosity had received a favourable mention in the Truro newspaper, *The Informer*, but now this…

'I received a note from Mr Princeton, the Stanforth lawyer, just after you went out,' Ben went on in a clipped voice. 'The Honourable lady had wasted no time, and Mr Princeton requested me to meet him with the county engineers and surveyors at Clay One works this afternoon.'

'What happened?' Morwen could imagine how Ben would hate this high-handed treatment. He was proud, the son of a self-made man, and very much in control of his kingdom. She sat down heavily on one of the damask-covered sofas, while Ben continued to prowl about the room, his dark eyes steely.

'We went over every inch of the track system,' he told her. 'There was no sign of subsidence, nor anything to make people think there was any danger. The hillside is as solid as the granite beneath it – except for one little item, of course.'

Morwen felt a cold trickle of apprehension wash over her. The casual way Ben said the words alerted her that it was far more serious than calling it one little item…

'And what is that?' Her voice was scratchy, waiting…

'Long before the china clay was discovered in such abundance around St Austell, the area was mined for tin,' Ben said shortly. 'The history of Cornish tin goes back centuries, Morwen, but there's no recorded evidence of shafts or tunnels on these particular moors. Tin was played out here long before the clayworkers moved in, even though there's many a tin-miner from other parts who scorns going a'claying, as they call it, thinking our industry so much less important than theirs—'

'Ben, what *happened*?' She realised suddenly that he was putting off the moment of telling her. Her heart seemed to beat in sickening bursts.

He shrugged, standing in front of the great fireplace now, hands tightly held behind his back, feet apart, chin jutting out aggressively, in the stance of old Charles Killigrew.

Morwen could see Charles in his son all over again at that moment. The same fierce pride in his clay works; the resentment at the accusation that he hadn't looked to the safety of all in his charge; the will to survive and be lord of his sky-tips, his white hills…

'I don't need to tell you of the clayworkers' reaction, do I? The news spread like a forest fire. I visited each pit in turn where the clay captains had called a noisy meeting of all the workers to explain what was happening. You'll know how hot-headed they are when a panic begins. So meanwhile all movement on the railway is halted until we get the say-so from the engineers and surveyors. I was obliged to agree to that, and I've no doubt the reporter from *The Informer* will be sniffing around pretty soon. But a detailed investigation with special instruments will start tomorrow. I insisted that I wasn't prepared to delay things while they are on their backsides in their offices and talked endlessly. If there's work to be done then I want action. I've no intention of seeing all my plans thwarted by some stupid woman's scare-mongering!'

He couldn't keep the bitterness out of his voice. Morwen went swiftly to his side. Even though the day was warm and a fire burned brightly in the hearth behind him, they were both chilled and dismayed by today's happening.

And into Morwen's head came a blurred snippet of memory, like a little ghost from the past. Years ago, old Zillah, the wise woman on the moors, had intimated in that mysterious way of hers that one day an earthquake could come… at the time Morwen had assumed that the earthquake prophesy had been fulfilled by the clay waggon crashing through old Nott's bakery.

That was upheaval enough… but now, suddenly, the half-remembered words took on a new and more sinister meaning. But she refused to think of them. Instead she wanted to comfort Ben, to replace the look of anxiety on his face with the special look of love he reserved for her alone. She leaned on tip-toe and kissed the hard line of his mouth, her arms around him like a protective mantle.

'Ben, there's nothing more you can do about it. It's happened, and we must have faith that everything will be all right. The rail tracks have been so beneficial for the town and the clayworkers. I refuse to believe that something that's brought so much good can turn bad.'

He breathed in the fragrant scent of her hair and tasted her soft lips, and some of his turbulent thoughts left him. She had a uniquely calming effect when he needed it most, and right now the simple logic of a clayworker's daughter eased his more educated mind better than all the ancient mining maps he and the county officials had studied over the moors and in the pit captain's hut that day. There was no real evidence yet of any ancient tin-mining activity beneath these moors… but not all of them may have been documented, and even the smallest doubt as to the safety of the Killigrew Clay rail tracks must be overcome.

Ben pushed it from his mind. Morwen was right. Tonight he could do no more than he had already done. His arms closed around her. His adored wife had the power to calm him and arouse him in equal measure when the need arose. Her kiss, begun so gently, suddenly deepened as though she melted into him. He felt the peaks of her breasts against his chest, and knew that for them both, passion was never far below the surface.

If all else perished, they had this… they were like two halves of the same coin, perfectly matched. Physically they were exquisitely in tune and, to Morwen's ever-receptive mind, the joy experienced in each other almost mystical. She felt the tightening of Ben's arms, and knew that supper could wait…

The tap on the drawing-room door was an intrusion into the sweetness of the moment, and Ben released her from his arms with a smothered oath as Mrs Tilley came apologetically into the room, though her eyes were alive with interest at her message.

'I'm sorry, Mr Ben, but there's a person come to see you from Truro. He asked me to give you his calling-card, so perhaps you'll tell me if you'm at home or not.'

Ben looked at the card, headed with the words *The Informer*, the hard-hitting Truro newspaper. Beneath it was the name of the caller, Lew Tregian, chief reporter and editor. Ben glanced at Morwen, who moved away from him as he told Mrs Tilley coldly to show the gentleman in. Already it had begun.

—

In the small snug Tremayne house Hal was relating the day's events to Bess, interrupted every minute or so by Freddie's excited questions, and by Jack's more sombre account. Jack had been on the main day shift, and was as ready to add his bits of news to his father's. Since Hal's rise in status to Works Manager of Killigrew Clay, Freddie had been attending the St Austell town school instead of working the clay like his brothers, and received more than the sketchy education of the rest of his family, but he was as eager as his mother to know of today's unexpected events. It was clear to all that Hal was deeply troubled by it all.

'Gil Dark at Clay Two works was up in arms at once,' Hal said. 'He never did think much to the townsfolk spying on the rest on us, dar—'

'Gil Dark was allus too stubborn a man for a pit captain,' Bess remarked. 'But what was Ben's feeling about these folk tramping over the works and the moors? He wouldn't take too kindly to it!'

'No, he didn't, Mammie,' Jack growled. 'Anybody could see that by the scowl on his face, though he didn't have much time for talking to we. And our Sam weren't saying a lot, neither. Keen to keep his job until he sees which way the land lies, I reckon—'

'That's enough of that kind of talk, our Jack,' Hal snapped. He didn't anger easily, but he hated to see the frequent quarrels between his two sons, when they had always been such close companions until lately. 'There's no sense in any of us getting our dander up until the folk that know about surveying and engineering see what's to do. If there's subsidence beneath the rail tracks as 'tis suggested, then 'twill cause a big enough outcry, but there's no sense in guessing until we know for certain sure. It may be no more than a scare. There's been no talk of any tin-mining around here in my recollection.'

'We've been learning about the tin-mining at school!' Freddie said importantly.

Jack snorted, still annoyed at being shouted down by his easy-going father. 'Tin-mining!' He scoffed, his blue eyes flashing. At seventeen he was a big, handsome boy, with a string of bal maidens anxious for his attentions, but so far he teased them all and favoured none. 'They old tin-miners thought themselves such fine feller-me-lads, and spent half their time afeared of the spirits under the earth—'

'Mr Pengelly told us about they too,' Freddie chirped up. 'Knockers, they was called. Supposed to look like little old men with screwed-up faces, who tormented the tin-miners unless they left 'em summat to eat on every shift—'

'I thought you was being taught the right way to speak, our Freddie,' Hal turned on his youngest son now. 'You'm not ready to grace any fine London school yet, I'm thinking!'

Bess spoke up in exasperation. 'I could box your heads together, the lot of you. We've more important things to consider besides Freddie's learning and our Jack's arguing. What's to be the outcome of today, Hal?'

'I can't tell 'ee that, dar,' Hal grunted. 'I'd need old Zillah's second sight to tell 'ee that. Mebbe one of us should go and ask her—'

'You know I don't like such talk!' Bess snapped, her face flushed with annoyance now.

Freddie darted a look at both his parents. He was tempted to say that his sister Morwen hadn't had such qualms about visiting old Zillah in the days when they had all lived in the cottage. Freddie hardly remembered how cramped and small it had been then, with all of them there. All the same, it had been a cottage filled with love and laughter.

The only black day Freddie could remember at the cottage was the day Celia Penry had drowned herself, and Matthew had found her and dumped her on Morwen's bed without realising that Morwen still lay there. He shivered. There had been many lurid tales of how terrible the once-pretty Celia had looked, all white-slimed with the slurry from the clay pool… he couldn't really recall her face, since he had been only eight years old at the time, but he remembered the nights that Morwen had cried…

'What be 'ee looking so gormless about now, our Freddie?' Jack baited him again.

'Oh, leave un alone, our Jack,' Bess rounded on him. 'I don't know what's got into 'ee these days.'

'Mebbe our Jack wanted to go to a posh school like me,' Freddie chanted, and was rewarded with a swipe from the back of Jack's powerful hand. Hal was quick to clip him back, and the boys glowered at each other, knowing when enough was enough.

'If we've all done wi' talk about the excitement at the works today, then we'd best talk of summat else,' Hal snapped. 'And first off, I'm warning the two of 'ee to keep the peace at the babby's baptising on Sunday. I want no nonsense, do 'ee both understand me?'

They both did, and went their separate ways in the small house: Jack to brood on why he felt so irritated all the time, especially with his older brother, Sam, whom he had once hero-worshipped; Freddie to sprawl on his bed in the tiny box-room that was all his own, and to dream of London and the brilliant future he could have if Mr Pengelly, the school-teacher, were to be believed.

Bess, meanwhile, spoke quietly to her man. 'Does it really look bad, Hal?'

'I fear that it does, dar,' he said heavily, using their special, shortened endearment. 'God knows how long these officials could be deciding what's what with the rail tracks. Thank the Lord the spring despatch of clay is done, and there's only Ben's excursions to come to grief for the next six months. But if they find proof of subsidence due to old tin workings and insist the present rail tracks must be dismantled and a new course laid, 'tis doubtful 'twould be ready in time for the autumn loadings. Killigrew's clay waggons would have to go through the town again.'

''Tis not a complete disaster,' Bess soothed him. 'Ben will put safety above all, dar, and it may only be one despatch of clay to go by the old method. Other pits still use it—'

'Ah, but Killigrew clay waggons will be bound to stir up hatred because o' the accident,' he growled. 'Memories can be short when it comes to putting blame, and 'twas a Killigrew waggon that killed so many folk, remember?'

Bess squared her shoulders resolutely. 'I think we've talked enough about it, Hal. It may all come to nothing yet.'

Privately Hal thought such a likelihood was doubtful, after the arguments that had gone on at the works that afternoon, but Bess was right. They had talked about it enough, and talk alone never solved anything. He was in full agreement with his son-in-law on that score.

-

News of any impending disaster, true or false, invariably spread to all corners with lightning speed. And to Truro in particular, where there was always a chance of being paid for information at the offices of *The Informer* newspaper. The chief reporter and editor had already departed for Killigrew House to interview the owner of Killigrew Clay, and town gossip among the townsladies taking an afternoon stroll down Lemon Street the following day had eventually reached Mary Carrick. Holding in a tight smile of satisfaction at Ben Killigrew's prospective downfall, she awaited her husband's homecoming from his legal chambers with much impatience.

'What did I tell you?' she finished triumphantly, when she had bombarded him with the garbled tales being bandied about Truro town. 'Ben Killigrew was always too big for his boots, and this is no more than he deserves—'

Richard Carrick looked at his wife with exasperation. He became less tolerant with her as the years went by, and simply closed his ears to anything he didn't want to hear. But this was something he couldn't ignore. More than the disturbing news about possible subsidence beneath Ben Killigrew's rail tracks at the clay works, Mary's sneering bitterness wounded him.

The Killigrews were his friends, and had always been his friends. And more than that. Until Ben had proved his astute business sense and gambled everything on owning Killigrew Clay outright, Richard Carrick had been a partner in the clay works with old Charles Killigrew.

Richard had only admiration for the way in which Ben took control at that time, settled an ugly strike and built the rail tracks St Austell so greatly appreciated. He would have liked a son like Ben Killigrew... and that was where all Mary's bitterness began, of course. From the time they were babies, she had dreamed of her daughter, Jane, marrying Ben Killigrew.

Mary seemed totally obsessed by the idea. It was almost less of an affront to her when Jane ran off with the terrible newspaperman to live in the Godforsaken wilds of Yorkshire, than when Ben himself married the common bal maiden. It was obviously on the rebound, Mary averred doggedly. No young man in his right senses could prefer the clayworker's black-haired daughter to her beautiful, golden-haired Jane!

No matter how many letters arrived from Jane, begging their forgiveness, and telling them how blissfully happy she was with her Tom, Mary never fully forgave her. It had taken Richard a long while, not because he didn't want his daughter's happiness, but because he had an inborn dislike of newspapermen.

But Tom Askhew had written private letters to Jane's father, and he finally admitted that the fellow seemed straight and honest. And when the Carricks were invited north to Yorkshire on the arrival of a golden-haired granddaughter, the image of her mother, his forgiveness was total. Even Mary had seemed to submit to the inevitable. Now, in a moment, it seemed as if all the old aggression towards Ben Killigrew was back again.

'Won't you ever forget, Mary?' he said angrily.

'Not as easily as you do, obviously!' She was furious at his lack of comment on the subsidence talk. Half of Truro was excited about it, and here was Richard, coldly glaring at her as if she had invented the whole thing. He used to be far more mild-mannered, more easy to manipulate, and she liked to get her own way. 'I don't forget the way Ben Killigrew came here and calmly bought you out, nor the way you let him! You've always been spineless, Richard!'

'If that's what you think, you're perfectly at liberty to go north and spend some time with Jane and Tom, my dear,' he said coolly. 'They're always asking you, and I assure you I shan't stop you.'

'I've no wish to live in the same house as Tom Askhew, as you very well know,' she snapped.

'Then you must stick to your guns if you've no wish to see your granddaughter either,' he went on. He knew for a fact that Tom was far too busy editing his fine Yorkshire newspaper, *The Northern Informer*, offshoot of the Truro newspaper he'd begun, to travel south-west to Cornwall for visits to his carping mother-in-law. Mary Carrick could visit them any time she pleased, but by not taking up the invitation, in common parlance, she was merely cutting off her nose to spite her face.

The look she gave him was one of almost pure hatred. If only Jane and dear sweet little Cathy would come visiting without that obnoxious husband of hers, whose flat nasal voice and blunt way of speaking so offended Mary's sensitive ears… but such a likelihood was as remote as pigs giving milk.

Mary felt her cheeks colour as the coarse simile came to her mind. It was that oaf, Tom Askhew's fault. She switched her annoyance from Ben Killigrew to Tom with consummate ease.

Tom could always bring out the worst in her. She wouldn't mind at all if she never saw him again.

–

The sentiments were in complete opposition to the ones her daughter Jane was expressing to her husband a few nights later. The news Tom brought home to their adorable little stone-built house on the edge of the Yorkshire dales was enough to make her turn as pale as death. She clung to him.

'You can't mean it, Tom!' Jane gasped, her pretty face almost bloodless at the determination in his eyes. He was a ruggedly-made man, a newspaperman to the core, and Jane adored him. Together they enjoyed a lusty marriage, an extension of the secret hours of passion in the Truro days, about which her mother would have been horrified.

Even more so had Mary Carrick known that Ben Killigrew had been a party to them, letting the illusion continue that he and Jane would eventually marry. For some reason Jane thought briefly of Ben in these anguished moments. She loved Ben as a brother, but it had never been with the tumultuous love she felt for Tom. And now he was telling her he was going to leave her… and she couldn't bear it… she just couldn't…

'Jane, listen to me!' Tom spoke harshly, holding her tightly as though he thought she would collapse if he didn't. He was probably right, she thought faintly.

She listened to the words he spoke in that flat voice of his, and they were all the more terrible because they conveyed so little expression. But Jane knew that for all his coolness, he felt very deeply, which was probably the reason for all this… she had felt a strange premonition when he had gone for a special meeting with Sir Garside Sefton that evening, the owner of *The Northern Informer*. She was Cornish, and felt such things.

'The soldiers in the Crimea need war correspondents, Jane. It's a new idea. They need good reporters to send back the truth about what's happening, instead of these rumours that distort everything. They need me, Jane, and Sir Garside knows I'm the best man to send for the paper.'

'You were never modest, were you?' She heard her voice break, knowing that if Sir Garside wanted it, then Tom would go. If the country needed him, he would go...

'Good God, lass, if young women are willing to go as nurses with Miss Nightingale, then you wouldn't have it said that your husband's afraid to go too, would you?'

'I'm the one who's afraid, Tom,' she whispered. 'Afraid you won't come back to me and Cathy—'

'I'll always come back, love,' Tom said roughly. 'But if 'tis what you want, I'd have no objections to your staying with your parents while I'm gone. God knows how long 'twill be, and that's a fact.'

Jane's eyes blurred with tears. 'You really want to do this, don't you, Tom?'

She could sense the longing in his voice now when he answered. A newspaperman would always have ambitions she didn't understand, she thought sorrowfully. Always that need to be where there was action and excitement. And for the past year and more it had all been concentrated in that distant, unknown part of the world, the Crimea.

'Perhaps I should enlist as a nurse for Miss Nightingale too, and come with you,' she said wistfully, and in answer he crushed her to him. The faint sweet scent of printers' ink and chemicals still lingered on his body.

'You have your own duties caring for our sweet little lass, Jane. I'll want you waiting here when I come home, whether in Cornwall or in Yorkshire, not in some hell-hole of a military hospital halfway around the world.'

No matter that that was where Tom would be, and most probably in far more dangerous and unsavoury places. Jane shivered, having heard something of this war from Tom's talk of it. They looked at each other without speaking for a moment.

Then, as though the thought struck them both that there may not be many more nights like this, they moved towards the stairs and into their bedroom, and Tom made love to his wife with a passion reminiscent of the first time they had lain together. Just as spectacular… just as wonderful… and for Jane, leaving her with tears dampening her eyes at the feeling that in the giving, she had also lost a little of herself.

Chapter Three

The April days had been alternately blustery and gentle, but on the Sunday of Primrose Tremayne's baptising, it seemed as though the spring weather had decided to be on its best behaviour for the occasion. Ben's father would want to know every detail of the day and its happenings when they got home again.

The air was almost as warm as summer, the moors soft and beautiful and bursting with new greenery and wild flowers. The pyramid peaks of the Killigrew Clay sky-tips on the crest of the hill above St Austell glinted in the sunlight, and the milky pools reflected the puffball clouds passing leisurely across the blue sky.

The talk among Killigrews and Tremaynes, clayworkers and townsfolk, had concentrated so much on the Honourable Mrs Stanforth's report recently, that it was a relief to put it behind them for a few hours. Ben had given the interview to the reporter from the Truro newspaper with a bad grace, knowing it would provoke more questions that he wasn't yet prepared or able to answer.

'For this one day, at least, try to forget the troubles, Ben,' Morwen begged, as they made the journey to Penwithick church in the Killigrew trap.

Ben glanced at his wife, as lovely as the spring day, and noted the way her hands were clenched tightly together in her lap. He put one hand over hers, and she felt its reassuring warmth.

And wondered fleetingly if this day, although so joyous in many ways, was something of an ordeal for her.

It was the third time they had acted as godparents for Sam and Dora's children, and vowed to care for babies not their own… he squeezed Morwen's hand, at least intending to make an effort, and put his own anxieties aside.

'Do you remember another time in Penwithick church?' he said suddenly. At last he saw her smile, and the faintly haunted look left her beautiful eyes.

'Would I ever forget, or wish to? 'Twas there that I first knew you loved me, Ben—' the voice was husky, liltingly soft. He had always loved her expressive voice.

He shook his head. 'The first time I put it into words, my Morwen. But it was something you always knew, wasn't it?'

Mischief suddenly danced in her eyes, because she could speak of things now that had wounded her years ago.

'Did I? I was as convinced as anyone that you were going to marry your Miss Finelady from Truro!'

Ben laughed, caught by her new mood, and forcing himself to forget the gnawing worry of the inspections of the rail tracks that were now going on daily, with no positive results as yet.

'And now you're my Fine Lady!' He twisted her own words. 'You always were, Morwen, from the day I saw you again after I came home from college. Remember that? When you tripped into my arms and scratched your face on my neck-tie pin?'

'And you said you had branded me—'

It was a good day for reminiscences. Blue and golden and sweetly scented. Even the tang of the sea was carried on the air as the breeze twisted and turned and danced among the bracken as they rode high above the town and towards their own white world.

Past the strange, evocative sky-tips; the sprawling landmarks of the four Killigrew Clay pits; the patchwork of clayworkers' cottages, snug and warm; the old Tremayne family cottage that was now Sam and Dora's; and the one where Celia and the Penrys once lived…

Morwen felt her throat thicken a little. She could never pass Celia's cottage without remembering how full of life her friend had been. How alive… and then how dead…

'Nearly there,' Ben said evenly, just as though he could read her thoughts. She smiled quickly, blinking back the shine of tears on her lids. She was the one who had said that today mustn't be spoiled by morbid thoughts. Today was a day for celebration.

She sought for something else to say, not wanting the day to slip into sadness. Killigrew House had been gloomy enough of late, what with the threat to Ben's rail tracks, and his obsession with the London newspapers with their current war reports from the Crimea, and the aftermath of the terrible winter the brave British soldiers had spent in atrocious conditions.

'I wonder what your Miss Finelady is doing now,' Morwen said lightly. 'Is Yorkshire a cold place, I wonder?'

'I daresay it's colder than Cornwall,' Ben commented. And then, as if Morwen's thoughts had been transmitted to him, he went on grimly, 'But not as cold as for those poor devils in the Crimea. Yesterday's account in *The Times* was nothing short of horrific.'

· He had read some of it aloud to Morwen and Charles, and she had shuddered, listening to the graphic words describing it. But she still couldn't really relate to it all.

'I can't think why you keep reading about it, Ben. You're always restless when the London newspapers arrive. There's nothing you can do about the war—'

'I'd probably be there with them if I didn't have a clay business to run,' he spoke harshly. 'The petty fuss about whether ancient tin-mines were worked beneath my rail tracks seems pathetic when you think of our soldiers in that hellish Turkish hospital—'

'Even with the wonderful Florence Nightingale coming to the rescue?'

Morwen didn't mean to be flippant, but she hated to hear Ben belittle his own achievements, when for his own small community he had done so much. She sensed the frustration in him when he read of others doing heroic deeds, and knew a secret womanly relief that Ben would never go to this war. He was needed here, and she needed him most of all. For a second, she imagined living without him. Her heart missed a beat and then raced on.

'Most of the wounded think the woman is a saint,' Ben retorted. 'Some of the sights and smells she must live with every single day are beyond belief—'

'Ben, please let's stop talking about it,' Morwen pleaded. 'I admire Miss Nightingale as much as you. Today, can't we just enjoy Primmy's baptism?'

For a second she thought he was still angry with her. His face was hard, the way it looked when he had trouble at the works. But now was not the time for dissent, and Ben slid one arm around his wife's tense shoulders, and pressed his lips to her soft cheek, as he halted the horse at Penwithick church.

'We'll just enjoy today,' he agreed. 'As long as you'll promise not to be haunted by ghosts of yesterday, I won't let myself worry about tomorrow.'

She couldn't quite promise that, when yesterday was all around them, and she knew just why she rarely came back to the old cottage, the moors around the clay works, and

Penwithick church. There were wonderful memories here, and dark ones too.

A sudden shout from the direction of the church made her look thankfully to where Sam's two youngest children were toddling towards the trap. Ben helped her alight, and she gathered up the tiny hurtling bodies of three-year-old Walter and two-year-old Albert.

'Don't let 'em dirty your pretty frock, Morwen,' Dora called from the church porch, where she held the shawl-wrapped Primrose in her arms. Beside her, Sam smiled proudly.

'Our Morwen's not too fine to worry about a bit of honest dirt,' he chuckled, and immediately she was in her old family place again. She was Morwen Tremayne, only girl in a family of lusty boys. She felt warm and welcome, and the brief constraint she still felt whenever Ben visited any of her family vanished at once.

Her parents were already inside the church, along with Jack and Freddie, slicked down for the day, though Jack was too old now for being told to wash behind his ears and to tidy himself. Morwen hadn't seen him for a while, and it gave her a shock to see how grown he was. No wonder her Mammie worried about him, she thought, before they all took their places, and the Vicar began intoning the words of the service.

Her mind wandered. They were all here except Matthew. Family occasions always accentuated those who were missing, and she knew her mother would be feeling his loss. She glanced at Bess, and knew she was right. She felt Ben's fingers creep around hers, and knew he was remembering that other time, when they had avowed their love here in this very church, cool and dark, and she had known then what she had always known. She had wanted Ben Killigrew all her life… and the miracle of it was that he wanted her too…

Primrose began squalling as the holy water was dribbled over her face, and Morwen guiltily reminded herself where she was. Though why God would condemn thoughts of love that had begun in His very house, she couldn't imagine. Even though that love was passionate and physical, it was God who had given them the joy in each other, and Morwen silently thanked Him for it.

Once it was all over and they were outside in the warm afternoon air, they prepared to go back to Sam's cottage for the modest feasting. The baby was already asleep.

Morwen's eyes sought the simple headstone in one corner of the churchyard, that she and Ben had put there in memory of her friend, Celia. Beside it were the graves of Celia's father and brother, who had both been mutilated and killed in the terrible disaster at Nott's bakery...

'No ghosts, Morwen,' Ben said gently in her ear. 'Dora wants you to hold the baby while we go back to the cottage.'

Dora passed the child across to her. Primrose had a deliciously warm, faintly milky baby smell, and Morwen felt her heart tug as she looked down at the perfect, sleeping face. She covered the dark downy head with the shawl, and tried not to imagine that Primmy was her child, hers and Ben's.

Coming back here was not always good for her peace of mind. She hadn't been to Penwithick church since young Albert's baptising, her nephew who had been named after the Prince. Before that it was Walter's... how many more would there be? How many more times would she feel these pangs, and never know the fulfilment of holding her own child in her arms?

As though what ailed her was suddenly illuminated, Morwen knew she was lonely. Ben had his own world, the way men did. Her brothers were settled with their own lives.

Her mother had made her own niche with her sewing, while Morwen…

She had once had a dear friend, and had never found another to replace her. Even with all the love that she and Ben shared, the time she spent with Charles Killigrew, and her loving family, she still missed Celia desperately.

She could take up Good Causes. She could maybe learn to play the pianoforte that stood idly in the drawing-room. She could try any of those things, but there would still be an emptiness in her life that only a child could fill…

At that moment Morwen made up her mind, even before the thought was really formed. But there was a way. There were potions to take. And there was someone who would give them to her. Someone with whom Morwen had had contact before.

She and Celia had twice visited old Zillah, and got different kinds of potions. Those had worked… her mind shied away from remembering the final outcome of those visits, but the resolve was already there. She would visit old Zillah and beg her help once more.

–

Sir Garside Sefton himself decided he would take Jane Askhew and her daughter home to Truro in Cornwall when they were ready to leave Yorkshire, while her husband Tom was in foreign parts. Since Tom had agreed so eagerly to take on the new role of War Correspondent in the Crimea for *The Northern Informer*, leaving his wife and young daughter behind, it was only right that Sir Garside should see to the young woman's safety on the arduous coach journey.

He had business as well as honour on his mind, of course. Sir Garside Sefton rarely did anything if he couldn't combine business with pleasure. It was how he had come across Tom Askhew in the first place, when an acquaintance visiting Cornwall had mentioned the vigorous young editor of the Truro newspaper, and said he was just the type they needed in the north.

Tom was described to Sir Garside as pithy and hard-hitting, and fearless in his reporting. Added to that, he was a Yorkshireman and no doubt willing to accept an editorial post on a brand new newspaper in his native county. Sir Garside had gone to Truro and made Tom an offer he couldn't refuse.

When the time had been right, he and Jane Carrick had eloped to Yorkshire in romantic fashion, against her family's approval or even knowledge, married and become established as a bright and well-liked young couple in the community. And under Tom's editorship *The Northern Informer* had flourished.

Now Sir Garside saw a way of linking the two newspapers successfully. Tom's war reports could be telegraphed from Yorkshire to the Truro newspaper. Sir Garside had no doubt that Tom's reports would be highly successful, and he had a notion to buy the Cornish paper out.

There was something to be said for having a finger in southern as well as northern pies, and he intended investigating this while in Truro, as well as discreetly checking the circulation figures. He was highly pleased with his new idea.

It was imperative to get Tom away as soon as possible. Other newspapers had already sent off reporters to be the new war correspondents and he had been short-sighted in not doing so before this – when the war was already more than a year old. Who had ever believed it would last so long?

Jane had barely had time to get used to the idea and dry her tears, when she was waving her husband good-bye, locking up the small house she loved, and boarding the coach for the long journey south-west, with little Cathy and the genial Sir Garside.

She hadn't even informed her parents she was coming, but she knew how delighted they would be at a prolonged visit.

Jane prayed that it wouldn't be for too long. She and her mother wouldn't be on good terms for months on end… and she wanted Tom back even before he had left England's shores. She felt obliged to invite Sir Garside to stay at her parents' home in Truro, and was enormously relieved when he said he had already made arrangements to stay at an hotel.

–

'You want to learn to play the pianoforte?' Ben couldn't remove the quirk of amusement at the corners of his mouth when they finally arrived home at Killigrew House on the evening after Primmy's first public occasion.

Morwen misconstrued the small smile and bridled at once. The very first time she had entered this house on her seventeenth birthday, summoned here by Charles Killigrew to a so-called social supper, Morwen had squirmed with embarrassment at being among so many fine folk.

She still remembered the way Miss Jane Carrick had been requested to play for the company, and had done so in such an accomplished manner, her slim supple fingers moving over the ivory keys as though she caressed a lover…

In her immediate jealousy of Jane Carrick, whom she had dubbed Miss Finelady, the thought had stormed through Morwen's mind then, and stormed through it now.

Did Ben think Morwen's bal maiden's hands weren't capable of caressing the keys so delicately? Didn't he recall the times she caressed him, to his groaning pleasure, and his assertions that the touch of her fingers on his skin was like fire rippling through him, warm and sensual and exciting?

He saw the sudden flush of anger on her cheeks, and the sparkle in her blue eyes as she leapt to her feet, and caught her hands in his before she could begin berating him.

'Darling, I'm not mocking you—'

'It feels as though you are! Have I said summat so queer? I thought it might please 'ee—'

In her distress she lapsed into the old way of talking. Four years of being a lady were suddenly wiped out in the feeling of inferiority Ben's reaction had given her. She was furious at recognising it. It had no place in their lives now. She was Ben's wife, his friend and lover, and yet in an instant she reverted to feeling as awkward as on that first night here.

Her mother had sewn gay trailing ribbons on to a cream-coloured dress for her to wear, and she had thought it so beautiful, until she saw the silk dresses of Jane Carrick and the other ladies… now she was Morwen Tremayne again, in a cream cambric dress with trailing ribbons sewn on for the occasion… she twisted away from Ben.

'Forget I mentioned it! 'Twas no more than a whim—'

'I won't forget it,' he said angrily. 'I think it's a very good idea. I love to hear someone play, and it's been a while since anyone did so. Aunt Hannah was the last one, and I'll arrange a tutor for you tomorrow.'

She was suddenly overcome with fright. 'I'll be no good at it. You'll be wasting your money, and the tutor will think me an idiot—'

He came close to her again. 'No-one will dare to think my wife is an idiot, Morwen Killigrew!'

His voice dropped to a lower pitch. 'Have you anything else to do tonight, my love? We've spoken with Father, and Nurse has settled him for the night. Are you tired?'

'Not a bit—' she was still ruffled, unsure of what she wanted now.

'Good. Neither am I. It's time we went to bed.'

She couldn't mistake the meaning in his voice, nor the way his arm curled around her waist and held her possessively. They were still attired in the fine clothes they had worn for the church service, but from the sudden flare of passion in Ben's eyes, she knew that in the privacy of their bedroom, those clothes would be discarded with the speed and urgency of lovers, needing fulfilment in each other's arms. The time for wrangling was over, and the anger died.

They left the drawing-room with their arms entwined. They had always been passionate lovers, but somehow tonight, the old associations with the moors and the church, and the memories of how their lives had been interwoven, gave an added dimension to their delight in each other.

Ben took his wife in his arms beneath the cool sheets, and held her naked body to his for long moments without moving, savouring the moments before his questing fingers began their familiar exploration of her. He loved every part of her. He loved her rounded softness and her smooth satiny skin, and the way in which her warm secret places opened up for him. He loved to bury himself in her breasts and taste their sweetness, to hear her breathing quicken and to feel the warmth of her breath against him. He loved to lose himself in her, and to feel himself wrapped in her. He loved her uninhibited responses, and the unerring way she pleasured him.

'God, but I love you, Morwen,' he murmured against her mouth as he felt the hardening of her nipples against his own chest. 'How many times have I told you that?'

'A million times, but never enough times,' she whispered back. 'Never stop telling me, Ben.'

'I love you! I love you. If I lost everything else, I'd still have the world as long as I had you—'

'You'll always have me. I've always belonged to you, and you know that. Oh, Ben, hold me tight—'

Her fingers began a tantalising trail down the length of his spine, moving over the firm hard buttocks and kneading them for a few moments. There was power in every part of him, and she sometimes marvelled that a man of such physical strength and iron will could also be so tender, so sensitive to her every mood, every need. He was everything a woman could ever want, and Morwen gloried in knowing that she was his woman, wanted and cherished and loved by Ben Killigrew...

The pattern of their loving was familiar, yet always new. The swift arousal of nerves and senses; the slowing-down of pace to give each other maximum pleasure; seeking new ways to prolong the ultimate union that Morwen believed implicitly was a God-given joy.

She was not deeply religious, except with a simple, natural belief. But the moment when male and female seeds fused had always seemed to her to be something not quite of this earth, to be compared with all things mystical and wonderful. Morwen was both exalted and humbled by it.

She felt that now, as Ben's body became part of hers, and the slow, rhythmic pleasuring began. Her whole being seemed to change, to glow, to melt into Ben's so effortlessly, as he gathered her to him. She wanted it to go on for ever; she wanted it to end; to take her further into that magical world that finally gave her a glimpse of ecstacy...

The movements quickened, the spiralling sensations carrying her to a pinnacle of desire, until she felt her fingernails biting into his flesh. The need of him was exquisite, almost unbearable, and then the sudden gush of his seed made her cry out.

She clung to him, eyelids flickering, hardly wanting to breathe, wanting to hold him for always like this, still part of her… cradling his head against her as he lay spent, his heartbeats drumming against her breasts.

At that moment Ben was her baby, her child, her lover… and all the wisdom of the ages couldn't compare with this knowledge…

They lay close, not speaking, for long moments afterwards. And then she felt his fingers gently stroking her cheek, and became aware of the dampness there.

'Why do you always cry, my Morwen?' Ben said softly.

He had asked her before, but she could never find the words to explain. She tried now.

'Perhaps because 'tis almost too much for me to bear, this one-ness I feel with 'ee, Ben,' she whispered, turning into his hand to kiss his palm. 'If we take too much happiness, I'm almost afraid 'twill be snatched away from us—'

Emotion thickened her voice. The nuance of it was pure Cornish. She had been wed for four years to Ben Killigrew, yet she recognised again that there were times she was still the fiery-tempered Morwen Tremayne, clayworker's daughter, who dared to aspire to a boss's love. A swine-herd looking at a king…

Ben rocked her in his arms as though she were the child now. Her loosened hair was soft as silk against his skin, her body warm and moist against his. He loved her more than life… his Morwen, whose mind could still reach out into places where he couldn't go.

As though he were bewitched by her – Ben sometimes wondered if that wasn't a fairly apt description. A London college education had ripped away much of his own Cornish belief in intuition, but never all. It was too deeply ingrained… but he could still laugh away Morwen's fears at this moment.

'How can you think for a moment that we'll ever change, my darling? Or that anything could come between us! I'd kill the man that tried!'

Or the woman? The question was never asked, and nor did it rate more than a second's thought in Morwen's mind. That anything or anyone could spoil their happiness was unthinkable. She was comforted by Ben's insistence on it. And by knowing that while they had lain together, suffused with love, he had been hers, totally. However troubled his world, near or far, there was always peace to be found in each other's arms.

Chapter Four

Hal Tremayne's pit captains demanded a general works meeting. The four of them had come to his office, alongside the pit captain's hut at clay one, which was now occupied by his eldest son, Sam.

All were agreed that Ben Killigrew had been a fair boss in the four years since he'd taken control from his father. Even fairer than many had expected, with his little bonus payments for the excursion trips to and from the town on the Killigrew railway.

And it was that very fairness that was causing much disturbance among the tough clay workers, the short-tempered kiln workers, the bal maidens who scraped and stacked the dried clay into blocks ready for despatching, and even the young kiddley boys who did the menial jobs of fetching and carrying and making tea for the others. Whole families were employed by Killigrew Clay, and when one member was upset, then so were the rest, and they were never slow in voicing their worries.

In the middle of the week following his granddaughter's baptising, Hal stood squarely in the large open area of clay one, near the clay pool, and faced the huge numbers of clayworkers jostling for space. For a minute or two it reminded him of the ugly scenes leading to the never-forgotten strike, but it had been Charles Killigrew then who had stubbornly refused to pay the extra pennies and twopences to make a man's wage-packet worth taking home.

Hal had to make them see that this new trouble was none of Ben's doing. He had a loyalty to both sides, and he had never been afraid to speak his mind.

He glanced at Sam and his fellow pit captains in their hard hats and dark jackets, symbols of their status, and felt a sharp pride that Sam had followed so stalwartly in his footsteps. He cleared his throat and called for order. The muttering voices died away as they looked towards Hal's tall, commanding figure for direction. The Tremaynes were a handsome family.

In the background there was still the hum of the beam engine, and the trundling of the little trucks to the sky-tips for those who must keep working and would have the words of the meeting related to them later. There was still the roar from the fire-hole, and the cursing from kiln workers, sweating profusely as they pushed and levered the wet clay for drying with their long-handled shovels.

There was no cause for work to stop completely, and Hal was glad to see his instructions had been carried out.

'We all know why we'm here,' Hal stated. 'And we all know that Ben Killigrew's as keen as the rest of us to get this thing settled.'

'He'd better be! My old woman's wanting to be rid o' the babbies for their annual trip to the sea. 'Tis her only day off in the year, and I be the one getting the stick, Hal Tremayne!'

Raucous laughter followed the plaintive shout from the back of the crowd, and Hal grinned as he waved his hands for quiet. At least the mood of the men was temporarily lifted.

'These engineer fellows say they'll be poking about for some while yet—' He had to pause until the angry shouting died down. 'I've also had words wi' Ben Killigrew, and he's agreed to make a token paying-out to those who'd normally be takin' the train on excursion trips and are deprived of it for the time being. He can't be fairer than that, can he?'

The few cheers were drowned in the demands to know how big the token payment would be. Hal glowered around at those who stirred up the rest of them, and guessed that Gilbert Dark, pit captain from Clay Two, would be amongst them. Gil Dark had a habit of opposing everything.

'It won't be much,' he snapped at them. 'But 'twill be payment for doing nothing, if you daft buggers will only think on it! What other clay boss pays out for bein' idle? Not Bultimore and Vine's, you can take it from me!'

The growling lessened. Payment for doing nothing was not to be sneezed at.

'So how long afore the rail tracks be called safe again, Hal Tremayne? 'Tis a lot of stuff and nonsense, all this inspecting 'em. No little train be going to fall through these moors, if the clay waggons ain't done so all these years. You tell Ben Killigrew that from we—'

''Tis they daft buggers sitting behind their desks in their fancy offices who'm to blame for all this, not young Killigrew. Ain't they got nothing else to do but interfere wi' other folk's business?'

Hal shouted for quiet again as the men argued among themselves.

'The fact is, Ben don't own these moors! He has to pay rent to the county for using the land where he's built the rail tracks. If 'tis proved that the land's unsafe, he'll have no choice. The tracks will have to change course.'

'Why didn't the stupid bugger find out how the land lay afore he built 'em then?'

Sam stepped in, adding his roars to his father's to keep the crowd under control.

'He did that! There was no evidence to show there was tin-mining under this part of the moors. But that ain't good enough for these official buggers. They mean to search out every little crack in the surface, and study every ancient map they can to make certain sure. And 'tis safety we want, when all's said an' done. We don't want the likes of the Honourable Mrs Stanforth falling down an old mine-shaft, do us?'

He provoked them, knowing it would bring on a string of bawdy comments as to where the Honourable Mrs Stanforth could go with the rest of the stuck-up townsfolk. The anger began to subside again. The pit captains of Clay Three and Four drew closer to Hal, giving him silent support.

'So now 'ee all know as much as me,' Hal bellowed to make his voice heard. 'Ben Killigrew's coming here this week to see what's to do, and I'm told he'll visit Truro and Bodmin to see some old county records. If nothing's found, then there's nobody to say the rail tracks ain't safe.'

More cheers followed at that, and as Hal moved away, the crowd began to disperse. For a few minutes he'd wondered if the men would get as obstinate as they'd been before the strike four years ago, and he heard Gil Dark mutter grudgingly that Ben's offer to make the token payment whether they worked the excursion train or not was a stroke of genius.

Hal smiled faintly, knowing he had been the one to put the idea in the boss's head on Sunday afternoon. It was sometimes useful to have the boss as one of the family.

–

Ben was irritated at the thought of visiting Truro and Bodmin on what he considered a fool's errand. He had made endless searches into records before he even started work on the rail tracks. He was convinced there was no danger, and he cursed the finicky matron who had imagined she heard creaking and movement beneath the surface of the hillside.

The ancients of the area would probably attribute the noises to the spirits of the mines, the so-called knockers, tapping away underground to frighten the miners and demand that there were tid-bits of food left out for them... Ben dismissed the idea, annoyed that it had even entered his head, and thought viciously that he wished they'd go and frighten the Honourable Mrs Stanforth instead.

Now he was forced to make numerous visits to the site while surveyors and engineers inspected and argued, bored holes and took away samples, and his frustration at getting no positive results made him irritable with everyone. At Killigrew House the staff avoided him whenever possible, knowing they'd get a flea in their ears as soon as he looked at them.

As the frustrating days went by Morwen began to wonder where the closeness between them had gone. It seemed as elusive as stardust. Ben was too preoccupied to think of anything but the problems facing him. Rightly so, of course. In her saner moments Morwen would not have him any other way. But there were other times when she was capricious enough to wish the whole damn clay works to kingdom come.

She assumed he had forgotten the matter of the piano tutor. She almost hoped he had. It was of so little importance compared with the outcry about the railway safety. The Truro newspaper article had stirred up strong feeling in the town, and several impromptu town meetings had already taken place in the market square.

St Austell's roads had suffered badly from the lumbering clay waggons in the past, and still did so from some clay works. The townsfolk clearly feared that with Killigrew railway being put out of action, there would be a recurrence of the bad times.

The times that had resulted in the terrible accident four years ago...

Ben had had too much on his mind to think about engaging a pianoforte tutor for his wife on the day after her heated reaction, but her unexpected request lingered in his head. A week later he held her in his arms, preparatory to riding into Bodmin for yet another meeting with the land surveyors. He kissed her good-bye, and murmured the words that made her jerk back with sudden fright.

Her eyes were large and round and intensely blue.

'A tutor will be coming here today?' She heard herself stammering. 'You should have warned me, Ben! I'll not know what to say to un! I'll be all fingers and thumbs—'

She felt the rumble of his laughter against her body as he gave her an impatient little shake.

'Morwen, it's the tutor's job to teach you! I thought it was what you wanted. You're like a leaf in the wind at times, sweetheart. There's no pleasing you—'

'I'm sorry, Ben,' she muttered, angry with herself for behaving like a failure before she had even set her fingers to the keys of the pianoforte.

It wasn't just that, though. It was the thought of some superior genius of a man thinking her a complete idiot, and getting above herself... the clayworkers' daughters she knew weren't refined enough for piano-playing... she felt Ben's hands holding her reassuringly, and reminded herself that she was Morwen Killigrew, wife of the china clay works owner... any tutor should be honoured to come to this lovely house and give her lessons. She managed a weak smile.

'You took me by surprise, that's all. I thought you'd forgotten. You've been so busy—'

'Not too busy to notice that my wife sometimes gets bored with playing the lady,' he retorted. She felt her cheeks start to burn with embarrassment.

'Do I appear so ungrateful?'

He let her go, annoyance on his face. 'I didn't marry you for your gratitude, Morwen, but I don't forget that until you came here, you led a very different life. I don't mean to look down on it. God knows the clay business is an essential part of my life too, but for all its privations, I'm aware that you had a freedom then that you don't have now.'

He was perceptive enough to know it. The life of a lady, however genteel and seemingly carefree, still couldn't compare with the wild freedom of the moorland creatures. And part of Morwen Tremayne's charm had always been that empathy with such creatures. She was a dancing nymph, fey as the morning mist, an enchanting wood sprite…

The clay folk had a peculiar rapport with each other too, a feeling that went beyond family ties. They nearly all had large families, and they were as close-knit as a weaver's mesh. In times of trouble they were one huge family that stood firm against all odds. In a strange way Ben envied them. He had everything, but there was still something intangible that was missing, and he hadn't yet discovered what it was. Or if he had he wouldn't admit it, even to himself.

'What do I want with freedom, Ben?' Morwen said huskily. 'I wouldn't know what to do with it! All right. I'll put on my best prim face and sit like a lady for when this old gentleman comes. Will that do for 'ee?'

She gave a mischievous smile. He suddenly laughed and kissed the end of her nose.

'You couldn't look prim if you tried, and I don't think you'll find Mr David Glass too overpowering. He'll be here at about three o'clock.'

'Oh!'

'Does that not fit in with your plans for the day?'

She shrugged. 'It doesn't matter. I'd thought of visiting Dora, but I can do it just as well tomorrow. I feel I should take more of an interest in them. Even if Dora and I don't always agree, I love to see the children.'

Even as she spoke she felt guilty, because visiting Dora was only an excuse to go deeper on to the moors, and pay her intended visit to old Zillah. Morwen was determined on it now.

'Then visit Dora tomorrow,' Ben agreed. 'And I had best be on my way. I may be late for dinner this evening, so don't wait for me. I've seen Father this morning. He'd like you to read the London newspaper to him, Morwen, so that will occupy you for an hour or so.'

'Must I? 'Tis always so gloomy and depressing. It can hardly cheer him!'

'News of war is always depressing, my love, but it's what he wants, so please humour him. I shall look forward to hearing you dazzle me with your piano-playing later!'

Another quick kiss, and he was gone, the set look returning to his face again, at the thought of the forthcoming meeting. Morwen sighed. If she had matured and changed in four years, how much more so had Ben. Sometimes she wondered if she would ever see the old Ben again, or if he still existed.

It wasn't that she loved him less. In fact it awed her to know how much she loved him, and that she was capable of such love. In a big family like the Tremaynes the love was spread wide. To concentrate it all on one person in married bliss was both spectacular and a little frightening. With that strange ripple of presentiment she sometimes felt, Morwen crossed her fingers at the thought, as though too much happiness still had to be accounted for in the future.

She took the London newspaper up to Charles Killigrew's room. At least reading about other folk would take her mind away from the fright of meeting Mr David Glass that afternoon.

How absurd she was being! He was just a man, for heaven's sake! Ben would have chosen a proper and respectable tutor for her. He wanted to please her, and she'd just show him she could do as well as Miss Finelady... she'd prove herself worthy of his admiration, just as Ben had admired Jane Carrick's trilling music so long ago in this very house.

Like the echo of that night, she seemed to hear Jane's polite voice remarking that she'd never met a bal maiden before, and Morwen's own snapping that they didn't have two heads... how gauche she had been then.

If she were to meet Jane Carrick now, she was serenely sure of her own poise and graciousness. It was easy to be serene, when the likelihood of such a meeting was remote.

–

Charles wanted to hear every bit of news about the Crimean war. The local rag, as he called *The Informer*, was filled with gossip these days, apart from the pompous 'News Despatches from Abroad'. Since much of these reports were gleaned from the returning wounded embarking at Falmouth, it was necessarily highly coloured, and not entirely reliable, as each hero put his own interpretation on events.

The London newspapers, now sending their own war correspondents to the battle areas, may not be as graphic, but were probably nearer the truth.

Even the ambience of wars had changed, with reports reaching distant shores almost as soon as incidents occurred. The electric telegraph had seen to that, as well as the steam-powered ships that brought the wounded home before they had forgotten the horrors they had seen.

'You don't really want me to go on reading about the cholera outbreaks and the terrible winter in the Crimea, do you, Father?' Morwen said at last. 'Winter's over now—'

'Mebbe it is here, but not for those poor devils,' Charles said painfully. 'They suffered some terrible losses, m' dear, from disease as well as in the fighting, and ships lost in heavy seas. We do well to remember it.'

'I don't want to remember it,' she said, suddenly angry. 'What does this war have to do with us here in Cornwall? It turns folk into fanatics. We know nothing of such places as Balaclava and Sevastopol, that I've been reading about to you. They're just names to us—'

'We still celebrate any victory—' he said smugly, and Morwen snorted inelegantly.

'You call it celebrating, when any bit o' news turns folk into dancing idiots, lighting bonfires on the moors and chanting round 'em? Even to making effigies of the Russian Tsar like heathens? I'm surprised you think well o' such goings on!'

The victory bonfires had started in London, lit partly to celebrate, and partly to revive flagging spirits. The idea of them had quickly spread until it seemed that for even the smallest triumph a trail of fires was lit from the capital to Cornwall. Townsfolk and countryfolk alike went wild, with any excuse for prancing like lunatics in city parks and open moors.

Charles's smile was lop-sided as a trail of spittle ran down the side of his chin, and Morwen quickly wiped it away.

'Any such goings on brightens my day, love.' As he spoke, sadness distorted his voice.

Morwen felt a swift shame, realising immediately that to Charles newspaper reports, however gory, were like a window on the outside world that he would never really know again.

She leaned forward and kissed his cheek, knowing that he was tiring. He tired with alarming suddenness, and Morwen knew she would soon be free to do anything she wished. She could walk in the sun, ride her mare along the sandy beach, visit her mother... she was free, as Charles would never again be free.

But she wanted to read no more war news. The new edition of the Truro paper, *The Informer*, had arrived that morning, and she picked it up, hoping to interest Charles in more local affairs. The 'Domestic Intelligence' column usually had some humorous bits in it, and some of the correspondence columns were ponderous and heavily anonymous...

'Has Ben read any of this to you?' she said quickly.

His head moved slowly from side to side. He liked to drop off to sleep with the sound of her soft voice still in his ears, so she picked up the paper and began to read, hoping the tremor in her voice wouldn't betray the unease she felt.

'It's a report by Lew Tregian, the editor who came here to interview Ben recently.' She began to read the printed words.

'It is announced that Mr Tom Askhew, former chief editor of *The Informer* here in Truro, and now of *The Northern Informer* in Yorkshire, is to become the official War Correspondent for both newspapers while the crisis in the Crimea continues. Mr Askhew left for the Crimea several weeks ago, and will be sending reports back with all speed. Mr Askhew's journalistic accomplishments have been widely praised in Cornwall and the North of England, and the owner of the Northern paper, Sir

Garside Sefton, has called him his right-hand man. Mr Askhew leaves behind his young wife, formerly Miss Jane Carrick of Truro, and their baby daughter, Cathy. It is to be hoped the parting will not be too prolonged, but we at *The Informer* feel privileged in our re-aquaintance with a fine master of the written word.'

Morwen supposed Lew Tregian felt obliged to be flowery in his praise of Tom Askhew, but she couldn't help feeling that part of his account was more like an obituary. She shivered.

Reading about Tom Askhew and his family revived all the old anxieties about Ben and Jane. She knew it was unworthy of her when Tom must be in very great danger now, and Jane deserving of everyone's sympathy, but it didn't stop her thoughts…

A sudden ragged snore made her realise that Charles was sleeping soundly, and had probably heard no more than a little of Lew Tregian's account. It didn't matter. For a second Morwen wished she dared screw up the newspaper and throw it away, so that Ben wouldn't read it, but that was being petty.

What did she have to fear from Jane Carrick Askhew after all these years? The parents had wanted Ben and Jane to marry, not the couple themselves. She knew it as well as she knew her own name, but she hoped fervently that the Crimean War would soon be over, and that Tom would come back safely. Morwen now had her own reason for wishing it.

She tip-toed out of the bedroom, whispering to the nurse in the adjoining small dressing-room she occupied, that Charles was asleep. The nurse was efficient and capable, but privately Morwen didn't think she had much heart.

Perhaps it was best for a nurse to be like that. It wouldn't do to get emotionally involved with patients. How would Florence

Nightingale fare amid the horrors of the Crimea if she wept over every wounded hero?

There was that wretched Crimea again, Morwen thought crossly. It slipped into everyone's thoughts, whether they wanted it to or not. She looked at the grandfather clock ticking away solemnly in the corner of the passageway.

It was a long while until lunch time, even longer until three o'clock and the piano lesson, but with not really enough time for her to visit her mother and be reassured that it wasn't incredibly foolish for a young married woman to learn to play an instrument when her days might be better occupied…

Thinking of her mother reminded Morwen of Matt at that moment. She had never traced her brother's movements on Ben's atlas from New York to California and the gold diggings after all. It would be something to do.

If Ben were here he could no doubt tell her in a trice which direction it would be, but she could surely find it for herself. Morwen went into Ben's study and across to the huge family atlas he kept on a side table.

It was open at the page showing the area of the Crimean war. Morwen put a marker in it, and quickly turned the pages until she found the American continent. New York was printed boldly, and she felt an odd sensation, just gazing at the name of the town where Matt had begun his new life. But where in the maze of place names was California?

Morwen was no scholar, and it took a long while before she finally found it; then she was aghast. It was as far from New York across land, as Cornwall was from New York over the ocean. It was so very far away… her eyes were damp as she left the atlas as she had found it.

Her mother had been so buoyant on hearing news of her lost lamb. It would break her heart all over again if she realised that Matt was now twice as far from them all. Morwen resolved there and then not to tell her.

It was a tedious day without Ben, even more so because of Morwen's growing nervousness as three o'clock approached. Her palms were clammy as the clock struck, and she was sure she would be useless on the pianoforte.

Mr David Glass would wash his hands of her after one lesson, and Ben would be angry at her stupidity. And somewhere in the north of England, as though some soft whisper on the air told her exactly what was happening, Jane Carrick Askhew would be laughing at her…

The rap of the heavy door knocker made Morwen jump, and she was furious to know how feebly she was reacting. She waited in the drawing-room with fast-beating heart as Mrs Tilley went to usher the tutor into the house. She smoothed down the cool fabric of the ice-blue afternoon dress she wore, and tucked a stray tendril of her black hair into its fashionable comb.

Footsteps neared the room and the door opened. Mrs Tilley was composed, her face blankly respectful.

'Mr David Glass, Ma'am.'

She moved aside and left the room, and a young man of about Ben's age stepped inside. He was quietly and elegantly dressed, and seemingly as nervous as herself. He was pale and good-looking. For some reason he instantly reminded Morwen of a poet. When he smiled, a nerve at the side of his mouth twitched, and it was Morwen who stretched out a hand to greet him. He held it almost reverently, and cleared his throat in some agitation.

'I'm delighted to make your acquaintance, Mrs Killigrew,' he said huskily. 'I was so pleased when your husband engaged me to instruct you. I've seen you many times about the town.'

57

'Have you?' She was taken aback as his face coloured, giving him the look of a young and eager fawn.

Her nerves disappeared. He seemed entranced by her physical appearance, yet Morwen knew instinctively that she had nothing to fear from David Glass. His adoration, if adoration it was, was of the ethereal kind. Ben had probably known that too, she guessed intuitively. She gave the young man a brilliant smile that made him swallow hastily.

'Should we not begin, Mr Glass?' she said gently. 'I'm sure you're an excellent teacher, and I'm a very eager pupil.'

He flushed with pleasure now, and Morwen thought how clever and sensitive her wonderful Ben had been, and how wickedly devious to let her go on thinking she was to be taught by some stuffy elderly gentleman. David Glass was almost childlike, and she was sure they were going to get along famously.

Chapter Five

Ben was well aware that there were few gentlemen with whom a lady could safely be left unchaperoned. They included the family doctor, lawyer, respected relatives, churchman and tutor. He had resisted his natural aversion on first meeting David Glass, and listened to the recommendations of others as to his teaching ability.

That David Glass reminded him all too well of those pale earnest youths at his London college was an undeniable fact. But it was never wise to go by looks alone. Besides which, there was no hint of scandal attached to his name in the town, where such things had an uncanny way of becoming public knowledge.

But by the time he got home to Killigrew House that evening, the pianoforte lesson was the last thing on Ben's mind. He was in a fury. The meeting in Bodmin hadn't gone well, and there seemed to be deadlock among all concerned. Even the surveyors and engineers were arguing among themselves now, each one refusing pointblank to give a firm decision until the specialist engineer was consulted. And he was at present 'travelling abroad'...

Ben made up his mind to go to Truro and consult Richard Carrick, bypassing the Killigrew lawyers, who seemed useless in advising him. Carrick was a one-time partner in Kiliigrew Clay, and always sympathetic towards Ben, despite his wife's antagonism with the whole family. More importantly, Carrick was eminently respected among the legal profession, and might well find a loophole no-one else had considered.

Morwen knew better than to discuss musical scales and arpeggios with Ben while he was in this mood. He raged over the absence of the chief engineer more than anything else.

'For all we know, he might be caught up in that bloody war in the Crimea,' Ben said savagely. He drank deeply, the level in the whisky decanter lowering rapidly as he poured himself yet another glass. He threw himself into a chair, his body tense with exhaustion and anger.

'Can't you do *anything* without him?' Morwen said anxiously.

He glowered at her. 'Do you ever listen when I speak? Watch my lips, Morwen! The bastards won't budge until we get the chief engineer's say-so, and that's final.'

Her face went a brilliant red. 'Don't treat me like a ninny, Ben—'

'Then don't act like one,' he retorted. 'How many times do I have to tell you before it sinks into your head? No matter how many times I plead and argue to keep the railway open, it's still stalemate—'

'Then it seems pointless to keep trying. Where's the sense in it?'

Her simple logic infuriated him even more.

'Stick to women's doings, will you? Mind your business, and leave me to mine!'

He shouted at her, sounding so much like his father in the old roaring days that she was shocked into silence for a moment. But not for long. She didn't have to listen to his insults. He could drown himself in whisky for all she cared. She leapt to her feet, her eyes blazing.

'I see 'twas a waste of time to wait up for you tonight! I had expected some interest in my afternoon, but there'd be no pleasing 'ee if I told 'ee I could play the entire works of Mozart after one lesson!'

She made to flounce away from him. His arm shot out, his hand catching hers and holding her fast.

'I'm sorry, love. My mind's a million miles from such things at present. Play for me tomorrow when I'm in a better humour.' He couldn't hide the tension in his voice.

He couldn't relax enough to make the words sound sufficiently contrite for Morwen. She snatched her hand away.

'I prefer to play for Mr Glass! He appreciates me!'

She saw the ghost of a smile on Ben's mouth, and completely misinterpreted it. She thought he was laughing at her, while the idea of David Glass appreciating any young woman, however beautiful, was the one thing that could amuse Ben at that moment. Morwen stormed away from him, her head held high.

She would show him! She would prove she didn't have to be born in a mansion to understand the rudiments of music! She would prove that other men could look at Ben Killigrew's wife and find her attractive, even if Ben was too busy to notice. She slammed the heavy door behind her childishly, and didn't care.

She lay shivering in the cold sheets for an hour, wishing Ben would come to bed and take her in his arms and tell her to forget all this nonsense that was causing the rift to widen between them. By the time he came upstairs, she was ready and willing to forgive him his bad temper. She longed for his tenderness, for him to be the Ben she loved...

'Next time you go into my study, please leave things the way you found them,' he snapped, as he got into the other side of the bed and turned his back on her.

Morwen lay wide-eyed and unmoving, staring up into the darkness. The harshness in his voice shocked her again. The soft tears slid down her cheek, and the thought churning about in her head was how two people who had been so much in love, could have grown so far apart with such little effort.

–

Ben was ready to leave early next morning. Morwen always rose early, and was eating breakfast when he told her briefly that he intended seeing Richard Carrick. She wondered at once if he had seen the piece in the Truro newspaper about Jane Carrick's husband, but pride stopped her asking him.

'When will you be back?' she said instead. 'Cook likes to be told if there will be one less for dinner.'

She was still upset from the previous night, and the words sounded prim and sarcastic.

'I don't give a damn for Cook's requirements,' he said curtly. 'She can prepare dinner for ten people and throw the lot to the street urchins for all I care. Don't bother me with such piffling matters—'

He looked at her coldly, very much his father's son at that moment – voice, words, attitude. Charles Killigrew had once been this arrogant, lord of his domain…

'And please don't be so unfeeling, Ben!' she said furiously. 'I asked a perfectly civil question, and I've a right to a civil answer!'

'I expect to be home later this evening. If not, then you'll see me tomorrow. I daresay Richard Carrick will offer me a bed for the night if necessary. Does that satisfy your domestic little mind?'

Her face burned at the insult. His railway might be under threat of closure, but it was no excuse for belittling her in this way. He had overcome crises before, and needed her support. She was bitterly hurt that he didn't seem to need her now.

'I daresay I'll manage to fill my time without you.'

She concentrated on her breakfast and didn't look at him. He pecked a swift kiss to her cheek, as though he couldn't wait to be out of the house and away from her.

Morwen resisted the temptation to grasp at his hand and hold it to her lips, and beg him not to leave her like this. But such sweet shared moments seemed far removed from the business of the day.

–

Morwen spent most of the morning with Charles, after assuring Cook that it didn't matter in the least if she had to throw good food away later, much to her own outraged sense of thrift. Bess Tremayne would be horrified if she could hear her daughter's airy instructions to Mrs Horn, but the days when Morwen Tremayne had to consider where every penny was spent were long gone. Whatever the outcome of the railway affair, she knew that as well as Ben. She thought he was taking the whole matter far too seriously. It would resolve itself, and meanwhile, Killigrew Clay was flourishing. There was an endless demand for china clay, and ships from far and near put into Charlestown port, eager to fill their holds with the white substance known fancifully by some as the porcelain earth.

And if their own clay waggons were forced to go through St Austell town's narrow hilly streets once, or even twice more, while a new railway course was being constructed, what would it matter? They had done so for many years before, and with only one bad accident... despite the trauma of that occasion, it had served to make other pits using the town route doubly careful, and no responsible waggoner would risk a second slur on the good name of Killigrew Clay...

There were times when lack of what was called 'a good education' was preferable to all the arguments and discussions such schooling produced, Morwen concluded scornfully.

Clay folk would see two sides to a question, consider the best course and act on it, not go all the way round the kiddleywinks to try to find a solution, and get nowhere!

After Morwen had eaten a light lunch, the stable-boy saddled her mare. She didn't want to arrive at Sam and Dora's cottage in any of the Killigrew vehicles, acting the lady. She wanted to ride, to feel the wind in her hair and capture the essence of springtime in her nostrils. She wanted to embrace the wild freedom of the moors and forget all the troubles that seemed to come with being the wife of a gentleman!

Most young girls thought that was the day all troubles ended... and they generally did, Morwen thought guiltily. But she couldn't quite feel that innocent euphoria today.

And no matter how she toned it down, there was a world of difference in the Morwen Tremayne who had once raced bareback on the wild moorland ponies, and the elegant Morwen Killigrew in her smart green velvet riding habit who dismounted at the old Tremayne cottage to visit her sister-in-law.

''Tis good to see 'ee, Morwen,' Dora said with forced heartiness. She surreptitiously wiped her hands on her apron, and gave Morwen an uneasy smile. Morwen smiled back, ignoring the faint smells of cabbage cooking and baby's urine. Dora was a loving wife to Sam, but she was none too clean in her habits.

'I thought I should visit my nephews and niece more often,' Morwen tried to be natural, but it was difficult with Dora's eyes assessing her fine clothes and the gloss of her hair with its silvery combs, and the string of pearls Ben had bought her on her last birthday gleaming around her neck.

She knew at once that she should have worn something even more demure. But why should she? Dora didn't dress up for her, so why should she dress down for Dora? The usual strained atmosphere existed between them, no matter how much Dora fussed over getting Morwen some refreshment, and the boys came hurtling down the stairs as soon as they heard Morwen's voice and scrambled on her knees, begging for a story.

'Don't 'ee go messing up Auntie Morwen's fine clobber now,' Dora said crossly, her embarrassment at Morwen's appearance making her take it out on the children. 'She don't want 'ee climbing all over 'er—'

'Oh, they don't worry me, Dora! Of course I'll tell them a story. Where's Primmy?'

'She be asleep,' Dora said abruptly, and then shrugged. 'I daresay 'twon't hurt waking her up just this once. She's near due for feedin' anyways. She's crochety wi' the colic when she wakes, so I'll feed 'er first, then 'ee can wind 'er if 'ee's a mind to it, and if 'twon't mess up your velvet.'

Morwen refused to take offence at Dora's obvious resent-ment. Instead, she held the two little boys on her lap, their large blue eyes fixed on her face as she related a story to them. She had to resist hugging them too closely, and to avoid letting her eyes stray too often to where Dora was by now nursing the baby to her breast, her voice softened and cooing to the child as she sucked. Morwen had to steel herself not to let the overwhelming ache of longing sweep over her, as Dora performed the personal and private task Morwen so dearly envied. When Primmy was satisfied, Dora deftly replaced her breast in her dress, and matter-of-factly handed the baby over to Morwen.

'Hold 'er over your shoulder,' she instructed. 'I'll fetch a cloth to put over 'ee first. She'll belch a few times.' Morwen looked down at the perfect little face, the mouth with a film of milk around it, the eyes half-closed with contentment. Did Dora have any inkling of how blessed she was? Morwen thought passionately. To have three beautiful children like these…

The boys had slid from her lap now, bored with the baby, and as Dora put the cloth on her shoulder, Morwen held Primmy against her body and patted her back. Primmy was heavy in her arms, her face warm against Morwen's, belching gently. It gradually dwindled to a faint hiccoughing, and Morwen sat the baby in her lap, facing her.

Her eyes opened wider now, as though she knew that these were different arms holding her. Morwen spoke softly to her, and her heart twisted as a sudden beatific smile spread over Primmy's heart-shaped face.

''Tis only more wind,' Dora said prosaically. 'She's the windiest babby in creation. If tain't one end, 'tis t'other!'

'She's beautiful, Dora,' Morwen said softly. 'You're so lucky!'

Dora stared at her, and sniffed.

'Sam don't allus think so when she wakes us up in the night to 'er squalling,' she retorted.

'You wouldn't be without her though, would you?'

As though she thought some demon spirit of the moors was going to snatch Primmy away that very instant, Dora immediately took the baby out of Morwen's arms.

''Course not. That's a daft thing to say! Be 'ee visiting the works while you'm away from the big house?'

The words were pointed, reminding Morwen that she had been here long enough. It wasn't her old home any longer. The furniture was different, the new family complete; Morwen's bed-space behind the curtain not used as in the old days. She got to her feet, and quickly kissed the boys good-bye. They bleated noisily about her leaving, clearly loving this unexpected visit.

"Til come and see you again,' Morwen promised. She glanced at Dora. 'That's all right, isn't it?'

"Tis your brother's cottage. That makes 'ee welcome.'

She didn't add her own welcome, and once out in the fresh afternoon air, Morwen was glad to be rid of the stuffiness of the place. Nothing stayed the same, she thought sadly, and then she dug her heels into her mare's flanks and raced him across the moors to try and dispel the burning emptiness inside her.

She was aware of a searing envy too... for while she had been at the cottage, she had felt a strange, fierce desire to keep those three children encircled in her arms for ever... she could love them as her own... and such longing was as futile as wishing for the moon. It was almost wicked too, for they were Dora's children, not hers. Sam's and Dora's...

The mare was lathering with the gallop. Morwen reined her in and slid off her back. Her own breathing was heavy and fast, both from the wildness of the ride, and the inborn need for it. She leaned against the mare's side, feeling her heave from exertion. And suddenly had to close her eyes against the brightness of the sun.

Her breathing gradually slowed down. Her hair had come loose from its combs and had tumbled down her back. She was on the crest of the moors, with Charles Killigrew's sky-tips, the white hills of the clay works, far away to the right of her, glinting in the sunlight.

Somewhere beyond was the granite bulk of the Larnie Stone, and far below was the busy town of St Austell, its buildings no more than stone huddles from this distance. Out of sight in the afternoon haze were the beautiful long sandy beaches, and the dust-white port of Charlestown, made prosperous by the export of china clay.

This was her world. From these moors she had gazed down on St Austell a million times with her friend Celia. Two carefree bal maidens, envying the townsfolk, and never thinking that one day one of them would be married to a clay boss, and the other would lie drowned in the slurry of a clay pool.

'Be 'ee lost, lady?'

The voice made Morwen jump. She knew its owner before she turned round. When she did, she saw the old crone's bead-like eyes narrow, and the breeze catching the scanty wisps of grey hair around the wizened face gave the old woman a scarecrow look.

'Don't 'ee know me, Zillah?' Morwen said huskily. ''Tis Morwen Killigrew who used to be Morwen Tremayne.'

'I mind 'ee well,' the woman nodded slowly. 'I mind the day 'ee came to see old Zillah wi' that pretty friend o' yourn. Not so pretty after, were she?'

'Don't – 'tis cruel to speak so—'

The old crone cocked her head on one side like a little bird. She had no time for niceties.

'What do 'ee want wi' old Zillah today then, lady? I'm thinking 'tis more'n chance that brings 'ee near to my cot.'

Morwen glanced behind the old woman and realised she had galloped nearer to her destination than she had known. The old hovel where Zillah lived with her cats and her evil potions was only a short distance away.

She took a sharp breath, suddenly hating the thought of stepping inside it again. The memories of the last time, when she and Celia had begged this old hag for a potion to rid Celia of Jude Pascoe's child were still too painful... it was ironic that Morwen should come here now for the very opposite.

'How long have 'ee been wed, lady?' Zillah asked suddenly, refusing to call her by name yet.

'Four years—'

'And no babbies yet?' As if she truly had the second sight of which she boasted, Zillah spoke shrewdly, nodding as Morwen's face reddened. 'So 'ee thinks to ask old Zillah for summat to make your man more amorous, be that it?'

'No!' Morwen said indignantly. Ben gave her all the loving a woman could ever need... until just recently, she admitted, when he was too concerned with other matters, but that wasn't something she cared to tell this evil old woman. Her Mammie had always been against consulting Zillah, and Morwen suddenly felt the need to be far away from here. Before she could move, the scrawny fingers gripped her wrist, fast as an eagle's talons.

''Tis the only thing I can do for 'ee, Morwen Killigrew,' Zillah said sternly, and then began to cackle in her unnerving manner. 'A potion to put in your man's drink to make him give 'ee more o' the loving if 'ee ain't getting enough. Even old Zillah can't improve a man's seed. Takes old Mother Earth to do that—'

Morwen twisted out of her grasp. 'I'm not tampering with Ben's drink,' she stuttered. 'And I don't want any more of your evil advice. Celia died because of it—'

She scrambled on to the mare's back and dug her heels in her again. She felt as young and vulnerable as on that bad day, imprinted in her memory for all time. Her hair streamed out in the wind as the mare whinnied in protest and then leapt to a gallop, but behind her she could still hear the old crone's cawing, parting words.

'The girl drowned herself, lady. 'Twas her own doing, not mine. 'Twas her destiny, same as 'tis yourn to be barren 'til the time be right—'

Sobs were tearing at Morwen's chest. She hardly registered the last few jeers, only that one hateful word. Barren, barren... the loneliest word in the English language.

She wished she had never come here today, to visit Dora and the children... to make this useless journey to see Zillah. The glory of the moors was lost on her, and all she wanted was to go home... but Ben wouldn't be there. He might not come home until tomorrow, and when he did, he still wouldn't be close to her in spirit. He wouldn't need her as she needed him.

She drove the mare on over the moors. The Larnie Stone, with its so-called mystical powers, seemed to rear up as she neared it. She barely glanced at it. It hadn't helped Celia in her quest for a true and noble lover, and Morwen was unwilling to remember right now that it was there that she and Ben Killigrew had first tasted the delights of one another.

Without noticing where she was going, she realised she was galloping along the leafy lanes towards her parents' home, and with the sobs still choking her, she finally slid off the animal's back and burst through the door of the house like a whirlwind, finding solace as she had always done, in Bess's arms.

–

'There, my lamb, whatever's wrong!' Bess exclaimed at once. 'Has summat hurt 'ee? You'm as flushed as a winter fire, yet your hands be cold as charity. Sit 'ee down and get your breath, and tell me what troubles 'ee.'

The urge to spill out everything was like a dam about to burst inside her. But it wasn't fair to burden Bess with it all. What good would it do? And knowing that Morwen had visited

Zillah would only antagonise her mother. Caution stopped her blurting out the words. Instead, she blamed her distress on missing Ben…

'What a ninny you be, Morwen,' Bess smiled gently with obvious relief that it was nothing worse. 'So Ben might be staying away for one night! 'Tis good to know you two still be lovebirds and want each other's company above all others. Be glad for the pain o' missin' him, love. 'Tis preferable to not caring if he's near or far!' Morwen forced a shaky smile to her lips. Did Ben care as much as she did? She wouldn't think of such doubts.

'I'm just being silly,' she mumbled. ''Tis just that I miss un so, and it seems that I hardly see him these days.' Bess gave her a quick hug. 'It takes a parting to have a sweet reunion, my love. Remember that! And I've no doubt Ben will be missin' 'ee too.'

Morwen tried not to sigh too audibly, and Bess spoke briskly, perhaps seeing more than her daughter imagined she did.

'Will 'ee both come for Sunday tea, Morwen? Freddie's school-teacher's calling on us, bein' the only time your Daddy feels free to see un, and neither of us be looking forward to it. If Ben's here, he'll mebbe help us on the decision about our Freddie going away to school.'

'All right.' Morwen relaxed. This was safer ground. 'What about Jack? Will he be puttin' his penn'orth in?'

'Jack's goin' over to Truro on Sunday. Seems he's met up with some folk who be more interesting than we clay folk. And Sam and Dora think 'twill be too much of a houseful wi' the babbies, so they be stayin' away too.'

Her voice was still crisp, and Morwen knew better than to question her further. But she meant to question Jack at the first opportunity. If he was drifting away from the family, it would break her Mammie's heart all over again, the way Matt had broken it when he'd gone off to America with Jude Pascoe.

'I'd best go, Mammie. I've been visiting Dora and the children, and Ben's father will be watching out for my return.'

'How is the poor man?' Now Bess was certain why Morwen had looked so distraught. Seeing Dora with her happy little brood must make the girl ache to hold a babby of her own.

Morwen shrugged. 'No better, no worse. Doctor Pender says he'll go on the way he is until his heart finally gives out.'

''Tis a poor prospect for a fine man,' Bess said sadly. 'But 'tis a blessing he has Ben to take on the burden of the clayworks. No man could ask for a better son, love.'

And what of the future if Ben had no son for the clay inheritance? The thought was constantly in Morwen's head, coupled with the undoubted fact that if he had married Jane Carrick, there would surely have been sons by now. Jane had proved her fertility by producing a daughter for Tom Askhew, and would probably have as large a brood as Sam and Dora in time.

'We'll see you on Sunday, Mammie,' Morwen promised quickly, and left the cosy little house feeling somewhat like Charles Killigrew. No better, no worse than before.

Chapter Six

Spring was already merging into summer. For once it wasn't a prospect that pleased Ben Killigrew. With every week that passed, the need to get his railway pronounced safe became more urgent. It was a matter of personal pride and integrity, as well as business sense.

He scarcely noticed the bursting forth of blossom and greenery as he rode to Truro to call on Richard Carrick on that fine May morning. His thoughts were still fraught over the unproductive meeting on the previous day.

There had been three others and himself poring over old maps and land proofs in the surveyors' offices at Bodmin. That there had been old tin-mine workings in the area where Killigrew and other clay works now flourished was undenied.

What concerned Ben was whether the underground working constituted a danger to the twice-yearly despatch of clay to Charlestown port, and for his railway to be carrying passengers at other times. He had little patience to listen to anything else. He wanted his questions answered, and these old fools seemed just as intent on dodging the issue.

'Mr Killigrew!' The surveyor, bewhiskered and pompous and constantly twirling his watch chain in his bulbous fingers, glowered at Ben in exasperation. 'We've told 'ee a hundred times. We dare not make a move on this until we hear from Chief Engineer Trent. 'Tis more'n we dare do, my dear sir.'

'Please don't patronise me, Mr Newton,' Ben snapped. 'I fail to see why you can't declare the area safe. There's been no trouble in the three years and more that the railway's been operating, and you can see for yourself that no tin mine workings exist beneath my tracks. I had the area checked before any navvying began. Good God, man, d'you take me for an idiot?'

'Please, Mr Killigrew,' one of the others, a red-faced site engineer, spoke nervously as Ben's voice rose. 'No-one's disputing your diligence, but you must have heard of rogue shafts. 'Tis they that we must investigate as far as possible—'

'No, I have not heard of rogue shafts.' Ben glared at the man. 'Are you trying to tell me there may be shafts that are uncharted and unregistered?'

'That's exactly it, Mr Killigrew,' the surveyor said triumphantly, as Ben himself put the problem into words. ''Twas illegal, o' course, but who was to know if a band o' miners found a tin stream underground leading off from the main shaft, and shored it up for themselves for the profits to line their own pockets? 'Twouldn't be the first time—'

'And there would be no evidence of it, see? Now that there's been a formal complaint, we daren't take a chance on it, until Engineer Trent comes back and deals wi' the problem—'

The smug tones of the third man made Ben fume with frustration. He rounded on the man, banging his fist on the table where the old maps and documents were spread about.

'Then where is this bloody engineer? Has no-one found out his whereabouts yet?'

Silas Newton's eyes glinted angrily at this show of temper. He began rolling up the documents one by one, precisely and methodically.

'Engineer Trent is on an extended trip abroad for his health,' he said sharply. 'His house is closed up, and I daresay only his doctor knows his exact movements—'

'Give me the doctor's name,' Ben said savagely. 'Have none of you heard of the electric telegraph? The man must have a forwarding address, and I mean to find it.'

The three looked at one another, then grudgingly gave Ben the name of a Bodmin doctor. He called on him immediately, to be told that Engineer Trent was in Europe suffering with consumption, and was not expected back in Cornwall for three months. The doctor refused to give Ben the address of the Swiss clinic, saying only that his patient had been very ill at the time of departure, and his wife had given strict instructions that he was not to be upset by news from home.

Ben only half believed the story. As he'd half hinted to Morwen, the man was probably swinging the lead and acting the hero, and had got himself caught up in the bloody Crimean war…

There must be some way to overrule the decisions of the Bodmin men. By now there were prominent notices all over the railway route, prohibiting the use of it while safety investigations went on.

Ben cursed the Honourable Mrs Stanforth a hundred times a day for creating unnecessary panic, and hoped to God that Richard Carrick's keen legal mind would help him find a solution.

–

By the time he reached Truro his temper was beginning to boil again. He knew he had treated Morwen badly, and that didn't help him. She had been so eager to show him her progress on the piano, and he had brushed her aside like a troublesome insect. He hated the world, and himself most of all.

Riding through the crowded streets of Truro, he felt an almost reckless urge to visit another house in the town where he'd been only once before. Where he had staked the fortunes of Killigrew Clay on the turn of a dice and won a fortune, enough to buy his father and his partner out, and assume control in the dark days of the clay strike.

If he had the nerve to gamble today, in his present frame of mind he would surely lose the lot. Right now, that didn't seem such a bad idea…

He told himself angrily not to be such a fool. It wasn't in his nature to admit defeat, and hopefully Carrick would give him solid guidance. Even if he had to take the damn surveyors to court to allow him to continue running his own railway, he would win in the end. He was determined on that.

He reached the Carrick house, hoping the lawyer would be there. He didn't normally go to his chambers until the afternoon. The door opened, and a maid bobbed politely on seeing him. She was new enough to show no surprise at this unexpected visitor.

The last time he had been here there had been a grudging admiration from the lawyer for the way in which young Ben had informed him of his intentions of winning control of the clay works. There had also been angry words between Ben and Mary, Carrick's haughty wife. He hoped he wouldn't have to encounter her right away…

'Would you please inform Mr Carrick that Ben Killigrew is here to see him?' he said shortly, and then a sudden rustle of skirts and a delighted exclamation made him temporarily forget why he had come.

For a moment it was as though a vision was moving towards him with arms outstretched. She was as bright as the sun, from her honey-gold hair to the delicate peach-coloured dress and slippers, and her pleasure at seeing him was like balm.

'Ben, how marvellous! We were only speaking about you last evening, and here you are! It's so good to see you again.'

He felt as though he smiled properly for the first time in weeks as Jane ran straight into his arms, and they kissed as old friends.

'Am I seeing things? How well you look, Jane! Marriage certainly suits you. I saw the piece about Tom in *The Informer* recently, but it said nothing about you coming home!'

She smiled up into his face and he saw how mature she had become in the four years since she ran off to marry Tom Askhew. How astonishingly pretty... she had always been that, but she was more so now.

And old friends they might be, but Ben was suddenly embarrassed to be holding her in his arms and gazing into her sparkling face like an adolescent boy. They were both adult now, and on Jane the word sat as beautifully as a summer morning on a sunlit beach. He released her with an awkward laugh.

'And I thought you had got wind of it, and come especially to see me,' she pretended to pout. 'I've been here several weeks now, and oh, Ben, I can't tell you how good it is to talk to you! Mama is driving me to distraction as usual, and she fusses over my poor Cathy until the child feels more like a little pet than a baby!'

Mention of Jane's daughter gave Ben a chance to collect his senses. 'Where is she – the child and the mama?' he added.

Jane gave a soft laugh. 'I'm afraid Mama's confined to her bed with a summer cold, and I know it's wicked of me, but it's quite refreshing not to have her stalk me around the house. She's sure I'm going to run off again at any minute. And Cathy's having a sleep in the nursery. Would you like to see her?'

'Of course. After I've spoken to your father, Jane—'

She stopped her prattling. 'Oh, I forgot that you were asking for Father. He had to go to Falmouth yesterday, but we expect him home this afternoon. You'll stay until he arrives, won't you? Take some lunch with me and Cathy, and then I won't feel so lonely.'

He agreed smilingly. He had never had any intention of leaving until he had consulted with Richard Carrick anyway. Being with Jane again would make a pleasant diversion.

'Then you must tell me all that's been happening since we last met, Ben. I know you married Morwen Tremayne, and I've heard something of your present troubles. Father still takes an interest in Killigrew Clay, even after all this time.'

'I'm glad to hear it,' Ben said, without giving anything away. 'I suppose it's hard for him not to. He was involved in it for long enough. And you seem to know everything of importance in my life already! I'd rather hear about you, and about how Tom is faring in the Crimea.'

Her face shadowed a little as she led the way to the nursery, and from the longing in her voice Ben didn't need to be a genius to know that she was as much in love as ever with her plain-speaking Yorkshire husband.

'I wish I knew. I miss him so, Ben. This new idea of news-paper war correspondents may be wonderful, but not for the women who know their husbands are in as much danger as the fighting men! I worry about him all the time, and I can't confide in Mama, who never had a good word for Tom as you well know.'

She hugged his arm. 'Of all the people in the world, Ben, you know how much Tom always meant to me. If it wasn't for you, I might never have known the happiness I've had with him.'

At her sudden indrawn breath, he kissed her cheek. She smelled of lavender and rose-water.

'We made a good pretence of being in love, didn't we?' He said lightly, 'Perhaps too good a job. It made it all the harder for your mama to bear when she discovered it wasn't me you meant to marry after all!'

'If she hadn't been so stuffy and narrow-minded she'd have welcomed the man I loved, not been so snobbish about him just because he's a newspaperman. Father managed to get over his resentment, but I don't think Mama ever will.'

She sighed, and they went into the airy nursery together. In the heavy oak cot a child was stirring. Ben watched as Jane spoke tenderly to her and lifted her out. The child was the image of her mother, with none of Tom Askhew's coarseness. At two years old, Jane's daughter already had her mother's grace and charm. He saw the small arms wrap themselves around Jane's neck, and felt a sharp and unfamiliar envy. Killigrew House, too, cried out for children to fill its rooms.

Long before Richard Carrick arrived from Falmouth in the late afternoon, Ben was cocooned in a very different atmosphere from the one he had left in St Austell. The Carrick house echoed to the sounds of Cathy's childish laughter, and Ben felt more alive than he had in weeks.

Somehow the fact that he'd been unable to plunge straight into his railway discussions made him feel as though he had been given a reprieve, in which he could play with this delightful child and her equally delightful mother.

Richard Carrick came home to find the extraordinary sight of Ben Killigrew on his hands and knees, with Richard's granddaughter clambering over him. It was such a domestic, intimate little scene, that for a few seconds, he felt the same regret as his wife, years ago, when they finally knew that the feelings of Ben and Jane weren't leading them towards marriage.

He came towards Ben with outstretched hands, the genuine fondness he'd felt for Charles Killigrew's son obvious in his eyes.

'How good it is to see you, m' boy!' he exclaimed at once. 'Though unfortunately I can guess what brings you to Truro and my door. It's sad that it takes a crisis to renew the acquaintance of old friends, Ben.'

'I regret it as much as you,' Ben said, the afternoon's interlude over. 'Can we speak privately, Richard?'

Jane got to her feet immediately.

'We'll leave you two alone. Cathy's allowed ten minutes in Mama's bedroom, and then it's time for her bath. Will I see you later, Ben? Can you stay for dinner?'

He was tempted. Morwen wouldn't expect him home after their short-tempered exchanges that morning. He could stay the night if it was offered, and he knew that it would be. They were all old friends.

But it was the very eagerness in Jane's face that stopped him. It was dangerous to slip so easily into this role that was Tom Askhew's by right… he was out of sorts with Morwen, and Jane was missing Tom…

He shook his head. 'I'm afraid not. But we must meet again, Jane. Perhaps you and Cathy could spend some time with us. My father would be delighted to see you again.' She nodded, as though she, too, sensed the danger in admitting to feelings that had temporarily thrown them closer together than they had ever been.

'We must arrange it,' she said. 'Give my warmest regards to your father, Ben.'

'And my greetings to your mother,' he said evenly.

Not by the wildest stretch of imagination could he send Mary Carrick warm regards, and they both knew it. Jane was still smiling as she gathered the protesting Cathy up in her arms and left the men to their discussion.

There was a small silence, and then Richard offered his visitor some brandy and suggested they go to his study. Both knew Ben was here on business, and the width of Richard's desk between them put it on a more comfortable footing than here in the drawing-room where Jane's fragrance still lingered in the air.

'So. I presume you think I can help you over this business with the railway, Ben.' Richard Carrick saved him the trouble of broaching the subject. Ben nodded.

'You've guessed why I came, then?'

'I've read the reports *The Informer* blazoned over its pages, to say nothing of Tregian dragging up the old fantasies about porcelain earth, and all the implications of its being so fragile,' Richard said drily. 'Your family lawyers can't help?'

'They say their hands are tied,' Ben said in annoyance. 'You've always been sympathetic to my cause, Richard, which is why I've come to you.'

Carrick looked at him through half-closed eyes. This was the young man he'd have liked for a son more than anything in the world. He was also the man who had bought him out of Killigrew Clay, and as good as snubbed his only daughter. If he took notice of his wife's wishes, he would tell him to go to hell and back, but the truth of it was, he admired Ben Killigrew now as much as he ever did and if there was any way to help him, Richard Carrick was the man to try.

'Tell me everything you've done so far,' the lawyer's voice became professional.

Ben related it all quickly, from appeasing the first outraged cries of the Honourable Mrs Stanforth to his latest efforts to find Chief Engineer Trent.

'We could get in a specialist engineer from another part of the country.' Richard shrugged, rubbing his fingers across the bridge of his nose. 'Or we could force the Bodmin doctor's hand by legal means to get the name of the clinic. Or we could simply go ahead with an independent surveyor's and engineer's report, take the whole thing to court and leave it to the judge to decide on it.'

'Let's go ahead with that,' Ben said at once, seeing a glimmer of daylight begin to emerge.

Richard smiled ruefully. 'I was thinking aloud, m' boy. Nothing's that simple, and nor could it be done in a matter of days or even weeks. The courts move slowly—'

'But quicker than waiting three months for the man to return from the clinic, surely?' Ben felt his blood pressure begin to rise again.

'The point is, will the judge be willing to listen to the case, when three months is a fairly short time, and in all honesty, won't affect your business? If the clay blocks were at a standstill and waiting to be shipped, it would be a different matter. But I'm well aware, and so is the town of St Austell, that the spring despatches have just been safely delivered to Charlestown, and there's no real need for movement on the railway until the autumn. The excursion trips that take place in between are merely goodwill on your part. I hardly think the small returns they bring in affect the fortunes of Killigrew Clay! Besides, the county mining officials would take a very poor view of our importing outsiders from upcountry. If it came to that, and they were to overrule our own folk's decisions, your name would be dragged through the mud. We Cornish are very insular. You know that as well as me—'

'I hadn't expected to be listening to a summing-up speech!' Ben said testily.

'Then you had better get used to it, Ben. This is a serious matter, and no matter how much I want to help you, I have to consider all the facts.'

'So you think I must sit it out for the three months until Engineer Trent gets home?'

'It would seem the sensible thing to do, and stand you in good stead with St Austell townsfolk,' Richard agreed. 'Especially if you let it be known through the newspaper that you've the well-being of all concerned at heart. Such words never hurt anyone's cause.'

Ben sighed heavily. 'I can't pretend to like what you've said, but I can see the sense in it. Can I call on you again to discuss it?'

'Any time. And if you want me to act for you, I shall be honoured. I have fond feelings towards your family, Ben.'

–

Dinner was over by the time Ben returned home. He was still in a state of frustration and indecision, and it didn't help his boorish mood to find the dining table cleared so that he was obliged to ring for food to be sent to him directly.

He could hear the sound of the pianoforte. Someone was practising scales with all the nervousness of a beginner, and the tuneless noise jarred on him. It would be Morwen, of course. She obviously hadn't heard him come in. He had expected her to be waiting for him. He had expected his dinner to be ready, the table set, a smile of welcome...

He crashed his chair, striding away as the maid scuttled about setting his place, and ignoring her quaking look. Killigrew men could be gentle and kind, and they could also be stubborn and aggressive. It didn't pay to be in the vicinity when the latter mood was on them, as servants knew very well.

He threw open the door of the drawing-room. Morwen was at the piano, her face puckered as she hit yet another wrong note. She was beginning to wish that she had never mentioned the instrument. She was so intent she didn't look up for a few seconds. Enough time for Ben's precarious temper to explode.

'Is it too much to expect my wife to welcome me home these days?' His voice throbbed with resentment. 'Am I no longer master in my own house? The food cleared away, and this caterwauling to greet me—'

Morwen felt colour flood her face. He was hateful to belittle her like this. More hateful than she ever thought he could be. She leapt up, banging down the lid of the piano in a fury. Her day too had been a bad one.

Seeing her sister-in-law Dora, and envying the happy little brood of children at the cottage… seeing old Zillah and getting nowhere. Being on the moors and finding the ghosts of the past less comfortable than she might have hoped…

'I'm sorry! I didn't know I was your servant, expected to hover at the window for my master's return!' She could be as sarcastic as he. 'I'm sorry if my playing doesn't please 'ee! I daresay even your Miss Finelady had to practise her scales before she became so perfect!'

'Will you please stop using that ridiculous name for Jane?' Ben snapped. 'It might have been quaintly charming once, but it sounds like the pique of a jealous woman now.'

Morwen gasped with shock.

'Perhaps that's what I am! Perhaps the feeling never really left me. Perhaps 'tis as well your *Jane* is away in Yorkshire, or I might be even more jealous—'

'Jane and her baby are staying with her parents in Truro indefinitely while her husband's away in the Crimea.' His voice was clipped and expressionless. 'If I had any sense I'd take the next boat to the war myself. At least I'd be acting like a man and doing something positive, instead of this bloody impotent feeling at being able to do nothing!' Morwen completely misunderstood him. Where she had been so flushed before, her face paled at his words. She stood taut and rigid, swamped in sudden misery.

'Why do you talk so? Do you want to get away from me so badly? Have I failed 'ee so much, Ben?'

He failed to see the hurt in her eyes.

'Why must women always relate things to themselves? God Almighty, but they must be the most self-centred creatures on this earth! Don't you know that I've more things on my mind than petty domestic squabbles—'

'But not so much that you couldn't spend some time visiting Jane Carrick, apparently!' Morwen flared at him. 'Was she the attraction that took you to Truro today and made you stay so long?'

'I won't listen to more of this. Perhaps when Jane comes to visit Killigrew House and to see my father, you'll see how a real lady behaves. You could take a few lessons from her, and not only on the piano, Morwen!'

It was the biggest insult he could have given her. She was still reeling from it when he banged out of the room, and went hollering about the house demanding food and drink.

Morwen felt the tears blur her vision. What was happening to them? They weren't just drifting apart. They seemed to be spinning away from each other at frightening speed.

She tried to understand Ben's problems with the rail tracks and the works. She knew how desperately he wanted to keep Killigrew Clay's good standing in the town, and that it must be a retrograde step to resort to the old clay waggons for the autumn despatches. If no-one else thought so, Ben would. Morwen knew all of that.

What she hadn't known was that Jane Carrick was back. Jane Carrick Askhew, Miss Finelady, whom she had always seen as her rival, no matter what Ben said. Jane was here, vulnerable without her husband. And Ben had invited her and her child here... ostensibly to see old Charles Killigrew, but in reality...?

Morwen's throat ached with the sobs she refused to allow. It was foolish to let the old jealousies taint the love she and Ben shared, but she didn't have the sophistication of a town girl. A girl like Jane Finelady.

Despite the jewels Ben had given her, the carriages and fine clothes, and her status in St Austell town, deep down she was still Morwen Tremayne, clayworker's daughter. The ring on her finger might have changed her name, but it hadn't changed the heart and soul of her. And not even all old Zillah's potions could do that.

She was still as lost and bewildered at that moment as the night she had first set foot in this house, so conscious of her humble gown decorated with bright ribbons, and seen how fine the Carrick ladies were in their silks.

But it was more than those memories that bruised Morwen now. It was the humiliating knowledge that she hadn't been born a lady, and nothing was ever going to change that. She despised herself even more for knowing how much it mattered.

Chapter Seven

Bess Tremayne still wasn't happy at the thought of her youngest going away to London to some posh school. She was afraid that too much education for one member of an ordinary family, especially clay folk like themselves, would inevitably alienate Freddie from the rest of them.

It was all very well for her son-in-law, Ben, whom she respected enormously, to give the scheme his full approval. Ben had probably profited from his own clever college, but if Freddie was merely having his head turned by the St Austell schoolteacher's glowing reports of him, then Bess couldn't help her misgivings.

'You wouldn't hold the boy back, would you?' Ben had asked, when they had all discussed the idea together in the schoolteacher's presence. 'At least let him take the exam. If he doesn't pass, there's an end to it.'

'And if he does?' Bess said.

'You've still got two choices. Let him go or let him stay. We can help with the clothes and books—'

Freddie saw his mother's eyes begin to glint, and put his own spoke in before they got on to another battle about money. When folk had none they always worried about it, Freddie thought, but they never wanted to take it from those who had more. He was young enough not to let such things worry him.

'Nobody asks me what I want!' he complained.

'What do 'ee want, our Freddie?' Jack jeered. 'To swank about like a little lord, and come back here telling we clay folk how to run our business?'

'Shut up, Jack,' Hal snapped, embarrassed that the schoolteacher should hear such talk, and hoping Ben Killigrew didn't think the words applied to himself.

'I think we should do as Ben says,' Morwen spoke up. 'At least let Freddie have his chance to pass the exam, and then decide.'

Her young brother gave her a grateful glance. He had always adored her, and even if he thought her very fine nowadays in her new clobber, he knew that she still championed him.

'Can we leave it there then, Mr and Mrs Tremayne?' The schoolteacher rose in some relief from these argumentative clay folk. 'Clearly you need to discuss it further, and you can let me have your decision in due course.'

'That we will,' Hal said heartily. He was slightly uncomfortable with the schoolteacher in the Tremayne house, and was glad to see him leave. He was long past feeling awkward with the Killigrews, but with an educated man like the schoolteacher, he always felt aware of his own lack of schooling.

–

The family discussions continued, and Morwen knew Ben was becoming irritated with them. They called at the little house on the Sunday after Ben had been to Truro to see Richard Carrick, and while Ben and Hal discussed the clay business, the two younger boys still wrangled. As usual, any mention of the school exam drew sneers from Jack.

'I don't see why 'ee wants to go away to London, anyway,' he scowled at Freddie. 'You'll only come back all poncified—'

'That's enough o' that talk, our Jack,' Bess said sharply. 'Go and get some sticks for the fire and cool your temper before we sit down to tea.'

Jack left the room, still glowering, and Morwen followed him outside after a glance at her mother. Something was definitely wrong with Jack. He'd stopped following his brother Sam about the way he used to, and apparently he'd lost interest in his work. Something had changed him and Morwen meant to find out what it was. She remembered she had meant to tackle him long before this.

She watched as he bent to throw the sticks into a basket. Jack was broodingly handsome, and she hated to see him so obviously unhappy.

'Are you going to tell me what's wrong, or shall we start a guessing game?' Morwen said calmly.

'What's it to you?' he retorted.

She snatched at the scruff of his neck and hauled him up from his bending position. He was a good deal taller than his sister, but she was older than him, and had as good a Tremayne temper as his, and her blue eyes blazed at him.

'It means a lot to me, when you're upsetting the whole household wi' your carryings-on! Mammie's upset, and Daddy don't know what's got into you, and I think you're just plain jealous of our Freddie—'

Jack hooted derisively.

'Jealous o' that little cow turd?'

He gave a sudden howl of rage as Morwen's hand shot out and slapped him hard across the cheek.

'It's pretty obvious he's got more brains than you, Jack, if all you can do is ridicule him. Maybe you'd have liked the chance to go away to school—'

'No, I wouldn't!' he said viciously, rubbing his cheek. 'I don't want to work the clay no more, neither, Miss Know-All! I want to work wi' wood, same as old Thomas Penry used to in his spare minutes, but a fat chance I'll ever get at that. Nobody ever asked what *I* want.' He echoed Freddie's words. 'I'm just meant to work the clay, same as the rest of 'em. Our Matt got out, and now 'tis our Freddie's turn. What chance would I have wi' all the upheaval they caused?'

Morwen looked at him in astonishment. It was about the longest speech she'd ever heard Jack make. Normally he was the more taciturn of the brothers. Or maybe none of them had ever stopped to listen. Then something in his words stirred her.

'What did you mean, about Thomas Penry? When did you ever watch him work wi' wood?'

He was still belligerent.

'Plenty o' times! I especially mind how he made a beautiful coffin one time. He said he were making it wi' love, and I watched how the golden wood shavings spun in the sunlight. The smell o' the wood was fresh and tickled my nose, and at the end of it all, he had a beautiful pale box wi' a snug-fitting lid, fit for a princess.'

He stopped abruptly, seeing the dawning look on Morwen's face. How could he have forgotten for a second? He cursed himself furiously.

'Fit for Celia, you mean,' Morwen said in a choked voice. Neither would she ever forget the sight of that lovely pale-coloured coffin, when the thought of her friend Celia lying inside it had haunted her dreams for weeks afterwards, and turned them into nightmares.

'I'm sorry, Morwen. I didn't mean to remind 'ee. But you asked me about the wood-carving—' Jack's voice was suddenly steeped in misery. She swallowed back her pain, and patted his arm as if she was the mother and he the child.

'It's all right. It took me by surprise, that's all. Have you said any of this to anyone?'

He shook his head. 'They wouldn't understand. They only understand the clay.'

He was filled with bitterness again.

'Will you let me talk to Ben about it, Jack? I don't think he'd want a clayworker who wasn't devoted to his job—'

'I don't want un giving me the push! Daddy 'ould be disgraced—'

Morwen heard the sudden panic in his voice.

'Ben won't do that, I promise,' she said quickly, though she had no guarantees how Ben would react to anything these days. 'It's just that we like to discuss things together. Like in our own family.'

'If that's the lane you follow, you'll come up wi' two and two making five, same as we!' Then he shrugged. 'Tell un if 'ee must. Just so long as 'ee don't tell Daddy.'

'Not until you want me to,' she promised, which Jack reckoned was neither one answer nor another. It had to satisfy him for the present, since Bess was calling for the firewood and telling them their tea was getting cold.

Morwen didn't mention what Jack had told her until much later. Ben had been quiet all the way home, and she knew his mind was still caught up with his railway problems and the absent engineer. It seemed no problem at all to Morwen to call in another one, but she refrained from giving her opinion, having been told shortly often enough that the clay was men's business.

She gave an unconscious sigh. Nobody thought so when they put their daughters to working with the clay, and their

wives and mothers too. Whole families under one clay boss…
the pretty-sounding name of bal maiden hid a dozen menial
jobs, from scraping the dried clay blocks, to stacking and drying
and loading… Jane Carrick had once asked her the meaning of
the name, and Morwen remembered snapping at her, thinking
the question patronising.

And so it was, Morwen thought freezingly now, refusing
ever to think of Jane Carrick as any kind of friend. And
certainly not now, when she had come home to Truro while
her Tom was away at the war, and Ben had obviously been
moonstruck at seeing her and the little girl…

'I've asked you the same question twice, Morwen,' she
started at Ben's annoyed voice, as the carriage clattered through
the gates of Killigrew House. 'I said what was wrong with Jack
tonight? He was even more morose than usual, if that's possible.'

She bridled at once, immediately on the defensive.

'You don't like Jack, do you?'

'I hardly know him. He doesn't give anyone a chance to
know him, does he? I always thought Matt was the secretive
one, but Jack comes a close second. Is he ill?'

She was tempted to tell him then, but she knew it wasn't the
right moment. She wondered if Ben was bored with Tremayne
family problems. It had never occurred to her before. She stuck
out her chin in a gesture of defiance.

'Jack's all right. He may just be a bit out of sorts lately, that's
all. He'll do his work properly, never fear—'

Ben spoke shortly as he helped her down and let the stable-
boy take the carriage away.

'Did I say that I doubted it? Don't read things that aren't
there, Morwen.'

'Why do you treat me like a child?' she said in a little rush. 'I'm not a child. I'm your wife. Or maybe you're regretting that now—'

'I don't know what on earth you're talking about. But I don't intend having an argument out here where my father can watch us and get upset.'

Morwen looked up to where Charles Killigrew's windows glinted in the early evening sun. She waved her hand and smiled. She couldn't see the occupant of the bed, but knew that he would be able to see her and Ben through the side mirrors.

'I've got some work to do in my study,' Ben went on. 'Ask Cook to send in my food on a tray, will you? I'd rather not be disturbed.'

So she was to dine alone. Morwen couldn't help thinking he did this deliberately, to punish her for something. Was it just because of her family, or the fact that his emotions were disturbed now that Jane Carrick Askhew had come back into his life, no matter how innocently? Or was it because of Morwen herself? Perhaps he had simply fallen out of love with her...

The thought filled her with a poignant pain. Such things happened, but she would never have believed it would happen to them. They had been such passionate lovers, such true kindred spirits. She wouldn't believe it... but the thought remained in her mind, like a recurring nightmare.

She went to bed early, wishing Ben would come to join her; that they would recapture the old sweet loving and he would kiss all her fears away. The night was warm, but she shivered beneath the sheets, needing his protective arms to hold her. Needing Ben as she had always needed him...

She must have drifted off to sleep before he came upstairs, because she felt the sudden dip of the bed as he slid in beside her, careful not to wake her.

Once, he would have pulled her into his arms, and asked her laughingly how she dared to sleep without him! Once, they would have gone upstairs together, arms entwined, because this was their special place and they never wanted to be apart.

She must have made a small sound because she felt him half turn towards her. Her hand reached out to touch his skin. Her hands were cold and the touch startled him, but to Morwen his instinctive flinching away was a rebuff. Her eyes were suddenly blinded with tears.

'Are you tired of me, Ben?' she said huskily.

'What are you fretting about now?' He pulled her close, enveloping her in his embrace, and the warm familiar smell of his body was more erotic than oriental spices. His voice was exasperated, teasing, and she nuzzled her face against his chest, finding comfort in the tangle of body hair beneath her fingers as she felt the smooth rhythm of his heartbeat.

'I don't know,' she mumbled, suddenly as insecure as the Morwen Tremayne she had been before she fell in love with the splendid Ben Killigrew, heir to Killigrew Clay.

She was still Morwen Tremayne, running barefoot across the moors with the wind in her face, her black hair streaming out behind her like a banner, young Freddie dancing at her heels and calling her as batty as old Zillah for believing in potions and miracles and the magic of the Larnie Stone.

The thought made her breath catch in her throat, and she felt Ben's finger lift her chin until her eyes met his in the soft moonlight cast across the bedroom. His face was very close, eyes searching hers, his mouth no more than a whisper away.

'I thought we always shared our secrets, my lovely,' he said gently. 'If there's something troubling you, then tell me.'

Here in his arms, she could tell him anything. It had always been that way, and the words suddenly tumbled out, and if she brought family problems to the sanctuary of their bedroom, then she prayed he would understand. She heard the rumble of low laughter in his chest.

'You Tremaynes always did make mountains out of mole-hills, didn't you?' She felt his hand stroke her dark hair, and shivered as his fingers gently raked through its glossy strands. The caress stopped her fiery retort. She didn't want to argue with Ben. Not tonight. Not now...

'Our Jack doesn't mean to be disloyal—'

'Morwen, nobody's accusing him of disloyalty! If he wants to make something of his life away from the clay works, then good for him!'

'You don't mind? If you don't, then 'twill be easier for Daddy to understand—'

Yes, she was still Morwen Tremayne, still with the clay-workers mentality deeply ingrained in her, Morwen thought ruefully. She couldn't adapt to sudden changes of fortune the way Ben did.

'Is Jack serious about this? It's not just a whim because of Freddie's chances?'

'I'm sure it's not. He really means it, Ben, and I don't like to see him unhappy. If I had my way, I'd like everybody in the world to be happy! I know it's foolish. It's no more than a child's dream—'

She was suddenly aware that his hands had moved lower down her body, curving the line of her waist and hips and kneading her rounded buttocks. His hands began slowly caressing every part of her body and his touch was telling her that he thought of her in no way as a child. She was his woman, his wife.

She felt a thrill shoot through her so unexpectedly it made her gasp aloud, and then his mouth was hard on hers. He prised it open, his tongue probing sweetly and seductively, and she could feel him hardening against her.

Without warning, he pulled her over him, so that the long fall of her hair covered them both like a blanket. She felt the power in his body as her own opened instinctively to enclose him inside. That first touch was as potent to her senses as it had ever been, as hot as fire, as sweet as honey.

He released his mouth from hers a fraction, just sufficiently enough to murmur against her lips.

'I think you talk too much. We have more important business to attend to, and I want your thoughts to concentrate solely on your husband for the present!'

Morwen felt the reckless laughter well up inside her at his arrogance and undisguised passion.

'Yes, clay boss!' she teased him as she sank down on him, and knew by his own indrawn breath how affected he was by her. She knew it and gloried in it.

'I'd say you were the boss at this moment,' Ben said hoarsely, his pulse beginning to race at her instant response.

He buried his face in the softness of her breasts, white and full above him, and tasted their sweetness. His hands pulled her into him, deeper and deeper, and Morwen felt every nerve-end throb with the pleasurable sensations flowing through her.

Sometimes their union was slow and languorous and more sensual than the finest tuning of an instrument. At other times, it was boisterous, exciting, the beating of drums, the pounding of flesh on flesh, heart on heart, a hungry, desperate need. It was that way now.

The flames spread wider, filling every part of her as she felt Ben gasp and twist beneath her, holding her tight in the sudden culmination, the rush of heat, the moment of release. They clung together without speaking until the pulsating movements eased. They rolled sideways to lie together, still part of each other, still joined in love.

They had been apart too long. Apart in spirit, and in such bodily contact as this, which was as God-given as the moon and stars and just as magical. The gift of procreation…

Morwen hid her damp face from his. Both their bodies glistened from exertions far more exhilarating than a gallop across the moors, but the simile made her smile. She had been the rider, he her willing steed… she mustn't spoil things now by an emotional reaction. But as their breathing slowed, and she became aware that Ben was already sleeping in her arms, she remembered that little phrase that had slipped so sweetly into her mind.

The gift of procreation…

Could any two people love more deeply than themselves?

They shared a physical love that was as spectacular as life itself, and yet they were denied the ultimate prize.

Morwen heard the sudden lashing of rain against the window. The day had been warm and beautiful, but the sound of the rain chilled her, and she moved gently away from Ben to slide into her nightgown. The rain was like a portent. Whenever she felt she had everything, something happened to spoil it. And always, the thing that she wanted most seemed ever out of reach.

–

It wasn't unusual for Morwen to awaken and find herself alone. Ben was too restless these days to stay in bed once he was awake.

But after last night, Morwen did think he'd still be beside her in the morning, to indulge in a few lazy, sleep-hazed moments of remembering how beautiful it had been…

She was disappointed to stretch out her hand and encounter nothing but his pillow. She sat up too quickly and felt her head swim. But the rain had stopped and the sun shone, and she brushed aside her brief pique and decided to take a ride along the shore after breakfast. It was a while since she had galloped across the sandy beach, and it might help to make last night's halcyon mood linger a little…

Ben would have looked in on his father, and once she had washed and dressed, Morwen went to pay him her morning visit too. Charles was scowling at the nurse, who flounced out as soon as Morwen appeared. Morwen hid a grin, knowing that for all Charles's indisposition, he could still send a servant off with a flea in her ear. He said so often enough.

'What have you been saying to Nurse Stevens, you wicked old man?' Morwen smiled at him when she had straightened the newspapers spread over the bed. Charles gave a snort.

'Blasted tyrant!' he said in his laboured manner. 'She makes me so tidy and tucked in that I can't even twitch. If I want my bed in a mess, I'll have it! Fool of a nurse says she'll go off to the war herself if I'm not careful and nurse soldiers who'll appreciate her. I told her good riddance!'

Charles was determined to have his say, though it took a while for the speech to end. Morwen wiped the dribble from his chin without comment, while her eyes took in the screaming headlines in the London newspaper on the bed, telling of more battles, more outrage at the appalling conditions in the hospitals, the cholera and the heroic efforts of Miss Nightingale to relieve the suffering.

Morwen felt a brief sympathy with Nurse Stevens, who might well feel that her services would be more appreciated elsewhere.

'Don't get upset, Father,' Morwen said evenly. 'It doesn't do you any good. How was Ben this morning? He'd already gone when I awoke. Has he gone to the works?'

'No. Gone to Truro,' Charles grunted.

Morwen felt her heart leap. To Truro? Where Jane lived now? Her thoughts spun. She couldn't think of anything else but that Ben must have gone to see Jane. Reason didn't enter her thinking.

After last night... after their wonderful night, when she had been transported somewhere close to heaven... she felt sick to her stomach, and her breakfast threatened to reappear. She forced the feeling down. She must be going mad to let such a small comment disturb her so. Was she really so unbalanced that she could feel physically sick with jealousy? It was degrading. She made herself speak naturally, seeing Charles's unblinking eyes watching her.

'Did he say why?' she asked.

'To see somebody,' he said, with such an infuriating blank expression that Morwen could have screamed.

Didn't the old fool see how vital all this was to her? She was immediately ashamed of her thoughts as she saw Charles's jaw slacken and the hated dribble begin again. She wiped it quickly.

'Did you know Jane Carrick's come home?' Charles suddenly perked up, and Morwen knew that Ben must have told him. Charles hadn't commented on it before, and the waves of jealousy washed over her again.

'He did mention it,' she muttered. Charles's face broke into a grotesque smile.

'She was always a lovely girl. Daughter of my old friend and his hag of a wife.'

Charles Killigrew had lost the art of discretion since his illness. Or perhaps since his listener was only Morwen Tremayne, it didn't matter. She felt less like Ben's wife right now, and more like the young girl Charles had brought to Killigrew House to be his housekeeper when he'd sent his sister Hannah packing. Holding out a helping hand to the bewildered Morwen Tremayne after her friend Celia had killed herself in his clay pool…

'Are you going to read to me or sit there mooning like a love-sick calf?' Charles suddenly complained.

Morwen clenched her hands. Sometimes she wanted to hit out at everyone, at anyone. Sometimes the frustration was just too much… she saw the watery old eyes that had once held such fire and swallowed her pride. She picked up the newspapers and read until Charles had had enough and her voice was hoarse.

And until she was so tired of reading about the war in the Crimea, that she couldn't wait to get out of the house and have her mare saddled up, and be away from the musty confines of the sickroom. Sometimes she felt that it stifled her as much as it must stifle Charles.

It wasn't too far to the wide sandy beaches bordering the ocean. The great granite cliffs were lashed by great curling waves that foamed against them. The sea was whipped up by the Atlantic wind, and for a second Morwen breathed in the salt breeze and wondered if her brother Matt breathed in the same air, all those miles away in America.

Then she remembered Hannah Pascoe's words. The letter from her son Jude had said that Matt had left New York and gone to the gold diggings in California. And Morwen had traced the state of California on the map of America and felt like weeping at discovering it was twice as far away as New York.

Matt had truly gone from their lives and they would never see him again. It was as though she heard it whispered in the rush of the waves on the shore, as though it was carried on the wind like an omen. And Morwen was too much a daughter of Cornwall to disbelieve in omens.

She raced her mare along the sands, her hair tumbling wildly about her. She leaned low, feeling the strength in the mare's body, and revelling in the freedom of the gallop. At that moment she felt free of all ties, loved or hated.

She deliberately pushed all thoughts of Ben and Jane Askhew out of her mind, but unwillingly then, her thoughts centred on her own family with a thrill of unease.

They were all changing. Matt had begun it. Now Freddie's head was being turned, and Jack wanted to leave the clay. Even her Mammie had taken up new work as a seamstress instead of working with the clay. A good thing she had, since Hal had become Works Manager, of course. It wouldn't have been seemly for his wife to continue being a bal maiden.

Morwen tried not to consider how she herself had changed, but she couldn't avoid it. Four years had made a huge difference in her life. From bal maiden to housekeeper for Charles Killigrew, to wife of his son, Ben, the new owner of Killigrew Clay. Ecstatic at seventeen, scared of being barren at twenty-one…

Only Sam stayed the same, she thought with a rush of thankfulness. Sam, the eldest, who had always wanted to be like their Daddy, and was now Captain of Number One pit, like Hal had been. Sam was always the same, like a rock in a stormy sea.

Chapter Eight

Sam Tremayne finally got the truth out of his brother Jack. Sam was tired of hints and snubs. If something was wrong, then he wanted to know of it, though it took a bit of goading to make Jack finally bawl out his frustration while they were both on the day shift.

Jack hated the thankless task of moving clay waste from one point to another. He did it carelessly, his mind far away from the non-productivity of what he was doing. When the two of them were far enough out of earshot not to be overheard, Sam rounded on his brother for his slipshod work.

Jack threw down the long-handled shovel with which he'd been piling waste into the little truck for tipping on to one of the white pyramids surrounding the works. Jack was shiny with sweat, his face grimed with dirt beneath the white clay-dust that lay over everything, workers and tools alike.

'I'm sorry I don't work fast enough for 'ee, our Sam!' Jack scowled. 'Mebbe not all of us are as besotted to make a fortune for the bosses! I do my work—'

'You don't do as much as the other men,' Sam snapped. 'You're lazy and insolent, and you shame our name wi' your ill-temper. Nobody gets a civil word from 'ee these days. If there's summat on your mind, let's have it!'

'You're a real boss's man, our Sam! You'm starting to sound just like 'em. Even Daddy never got so uppity. I wonder you don't wipe Ben Killigrew's arse for un—'

One minute he was standing with his hands on his hips, glaring at Sam. The next, he was feeling a great crack across his nose and seeing stars. He staggered backwards as blood spurted out. He would have fallen, if Sam hadn't lugged at his collar so tightly he could hardly breathe.

'You snot-faced little bugger!' Sam bellowed. 'I'll wipe the ground with *you* if you don't wake up your ideas! What in God's name is wrong with 'ee, Jack? We used to be such good uns together, but I don't know 'ee any more—'

'I want to get out o' the clay!' Jack almost screamed the words at him, his eyes bulging in a face suddenly scarlet as Sam shook him by the throat in his fury. 'I want to get out, like our Matt did! Don't 'ee understand? I can't make it plainer—'

Sam suddenly let him go, and Jack fell back against the clay truck, breathing heavily to get back his wind. His throat was sore where Sam had near to throttled him, and the blood from his nose ran into his mouth. He tasted it with disgust.

Sam handed him a rag in silence, digesting what his brother had just said. Jack looked at him warily as he wiped the mess from his face.

'Is that what 'tis all about?' Sam demanded. He had never even considered this possibility, and couldn't think straight for a few minutes. The clay was his life, same as Hal's, and it still surprised him that anyone brought up in a clay-working family could want to leave. There were comparatively few who did.

'That's it,' Jack muttered. 'Now I s'pose you'm going to laugh at me about that! 'Tis as funny as our Freddie wanting to go to some posh London school, ain't it?'

Sam remembered that this was the brother who'd once followed him closer than a shadow, who had once wanted only to be like Sam… he felt an odd lump in his throat, seeing the defensiveness in his brother's eyes. They had grown apart, but

Jack still needed Sam's approval. That, too, was part of what ailed him. He expected Sam's anger — that was painfully clear.

'I'm not laughing, Jack. It saddens me that 'ee didn't confide in me before now. We might have managed not to snarl at each other quite so much of late.'

Each felt a sudden embarrassment, and Jack quickly turned away as another truck came trundling towards them with its handler and its load.

'Well, now you know, and I'd thank 'ee to say nothing to Daddy. I've as much chance of going my own way as a snowball in hell, and there's enough upset for now wi' Freddie's schooling.'

'Does anyone else know of it?'

'Only Morwen,' Jack muttered, suddenly wishing he'd held his tongue then and now. It had been his secret and he could brood on it with some dignity. Now it was shared, and he hated to sense pity from anyone. It was a family failing often misconstrued as false pride. He glared at Sam, daring him to sympathise with him.

And Sam, knowing him too well, shrugged and turned away as someone called for assistance from Clay One's pit captain.

'I'll not tell folk. Just as long as you do your work while you're here. There's no room for idlers, especially one of my family. Just remember it, Jack.'

If that was a hint that he'd be thrown out if he didn't pull his weight, Jack knew it wasn't a straw he could grasp. The disgrace would be too much. No Tremayne had been forced to leave their employ because of bad work. Sam knew it as well as he did.

Jack stared broodingly after his tall brother, tenderly tested his nose and decided it wasn't broken, and began to shovel the clay waste into the truck again with a savage fury.

It was late afternoon when Ben came home from Truro. Morwen had whiled away an hour with her mother in Miss Fielding's Tea Rooms, then strolled about the town, trying to take an interest in shops and gardens and acquaintances.

And all the time her mind was miles away, wondering what Ben was doing, and more importantly, whom he was meeting. She moved listlessly in the St Austell street when someone blocked her path. She did not look up to see who it was, her mind being too full of personal matters.

'I see we're too fine now to say good-afternoon to our husband's relatives,' said a frosty voice she hated intensely.

Morwen looked into the face of Hannah Pascoe, Ben's aunt and forced a dutiful half-smile. There was no reason she should pretend real warmth towards this woman, who had never shown her anything but dislike and reminded her all too vividly of an episode in her life that was still painful.

'Good-afternoon, Mrs Pascoe,' Morwen said evenly, and made to pass, but Hannah Pascoe still stood in front of her, and Morwen saw her narrowed eyes rake Morwen's trim shape. Morwen could swear that there was a distinct smell of whisky coming from the woman's lips.

'No child expected yet, I see,' Hannah sniffed. 'I wouldn't have thought Ben lacking in that direction. My brother would be glad to see a grandson, I daresay. It would be a poor do if he went to his grave without seeing the fortunes of Killigrew Clay assured, Morwen Tremayne, even by one of your family!'

'It's Morwen Killigrew, Ma'am! If you'll please let me pass—' Her face flamed with angry colour, but there were enough curious bystanders already turning round at Hannah Pascoe's shrill voice, without adding to the peep-show. What in God's name had got into Ben's aunt today?

'I'll excuse you nothing!' Hannah suddenly hissed. 'You're nought but an upstart worming your way into my brother's household. Making my own brother turn me out—'

'That was done by your own efforts, Mrs Pascoe,' Morwen snapped, too reckless now to mince her words. 'You were always an unpleasant woman, and Charles Killigrew was well rid of 'ee. He'd have been dead long before now with all the upset you'd have brought him!'

'Well! Such talk from a clayworker's daughter!' Hannah glanced around, noted a few nods from some elderly dames, and drew courage from them.

Hannah swayed slightly, and Morwen was certain now that she had been drinking. She was filled with disgust. It had been Jude Pascoe's weakness. She had never thought it would be his mother's too. It seemed infinitely worse for a woman to take to drink. The street women did it, but not ladies of quality.

'I wanted words with you, Morwen Tremayne,' Hannah went on, her hand gripping Morwen's arm.

'Then say what you have to, and let me go,' Morwen said shortly. The sooner she could get away from this odious woman, the better. Hannah's face suddenly crumpled, and to Morwen's horror, two large tears trickled down her angular face.

'My friend is dying,' Hannah said abruptly.

Morwen stared at her. The words were totally unexpected.

'I'm sorry. But what has this to do with me?' She didn't want to know this woman's problems.

Charles Killigrew had paid her off when he dismissed her from his house, and she lived comfortably enough with her woman friend in St Austell town. There was no reason to think Ben would do less for his aunt when his father died.

'My friend. Miss Emily Ford,' Hannah mumbled. 'She's dying. When she goes, I'll have no-one. Jude won't ever come back from America, and I'll be lonely. I don't want to be lonely. Not when I've got family living close by. What do you think my chances are, Morwen Tremayne, for Charles taking me back?'

Morwen listened in horror. This terrible old woman wanted to come back to Killigrew House! She couldn't imagine Charles Killigrew ever agreeing to it. Nor Ben… she swallowed drily. She couldn't be sure of Ben. He had a soft heart, and Hannah could wheedle when she chose, putting on that pathetic tone…

Morwen's thoughts seemed to streak ahead. If Hannah Pascoe moved back to Killigrew House, and if her son ever took it in his head to come back to England, he'd naturally expect to move in too. Morwen would be under the same roof as the man she loathed, the man who had raped her dearest friend, Celia Penry, and caused her to drown herself because of the shame…

She shivered as she heard a cackling laugh.

'Your face is a picture, Morwen *Killigrew*! I take it you won't speak up for your old auntie, then?'

Morwen shook her off as if she was a poisonous insect.

'I'd as soon speak up for a plague rat,' Morwen snapped. She thrust past the spiteful old woman, holding her head high as she heard the tut-tutting of the town dames nearby.

Let them think Morwen Killigrew was heartless to her husband's relative, she thought furiously. They didn't know Hannah Pascoe like the family did. They didn't know her devious ways…

Morwen felt a shiver run through her. What if the friend where Hannah lived – Miss Emily Ford – was really dying?

What if she did come to the house, relying on Ben's generosity, and he allowed her back?

She remembered Hannah's own raging words when Charles Killigrew had hired Morwen to be his new housekeeper. She had said then that she'd never live under the same roof as Morwen, and Charles had told her good riddance. But the fact was as true from Morwen's angle. She couldn't and wouldn't live under the same roof as Hannah Pascoe. If she moved in, then Morwen would have to leave.

She tried to tell herself how foolish she was being. She knew it, but the nagging thought wouldn't leave her. Somehow, the feeling that if Hannah came back, then so would Jude, seemed an inescapable nightmare.

-

Morwen put on a smile as she glanced up towards Charles's windows, but the smile dropped as soon as she went inside the house. She wished Ben were here. She felt suddenly adrift, like a small boat tossed about on a vast ocean.

Then she heard Ben calling her name, and wondered if she was dreaming until she saw him come out of the drawing-room. His arms opened and everything shifted back into place again as she went into them, safe in her own world.

'I hoped you'd be at home when I got back from Truro, darling,' he said.

'You went off without telling me! I was so anxious.' She bit her lip, not wanting to betray her anxiety that he had been visiting Jane Askhew. Minutes later, she thanked God that she hadn't, as Ben revealed where he had been.

'I went to see an old gambling friend of mine,' he went on. 'He has a flourishing boatyard in Truro, and I wondered if he might have a place for a young apprentice. Building boats is a fine career for a young man who has a feeling for wood—'

Morwen felt her heart leap with joy.

'You did this for our Jack!' Her eyes shone brighter than they had in weeks. 'Oh, Ben, what did your friend say? Was he agreeable to it?'

Ben laughed, holding her close, loving the quick excitement in her eyes, and the rosy flush on her cheeks. Seconds ago she had looked so flustered, but the anxiety on her face had vanished now.

'Why shouldn't he agree to it? He owes me a few favours. I told him the young man in question was my wife's brother, and would be a keen worker. He's willing to see Jack and take him on right away if they find themselves in agreement. He'll need lodgings in Truro, of course, but that's no hardship. There's plenty of homely places ready to take in a personable young man who can pay his way.'

He felt Morwen's arms around his neck, and her soft warm mouth pressed to his in her pleasure.

'Thank you! I had no idea you were going to do this—'

'You thought I was off visiting my lady Jane, didn't you?' He couldn't resist teasing. Suddenly it didn't matter. She laughed, secure in Ben's love.

'I didn't think it for a minute,' she said airily, crossing her fingers behind his neck as she did so.

'Don't you know that your tongue will drop out if you tell such lies?' Ben grinned. He wished he could fulfil all her desires so easily, if it produced this sudden blaze of passion, this echo of the Morwen he had always loved more than life, and who seemed to have got lost in the everyday business of living.

She pouted, saying that it was only a little white lie, and that didn't count. Ben laughed again, and scooped her up in his arms to put her laughingly on to the sofa and to drop down beside her. Suddenly they both felt and acted like reckless children, instead of respectably married people, and it was a good and heady feeling.

Ben teased her neck with his lips, sending warm shivers over her. Last night's euphoria was still there after all, and all the Hannah Pascoes in the world couldn't take that away from her. She opened her mouth to tell him of the afternoon's meeting with his aunt, and closed it again. Why spoil these moments? There was time enough for talking.

She wondered when he was going to stop kissing her... but she wasn't complaining. It was ecstatically exciting, like the wonderful days when they were first married...

'As a matter of fact, I did see Jane today,' Ben said eventually. Morwen's heart gave a jolt.

'Now, get that mutinous look off your face!' Ben went on, still laughing. 'Father's keen to see her, and I don't see why he shouldn't. Why should the mistress of Killigrew House fear the visit of an old friend of the family?'

'I don't fear it—' Morwen said quickly. He shook her shoulders gently.

'Then don't act so jealously. It doesn't become my lady.'

'Your lady?'

His arms held her more tightly. She could feel the strength in them. She could see the hunger in his eyes and feel the passion in every pore of him as his fingers moved to the soft swell of her breasts.

'There's no lady in the world can compare with mine,' he said seductively. 'Must I repeat it every day of my life before you believe it?'

'Yes!' she said joyfully, laughing back at her strong, passionate husband who was making it very plain that he desired nothing more at that moment than to possess her. He wanted her as she wanted him, with a wildness and a tenderness more beautiful than life itself.

'Ben—' she said weakly, 'you just reminded me that I'm the lady of the house – and this is our drawing-room. The servants may come in at any minute—'

'Then we had best continue this delightful interlude in the privacy of our bedroom. And if it takes all night, then dinner can wait!'

And before she had time or wish to say another word, he had lifted her in his arms and taken her towards the stairs, and begun to carry out his promise.

–

Jack Tremayne's problems were now out in the open, and his parents hadn't been as distressed as Jack had expected. If Hal and Bess were sadder than they let on because Jack was moving to lodgings in Truro, they could hardly deny the joy in the boy now, and know that the apprenticeship in the boat-building was right for him.

Since Ben's intervention, it was all settled with great speed, and Jack became apprenticed to the Boskelly Boat Builders, Truro, and shook himself free of the clay at last. The Boskelly brothers were pleased with his enthusiasm and surprised at his natural skill and feeling for wood, and felt they had got themselves a bargain.

A few days later, Ben had business with the Killigrew Clay accountants, and went on to the works to consult with Hal and the pit captains. Morwen was feeling more content than she'd been in weeks, sure of Ben's love, chiding herself for ever doubting him.

How could she be so foolish as to continue fretting over Jane Askhew? Morwen was Ben's wife, and nothing could change that. Ben had chosen her out of all the world. It was a thought that continued to charm her.

That afternoon she had her pianoforte lesson with David Glass. She was a quick but impatient learner. She knew where to put her fingers on the keys, but her mind was always on the next chord, the next sequence, so that time and again the young tutor sighed inwardly, wishing that the beautiful Mrs Killigrew would realise that what had taken him years of study and practice couldn't be taught in a day!

'I'm tired of scales, Mr Glass!' she exclaimed in frustration. 'And the little tunes you've taught me are for babies! Teach me something more lively, won't 'ee? Won't you?'

She corrected herself quickly, trying very hard of late to live up to Ben's image of the lady of Killigrew House. Her soft Cornish accent would never change, and nor would she want it to, but she could learn to speak more correctly.

David Glass sighed audibly now. He had the forlorn look of a chastised puppy when he despaired of a pupil. Mrs Killigrew wanted to run before she could walk, but he was learning that when her lovely mouth set in that obstinate line, he may as well comply with her wishes, or he'd hear nothing but crashing discords for the rest of the lesson. He rummaged in his music bag for a simplified jig and placed it in front of her.

'I fear you may be just as frustrated when you try to play this as you appear to be with the scales, dear lady,' he said bluntly, his round face flushed. Morwen looked at him, putting a hand on his arm and making him blush even more.

'Mr Glass, 'tis not you I'm angry with, but myself! I do so want to play for my husband, and I fear he's tired of hearing boring runs up and down the piano! Please don't lose patience with me. I'm impatient enough for us both!'

He cleared his throat. He could hardly bear to see the melting plea in her lovely eyes. If he was a young man eager for a woman's love, it would be sheer torment just to be near her once a week.

As it was, he loved the gentleness and the fire in her, the scent of her skin, the contours of her body, but she need never fear more ardent attentions from him. He guessed that she was as innocent of his inclinations as her husband was aware of them. In David Glass's eyes, Morwen Killigrew was perfection, but as untouchable as the stars.

If she sometimes wondered about the waft of perfume from the young man's body as he stretched out a hand to point out the notes on the music, then Morwen put it down to a thoughtfulness on the tutor's part not to offend his pupils, and nothing more.

'Teach me the jig, Mr Glass!' Morwen said determinedly, and David put all other thoughts aside and concentrated on trying to get the erratic rhythm of the jig into Morwen Killigrew's uncertain fingers.

–

She was being far too ambitious. She should have listened to the tutor's words of caution. She knew it now, an hour after David had gone, and no matter how she tried, her performance still sounded more like caterwauling than a recognisable tune!

How could she be so foolish as to think she could play it? Or anything at all? In a fury, she crashed both hands over the keys, her loosened hair flying about her shoulders, her face flushed with anger at herself.

'That's no way to treat a sensitive instrument, Morwen!'

She heard the faintly amused voice with a sick feeling in her stomach. She swivelled round on the piano stool. She knew at once who the visitor would be.

Jane Askhew... Miss Finelady... shown into the house by the servants as an old friend. Finding her own way to the drawing-room, and hearing Morwen's pathetic efforts to perform like a lady. Like the lady she was not, nor ever would be.

Morwen reached behind her and crashed down the lid of the instrument, knowing her face was even more fiery. She caught the flash of sympathy in the other girl's eyes, and it shamed her even more.

She hardly noticed the small child hiding behind her mother's fine skirts at the awful noise that had led them to the right room. All she registered was the difference between them. The cultured young lady and the clayworker's daughter.

'That's a terribly hard piece to play, isn't it?' Jane said quickly. 'It took me ages to master it. Perhaps I could help you a little. May I, Morwen? You're forgetting to play sharps instead of naturals.'

Morwen hardly knew how she came to be standing, and Jane at her place on the stool. The lid was opened, and Jane's agile fingers were trilling over the keys and transforming Morwen's noise into the jig tune. At each difficult passage, Jane paused and pointed out where Morwen was going wrong.

Jane only meant to be helpful, but to Morwen, the gall of being overheard by this girl in her moments of temper made things a hundred times worse. She couldn't take in anything Jane told her, and stood tautly beside her, her eyes stormy.

She heard Ben speaking to Mrs Tilley outside the room, and the next minute he was inside it, smiling delightedly.

'Your tutor deserves a medal, darling! The improvement is nothing short of miraculous—'

Ben stopped, suddenly aware of the three people in the room, and even more aware of the tension there. Morwen, scarlet-faced and furious at his mistake. Jane, acutely embarrassed and realising what she had done.

The little girl recognised the nice man who had played with her, released her mother's skirt and ran towards him. Ben automatically scooped her up in his arms, and with a choked sound in her throat, Morwen rushed from the room.

'Morwen, come back!' Ben ordered. 'We have guests—'

'Then you entertain 'em. They be your guests, not mine!' she shouted back furiously, tears stinging her eyes.

The little tableau left in the drawing-room, Jane and Ben, the child in his arms, was the right one, the fitting one. In a second, the confidence of the last four years was wiped from her mind, and she was Morwen Tremayne, the clayworker's daughter, and nothing more. She would never be anything more.

A short while later Ben came crashing into their bedroom, angrier than Morwen had ever seen him. He kicked the door shut behind him and strode across to where she lay dry-eyed and staring up at the ceiling. She flinched as he jerked her to a sitting position by her wrists.

'You're hurting me!'

'What in God's name got into you just now? Jane felt terrible—'

'*Jane* felt terrible? What about me? What about your wife? Don't my feelings count, when your lady-friend comes mincing into the house as though she owns it, and shows me up for the ninny that I am!'

'You're more than a ninny if you can let your bloody insane jealousy take over any semblance of good manners. I was ashamed of you—'

'I don't doubt it,' she retorted bitterly. 'I'll bet 'ee regretted ever marrying me when 'ee saw the two of us together. Her so fine, and me so plain-speaking. I was born to the clay and 'twas a bad day when 'ee ever dragged me out of it and thought 'ee could turn me into a lady, wasn't it?'

She heard her own voice become more countrified by the second and couldn't seem to stop it. It had a will of its own, as though it possessed her. Reminding her that deep down she was still what she had always been. She gasped as Ben shook her until her teeth rattled and the room spun.

'I never thought I was married to an imbecile, but I'm beginning to think so now!' he raged at her. 'Don't act the simpleton with me, Morwen. Have some respect for yourself, and others will respect you in return.'

He let her go suddenly. She fell back against the pillows where they had loved so passionately in what seemed like another life. His eyes looked her up and down contemptuously. He spoke in a clipped, contained voice.

'We have guests in this house. They came to visit my father and pay their respects to you, the way civilised people do. I expect you to receive them and to offer them refreshment. At present Jane is sitting with my father and introducing her daughter to him. I expect to see you tidied and downstairs in half an hour, and making our visitors welcome.'

He was gone before she could throw something at him.

He couldn't make her do this, she raged. She would leave Killigrew House before she submitted to such humiliation…

Very slowly, her fury subsided. It was what they would expect of a clayworker's daughter, wasn't it? That she couldn't handle such a situation. That she would flounce and sulk and weep… exactly the way she had already done, Morwen thought in mortification.

They wouldn't think she could rise above it all, and act as though nothing had ever happened. They would never expect her to ask Jane to play for them, and listen attentively, and enquire politely about her husband, Tom, away at the Crimea. They would never believe she had the aplomb to behave like a lady after showing her claws like an alley cat…

Her chin lifted, and her blue eyes gleamed at the challenge. She moved away from the bed and caught sight of herself in the mirror. Black flowing hair as unkempt as a horse's mane, her face like roses in full bloom, her mouth still trembling. But she would show them. She would show them all.

Chapter Nine

It was hard to tell who was more surprised at the serene vision who graced the Killigrew drawing-room half an hour later. Morwen ordered tea and biscuits to be sent in, and presided over them as if she had been doing so all her life. Her lemon afternoon gown was immaculate, her face cooled with rose-water and fanning, her hair coiled becomingly around her head.

Cathy Askhew's small face had shown bewilderment when the beautiful poised lady entered the room, as if wondering if this could really be the same person who had swept out like a hoyden.

Morwen's appearance was a total triumph, and her ragged nerves gradually settled down as she saw the undoubted admiration on Jane's face, and the distinct surprise and approval on Ben's.

'Have you had news of your husband lately?' she asked Jane politely, every inch the hostess.

'Nothing very positive,' Jane said unhappily, and although she covered her sadness quickly, Morwen felt guiltily cheered by the realisation that Jane was missing her husband very much. 'His letters are guarded, but the true reports of the dreadful war are what he sends home for the newspaper. He tries to shield me, but he doesn't try to dress things up for his readers. You'll know that from the Despatches From Abroad columns he writes, of course.'

Morwen kept the interest fixed on her face, though she rarely read the war columns under Tom Askhew's name, or anyone else's. She was appallingly ignorant of the progress in the Crimea, and felt an unexpected shame to know it.

'It was never Tom's way to gloss over bad news for his readers. He was always a blunt-speaking man—' Ben put in.

'Yes, he was,' Jane said with a half-smile.

'Please stop speaking of him in the past tense!' Morwen said quickly. Such talk was almost an omen to her superstitious mind. 'I'm sure you'll be seeing him again very soon.'

'I hope so,' Jane said. 'Cathy misses her father. I'd like to come here now and then, Morwen, if only to let Cathy see Ben and old Mr Killigrew. My father is awkward with children, and it's good for her to have a younger man to tease her and play with her. I'm afraid that when Tom comes home, she'll have forgotten how to play, how to be a child!'

Morwen felt even more guilty as Jane's calm, frank voice went on. She clearly wanted no more from Ben than to be a substitute uncle to Cathy. She saw Ben's eyes watching her. Did he expect her to snub Jane now?

'Please come here whenever you wish,' Morwen said evenly. 'I know little about the war, but Ben is very interested in its progress. To hear more of it first-hand from your husband's letters will interest him, I'm sure.'

'That's very kind of you, Morwen. And perhaps you could visit me in Truro sometime? I'd like to think we were friends. Ben tells me your brother has begun work for Boskellys. If you're visiting him at all, come and take tea with me.'

'Why – thank you. That would be very nice.' The invitation took her by surprise, and Morwen mumbled for the first time since her reappearance. She took a deep breath, and spoke more warmly.

'Thank you, Jane.' It was also the first time she had ever spoken the other girl's name to her face.

It was still a relief when the visit ended. By then Cathy had decided that the pretty lady wasn't such an ogre after all and had taken a liking to Morwen, climbing on to her lap and fingering the necklace around her throat.

And Morwen had found it bittersweet to be holding Jane Askhew's daughter, feeling her warm little body pressed close to hers and seeing the trusting eyes so like her mother's. She had disliked this child before even seeing her, she remembered with a stab of guilt. But she couldn't dislike her any more. Cathy was a little charmer, and Morwen could only yearn that one day she too would be blessed to have such a child...

Ben took his wife in his arms when the Carrick family carriage had taken the visitors back to Truro. Morwen waited almost fearfully for what he had to say. Were they to have an inquest on the events of the afternoon?

'You constantly surprise me, Morwen Killigrew,' Ben said softly. 'But then, you always did, which was one of the things that made me love you in the first place.'

'Only one of the things?' she said huskily. Ben gave a low laugh.

'Oh, there are a few more,' he commented. 'Some of them madden me, and some of them fill me with such pride I wonder just how so much intelligence can be closeted in that beautiful head.'

Her mouth curved into a smile. Her heart lifted.

'Intelligence? I thought I was an imbecile—'

'You shouldn't believe everything you hear. I think we'll forget a few of today's happenings, and begin again from right this minute. Agreed?'

'Agreed!' Morwen said with vast relief.

Even though she had sunk her boats. She had held out the hand of friendship to Jane Askhew, because she had had no other choice. She had invited her here, and received invitations in return, and she still wasn't sure how it had all come about.

But it was done, and there was no undoing it without causing a bigger rift between her and Ben. For the moment the rift was healed, and Morwen had no wish to breach it again. And the visits didn't have to begin at once. They could be delayed on any number of reasons...

–

It seemed that Jane didn't feel the same way. In the next few weeks she called at Killigrew House three times, and Morwen was forced to smile and entertain, and wonder at the eagerness with which Ben greeted her, wanting news about Tom, and of the ships docking at Falmouth spilling out their wounded with even more lurid tales of the Crimea to be related in *The Informer*, and tossing Cathy into the air to her squeals of delight.

Morwen's serenity didn't last. She was irritated by Ben's change of manner whenever Cathy was running about the house, and ached to fill the house with their own children, not someone else's. Ben seemed so attached to the child...

She snapped at him when he suggested a picnic by the sea the next time Jane came.

'I'm sick of making arrangements for Jane and her daughter. When did we last take a picnic to the sea? It would be nice for the two of us to go there—'

'Very well. Ask Cook to fill a basket and we'll go,' Ben said coolly. 'When do you suggest? Today? Tomorrow? We have every day at our disposal, Morwen. I'm your puppy-dog, to be called to heel whenever you wish.'

'Now you're being ridiculous—'

'And you're showing the green of your eyes again. Do you realise how much time Jane spends with Father when she comes here? Hours spent with a sick old man, Morwen. I just thought it would be nice to give her and Cathy a little treat in return for her kindness in sitting and reading to him.'

'I see. I take it you've never counted up the hours I've done the same thing.'

Ben's face darkened. 'That's entirely different. You're his daughter-in-law. He cares for you, and I thought it was mutual. Sometimes I wonder if I know you at all. You seem too concerned for yourself to think of anyone else. How long is it since you've asked after my battles for the rail tracks, or when the engineer will return, or if I'm taking it to court to see if I can get the excursions started again? You haven't even bothered to go to Truro to see your own brother, when you were so all-fired concerned about him.'

'That's unfair! You know I want to see our Jack. The next time you have to go to Truro, I'll come too—'

And if you dare to say it's because I think you'll be visiting Jane Askhew, I shall hit you, she thought furiously...

'Good. Be ready tomorrow morning. We'll take luncheon in a tea room, and I'll take you to the boatyard. I'm sure Jane will be delighted to see you in the afternoon for some tea, and I'll collect you from there.'

He pecked her on the cheek before she could think of a good excuse. It was just as if it was all planned beforehand, Morwen thought furiously. But she did want to see Jack. She wanted to be sure he was happy. It would be nice to think one of the Tremayne family was happy...

Although, if she thought about it, perhaps she was the only one who wasn't. And she had no right to be miserable, when she had her heart's desire. But that desire had just walked away from her with about as much passion in his kiss as if he'd caressed a maiden aunt, and it wasn't much comfort to know it.

–

The events of that night took all thoughts of a visit to Truro from both their minds. They were awoken in the early hours of the morning by a rapid hammering on the door of Killigrew House. Ben swore angrily as he threw on a dressing-robe and went downstairs to see what the commotion was all about.

Not more trouble at the clay works, Morwen thought fearfully. They had had enough already…

Mrs Tilley came hurrying to the foot of the stairs, her face ashen. Morwen, behind Ben, heard her stammering words.

'Oh, Sir, there's a man here says there's been a terrible accident in the town on the seaward side. A house has burned down and there's nobody saved in it, and the constable sent un out here to alarm 'ee of the news—'

'What house? Why should it be of any interest to me, save for feeling sorry for those that perished—' Ben snapped as the woman seemed to lose control of her voice.

'Oh, Sir, oh, Sir—'

Morwen smothered the surge of fear in her stomach.

Her thoughts leapt ahead. Not the Tremayne house… that was outside the town, below the hill between St Austell and the clay works. Yet she had a strange presentiment that seemed to seep into her very bones. If not her family, then whose…?

Almost before the townsman pushed past Mrs Tilley, cap twisting in his hand at facing these fine folk in their posh house, Morwen knew.

She listened in a kind of guilty fascination as the tale unfolded. Part of her was glad… *glad*… She knew how wicked she was to feel so, but she couldn't help it…

'Mr Killigrew, Sir,' the man stuttered, 'I'm sent to tell 'ee as how 'tis your aunt that's dead and burned. Her and that Miss Ford who lived in the house on Trehidy Street. The house went up like a tinder-box, and there was no savin' 'em. Burnt to a crisp, by all accounts, beggin' your pardon, lady.'

He added the words apologetically as he became aware of Morwen behind Ben. He needn't have bothered, she thought hysterically. If she dared to say so, she'd have screamed out that she was glad Hannah Pascoe was dead! That it was probably her drunkenness that had sent her lurching about, overturning an oil-lamp and setting the small house ablaze.

Or perhaps there had been a pact between them. The dying Miss Ford and the outcast Mrs Pascoe… or maybe it was nothing like that at all. Simply a terrible accident…

'Morwen, put your head between your knees,' she heard Ben's instruction. 'Mrs Tilley, fetch some brandy, please. Some for this fellow too. He looks shaken enough.'

Why did she need brandy? She wasn't ill. She wasn't sad! Morwen suddenly heard the sound of laughing, shrill and wild, and realised with horror that it came from her own lips. She was truly hysterical, and the realisation stopped the awful sounds at once. She was bitterly ashamed of herself, especially with the poor man who'd brought the message looking hunted, and no doubt wishing himself anywhere but here.

'I'm sorry. I'm all right,' she gasped, her lips white.

'You're anything but all right.' Ben pushed the cold glass to her mouth and instructed her to drink. The spirit burned like fire as it trickled down her throat. Fire and burning… was this how Hannah Pascoe had felt when the flames caressed her skin and began to shrivel it?

Stop it, she told herself!

She forced her limbs to stop trembling with a great effort. The poor messenger shifted from foot to foot, clearly wondering how to get away from this house with the madwoman in it. There would be a tale to tell in the town. Of how poor young Mrs Killigrew had gone to pieces on hearing of the fate of her husband's aunt. Perhaps a real affection existed between the two of them after all, despite the rumours…

'I'll take my wife upstairs, and be with you in five minutes,' Ben told the townsman. 'Wait for me here.'

Morwen was propelled back to the bedroom. Should she offer to go with Ben? She knew it was more than she could do. The last time they had been involved in a terrible accident it had been so different.

Then it had been the clay waggon hurtling through poor old Nott's bakery, and the men killed had been her friends. She couldn't be hypocritical in pretending to be sorry Hannah Pascoe was dead, although she wouldn't wish such a horrible fate on anyone. Except perhaps one person.

Even as she thought it, Morwen's mind cleared. It was as though she had been exorcised in some way. Hadn't she been thinking only recently that if the odious Hannah Pascoe came back to Killigrew House, then it would open the doors for her son Jude to come back too? And now one of them was gone, and there was no reason for the other to enter their lives again.

She couldn't tell Ben of the certainty. Not yet. Hannah had been his aunt, and family feeling still meant something. She pushed her own feelings aside, and held on to his arm as he gently tucked her back into bed.

'Ben, I'm so sorry,' she whispered. 'You'll have a bad time ahead of you.'

He leaned down and kissed her. She saw that he was pale, but his face was set and controlled. He was strong, as strong as

Charles Killigrew had ever been. As if thoughts of Ben's father entered both their minds at the same instant, he spoke rapidly.

'Morwen, there's something you can do too. I see no reason why Father should know what's happened. It will set him back months, and he's already losing his grip on reality.'

It had become evident in recent weeks. There were days when it seemed as if Charles no longer knew where or who he was. They had never thought such a happening might be a blessing, but listening to Ben now, she saw the sense in his words.

'Rest for a while, darling. The servants will need to know, but you can instruct them that on no account is my father to learn of his sister's death. He has few visitors outside the household, and can no longer read for himself, so any account in the newspaper can be kept from him. It's little enough we can do, Morwen, but I'm sure the doctor will agree.'

'You're right, Ben,' she said slowly. 'And we can't even inform your cousin, since we don't know where he is. What of Miss Ford's relatives?'

'I remember my aunt saying there are none. The two of them only had each other.'

Morwen clung to him for a moment, the sadness of it all washing over her, temporarily clouding the guilty relief that the Pascoe woman was no longer a thorn in her flesh. Her generous heart could still feel sorrow at such an end, and to have no-one in the world to mourn was surely the saddest thing of all.

'I'll be back as soon as I can,' Ben said, throwing on some clothes. 'There's nothing anyone can do by the sound of it, but someone will need to officially identify what's left, I suppose, and make the formal arrangements.'

Morwen shuddered, her imagination filling in the details. Ben seemed to be talking almost to himself now.

'There was no love lost between us, but I can't let my aunt have a pauper's funeral. It will be as small as possible, and you and I will be the only mourners, Morwen. It's the last thing we can do for them both.'

Morwen nodded. It would be a farce, but it had to be done. She would do it for Ben, for the family honour. The whole town would know of the accident, all except Charles Killigrew, Hannah's brother. That was bizarre enough, and it was even more ironic that she should predecease him. She had seemed wiry enough to live for ever.

It was impossible for Morwen to sleep after Ben had left the house. How could she sleep? A thousand memories crowded her head. Where Hannah Pascoe was concerned, none of them was good. Where her son Jude was concerned, none of them was even tolerable. She blotted them out of her mind, and inevitably her thoughts turned to her friend, Celia.

The carefree days of laughter and shared childhood seemed an eternity ago. Bal maidens together for Killigrew Clay, running wild and free across the summer moors and flirting with the young clayworkers who all had an eye for the two prettiest girls at Clay One pit, making girlish plans for the future that could never come true…

Yet for one of them, the impossible dream had come true. Morwen had married the boss of Killigrew Clay and begun her life of happy-ever-after… and Celia had drowned in the slurry of a clay pit because of the evil Jude Pascoe, Ben's cousin…

A sob was wrenched from Morwen's throat. *No*, however much she tried, she couldn't regret Hannah Pascoe's death! The woman had been as wicked as her son.

–

'Can't 'ee spare the woman even a morsel of pity, Morwen?' Bess said sadly, when Morwen had taken the news to the Tremayne house that morning. 'I know she were never your favourite, but 'tis a terrible sad way to end—'

'I'm sorry for her friend, Mammie. Isn't that pity enough?'

Bess sighed, eyeing her daughter and the proud set of her head. She shook her head slightly.

'You've become hard, my lamb, and I'm sorry to see it. But no doubt you and Ben have your reasons for keeping the send-off small, and not wanting to invite folk. What does Mr Killigrew say to it all? Is he sore upset?'

Her face dropped when Morwen told her tersely of Ben's orders. These ways were new-fangled to Bess, who firmly believed that a man or woman's send-off was the last dignity on this earth, and to be deprived of that was near to blasphemy.

'It's Ben's wish, Mammie,' Morwen rushed on, seeing the look on her mother's face. 'We don't want to distress his father, nor do we want to turn the funeral into a peep-show. It's to be private and there's an end to it.'

'All right! Don't go on so!' Bess said in a huff. 'I just hope that when 'tis my turn, and your Daddy's, that you won't be hustling us off behind closed doors as if we'm a shame to 'ee.'

Morwen ran to hug her mother, her eyes damp.

'How can 'ee think that way? 'Tis not like that at all. If I could only tell 'ee my own reasons for not opposing it, you'd understand. But I can't! 'Tis too private. But don't be talking about you and Daddy in that way! I can't bear it!'

Bess was shaken by the passion in her voice, and the hinting at secrets too deep and painful to be shared. What they were, Bess couldn't begin to guess, but she respected another's wish for privacy, and she folded her daughter in her comforting arms, and hushed her tears the way she had always done.

It was a harrowing week for Ben. The doctor entirely agreed that there was no useful purpose in telling Charles Killigrew of his sister's death. The old man lived in a world of his own for much of the time, and all about him were anxious to keep him as serene as possible, for their own sakes as much as his own. When he became agitated Charles was a trial to them all.

The inquest on the two women was brief, with a verdict of misadventure. There was nothing else to be said, considering the lack of evidence to the cause of the fire. The house was charred to a cinder, the debris already disposed of. The sad little funeral service was attended only by Ben Killigrew and his wife, and the family doctor. No formal notice of the date was given in order to deter the curious.

A brief account was published in *The Informer* newspaper, and Lew Tregian, the chief reporter and editor, came to Killigrew House personally, to interview Ben on the story.

'I can tell you very little,' Ben said frankly. 'Two elderly ladies died tragically in a house fire, and there were no suspicious circumstances. I'm sorry I can't give you any more drama for your paper, Tregian.'

Ever hungry for news, the reporter saw no reason why he shouldn't capitalise on this meeting.

'And what of your own progress with the subsidence beneath the Killigrew rail tracks?'

'That has yet to be proven,' Ben snapped. 'Such a statement could be called libellous—'

'My dear Sir, I mean no disrespect! But it's some while since we've had any word on the findings, and I wondered if you'd care to give me a statement while I'm here.'

'Since the findings amount to nothing as yet, there's little to tell,' Ben retorted. 'However, I agree with you that a further statement might be of interest.'

He recalled Richard Carrick's comment that an assurance to the town that Killigrew Clay was doing everything possible to ensure future safety for the works and the rail excursions could only stand Ben in good stead.

He had done nothing about it. But he had thought long and hard, debating on whether or not to call in an independent surveyor and engineer, or to wait for Engineer Trent's return. The decision had been half-formed and he acted on it now.

'The summer excursions will be suspended for the time being. Engineer Trent is due back from Europe in a month or so, and will make a full inspection of the site, though preliminary investigations have shown nothing untoward. I am convinced there's no danger, but in respect of town feeling, I'm willing to show my goodwill in the matter. In order not to disappoint the clayworker's children over the annual train excursion to the sea at the end of the summer, I sincerely hope that all will be resolved by then.'

He looked at the reporter, head bent as he rapidly scribbled down Ben's words.

'Will that suffice, Tregian?'

'Excellent, Mr Killigrew,' the reporter beamed. 'If I may say so, it will be a welcome piece of news to offset the tragedy of the other, though naturally you have my condolences on the demise of your aunt.'

Ben nodded, wanting now to be rid of the man. The statement had been dictated on the spur of the moment, but he felt it had been the only one possible, and he knew he had been stubbornly putting off the moment of giving it.

Now that it was done, he wanted to tell Morwen of it, knowing that she would be relieved, and so would her family. So, too, would the clayworkers, he guessed, despite the small losses in their wage packets from the excursion money. He could afford to make them up with an occasional bonus payment, he thought quickly. Better that than disgruntled employees.

A boss's indecision was no good for anyone, and even if the action was an unwelcome one, a firm hand on the tiller was better than a restless one. It had been one of Charles Killigrew's sayings, and Ben began to realise the truth of it.

The reporter left the house, and Ben found Morwen in the drawing-room, frowning over one of the London newspapers he had sent down every week. Her brow was puckered at the unfamiliar names of places far away, the little sketch maps of the Crimea still making it seem as distant as the moon to her.

But she did try to follow some of it. It pleased Ben to know that she did so, and she wouldn't want folk to think his wife an ignoramus. She did try...

She felt his arms around her waist, and turned quickly, her face colouring. She hadn't heard him come in, and thought he was still with that funny little man from the Truro newspaper who'd taken over from Tom Askhew, telling him the details of Hannah Pascoe's terrible end, for the avid readers of such things...

'Has he gone?' she asked quickly.

'He has, and it's all over, darling. I gave him an extra bit of news for his rag too. Something that will please you, and give us all a breathing-space. I think we all deserve it.'

'What are you talking about, Ben?'

She didn't understand yet, but she knew it was something good. She could tell by the way he seemed more relaxed, his eyes clearer than they'd been in weeks, as if a weight had lifted from his shoulders. He looked somehow different...

She twisted into his arms, fitting against his body as smooth as silk. She could feel his heart against hers. She saw his head dip slowly towards hers, and tasted his mouth as it claimed hers in a long, lingering kiss.

There was good news to be told, and after this past terrible week, she felt they were due for good news. For happiness, for time for themselves. She didn't know yet what Ben had to tell her, but the moment of telling could wait. This was more important, this unspoken renewal of love between them, as deep and enduring as the ocean.

Chapter Ten

So for the time being, there were to be no more blistering tempers. No more frustrating meetings with surveyors and land agents. There was a temporary respite, and Morwen breathed a huge sigh of relief when Ben finally told her of the statement he had given to Lew Tregian.

She knew Ben was being generous in allowing the clay-workers the small bonus too. They would appreciate that. The world was becoming a sunnier place in every respect.

It was as though the tardy summer had decided to make its appearance at last, and catching Morwen's own mood, it was Ben who suggested a picnic by the sea, several weeks after his aunt's death had ceased to be news. There was no mention of including Jane Askhew in the invitation, which guiltily pleased Morwen even more.

'Didn't you say young Freddie was coming for the day on Sunday? He can come with us, if you like.'

'Oh, he'll like that, Ben!' Morwen said, her blue eyes glowing. 'Mammie said he was complaining only this week that he hardly ever sees you.'

'Is it that important to him?' Ben said in surprise. Morwen laughed, hugging his arm.

'Don't you know by now that you're his hero, darling? I suspect that all this talk of going away to a London school is partly because he wants to be just like you! Though I still think the rest of my family has reservations about it.'

'Thinking he's going up in the world? Freddie's got a sensible head on his shoulders, my love. He'll do all right.'

The townsfolk smiled with discreet sympathy when they saw her, on account of the Pascoe tragedy, and with approval on account of Ben's statement to the Truro newspaper. The Killigrews were popular folk once more.

–

Freddie arrived at Killigrew House on Sunday morning, agog to hear at first-hand about the recent house fire. He hadn't been able to catch his sister alone since then, and his parents had hushed him up whenever he wanted to talk about the accident, but Morwen could usually be persuaded to tell him more. He was aggrieved when it didn't seem to be the case this time.

'But what happened to the old biddies, our Morwen—?'

'You're not to talk about the ladies like that, do you hear?' she said crossly, knowing it was exactly how she thought of them herself! 'It will upset Ben to hear you speak so of his aunt and her friend—'

'Ben ain't here yet, is he?' Freddie sulked. 'You never used to be so feared o' telling the gory details, our Morwen. Did they frizzle like mushrooms in a pan, do 'ee suppose?'

'Freddie, will you stop it!' she snapped. 'You're not a child, and you know well enough why we don't talk of it in this house. Poor Mr Killigrew's not well enough to know of it.'

'I ain't telling un. I just want to know it all!'

'Well, you know as much as I do, and if you want to come with us for the picnic, you'll keep quiet about it, or I'll send you packing, do you understand?'

Freddie scowled at her. He was so like Jack at that moment, she almost laughed out loud. She felt an odd lump in her throat at seeing his look.

'You'm a snob, our Morwen. I don't like 'ee much any more. You ain't so nice as 'ee used to be.'

'Oh, Freddie, don't say that. Families should love each other, not fight—'

'Why?' he said mutinously.

Why indeed? If she thought about it, the Killigrews and the Pascoes didn't love each other! She couldn't answer his question, and was relieved when Ben came breezing in with the picnic basket, asking if they were ready or if they were going to sit around indoors all day when there was glorious summer sunshine waiting for them outside, and Freddie could gallop his horse along the beach if he was careful.

Freddie perked up at once. Ben threw a quick smile at Morwen, as if to acknowledge her remark. At that moment Ben was definitely Freddie's hero.

And the beach was so beautiful that day, as if it had been specially spruced and polished for the occasion. The sands were soft, but still springy where the incoming tide had recently washed them clean.

The tang of salt was sharp and refreshing, the ocean a glittering sheet of diamond points where the sun struck its rippling waves, the sun high in a clear blue sky, the distant horizon gently hazed, and beyond it… beyond it…

Morwen listened to the horse's thundering hooves as Freddie galloped him along the sands, kicking up the virginal sand in golden flurries, her brother's young voice squealing and shouting with pleasure. Ben watched and encouraged him, calling instructions, hands on hips, boots shining, hair ruffling in the warm breeze, master of all he surveyed.

Morwen watched the two of them as she sat back on her heels, spreading out the cloth and opening the luncheon basket. They were perhaps the two she loved best of all, she thought suddenly, and it was as if she had never realised until now just how dear her youngest brother was to her.

Ben, of course, she loved more than life, but the rush of emotion she felt for Freddie in those moments took her by surprise. Why should it be so? And suddenly she knew.

It was all wrapped up in the feeling of the morning. Being here, close to the sea, carefree and child-like, the distant horizon reminding her of other days, other times…

If Freddie had looked like Jack in his black mood, then how much more did he remind her of Matt right now! Her dreaming brother, who hadn't been content with Cornwall, but wanted a different life, needing to be free and unfettered. The first one of the Tremaynes to break the ties with the clay, followed incredibly by her Mammie, giving up the rough job of bal maiden and taking in the sewing for the genteel ladies of St Austell town. Then Morwen herself, becoming housekeeper for old Charles Killigrew, and eventually marrying the young boss. Now Jack had left to train as a boat-builder, and if all went as planned, then soon it would be Freddie's turn to leave… So many changes… and only Sam the eldest stayed the same. Sam, following in her father's footsteps so squarely…

'What ghosts are you laying this morning, my darling?'

She jumped as she heard Ben's gentle voice, and yet it seemed as if she turned her head in slow motion, as if she could hardly bear to lose the images forming in her mind. It brought them all so close, these water-colour ghosts, Sam and Jack and Matt… and Freddie, hurtling along St Austell sands…

She met Ben's eyes as she knelt on the damp sands, her hands immobile in her lap. Soft hands now, that had once been as roughened as her Mammie's used to be, working with the clay blocks, drying and stacking and loading, for the prosperity of Killigrew Clay.

And Ben saw the darkness in her blue eyes, the emotions that she could never hide from him, and caught his breath at the loveliness of his fey and beautiful wife. He dropped down beside her and gathered her roughly to him, rocking her for long private moments, the two of them enclosed in a warm, magical world of their own, where words were superfluous.

Sand suddenly stung her face as Freddie laughingly flipped it over them, and shrieked out that he was starving, that the horse was tired, and when were they going to eat the picnic?

The spell was broken, and Ben broke away from her with a bellow that Morwen knew covered his own emotions, as he told Freddie to come and help if he wanted food.

Morwen turned away, inexplicable tears misting her eyes for a moment. Knowing that she thought of her brother Matt that day as she hadn't thought of him for a long time. Wondering how he fared, if he prospered or ailed. They didn't even know if he was married or had children. She caught her breath at the thought of Matt's imaginary little American children.

The one thing they did know, according to the late Hannah Pascoe, was that Matt had broken the bonds with her son Jude, and to Morwen that was the best news of all.

She had always suspected that the two of them had boarded the ship for America in unnecessary haste, all those years ago. It had coincided rather too timely with a wrecking along the coast, where a man had been killed and no culprit had been found.

She would never believe her gentlest brother capable of killing anyone... just as she would always believe anything of Jude Pascoe.

But she realised now just how her mother felt, missing her lost lamb so badly at times. Bess rarely spoke of Matt, but the memories didn't die. A son was always a son, no matter what he did or where he went. The cord was never really severed.

'Come on then, if you're starving!'

She spoke brightly to Freddie, when the day threatened to turn into a maudlin one, at least on her account. 'There's pasties and jellies and fruit drink, and apples and cheese. Enough to satisfy an army of greedy schoolboys!'

'I want to swim afterwards. Is it all right, Ben?'

Freddie bypassed his sister on that score as his teeth sank into one of Mrs Horn's juicy pasties, the meat and potatoes at one end, the jam at the other, in true Cornish tradition. Miners' fare, for a complete meal in one tasty pastry package while they toiled underground in poor lighting and dank conditions. More happily enjoyed on this summer day on a sunlit Cornish beach with the scent of the breeze lifting their spirits.

'It's all right by me!' Ben stretched out on the sand. 'There's no work today so we may as well enjoy ourselves as long as you stay decent and don't alarm other folks, nor the horse.'

Freddie laughed at his teasing.

'We've got the beach to ourselves, by the looks on it. Mammie gave me a towel in case I got wet, and said I was to keep me underpinnings on at all costs.'

Morwen burst out laughing. 'A lot of good they'll do you afterwards if you swim in them, ninny.'

'Don't stop him or he'll take them off, and I can't bear such a sight so early in the day,' Ben grinned.

They were just like a family, Morwen thought later, as Freddie scampered off to the water's edge in his ridiculous long underpants, his skin weathered to a deep bronze by the moorland winds, the young muscles tensed and strong as his screaming leap into the waves made the cotton fabric cling wetly to his body.

She couldn't avoid seeing the bulging shape of him, and realised that her baby brother was fast growing up. She felt a great tenderness towards him to know it, and averted her eyes so that he wouldn't know she was aware of it.

Ben was aware of it too. He hadn't realised how quickly Freddie was growing either. He was a young man already. Sam's children were the only babies in the combined Tremayne and Killigrew families now. The days merged into years under their noses, and no-one ever realised how it changed people until suddenly confronted with a man who only yesterday had been a boy.

It must be the relaxing sea air that was filling him with such introspection, Ben thought. That, and the strange, wistful look he had glimpsed earlier on Morwen's face. He knew that look when she gazed towards the horizon.

It was Matt she missed then. Ben would give her the moon if he could, but he couldn't give her the two things he knew she yearned for most. News of Matt Tremayne, and a child of her own to fill her empty arms. The anguished thought was in his head before he could stop it.

'It's time we were leaving,' he said abruptly, when Freddie had rubbed himself dry with the rough towel and draped his underpinnings over a rock to dry in the sun; Ben's own thoughts were less than comfortable.

Freddie gave a howl of protest, but Ben was adamant; obediently, Morwen began to gather up the remains of the picnic and thrust everything into the basket.

'Don't argue, our Freddie. We've been here several hours already. The sun's prickling my skin, and a lady has to protect her white skin at all times.' She laughed up into Ben's eyes as she spoke, seeing the answering smile there.

Freddie snorted. 'You'm turning soft, that's what! You ain't a real lady, anyway. You'm just our Morwen—'

Ben gave him a friendly cuff about the ear. 'That's just where you're wrong, then,' he said smartly. 'Morwen is my lady. What's more, I'm not so sure about her being "our Morwen", either. I prefer to think of her as *my* Morwen.'

The little glow Ben's words gave her softened with sympathy as she saw Freddie's glum look at being chastised by his hero. She gave him a quick hug. He wasn't too big for that yet, even though he squirmed away almost immediately.

'He'll never stop me being "our Morwen", will he, lamb? Part of me will always belong to you and Mammie and Daddy and—'

'Now you'm really being soft, our Morwen!' He was hot with embarrassment, and started to laugh as the old familiar phrase tripped off his lips.

He felt an odd satisfaction. For all Ben's cleverness, he couldn't separate the Tremaynes, even if he wanted to. Deep down, they still belonged together, however many wives and husbands and oceans parted them. Even Freddie knew that.

'Can I come into your study with 'ee when we get back to the house, Ben?' he said eagerly now.

Ben ruffled the boy's dark hair affectionately.

'Why not? I suppose you want to look at my London news-papers, do you?'

Freddie grinned. ''Tis not only the war doings I like to see. 'Tis all the grand places I'll be able to visit if I go to the posh school. Mr Pengelly said he had a quick look at my examination paper, and thought I did well enough.'

'He shouldn't have done that. It should be sent straight to London—'

'Ben, don't be so pompous,' Morwen protested. 'What harm does it do for Freddie to know he's done well?'

Ben shrugged, shaking the sand from the cloth and fastening the picnic basket securely.

'Probably none at all, but it's not the way things are done. Freddie will need to learn that if he goes away to school. The lazy country ways are very different, and it's not only his formal education that will need attention.'

'What a funny remark to make!'

'Then forget I made it,' he said lightly, before he said more than he intended, and alarmed her needlessly. There was no point in stirring up trouble before trouble was upon them.

–

They reached Killigrew House, tired and dusty and gritty with sand. Morwen said that she must brush it out of her hair immediately, and that Freddie must wash himself properly before setting foot in such elegant surroundings.

'I were washed enough in the sea!' he howled. 'Besides, Ben said I can go with un to his study, our Morwen—'

Mrs Tilley appeared before she could take him by the ear and march him right upstairs to a jug and basin and attend to his ablutions personally.

'Begging your pardon, Sir and Madam, but a visitor's come while you were out.'

She sounded flustered and a touch excited. Not Jane Askhew again, surely… but Mrs Tilley was used to that young lady's visits now, and wouldn't be in such a tizz about that.

Ben exclaimed impatiently. It had been a good day so far, and he wanted nothing more now than to relax in his study for an hour or so, and perhaps take an evening stroll with Morwen after dinner that evening. He wasn't in the mood for company.

Freddie Tremayne was lively enough, but by the middle of the afternoon, Ben had had enough chatter for one day.

'Who is it, Mrs Tilley? And where have you put the person?'

'I didn't know what to do with un, Sir. In the end, he asked to see your father, and I thought it would be all right, him being such a splendid gent an' all, and wearing the uniform of an officer of the Queen—'

'Who the devil is it? Didn't he give his name, woman?' Ben demanded, as she continued to flounder at the way the young master glowered impatiently at her.

'O' course, Sir. I have his calling card here,' she said stiffly, annoyed that Mr Ben thought she was slipping in her duty. Unannounced visitors on a Sunday when she was trying to take a catnap didn't endear her to her role as housekeeper, for all her fondness for the Killigrew family.

She thrust the card on the little silver tray under Ben's nose. He stared at it for a few seconds, not recognising the name immediately. Nor would he, he thought, when recollection came. The last time he had seen it there was no prefix of Captain before it, nor the proud name of an army regiment beneath it.

'Good God!'

Neville Peterson... Captain Peterson now, he amended grimly. Images spun through his mind. He recalled a tall, well-built young man with corn-fair hair. Good-looking, authoritative, and with a family well-heeled enough to buy him into any rank of any regiment he preferred. Money that had always bought him out of any scrapes, large or small...

Neville Peterson, one-time scourge of a class of elite sons, whose parents were all politicians or minor royalty or something vaguely important in the city... one of an even more exclusive band that Ben had hoped fervently never to meet again in his lifetime…

'Who is it, Ben?' Morwen said curiously, when he seemed to do nothing but stare at the gilt-edged calling card.

'Someone I used to know at college in London,' he muttered, since there was no help for it. 'How in God's name did he find his way here?'

'You don't sound very pleased about it! He must have been a friend of yours.'

Ben suddenly looked at him as if seeing him for the first time. His voice was suddenly harsh.

'You'd best go home, boy. I can't entertain you any more today if we've got a visitor. Come back some other time, and I'll show you my maps and papers.'

'And the pictures of the coffee-houses in London where 'ee used to go?'

'Get off home, Freddie. Tell your mother you've been tolerably good for once.'

He smiled as he spoke to take the sting out of his words, hoping he didn't betray his eagerness to get Freddie away from the house. His own actions annoyed him. He was over-reacting to a visit from someone he hadn't seen for over five years. People changed. Neville Peterson might well have changed too.

Morwen saw her brother out, glancing back at Ben and wondering just why he seemed so agitated. He covered it well, but she knew the signs. She noted the twitching nerve at the side of his mouth, and way his hands clenched and unclenched without his realising that they did so.

Ben wasn't pleased that this old school-friend had called on him, and she was wise enough not to comment until she met the man for herself.

'I'd best go up to Father's room and join them,' Ben said tersely. 'I hope it hasn't been too much excitement for him.'

'Nurse Stevens will soon hoist the visitor out of the room if she thinks that, my love,' Morwen said lightly. 'I'll go and tidy myself. I look forward to meeting this old friend of yours, Ben.'

She hoped to remind him delicately that a guest in the house deserved hospitality, however uninvited. He had expected Morwen to welcome Jane Askhew. The least he could do was show a welcome to this unexpected visitor. It puzzled her that he seemed so reluctant to do so.

—

Ben took the stairs two at a time, knowing he couldn't put off the moment any longer. Before he reached his father's bedroom, he heard the old man's gurgling laughter, and remembered that Neville Peterson had always been able to tell a fine story to amuse his listeners.

The thought mollified him a little. It would have been a long day for Charles, with his family away at the beach for most of the day. Ben put a determined smile on his face as he walked into the room, and the tall figure seated beside the bed rose at once and turned to greet him.

Ben's instant thought was that at least Captain Peterson looked more manly than the boy he remembered. The chin was firmer, the mouth less full, the eyes keener and not so damnably alluring in a way that would have looked better on a woman…

The uniform helped, of course. The man was as dashing a figure as ever graced a society ballroom, Ben had to admit, as Neville came towards him, arms outstretched. In those first moments, Ben barely registered the way one of the officer's legs dragged behind the other in the elegantly-fitting trousers.

'Ben, my dear old chap, it's good to see you again. Bit of a surprise, my turning up here out of the blue, I daresay, what?' The voice was the same, deep and charming and persuasive.

He forced an answering smile as his hand was pumped up and down exuberantly.

'More of a shock, I'd say!' Ben tried not to sound too rattled. The other laughed.

'So your father said – or tried to. I say, old chap,' he lowered his voice as if Charles was merely hard of hearing and couldn't understand plain English any longer. 'This is a rum do. Wasn't the old boy head of some tin-mining concern?'

'Not tin mining. Killigrew Clay produces much of the Cornish china clay that goes into the manufacture of pottery and medicines and newspaper chemicals,' Ben said shortly. 'The business belongs to me now.'

'Is that so? Well, well.' Captain Peterson nodded thought-fully, as if such manufacture was of immense interest to him. Ben remembered that studied look of old. It meant nothing. Peterson's only interest was in Neville Peterson. At college, his self-indulgence had been legendary.

'What about you?' Ben said. 'I don't need a crystal ball to tell me what you've been doing, but what brings you to this part of the world?'

And more importantly, for how long…?

Captain Peterson swayed sideways a little, and hobbled back to the bedside chair, where Charles was already waving at him to rejoin him, clearly enjoying the interruption to his dull day, and gibbering something completely unintelligible.

'You'll forgive me, Killigrew,' Neville apologised to Ben. 'The old leg gives me hell at times. Got shot up a bit at Sevastopol, d'you see, and got shipped home from the Crimea as a bit of a bloody wounded hero. I arrived in Falmouth on a troop ship a week ago, and suddenly remembered it was your part of the country. I thought you might remember an old school chum and be willing to offer me a bed for a night or two. The parents are doing the grand tour in Europe at present. War or no war, the old pater enjoys his summer visits, so I'm at a loose end for a month, d'you see?'

Ben listened in a kind of horrified stupor as the mesmeric voice rumbled on, and Charles continued to wave his stick arms as though demented, while Ben deliberately ignored the garbled insistence on giving the officer a room and bed for as long as he wished… it was the very last thing Ben wished…

'I say, old boy! You may be buried in the depths of the old backwoods, but you don't run short when it comes to beauty, do you? Won't you introduce me to this lovely lady?'

Ben started as Neville rose to his feet again, a smile widening the handsome face. A face to charm any woman off her feet, Ben thought ironically.

Right now, the woman taking the full brunt of those admiring eyes was Morwen, framed by the doorway, and looking a picture of loveliness in a freshly laundered gown, the sand brushed out of her hair, a welcoming smile on her lips.

She didn't wait for Ben to introduce her, but walked straight to his side, linking her arm in his.

'I'm Morwen – I'm Ben's wife – and I know that we'd be very honoured to have you stay with us for as long as you wish, Captain. It's such a pleasure for me to meet one of my husband's old college friends.'

She was as gracious as any well-bred lady. Not even Jane Carrick Askhew could have done better, Morwen thought serenely. She was proud of the way she was handling this first visit from a stranger. Ben would be proud of her too.

Captain Peterson limped forward to take her hand in his for a moment, and murmured how enchanted he was to make her acquaintance.

And Morwen was completely unaware that Ben had once considered him the most treacherous of young men, and least of all a friend.

Chapter Eleven

'But *why* don't you want Captain Peterson here?' Morwen said in exasperation, as she slid between the sheets and hunched up in the bed watching Ben strip off his clothes for the night.

Her dark hair fell over her arms and knees like a silk curtain, and she tossed its tickling tresses away impatiently. For the life of her, she couldn't see what Ben's objections to his friend's presence could be.

The evening had been perfectly fascinating, and listening to the tales of an officer's life in the midst of the Crimean war had brought it all more vividly to life than any dull old newspaper account ever could.

It amazed her that Ben didn't see it in the same light, considering the hours he pored over his stuffy London papers, and exclaimed harshly at the waste of so many lives, especially when one and then another that were familiar to him from his college days appeared in the deceased columns.

Captain Peterson was bright and charming, and was already insisting that she must call him Neville, since he and Ben were such old friends.

Morwen could still hear her husband's undignified snort at the remark, and simply couldn't understand it. She would have expected him to be intent on Captain Peterson's every word, instead of cutting him short at every opportunity.

Morwen wondered suddenly if after all, Ben regretted the fact that he had never been at liberty to seek an army commission himself, instead of being stuck with the ownership of Killigrew Clay, and therefore couldn't bear to hear such first-hand accounts. There were few enough clayworkers who would agree with such sentiments, but Ben's ideas were far removed from theirs.

Wars in distant shores seemed part of another world to humble clayworkers who worked hard enough to earn a crust to fill hungry bellies, and considered their duty began at home and not fighting overseas. They would leave that to those who had fighting in their blood, or ambitions to fill officers' uniforms.

Was Ben wishing he had been able to do just that after all? The very thought made Morwen uneasy. The Captain was gallant and charming, but she would hate to be the wife of such a man. Morwen wanted her husband at home, by her side, in her bed at night. The knowledge was too natural to make her blush.

'I don't wish to discuss Neville Peterson,' Ben said as he joined her in the bed. 'It's enough that he's here, and thanks to you he's going to stay until God knows when! I'll thank you in future to leave me to issue my own invitations.'

Morwen swallowed. The harsh words hardly echoed her own romantic sentiments of moments before. This day had begun so beautifully, and she thought she had done what Ben would want. Somehow it was all turning sour. As if to add to her dismay, she heard the soft patter of rain on the windows and shivered. She tried to summon up an angry retort and failed.

'I'm sorry. I only meant to act graciously,' she muttered. 'I thought it was what you'd want of me—'

He suddenly turned to her, pulling her into his arms and holding her so tightly she could hardly breathe. His heart beat so loudly it was like a drumbeat against her own.

His mouth was very close to hers, his breath warm on her skin. He spoke oddly, with a rough arrogance that had sent many a clayworker scurrying to do his bidding.

'What I want you to do is forget everyone else in this house but you and me. Especially do I want you to forget Neville Peterson. I don't want even his mental presence in this room that belongs to no-one but we two. Here and now, no-one else exists in the world but you and me. Do I need to make it any plainer?'

'No – oh, no—'

She opened her mouth to speak, and Ben's mouth covered it, his tongue moving sensuously against her soft inner skin and rousing her to a flame of answering desire in an instant. Such was the passion that had always existed between them that it took no more than that, a whisper of sweet seduction, a tingling touch of flesh on flesh, a slow intimate caress…

Morwen soon realised that Ben had no wish for slow intimate caresses that night. She had no experience of how a whore behaved, those dubious ladies of the night who frequented every waterfront, yet somehow her responsive mind knew that what Ben wanted from her was the response of a wanton, an abandonment that was even wilder than the frenzied performance their love-making frequently took.

Tonight it seemed as if he needed to explore every part of her as if it was new to him, touching, kissing, caressing, yet with that strange urgency that was beginning to set Morwen's senses on fire.

She gave him everything he wanted, and felt the pulsing core of her respond to it all. He thrust into her as though possessed by demons, and she gloried in the pleasurable sensations rippling through her. His mumbled words were a mixture of love and blasphemy, and neither shocked her. When the moments of his release came, he clung to her, his fingers kneading the tender skin of her breasts and hardly noticing what he did.

Gradually the exertions stopped, and he rolled over on to his side, still holding her close, still part of her, as if he couldn't bear to let her go. And Morwen's eyes were damp, not understanding why he had felt this fierce, almost brutal need of her, and unable to question him.

There was something deep in Ben's soul that had tortured him tonight, and she felt instinctively that she would learn of it when the time was right. But now was not the time… he was releasing his hold on her at last, as exhausted as she.

Morwen touched her breasts tenderly. They felt bruised.

Once, she had almost cried out at his treatment. Yet some instinct told her it was almost as though Ben desperately needed her womanliness to reassure him. For an odd moment she had felt like a mother with a child, and the weird thought had stopped her crying out.

Morwen smiled crookedly into the darkness. A mother with a child… no, that was not the sum total of her feelings! Not when her man was filling her with so much love… or was it lust? It didn't matter. In their passionate marriage the one was too bound up with the other to make the distinction. One complemented the other, the love and the lust, and the love…

Morwen drifted into sleep, but he lay wide awake long after her breathing had slowed and deepened. He listened to her breathing, his beautiful Morwen, dearer to him than life, the other half of him…

His hands tightened unconsciously at his sides as unwanted images, long forgotten, swirled into his mind.

–

In his restless waking dream he was no longer the powerful owner of Killigrew Clay, but a frightened boy, newly arrived at the huge London college, where everyone spoke with strange quick accents, and a good many of the older boys whispered behind their hands at this newcomer from faraway Cornwall.

'What's this?' One of the thick-set youths chortled when a group of them saw Ben trying to become as inconspicuous as possible. He tweaked him out into the open by his ear, and the group closed in on him.

'By all that's holy, it's a new boy,' another exclaimed in mock astonishment. 'A fresh-faced callow lad from the country, don't y' know, chaps? And what shall we do with this tasty morsel still wet behind the ears?'

'This one's for Neville,' sniggered the first one. 'He's partial to country boys.'

Ben had looked suspiciously from one to the other, hating their leering mouths, and inferences he didn't fully understand.

His father had made a few halting references to the dangers of a dosed society where the college boys made their own rules, but Charles had been reluctant to speak frankly on a subject that had never bothered him. Ben was handy enough with his fists, and could take care of himself.

Charles had consoled himself with the thought that it would strengthen the boy's character to learn the seamier side of life for himself. Not that there could be much of it, in a college that catered for the sons of gentle-folk, Charles had thought with innocent complacency.

'Very partial, old boy,' the one called Neville had breathed. 'My room tonight for the old initiation ceremony, country boy. You'll be shown the way. Someone will come to fetch you after lights out.'

Ben found his voice. 'What initiation ceremony?' He growled hoarsely with sheer terror, which made the group scream with laughter. Their snide glances sickened him, and when one of them put an arm around his shoulders and squeezed it hard, his urge was to twist away and run, and run and run...

'You'll find out,' the other said softly. 'I promise you it'll be a night to remember!'

The group had dispersed as quickly as it had surrounded him, and he had been suddenly alone. He'd heard a low whistle from the side of the building, and had a lucky warning from an earlier sufferer on just what form the initiation ceremony took.

Ben's face had turned a furious scarlet.

'I just wanted to warn you, Killigrew. If they've set their sights on you, you stand no chance, and I could see by their faces that you're next on their list.'

'Does nobody fight them?'

'There are six of them, and they always pick on scared new boys. Who would report to a master that he's been assaulted? The six would defend each other as always. It would be their word against one. Better to go through with it until the next pretty boy arrives.'

Ben's eyes flashed furiously. 'No chinless wonders are sticking me up against a wall without a fight!'

'Oh, it won't be against a wall, Killigrew,' the boy said quite seriously. 'They feather-bed the ones they like. You'll be treated like a queen bee—'

'Like hell I will!' Ben raged. 'Get out of my way, you slimy bastard—'

He pushed the boy, who staggered against the wall, affronted at this reaction. To Ben's horror, he began to cry.

'Don't say I didn't warn you. They rule here. You stand no chance—'

Ben strode off. His heart thumped sickeningly. He looked at the clock-face on the college tower. It was a free afternoon, and tonight he was to undergo an ordeal more degrading than anything he had ever imagined.

He swore savagely under his breath. He shut out any kind of imagining. Nor would he spend the rest of the day cowering in terror like the thin boy who had glided away in the shadows just now. He had a tongue in his head, and there was time to prepare himself.

He left the college grounds and called a hansom cab. The driver's eyes widened at the strange request. Cabbies were used to taking college boys to the theatres, to the Ritz and other high-class hotels, and conversely to the shady places where the buckos cavorted with prostitutes, spending their rich Daddies' money as if it was water… but this cabby had never had such a request as this before. He peered back at the good-looking boy with the lazy accent he didn't readily identify.

'You sure that's what you want, young sir?'

'I'm quite sure. You know of such a place, don't you? I thought London cabbies knew everything—'

''Course I do, mate. I was just wond'ring what a fine young gent like yerself would be wanting with an establishment that teaches the Japanese Martial Arts!'

He mimicked Ben's determined request.

'Just get me there, will you? And hurry up, please.'

The cabby shrugged and clicked the horse into action. Ben sat back. He had no idea what it would cost to learn the rudiments of the craft, but by God, it would be worth a king's ransom to surprise Peterson tonight. He smiled grimly at the thought.

Three hours later he almost staggered out of the side street and into another cab. The inscrutable instructors had looked shocked when Ben had stated he needed to learn everything in one afternoon.

How could this be done, when it had taken centuries to perfect the finer points of the martial arts? The young sir was presumptuous. Perhaps this initial lesson would open the way to further study...

'I don't have centuries,' Ben had snapped. 'I have a couple of hours. Teach me all you can to deal with six opponents. Don't be soft with me, and don't give me basics. I want to hit where it hurts most. I can pay whatever fee you ask. If I'm wasting my time here I'll go elsewhere.'

—

He had heard his door open some time after lights out. One of the six who had accosted him earlier told him to follow him quietly. Ben slid out of bed. He was fully dressed. Around his wrist he had wound a leather belt, concealing the heavy buckle in his palm. The feel of it gave him comfort.

Earlier, he had grabbed the thin boy to ask how the group operated. He learned that there were only three inside the room at any one time. The others kept watch outside the door and in corridors, should any untoward noise alert the staff. There would be plenty of noise tonight, Ben thought tensely.

'Inside, country boy.' The youth pushed Ben inside the room and took up his station outside it.

Ben's heart lurched. Neville Peterson lounged on the bed, clad only in a Chinese silk kimono. Two others were similarly dressed, and the room smelled of a sickly perfume. It almost made Ben retch. Neville beckoned him forward into the pool of light thrown by a sputtering gas light.

'Come and join us, country boy,' he said softly. 'This is to be your night of pleasure – and ours too, what?'

He heard the creaking of the bed-springs as they made room for him, and it was the sound that moved him into sudden action.

He gave a battle shriek loud enough to waken the dead, letting the belt snake out from his wrist like a whip. The ornate buckle struck Neville Peterson cruelly in the throat. He gave a strangled gurgling scream as blood spurted out from a vicious jagged cut.

The other two closed in on Ben from both sides, but he was ready for them. He remembered frantically the moves he had been taught that afternoon, the kicks, the punches, the painful pressure points whenever he was near enough to apply them. What he hadn't learned that day, his own fury supplied.

Neville Peterson crouched on the bed. His throat bled over the expensive silk kimono, but he was less interested in that than in rocking over the excruciating pain in his crotch. One of the others moaned on the floor in similar position. The third screamed at the companion outside the door to come and help them with this madman.

Ben swivelled to meet him, leaping clear off the ground as the boy rushed in. His feet caught him in the belly, his fist following with an almighty crash on to the boy's nose. Blood gushed out as he dropped to the floor with a howl of pain.

Ben heard the sound of running footsteps in the corridor, and there were bells ringing in his head. Or was the sound coming from other parts of the college? He couldn't be sure… but the group of boys in the room were sure. They screamed in panic at him to get out, and never to come near them again.

He didn't need telling twice. He turned and ran, sobs tearing at his chest. It would be appalling to be hauled up before the college professors in his first week. Even worse to be sent packing in disgrace. His father would be shamed, and so would Ben.

Somehow he reached his own room, uncaring what holocaust went on behind him. He lay beneath the bedcovers, awake for hours, expecting his door to be thrust open at any minute and for accusations to be poured on him. He knew bitterly that blame would be attached to him as well as the others. Dirt stuck, no matter how innocent he was. It was another lesson to be learned.

Incredibly, no-one came to his room. Nothing was said about any incident, and if four boys in the elite class went about with bruised and battered faces and careful footsteps for the next few weeks, no-one remarked on it.

It amazed and appalled him that such happenings could be covered up. But the longer he stayed at the college, the less he ceased to be amazed. His education widened his eyes to the rottenness of life as well as its advantages.

The one thing that gratified him was that from that night on, he was left strictly alone by Peterson's gang. They had a healthy respect for his response, and he went his own way.

Ben wasn't sorry when they left, being one class above him, and never expected to see any of them again.

And now that same Neville Peterson was installed in his own house, older, more handsome than ever, as gallant to Ben's wife as any young officer could be.

Ben wondered suspiciously just how genuine it was. Did such people ever change? And if they did, then Ben wasn't at all sure he wanted the man playing court to Morwen!

Whatever Neville's present inclinations, he appeared to have forgotten that any antagonism ever existed between himself and Ben Killigrew. An incident that was imprinted so deeply on Ben's mind was evidently just one of many in Peterson's shady student past, and meant nothing more than a night's excitement.

Whatever the case, Ben had felt that extraordinary urge to take Morwen in his arms that night, and express his full sexual power onto her.

And remembering just how perfect that expression of love had been earlier, with Morwen rising to meet him in every way, Ben finally slept.

—

'Had you forgotten that Jane and Cathy are coming to visit one day this week?' Morwen asked Ben, slightly annoyed that he was home so little during that first week of Captain Peterson's arrival.

She had expected him to be taking his friend about, showing him the town, and certainly the clay works. But Ben seemed to have little interest in acting the gentleman host, and left much of the entertaining to Morwen, and to the unlikely assistance of his father from his sickbed.

'I hadn't forgotten,' Ben said briefly. 'I daresay Jane will be especially interested to meet Neville, and question him about conditions in the Crimea. You might suggest that he tempers things down a little, in order not to disturb her too much. She worries enough on Tom's account already.'

Morwen resented the fact that he was giving her orders as hostess. He should be here, showing Neville around himself. She resented the fact that she must act as an intermediary between Jane Askhew and their guest, when it was Ben's job to do so.

In fact, since that one glorious night after Captain Peterson's arrival, Morwen realised that Ben had become very edgy, and she had no idea of the reason. Unless it was because he disliked the way Neville paid her little compliments, and clearly enjoyed her company. Unless Ben were jealous of his old friend!

He had absolutely no reason to be, but Morwen couldn't help a feeling of pleasure if it were so. It didn't hurt for Ben to think another man found her attractive and feminine. It didn't hurt at all.

She completely misunderstood his scowling face whenever Neville smiled winningly across the dinner table at her, or took the liberty of picking her a late summer rose from the garden and telling her its perfection was only surpassed by her own. It was like balm to her senses to hear such gallantries.

Neville complimented her on her piano-playing, and told David Glass he considered Morwen to be an ideal pupil, quick and eager to learn. David was gratified that at least one person in the Killigrew household was genteel enough to appreciate his patience in teaching a stormy young lady, and managed to convey the fact discreetly.

'Would you care to see the Killigrew clay works, Captain Peterson – Neville?' Morwen asked one morning, when Ben had ridden from the house early for a meeting with the accountants about the bonuses paid to the clayworkers.

Neville hid a sigh. Clay works weren't of the least interest to him, but he was tired of the dribbling old man upstairs, and Ben as a country squire was becoming a bore. At least the wife was pretty to look at, and country air would be better than idling indoors yet again.

'It would be a pleasure,' he said. 'Ben kept his business a mystery in our college days, dear lady. We all wondered what on earth happened down here among the hay stacks. Does your own family live near to Killigrew House?'

Morwen smiled at his snobbery. Intentional or not, she was very aware of it, and she was surprised to know it didn't trouble her. Nor was she ashamed of her background, and was ready to let Captain Peterson know it.

'My family all worked for Killigrew Clay in very humble capacities,' she said with quiet dignity. 'I was a bal maiden and so was my mother. At one time my father was pit captain of Clay One, the biggest of the Killigrew Clay Works, and my brothers were all clayworkers. My father is manager now, and my eldest brother is pit captain in his place. The rest of us have different roles in life,' she finished with a slight smile.

'Gracious me,' Neville stared at her. 'I must say, you don't have any reticence in telling the facts, dear lady.'

'Should I?' Her blue eyes were as candid as ever. 'We are what we are, Captain Peterson.'

His hand closed over hers and squeezed it for a second. She wasn't sure if it was meant to be a gesture of understanding, but the touch of his hand was clammy, and she had the strangest urge to fling it away from hers.

'That's so profound, Morwen.'

'Is it? I thought it was perfectly obvious!'

He began to learn the logic of her thinking, as Ben and his father had done long ago. She had no patience with devious minds, and her reasoning was as clear as the cloudless blue sky. She recognised his sudden embarrassment, and sought to put him at ease, since he was a guest in the house.

'My youngest brother Freddie is hoping to go away to college in London if he passes the entrance examination. He's thirteen now, and doesn't want to spend his life working with the clay. He's a bright boy, and Ben wants him to have his chance. We can call at my parents' house on our way to the clay works if you wish, and you can meet Freddie and my mother. I know they'll be thrilled to meet an army officer.'

Neville smiled his most charming smile.

'It sounds delightful, Morwen. And if your brother does get his place at college, I'll be sure to give him my London address. I have a very nice mews house with plenty of space for overnight visitors. It would be my pleasure to entertain him occasionally as a break from his studies, and to show him something of our capital city.'

'That's very kind of you, Sir!' Morwen exclaimed. 'Freddie will be feeling lost in London, I'm sure. It will be good to know he has one friend.'

Neville smiled again, patting her hand as they walked out into the sunshine to the stables, where he handed her up into the Killigrew trap.

'It will be my pleasure, dear lady.'

He climbed into the trap beside her and took the reins in his beautifully manicured hands, and as he turned his head Morwen suddenly noticed the scar across his throat, the jagged line of it caught by the sunlight. She wondered fleetingly if it was the result of a battle skirmish in the awful Crimea.

How little the Captain made of his war experiences, she thought suddenly. And what surprisingly little interest Ben showed in it. She was suddenly indignant on her husband's behalf, and determined to show the Captain every consideration and feeling of welcome.

Chapter Twelve

Freddie was excited at the thought of visiting Captain Peterson in London. He asked endless questions about college life, about the Crimean war, about the wound in Captain Peterson's leg, until Bess was obliged to stop him.

She was already flustered at Morwen bringing the gentleman to the Tremayne house unannounced, and had hastily whisked away her sewing and rushed to offer cool drinks and bring out some scones and jam, even though it was only mid-morning.

'Stop bothering the gentleman, Freddie,' Bess hissed in his ear. 'He'll be tired o' your questioning, and regret that he ever asked 'ee to call on un.'

Neville smiled in kindly fashion. 'Nonsense. It's good to find a boy with a keen mind, Mrs Tremayne. We should never stop the young from enquiring. It's the only way they discover things.'

'Did 'ee get that throat-cut in a battle, Captain Sir?' Freddie said eagerly, echoing Morwen's own thoughts, and ignoring his mother's glare for his rudeness at being so personal.

Neville touched the scar absently. He'd long forgotten the true circumstances of the wound. It was in some college brawl, but such things had been commonplace. He had plenty of battle-scars apart from those inflicted by a foreign enemy. But there was no harm in embellishing it for the boy.

'I did, Freddie. A fellow twisted a knife in me and left me for dead. But I was tougher than he thought—'

'Oh, please, Captain Peterson, don't fill our Freddie's head with such tales. He has enough taste for the gory already,' Bess said feelingly.

Neville apologised at once, winking at Freddie behind his mother's back as if to promise that such tales would continue when the opportunity arose. Morwen could see that her mother wasn't altogether happy at this interruption in her day, and suggested that the visit should be a short one, since they were their way to inspect the clay works.

'Can I come with 'ee, our Morwen?' Freddie said at once.

'No, you can't,' she said crossly. 'There's only room in the trap for two—'

'I can ride the horse. Ben don't mind it—'

'Oh, do let him come.' Neville's voice was lazily persuasive. 'Unless his mother needs him at home, of course?'

'Not at all,' Bess said smartly. 'The less he's under my feet, the better!'

'That's settled then.' He took Bess's hand in his, and touched it to his lips. 'I hope we'll meet again, dear lady.'

Bess watched them go, faintly unsettled at such exaggerated charm. She and Hal didn't go in for such finesse, and not even Ben put on such fancy airs and graces. If this fine gent was the kind Ben had associated with in his college days, then Bess was thankful that not too much of it had rubbed off on her down-to-earth son-in-law.

Freddie leapt on to the back of the horse with ease. He was growing tall, Morwen thought suddenly. He sat astride the horse with a gangling grace. Captain Peterson evidently thought so, from the approving look he gave to Freddie's confident seat.

They rode up the winding track leading to the moors above St Austell town, to where Charles Killigrew's sky-tips glistened in the sunlight. Morwen pointed them out as they appeared on the sky-line.

'The townsfolk call them the white hills,' she commented. ''Tis a fancy name for the clay waste, that's all. I take it you've never seen clay works before, Neville?'

He shook his head. Morwen briefly described the scenes that had once been part of her everyday life, trying to make them interesting to a city gentleman. The words came out in a rush at the sudden thought that it could all be of no possible interest to him anyway!

'There's a milky-green clay pool surrounded by the sky-tips, and a kiln and a murderously hot fire-hole, and little trucks trundling up and down all day long with clayworkers tipping the waste, and bal maidens in white bonnets laying the clay blocks out to dry before they're transported to Charlestown port. There's the engine-house and the pumping equipment, o' course, and everyone gets covered in white claydust and look more like ghosts by the end of their shifts—'

'I think I begin to know what to expect!' Neville was laughing at her, and she stopped her chattering abruptly.

'Our Morwen used to be a bal maiden,' Freddie threw back at them. 'They said she were the prettiest at Clay One—'

'I can imagine that,' Neville said approvingly.

'Don't be so silly, our Freddie,' Morwen snapped. 'You can't even remember me working there. It was a long time ago.'

So long ago... a wave of nostalgia swept over her for the old days, that always seemed sunny in retrospect. For days that were warm and carefree, when she and Freddie ran barefoot over the moors with the soft summer turf beneath their feet. Days before any Tremayne had ambitions to be away from the clay. When the little house that now belonged to Sam and Dora had bulged happily at the seams with Hal and Bess's family, and Morwen and her friend Celia Penry had gaily whispered their secrets in the seclusion of the sky-tips, and never looked for anything more than the admiration of a lusty young clayworker...

'We'm here, Morwen.' Freddie gave up resenting his sister's irritation and scrambled down from the horse's back, and she saw with a start that they had reached Clay One. Hal had seen them coming from his manager's hut, and came out to greet them curiously. Morwen introduced the two men.

''Tis an honour to meet you, Captain Peterson,' Hal said. 'If you'd care for a guided tour, I'd be happy to take you around myself. I know 'tis what Ben would wish.'

Morwen doubted that, but she said quickly that if her Daddy would do the honours, she would call on Dora and the children for half an hour, knowing guiltily that she had neglected them again. Freddie had no interest in babies, and said he'd go with the men.

Neville put an arm loosely around Freddie's shoulders, and promised that they would be at the gate whenever Morwen wanted to meet them.

'No more than half an hour then. That will be enough for me,' she answered.

She enjoyed the children, but Dora would probably be as prickly as ever. She climbed back into the trap as the three of them walked off, with her Daddy pointing out the boundaries of the works with as much pride as if he owned it himself.

She was slightly ruffled by the time she returned. Dora had been in a bad mood and Primmy was teething, and the little boys had whined the whole time Morwen was there. Was this the domestic life Morwen wanted for herself and Ben? But despite the trauma of the visit to the cottage, she knew that it was...

'How about a ride over the moors?' Neville asked. 'Do we have time before luncheon?'

Morwen grinned. 'Did Daddy blind you with clay talk?'

'Not at all,' Neville smiled back. 'It was all very interesting.' They both knew he was lying.

'Let's take un to see old Zillah's cottage, Morwen,' Freddie said. 'And the Larnie Stone.'

Morwen's heart jumped. Why did he have to remind her? Why lump the two places together so that she would always connect them in her mind with Celia?

'It sounds intriguing. Tell me more,' Neville prompted.

'Some say old Zillah's a witch.' Freddie was puffed up with importance now. 'Morwen's been to see her plenty times, though Mammie don't really allow it—'

'Shut up, Freddie—'

'And what's this Larnie Stone?'

''Tis a big standing stone wi' a hole in the middle, and you can see the sea through it. 'Tis supposed to have magical powers, and old Zillah can tell 'ee more on it—'

'Well, nobody's going to talk with old Zillah!' Morwen snapped. 'We'll ride over the moors if we must, but we'll keep our distance, or we won't be back in time for our midday meal, and Mrs Horn will be cross.'

'I thought you was meant to be the mistress in that posh house, our Morwen,' Freddie jeered.

'You know nothing about the way folk in big houses live, so mind your business,' she retorted, knowing she was showing herself in a bad light to Captain Peterson, and furious with her brother for making her act so. But Neville seemed quite unconcerned, and smoothed things down with practised ease.

'We must do as your sister says, Freddie, but you can point out the places to me. Perhaps if we meet again, you can explain more about your Cornish customs. We don't have magical stones in London, I'm afraid.'

Morwen wasn't sure if he was mocking them or not, but he spoke sincerely enough. And Freddie was quite mollified.

''Tis only a tale, but I can tell 'ee of plenty more, Captain. Cornwall's riddled with 'em.'

'Good. Then I see that we shall have some delightful hours together,' Neville said smilingly.

Morwen sat back, feeling oddly now as if she was the third person in this expedition. She barely needed to say a word as Freddie pointed out Zillah's grey hovel, smoke still curling from its chimney regardless of the summer weather, and later, the gaunt solidity of the Larnie Stone.

The stone where she and Celia had taken their potions and circled it at midnight, hoping to see the face of their true loves through the hole in the stone. Celia had seen Jude Pascoe's leering face, and she had seen Ben Killigrew…

'We really had best be going, Neville,' she said quickly, and he nodded at once.

'Can I come to Killigrew House with 'ee?' Freddie asked.

'No. Jane Askhew's coming over from Truro one day, and she'll want to talk with Captain Peterson. You're not to come until you're given an invitation, you hear?'

No matter how he sulked, she was adamant. Neville told him breezily that there would be plenty of other occasions, and he gave in.

'Freddie's quite taken to you,' Morwen commented when they left her brother at the Tremayne house. 'Normally he argues far more vehemently!'

Neville laughed. 'He's a fine boy. I liked him.'

–

'He said *what*?' Ben almost exploded when Morwen related all that had happened that day. Neville had gone into the town on his own for the evening, as he had done on several other occasions, and they were having dinner alone. Morwen was alarmed at the sudden blaze of fury in her husband's eyes. It was a fury that was totally inexplicable to her.

'Neville said that if Freddie goes to London, he'll give him his address and he can visit him at his mews house. He also said he'd show him something of London,' she repeated. 'I don't know why you're getting so hot and bothered about it, Ben. I think it's very kind of Neville to take so much trouble—'

'Oh, it'll be no trouble, I assure you, my darling!'

'Don't call me your darling in that patronising way. If you want to have an argument, then at least will you tell me what I've done wrong, for I haven't the least idea how I've displeased 'ee yet again!'

She jumped up from the table, pushing her plate away and having no more appetite for food. She meant to rush out of the dining-room, when Ben's voice stopped her.

'Morwen, come back here at once!'

She whipped round, bright spots of angry colour staining her cheeks.

'Do 'ee talk to me as if I'm one o' your bal maidens again then? Am I doin' summat wrong that has to be accounted for to my lord and master?'

She bit her mouth, feeling it tremble as the old dialect tripped off her tongue. For some reason, the remark she had made to Captain Peterson earlier that day flashed into her mind. *We are what we are.*

And right now Morwen felt as lowly as the imperious young Killigrew boy had ever made her feel in the days when he'd come lording about the clay works fresh from college, and the sniggers had followed him around Clay One... even the day he and his cousin Jude had been sent to do an honest day's work, and Ben had boiled and sweated in the kiln... he had still been a cut above the rest, and they all knew it. Hal Tremayne had wisely insisted to Charles Killigrew that a boss's place was not working beside the men. There were bosses and workers, and the two should be kept strictly in their places for harmony between them.

Right now, with Ben on his feet and towering above the dinner table, his face dark with anger, Morwen felt exactly as she had done in those far-off days.

She felt as her Daddy had felt. She had no place here, in this fine house, with this fine gentleman...

'For God's sake, don't speak such rubbish!'

'I'm sorry if 'ee don't like my words now. 'Tis hard to act the lady every minute of the day.'

'I'm sorry if I was rude to you. It wasn't my intention, but you can be so almighty stubborn at times, Morwen. You just don't listen—'

'Listen to what? You're talking in riddles, Ben! We were having a normal conversation, and I was telling you how sweet Neville was to Freddie this morning—'

'Neville Peterson was never sweet to anyone except for his own gratification,' Ben stated flatly.

Morwen said nothing for a moment.

'I don't understand you.'

'I didn't want you to understand me. I had hoped this disastrous visit would end without the need for it. But now I see that there are things that must be told, so you'll please follow me to my study and close the door behind you.'

It was more than a request. It was an order. And Ben's set face told her more than words that it was no time for further arguing. She followed him, still perplexed, and sat on the chair on the opposite side of the desk from him. Ben didn't sit. He prowled about the room, conscious of her unwavering eyes on him.

'I don't need to tell you I was angry when Neville Peterson arrived here, and discovered you had invited him to stay for as long as he likes, do I?'

'You do not. I couldn't think why! You invite Jane Finelady here often enough—' She was furious to hear the old name on her lips before she could stop it.

It was a measure of the seriousness of this discussion that he made no comment on it. He spoke tersely.

'Neville Peterson was in a class above me at college. He and his cronies formed an elite kind of group. They were all the sons of rich fathers and thought the world was their playground. They specialised in making new boys welcome. Any young, vulnerable boy was in danger of coming under their control—'

'I still don't understand what you're saying. It sounds no more than horseplay—'

'Perhaps I should make it plainer, then. Perhaps you'd prefer me to say outright that Neville Peterson and his gang tried to get every young frightened boy into their evil clutches. I know exactly what I'm talking about—'

'Dear God, Ben—' Her voice was hoarse with shock.

'No, not me, love! I was one of the lucky ones who was warned beforehand. But they tried. Believe me, they tried! Have you noticed the scar on Peterson's throat?'

She nodded dumbly, her eyes wide with horror. Only that morning Neville had told Freddie glibly that it was caused in battle by some black fellow or other...

'It was caused by my belt buckle. I still have it. I can show it to you. I consider it a worthy trophy.'

'I can't believe what you're saying, Ben.' Her thoughts were spinning, her heart thudding sickly. 'Neither can I believe it of Neville—'

'You think a cultured voice and good manners and a fine masculine uniform changes the habits of a lifetime?'

She was suddenly angry. All she knew of Captain Peterson was the image he'd presented to her, but she had no reason to doubt that he was anything but a charming, entertaining if rather frothy young man.

'How do you know such habits remain? Perhaps it was all harmless college games. I know nothing of such things, but—'

'No, you don't. But your championship of Peterson could be the most dangerous thing you've ever done, Morwen.'

'How can it be?'

'Will you still think of harmless college games when Freddie goes away to London and Peterson invites him to his home? I've no doubt there's still an elite group who'll be only too delighted to have a young buck to sport between them. How will you feel about your favourite then?'

Morwen jumped to her feet.

'I think you're evil to even suggest such a thing! I refuse to listen to any more of it.' She put her hands over her ears, and Ben pulled them roughly away.

'You must, Morwen. It's Freddie I'm concerned about.'

Tears blinded her eyes. Was Freddie's lovely dream to be tarnished as well?

'He may not even get a place at the school,' she said chokingly. 'It may not even happen—'

'If it does, then we must think seriously about telling him, Morwen, and I'll call on Peterson in London myself to warn him off.'

'I still won't believe it. I don't want to believe it. I wish he'd never come here, but I can't ask him to go with no reason.' Her voice rose hysterically, and she tried to think calmly. 'Anyway, I think he's already tiring of the country life. I'm sure he'll want to go back to London soon.'

'The sooner the better.'

'Well, I can't condemn the man without proof!' she said, still incensed and upset. She made an attempt to be flippant. 'Anyway, he's the only war hero we've got! Surely that must count in his favour. I won't ruin his visit, Ben—'

Ben didn't respond to her flippancy. 'Just as long as it's not Freddie who's ruined.'

Morwen felt like weeping. Such ugliness hadn't entered her life before, and she hated Ben for telling her, even though he'd felt it had to be told. However pleasant Captain Peterson was now, the knowledge was going to colour their relationship.

She was thankful he had found some acquaintances in St Austell town and was not seeking her company quite so often. But for the time being he still remained in the house, and she was conscious of an awkwardness that hadn't been there before.

–

It was an unexpected relief when Jane Askhew came calling with her daughter a week or so later, and brought with her an uninvited visitor. Morwen was sitting upstairs with Charles Killigrew, and Ben was making grudging conversation with Neville in the garden. Jane smiled a little diffidently.

'Ben, I'm sorry to come unannounced like this, but you know Mr Tregian of *The Informer*, don't you?'

The two men nodded to one another. Jane rushed on.

'Mr Tregian was in Falmouth recently, hoping to glean first-hand news for the paper from returning soldiers, and he heard that an officer was asking for directions for Killigrew House, saying he was an old friend of yours. I hope you don't think it a liberty, Ben, but Lew would very much like an interview, if the Captain is agreeable.'

'I think it's Captain Peterson you should be asking about that,' Ben said non-committally.

'I've got no objections,' Neville answered at once. 'But may I be introduced to this charming young lady?'

Ben was crisp. 'Mrs Jane Askhew and her daughter Cathy – Captain Neville Peterson, late of the Crimea. If you'll excuse me, I'll have some refreshment sent out to you. It's pleasant enough in the garden for your purposes, isn't it, Tregian?'

'Oh, admirably, Mr Killigrew,' the man said hastily. 'Mrs Askhew wishes to listen to the Captain's reports. Does that meet with your approval, Sir?'

'I can think of nothing I'd like better.' Neville's smiles were dazzling. 'Every soldier likes to bend the ear of a pretty woman and gain her admiration for his courage!'

'Jane's husband is a war correspondent for the newspaper,' Ben heard himself say sourly. 'You may have come across him. Tom Askhew.'

'I don't believe so.' Neville's smile didn't waver. He turned to Lew Tregian, becoming businesslike. 'Now then, dear fellow, where shall we begin?'

'Please tell us of the true conditions in the Crimea, Captain,' Jane's soft voice said at once. 'Was it very bad?'

Neville looked at her troubled face and began to speak earnestly, while Lew Tregian scribbled furiously, jubilant that he had a real scoop for his paper at last.

He knew the basics, of course. The French were unwilling allies of the British against the Russian forces, and both armies were scathing of each other. The last assault on Sevastopol in

June that year had failed, and each of the allied armies blamed the other for the fact that the town was partly in ruins but still unconquered from the enemy.

'So the hospitals are overcrowded and rife with disease as well as being totally unable to cope with all the wounded?' Lew prompted when Neville had exhausted the battle details and gone on to more human stories. 'What of the indomitable Miss Nightingale and her nurses?'

'An excellent lady if one can stomach the hearty type!'

'I hardly think the poor soldiers would care about that, as long as their needs are catered for,' Jane said, visibly upset at hearing of the dysentery and cholera and the last terrible winter that had finished off many of the weakened men, when morale was at its lowest.

Tom hadn't gone to the Crimea until the spring, but he had said little of the squalor and disease that Captain Peterson was reporting now, keeping his despatches strictly impersonal and factual so as not to unduly alarm people at home.

'Oh, of course, of course! And a firm approach is probably better than trying to be too soft with dying men. It does them no good to be wept over, does it?'

'Darling, run along indoors and find Aunt Morwen,' Jane said quickly to Cathy, as the child's eyes widened. Cathy had been quite occupied with picking daisies until moments ago, but now she was listening too intently for Jane's comfort.

'I think I have plenty of interesting information here for a lead article, Captain Peterson,' Lew Tregian said at last. 'I'd be honoured to use your name as told to our reporter.'

'By all means,' Neville said.

The editor turned to Jane. 'I won't wait for refreshment, Mrs Askhew, if you'll make my farewells to Mr Killigrew. I'm anxious to get back to Truro and set up this article.'

Jane smiled at Neville when the man had gone.

'You must forgive him his enthusiasm, Captain. He has printer's ink in his veins, the same as my husband.'

'Please don't apologise, dear lady. I like a man with enthusiasm. There are enough milksops in the world.'

Jane looked at him with approval. He had spoken so bravely of that terrible war and the appalling conditions of the hospital at Scutari on the Turkish mainland, where the poor soldiers had to be taken by boat from the Crimea, encountering even more discomfort on the rough sea journey.

She prayed that her Tom was safe. She prayed that there were more brave heroes like Captain Peterson. In her innocence, Jane thought humbly that milksop was certainly not a name to be applied to this man!

Chapter Thirteen

Hal Tremayne arrived on the day shift at Clay One to find an angry impromptu meeting among the clayworkers. Sam was already there. He pushed his way through the mob to reach his father.

'We might have expected summat of the sort when Ben announced the bonuses,' Sam stormed. 'Them that normally take the excursion passengers on the rail tracks are grumbling that the bonus is no more than a pittance, and cussing even louder that the rest on 'em shouldn't get what's normally theirs, for doin' no extra work at all.'

'What of the rest? What's their argument, for God's sake?'

'They'm all up on their high horses, saying they've as much right to bonuses as the excursion men, since they'm all Clay One workers. And there's summat else too. They want to know what's to happen wi' the autumn clay despatches. If the rail tracks be still silent, and we have to use the old clay waggons again, they'll need repairing after four years of disuse, and the horses be unused to the narrow town streets after all this time.'

Hal's reply was swallowed up as the men closed round. 'Now then, Hal Tremayne, you be works manager and spokesman, so you'm just the man to settle this!'

'And we don't want no fobbing off with tales to Ben Killigrew that don't get no results—'

'When did that ever happen?' Hal shouted above the din. 'Ben's always stuck out for fair dues for the lot of 'ee—'

'You've got bloody short memories if 'ee don't know 'tis true enough,' Sam yelled. 'What of the march to St Austell town to demand wage rises some years back? Didn't Ben Killigrew march wi' us?'

'Oh ah! If 'ee call it marching when he's sat on his arse on his fancy horse and riding alongside us—'

'Shut your bloody noise, the lot of 'ee!' Hal roared with enough gusto to do credit to old Charles Killigrew. 'If there's a complaint to be made, then I'll hear it, and 'twill be forwarded to the boss in the usual way. I'll have no trouble at my pit, and the first one that whispers strike will have my boot up his arse quicker than blinking. Is it clear to 'ee?'

The clayworkers shuffled, their long leather boots that were so necessary in the damper conditions of the pit scuffing up dirt and dust now. The catcalls died away to angry mutterings. There wasn't one there who didn't know Hal Tremayne for a fair man, nor one who doubted that he'd make good his threat.

But there were still the few who wanted to make sure Hal knew his place, and remind him that he didn't wear boss's gaiters yet. In the scale of things, Hal had more status than they, but he was still answerable to the Killigrews.

'Do 'ee scratch the boss's arse for un now then, Hal Tremayne?' a young clayworker near to him sneered daringly.

Hal was quicker to anger than of old, and his answer was to haul the boy close by the scruff of his neck, and twist the neckcloth he wore until the other's eyes bulged.

'Would 'ee like me to scratch yours, Davey Lee? If there's a clay scraper handy, somebody can soon hold 'ee down for me, if 'ee fancy a branding—'

'You'm a real boss's man now, ain't 'ee, Hal Tremayne?' the boy choked out. 'You and your family, what's left of 'em—'

'Leave our family out on it,' Sam snapped.

''Tis a good thing you'm still here to back up your Daddy, Sam Tremayne!' another jeered. 'When be you finding the clay too heavy for your white hands like the rest of your fine brothers? And your sister, Morwen, visiting us with some fancy officer and acting the real lady—'

Sam lashed out at him with the back of his hand.

'This here meeting was about bonuses, and 'tis high time it ended and you buggers got back to work. When me and my Daddy start criticising your families, you can do the same about ours. Till then, keep your traps tight shut, or you'll find my fist in 'em, and I'm not fussy who's first.'

'Sam's right,' one of the older men growled. 'We've no grudge against him and Hal. You young bucks need putting in your places. There's some here who don't like to hear Morwen Tremayne spoken of that way neither. She be a fine maid.'

''Twas a long while since since she were a maid, unless Ben Killigrew's got nought but string between his legs,' came the sniggering reply.

'Leave it, Sam!' Hal rapped out, as his son turned murderous eyes on the taunting kilnworker. 'We've had enough arguments for one morning. Ben will have to sort out the rights and wrongs of the bonuses, and 'tis time to get some order here.'

'I'd prefer to break yon bastard's head, but I suppose you're right,' Sam muttered savagely. He turned to the men and raised his voice above the rumpus.

'Tea-break will be taken now while your tempers cool down, then I want to see all you buggers hard at work for the rest o' the shift, or I'll be reporting to Ben Killigrew those who ain't deserving of any wages at all. Do 'ee all understand me?'

He gave the tea-break whistle a piercing blow, and the kiddley boys began to scurry about with boiling water and mugs. The unofficial meeting slowly dispersed as the men went back to their own corners of the pit, the bal maidens giggling and chattering at the unexpected lull in the boredom of the shift and the fuss the men made over nothing.

The men considered it a legitimate grudge, and as ever, were prepared to make a stand for their rights. But they'd had their say, and they knew when it was time to let things simmer. Once the atmosphere was calmer, Sam slammed his father's hut door shut behind them both and glowered at Hal.

''Twas a fair compromise, Daddy, but how the devil will 'ee back it up wi' Ben Killigrew?'

Hal shrugged. 'It's Ben's problem, not mine. He should make the bonuses fairer anyway, so those who'd get more from the excursions get a bit more than the rest who do nothing. I can see the sense in their argument. Either that or pay no extras at all. I doubt that other pits would be as generous.'

'Ben won't like having his head held to the wall. He never did.'

'No more do I,' Hal snapped. 'But if I was in the clayworkers' boots, I daresay I'd feel as they do. Don't ever get so high and mighty that 'ee forget their feelings, Sam.'

'Was I ever so block-headed?'

Hal grinned. 'Who said you ever got any different?'

Sam smiled grudgingly, accepting the jibe.

'All the same, I don't like 'em leering at our family. There's no call for it, when they'm not here to defend themselves, and nobody could call our Jack soft for one!'

'Building boats is as honourable a profession as digging clay,' Hal agreed. 'I'm 'mazed that they haven't picked on young Freddie yet, for bein' at a proper school instead of still being a kiddley boy like most o' the young uns. As for him goin' away to London—'

'I doubt that many know of it yet,' Sam grunted.

Sam didn't hold with the idea of Freddie going away to London. Matt had already split the family by going off to America with Jude Pascoe. To Sam, London was no less distant. If you had a horse beneath you, or the inclination for a day's walk, then Jack was no more than a spit away in Truro, so that was all right. And Morwen was still part of Killigrew Clay, being the boss's wife.

They could do nothing about Matt, but the others still had a hold on the old life, and privately Sam thought that his Daddy should put a stop to Freddie's ambitions before he grew above himself and everybody else.

—

Freddie buzzed around Morwen as irritatingly as a bee, wanting to know when he could spend a day at Killigrew House. It wasn't that she didn't want him there. In fact his presence could usually be relied on to keep her cheerful, and old Charles Killigrew liked a brief visit from the chirpy young Tremayne boy. But now that Morwen shared the secret regarding Captain Peterson, she found herself constantly on edge whenever Freddie badgered her for a visit. But she couldn't fob him off forever, especially when Bess said pointedly that she hoped Morwen wasn't getting above herself and not wanting her family at the big house.

'You know it's not that!' Morwen said crossly, when she and Bess met for their weekly tea and buns at Fielding's Tea Rooms. 'I haven't had a day lately when it was convenient—'

'Convenient now, is it?' Bess said tartly. ''Tis your little brother you're speaking of, Morwen, not some posh lord or other.'

Morwen felt her cheeks burn with colour. Her mother had always had the knack of putting her in her place with the briefest of phrases. She spoke quickly.

'He can come tomorrow. It's the day for my pianoforte lesson, but he can read to Ben's father whilst I'm engaged with Mr Glass. Will that suit, Mammie?'

''Twill suit fine, so long as it suits you,' Bess said drily.

'Why don't you come as well? You hardly ever visit us.'

'I've my own house to look after, and work to do. I've promised a gown for my new client, Miss Wellesly, and I've never been late with an order yet.'

The quiet pride was in her voice, and Morwen felt a rush of love for her mother. She leaned across the table and squeezed her hand.

'I'll ask Ben if we can have a tea-party soon, and you'll all come. Once Captain Peterson has gone, and we have the house to ourselves again—' she stopped, knowing it sounded slightly ludicrous, for in a place the size of Killigrew House, one extra person made as little difference as an extra grain of sand on a beach.

'You don't like him, do 'ee, Morwen? Our Freddie seems quite struck wi' him. He's not been improper towards 'ee, has he?' Bess lowered her voice, so that the good dames of St Austell town who frequented Fielding's Tea Rooms shouldn't overhear.

Morwen felt the laughter bubbling inside her and blamed it on the tears pricking her eyes as she shook her head.

'Of course not, Mammie! What an idea! You're imagining things. Don't forget now, tell Freddie he can come for the day tomorrow, and to slick his hair down before he leaves home!'

She turned the conversation quickly. The last thing she wanted to do was to dwell on thoughts of Captain Peterson, and she could hardly tell her mother that it was highly unlikely that Captain Peterson would be making advances towards Morwen!

As she raised her tea-cup to her lips, Morwen realised that she had accepted Ben's assessment of the man, and wished with all her heart that he would leave Killigrew House soon.

—

The day of Freddie's visit was blisteringly hot and still, without a breath of air to relieve the oppressive heat. It was a day for taking a picnic to the shore… Morwen thought longingly of cool salt breezes and the shifting sand beneath her feet, and she and Ben together in an idyllic world of their own…

'Mrs Killigrew, I think we had better play that piece once more, if we are to get it right.'

Morwen heard the soft, apologetic voice of David Glass, the pianoforte tutor, as if through a cloud of cotton. It was impossibly hard to concentrate today, and she dimly realised that she had played the wrong notes for the third time in the piece of music she was trying to master. She rubbed her damp hands against the thin fabric of her gown.

'Why do you always instruct me as if there are a group of us playing the instrument?' she sulked at him. ''Tis not *we* playing the wrong notes. 'Tis *me*!'

'I apologise, dear lady. I fear that it's a habit I've developed when I'm teaching younger children. I find it gives them a little more confidence in their ability.'

'Well, it does not give me confidence,' Morwen said crossly. 'And it makes me feel even more inadequate to know that you class me with younger children!'

'Oh, my dear Mrs Killigrew, I meant no offence!' David Glass said in consternation, his pale face flushing. 'You have improved tremendously, as you well know. Please forgive me if I have upset you unduly!'

'You'll upset me more if you go on so,' Morwen found him increasingly irritating in his fatuous attempts to be pleasant. Had he always been this ingratiating? Or was it simply the heat that was trying her patience with him?

She twirled round on the pianoforte stool.

'I have had enough of this lesson for today, Mr Glass. I know I have not been the best of pupils, but perhaps we shall both be in a better humour when the heat is less bothersome. If you would care to retire to the summerhouse where it is cooler, I will have some lemonade sent out to you.'

The tutor didn't hide his relief.

'As you wish, dear lady. I believe I saw your houseguest in the garden earlier. I will join him, if I may.'

'Please do.' The man was irritating her more than ever. 'Tell Captain Peterson some refreshment will be forthcoming, if you please.'

She flounced from the room, annoyed that the tutor seemed to be so well acquainted with the Captain. Everything seemed to annoy her today. She tried to relax, and failed miserably. When David Glass was out of earshot, she made one last private attempt to make the jumbled notes become a melody, and finished by crashing down the lid of the instrument in a fury. She would never be a Jane Askhew, she raged. She would never be a lady...

She met Freddie in the doorway as he came hurtling down the stairs from his sojourn with Charles Killigrew, tired of acting nursemaid, and eager for more exuberant pursuits. He cannoned into Morwen, who was sorely tempted to box his ears, and restrained herself with an effort, merely shaking him instead.

'Go into the kitchen and ask Cook for some lemonade for the gentlemen,' she snapped. 'Mr Glass and Captain Peterson are probably in the summer-house. Take a tray out to them, and try to be still, for heaven's sake, Freddie. You make my head ache!'

He turned readily enough, and Morwen thought guiltily what a grouch she was becoming. He was eager enough to please, and it was his treat to be here for the day. She would make it up to him later. She would suggest a ride to the sea. Freddie loved to ride along the water's edge, with the horse's hooves sending the salt spray flying into his face... she would just sit in the cool of the drawing-room for a little time, while she let the humiliation of the pianoforte lesson disperse... she would just close her eyes for a moment or two...

–

A horrendous scream and the sound of splintering glass brought Morwen jumping to her feet, her heart pounding. Dear God, what had happened? Her first thought was that it must be one of the servants, and that Charles Killigrew's end had come...

Her brother tore into the room, his eyes wild. Morwen grabbed at his shoulder, shouting at him to know what was wrong.

'What is it, Freddie? Tell me at once! Is someone hurt?'

He gawped at her, his face as red as beetroots. His mouth trembled, and she could feel him shivering as though he had the ague. He seemed unable to speak. She shook him hard.

'I can't tell 'ee, our Morwen,' he gasped out at last. ''Tis just like the boys at school were sniggering about—'

He twisted away from her, darting under her arm and rushing through the house and out of the front door. Morwen raced after him, knowing he couldn't go tearing about the town like this. People would think he was demented, and he'd probably come to grief beneath the wheels of a vehicle or the flailing hooves of a horse...

Besides, from his brief intimation, she knew what was amiss. As though she was gifted with old Zillah's sixth sense, she knew what Freddie must have seen. She wondered why the clarity of it hadn't been obvious to her before.

David Glass had been here so often, and each time Neville Peterson had been hovering about. The two men had smiled politely at one another. Several times David Glass had offered the Captain a lift into town in his modest vehicle. Peterson had made friends in St Austell remarkably quickly. Or had it been just one friend? A friend he had met in this very house, under Ben Killigrew's roof?

Morwen caught up with Freddie before he reached the front gate, and hauled him back the way he had run. Out of breath herself, she pulled him into the shade of the shrubbery, and slapped his face hard. He was already shocked. She could see it by the dilation of his blue eyes.

Morwen held Freddie's arms tightly as though he would take flight at the slightest chance. Indeed, she was certain that he would if she didn't hold him captive.

'Freddie, listen to me,' she said, praying that her voice wouldn't waver. 'You must tell me what happened to make you scream. You must tell me, Freddie.'

'I can't tell 'ee, Morwen. 'Tis not for women's ears.'

'Love, forget that I'm a woman,' she said gently. 'Ben would want to know if something has happened at Killigrew House, and since Ben's not here right now, I'm the one you should tell. Ben will deal with it, but by the time he comes home, you may have forgotten it—'

185

'No, I won't.' Freddie shuddered. 'I won't ever forget. It was Captain Peterson and Mr Glass, Morwen. They were in the summer-house – together. They were touching each other – in private places, our Morwen.' Freddie was scarlet with embarrassment. 'They were kissing on the mouth. Mr Glass was bent back over the shrubs in the corner and Captain Peterson was whispering things to un. I thought it was a game at first, and I watched, and then I knew it weren't a game. I dropped the tray and Captain Peterson yelled awful things at me, and I ran off. Don't make me see him again, Morwen.'

She folded her arms around him. 'You won't ever have to see him again, Freddie,' she vowed. 'And neither will I. We'll go to the stables and get the horses, and we'll go to the beach right this minute. I'll leave a message for Ben to meet us there. We'll tell him together. He'll know what to do, my lamb.'

She ached to put things right for him, to make things as they were this morning when he had arrived, young and full of life, before the pain of awareness clouded his whole being. The total loss of innocence, the fear of Colonel Peterson's savage words.

God, but she hated that man. If she had the means to strangle him with her bare hands, she would gladly do it now.

She kept her arm around Freddie as they walked around the house to the stables. She talked soothingly to him all the while, and tried to calm her own jangling nerves.

An hour later the two of them had ridden for the tenth time along the length of the sandy bay, and Morwen was straining her eyes desperately for the sight of Ben's horse winding its way down the sandy path towards them. Would he never come? He must have got the message by now.

He had been due home long ago, and she had instructed the stable-boy to go at once to the housekeeper and deliver Morwen's words. Ben was to come at once to the bay where she and Freddie were waiting for him, and it was on a matter of great urgency. How could he fail to know it was desperately important?

He couldn't fail her now. They had been so much at loggerheads of late, but surely he knew she would never send such a message for a frivolous reason? Had they grown so far apart that he couldn't sense the panic in it...?

'Here he comes,' Freddie said suddenly.

He had grown tired of riding and was disconsolately scratching in the sand with a piece of driftwood. But at the sight of Ben approaching, he jumped to his feet and all the agitation was back in his eyes again.

'Morwen, I'm afraid,' he stuttered. 'Supposing he don't believe me? The Captain be his friend—'

'You must trust Ben, the way you trusted me.'

She felt the same sense of relief that she always felt when Ben came striding over the firm sand towards her. Ben would put things right, and send Neville Peterson packing for the horrors he had shouted at Freddie.

'What's happened?' Ben said at once. 'I haven't been inside the house. The stable-boy passed on your message so you'd best tell me at once. I presume it's not my father, since you chose to meet me here. Is Freddie in disgrace?'

He couldn't have said anything worse in his attempt to brighten the two gloomy faces in front of him. Morwen pulled her brother towards her at once and Freddie's wan face crumpled.

'Ben, you'd best listen to what Freddie has to say,' she said quickly, but she could feel his shivering again, and wondered if they would get anything coherent out of him. 'Go on, Freddie. Tell Ben what you saw in the summerhouse.'

'I – I can't,' the boy said chokingly.

Ben's eyes met Morwen's above Freddie's head. He moved forward and drew Freddie away from her, sitting down on the warm sand beside him.

'Freddie, you're Morwen's brother, and that makes you part of my family. Anything that hurts you hurts me too, but if you don't tell me what it is, I can't put it right. This friend that you speak of – is it Captain Peterson? And if it is, let me tell you at once that he is no true friend of mine, and never has been. I knew him at college, that's all, and I did not invite him to stay at Killigrew House.' He avoided looking at Morwen. 'If Captain Peterson has said anything to upset you, let's hear it.'

Freddie looked desperately at Morwen.

'Tell him, Freddie,' she ordered.

He took a deep breath, and the words tumbled out. 'They were kissing, and whispering, and doing... and then he said awful things—'

'All right, boy, don't worry.' Ben's instinct was to pull Freddie into his arms, and yet he knew it was better that he did not. The boy's nerves were too fragile as yet. Instead he spoke crisply and decisively.

'Freddie, this has been a shock to you, the things he said to you so viciously.' Freddie nodded, still scarlet-faced.

He went on in an even voice. 'I promise you that Captain Peterson will leave Killigrew House immediately, and we will never see him again. As for you, Freddie, I am wondering what we should do with you?'

Freddie looked at him in alarm.

'I did nothing, Ben. I weren't spying, truly!'

Ben gave a short laugh. 'I know that you weren't! But does the London school still appeal to you, or would you prefer to stay in dull old Cornwall after all? If you don't like the idea of working for Killigrew Clay, I'm sure we can find some other worthy employment for you. I'll speak to your father about it. But if you still want London, Freddie, it's your choice, and at least you'll be alert to certain dangers—'

This time it was Freddie who hurled himself into Ben's arms. The tears he'd been too old to cry streamed down his cheeks as he wept against his champion.

'Oh, don't let them send me away, Ben! I don't want to go to London any more. I want to stay here with you and Morwen and Mammie and Daddy and the rest on 'em.'

'Nobody's going to send you anywhere, Freddie,' Ben said calmly. 'We'll have to think about your future, though. You're too bright to be a kiddley boy for ever, and your Daddy tells me you're good with your hands. As good as Jack, I hear.'

Morwen listened to him, turning her brother's attention away from the shock of the afternoon, and thanked God for Ben's cool head. She knew him well enough to know how he seethed inside at the indiscretion of the two men in his own house. Peterson would be turned out at once, if he hadn't already left.

'Perhaps I could work wi' Jack in Truro,' Freddie quavered, as the new thought struck him. 'I'm good at whittling toy boats out o' wood. There ain't such a difference in making real ones, I daresay.'

'I daresay there's not,' Ben said gravely. He smiled briefly at Morwen. His confrontation with Neville Peterson was yet to come, but mercifully the day may not have been a complete disaster for Freddie after all. He had the resilience of the Tremaynes in his blood, and Ben knew full well what an asset that could be.

As Freddie snuffled against his chest, his hand reached out for Morwen's, and she knew he forgave her for insisting that the charming but evil Neville Peterson be a guest in Killigrew House. The visit was over.

Chapter Fourteen

Ben threw down the Truro *Informer* in disgust. Morwen was used to his moods regarding the war in the Crimea now, but since what was delicately referred to as the Peterson affair, his attitude had changed slightly.

Morwen knew he could be as dogmatic as his father. Just as much a champion for what he considered right. Just as intolerant of the weaknesses of others. But she couldn't blame him in any way for his reaction towards Neville Peterson.

Her own brother's tetchiness in the few weeks since Captain Peterson had quit the house was enough for that. For Freddie, the trauma of seeing Peterson and David Glass together, and of being subjected to Peterson's tirade, had lasted only a few minutes, but the shock of it was taking longer to erase.

It was a constant worry to Morwen, especially since she and Ben and Freddie had come to a mutual agreement that they should tell no-one else of the incident. Morwen would dearly have liked to confide in her mother why Freddie was so out of sorts with everyone of late, but it was too embarrassing a tale.

But it was not thoughts of Freddie, nor yet another newspaper report of the war that was irritating Ben this morning. It was August. The days in Cornwall were long and hot, and seemingly so in another part of the world. Ben picked up the newspaper again at Morwen's terse enquiry as to what was annoying him now.

'Just listen to this. They print this rubbish as an antidote to war. They think we'll forget what's happening to our soldiers by filling our heads with it!'

'Since I have no idea what you're talking about yet, I can hardly comment on it,' Morwen said tartly.

He began to read the piece aloud. 'The Queen and Prince Albert are enjoying the blazing sunlit days in Paris. Together with the young Prince of Wales and the Princess Royal, they are receiving the accolade of the French people. Paris is full of banners, flags, arches of flowers and illuminations for the royal visit.'

'It sounds wonderful!' Morwen said wistfully, a faraway look in her blue eyes as she tried to picture it all. Visiting any foreign country was an excitement Morwen hadn't yet discovered.

'Wonderful for the few, I daresay. Amid all the glitter of a royal occasion, the French are easily able to forget that they are unwilling allies of the British in the war.'

'Isn't that a good thing?' Morwen demanded. 'We should do anything we can to stay on good terms with our allies. The Queen and Prince Albert do us proud by visiting abroad in troubled times.'

'You understand nothing,' Ben snapped. 'They waste the country's money which could be put to better use providing more hospitals for the sick and wounded. While they drive about like poppycocks in their pretty carriages, men are dying in the Crimea. The royal party don't go to the front, do they? They don't risk contracting Asiatic cholera the way our soldiers do.'

'They give people hope for a better future, Ben. That's worth a good deal to ordinary folk. But you've never quite understood the way ordinary folk think, have you?'

She could feel the tension growing between them. Another simple discussion was in danger of turning into a blazing argument if it wasn't stopped immediately. She saw the glint in Ben's handsome eyes, and knew it was too late.

'And you do, I suppose? You have insight into every poor bugger who lies dying in the mud and filth of a battlefield, do you? Can you guess at his thoughts at knowing his queen is graciously bestowing her favours on the French at this time? Wouldn't he rather have an extra bandage to soak up his blood?'

'Ben, stop it,' Morwen snapped back. 'You're talking nonsense. And please don't swear. You demean yourself—'

'I apologise! I was under the impression I could speak as I liked in my own house!' He spoke with exaggerated sarcasm. 'I know your precious queen rules the country, but I hadn't realised that petticoat rule had reached the backwaters of Cornwall yet. Perhaps you'd like me to walk backwards when I leave your presence, my lady?'

'I'd like you to stop acting the goat and stop treating me as if I'm a complete ninny!' Morwen leapt to her feet, her eyes blazing. 'As to being your lady – sometimes I think you forget that's what I'm supposed to be. I'm sorry if I don't always live up to your expectations.'

She stormed out of the room, not heeding his angry shout after her. Her eyes stung. She was as badly out of sorts as Freddie. She wished she could run to the moors and shout out her frustration to the wind and the wild gorse, but those days were past. She was Killigrew's lady now… and she had never felt less like it.

If only she could have spent the day in her Mammie's calming company… but that too was denied her. Jane Askhew was coming to stay for a week, bringing her little daughter, Cathy, with her. It was an added indignity. Especially, as in a rash moment, Morwen herself had given the invitation, knowing it would please Ben and old Charles Killigrew, who constantly complained that he saw so few people outside the household. He had become a trial to all of them, and to his nurse in particular, who threatened daily to leave him.

—

Ben banged out of the house a short while later. He didn't even bother to say good-bye. Morwen bit her lip to stop it trembling, wondering what was happening to them. They were together as they had always wanted to be. They had each other... and they did nothing but wrangle.

He still had to sort out the problems with the clayworkers after Hal had come to Killigrew House and told Ben bluntly all that had gone on at the meeting among the men. Ben had reluctantly agreed to Hal's suggestions and was going to the works today to give his new orders to the men himself. He was never one to shirk a duty or to pass it on to someone else.

Morwen gave a small sigh. Would he have been any different if he had gone to the war after all? Would his masculine needs have been satisfied then? Perhaps all men needed to be involved in the battle for survival on a larger scale than the comparatively small demands of a clay works.

She was still sitting on her bed staring aimlessly into space, when one of the servants came with a message.

'Mrs Tilley says I'm to tell 'ee the bags have been sent up to the guest room, Ma'am, and the young lady and the little un be waiting for 'ee in the drawing-room.'

'Thank you, Fanny,' Morwen answered.

Why couldn't Jane have waited a little longer until she felt more composed, she thought crossly. A quick glance in the mirror showed all the marks of a previous argument on her face. Flushed cheeks; sparkling eyes; full mouth… Ben always said she looked almost at her most beautiful after an argument… her most beautiful being after they had made it up…

Morwen pushed such bitter-sweet thoughts from her mind and went downstairs to greet the visitors. Jane was as immaculate as ever, cool and fair, the little girl a small replica of her mother. To ease the moment, Morwen exclaimed at once on how much Cathy had grown since the last time she saw her.

To her surprise, the child hung back. By now she was more usually a little chatterbox at Killigrew House.

'She's been complaining of not feeling well, Morwen,' Jane said anxiously. 'I was in two minds whether to come or not, but she insisted so much that she wanted to see the old gentleman, that I didn't have the heart to refuse.'

'Didn't you want to see Ben and me too, Cathy?' Morwen teased her. 'And the horses?'

Cathy clung even more to Jane's skirts, and looked pleadingly into her mother's face. She was definitely flushed, Morwen thought uneasily, and hoped there was nothing really wrong.

'Drink, Mama,' she spoke in a thin reedy voice.

'I'll send for some barley water,' Morwen said at once. 'Perhaps 'tis just the journey that's tired her. Does she have a sleep during the day? My brother's babby does.'

She bit her lip. Why couldn't she remember to say baby the way Jane would? But Jane merely nodded.

'I think we'd both like to go to our room and settle down, Morwen. Perhaps you'd send the barley water up. When Cathy's asleep, I'll look in on Mr Killigrew, and then you and I can have a talk. You must tell me how your pianoforte lessons are progressing.'

Morwen realised with a start that of course Jane would know nothing of the summer-house incident. She knew that Captain Peterson had gone, but not the real reason for it. There was a need for more lying…

The memory of how painfully Morwen had had to lie to cover up her friend Celia's pregnancy before and after the girl's death swept into her mind. Lies and deceit were abhorrent to Morwen's honest open nature, yet it seemed that the devil plagued her with the need for them.

'I'll see that there's some tea waiting for 'ee – you – when you're ready,' Morwen said quickly.

When would she ever lose the memories? When too would she ever rid herself of this feeling of inadequacy whenever Jane Carrick – Jane Askhew – was around?

She watched her carry her tired little daughter upstairs, and felt a stab of jealousy, not for the young lady this time, but for the completeness of her life. She had her adored Tom, and she had their child…

–

'Fanny!' She snapped in her frustration, as the maid appeared in the doorway. 'Take some barley water to Mrs Askhew's room at once, and tell Mrs Horn to have some tea brewing in about half an hour for the lady and myself.'

'Yes, Ma'am,' Fanny bobbed, and sped to the kitchen, to relate that the mistress was in a foul humour and they had all best steer clear of her.

–

The next hour was tedious for Morwen. She was obliged to sit about and wait for Jane to reappear, and the day dragged. When her one-time rival finally came into the drawing-room with a rustle of skirts, it was obvious at once that she was disturbed.

'Morwen, I've spent some time with Mr Killigrew, and just looked in at Cathy, and I fear she is ill. She's feverish and rambling, and I would deem it a great kindness if you would send for Doctor Pender to take a look at her. I'm so sorry to be a burden to you—'

'Don't be foolish! Of course you're not a burden. Fanny shall go for the doctor at once!'

Morwen tugged at the bell pull and the maid came running, fearful of more acid from her mistress's tongue. But once told what to do, she scurried off at once, and Morwen gave instructions for the doctor to be taken straight up to Miss Cathy's bed.

'May I sit with her for a while?' Morwen said at once. ''Tis said I have the calming touch in my hands, Jane.'

'I would be so grateful,' Jane said at once. 'I always feel so helpless when she is ill, and I fear so that it might be the measles. There's so much of it raging in the towns, and I thought we had escaped it. I shall be in such distress if we've brought it into this house, Morwen.'

'There's little you can do about it if 'tis so, but we should not count chickens until 'tis confirmed,' Morwen said, although her heart leapt at Jane's words. Measles had already killed many...

Upstairs, one look at little Cathy Askhew's raging cheeks, and Morwen had little doubt that this indeed was what ailed the child.

She soothed her hot forehead with a damp cloth and gently lifted the child's nightgown where the tell-tale spots were already spreading over the small body. As Jane saw them too, Morwen heard her muffled weeping.

'That won't help the child,' she snapped.

'I know!' Jane wept. 'But if Cathy's really ill – oh, you don't know what it's been like for me all this time without Tom. At times of crisis I want my husband with me. I miss him so!'

Morwen was momentarily ashamed of her harshness, and even more shamed at the guilty thought that she couldn't ignore. *Just as long as Jane didn't turn to Ben as a substitute for Tom…*

It was a recurring thought, and was as much a thorn in her flesh now as ever. And it was wrong to feel that way, when this poor sick child looked so tiny and pathetic, with hardly the strength to fight a virulent illness…

–

Doctor Pender confirmed that Cathy had the measles, and instructed the women to keep the child warm and in bed, and to drink as much fluid as she could. There was little else anyone could do, until the disease had either run its course, or…

Ben arrived back at the house to find Jane in a state of total collapse. Morwen felt sorry for her, but was impatient at her lack of control. Jane was the butterfly; Morwen the practical one; and this kind of hysteria helped no-one.

'You'd be more use to Cathy by sitting and reading to her instead of wallowing in self-pity, Jane,' she finally said testily, thinking this a fine way to spend the evening.

Ben rounded on his wife. 'How can you speak so cruelly, Morwen? If you had a child who was sick, you'd know what Jane was suffering!'

He spoke angrily, twisting a knife in the wound. Jane seemed quite content to let him comfort her as an old friend, and the sight of Ben holding her and protecting her, seemingly against the sharp tongue of his barren wife, was suddenly too much for Morwen.

'Well, someone should be sitting with Cathy, and since no-one else seems capable, I suppose it had best be me! 'Tis all I'm fit for, after all, to be someone's skivvy!'

'Morwen, don't be ridiculous!' Ben's rasping voice came after her, but she sped on up the stairs and into the child's room. Why, oh, why did she always let Jane Askhew make her react in this way? Even now, when Jane was clearly upset, the hated jealousy was still a part of Morwen.

'Is it you, Morwen?' Cathy's weak little voice came from the bed. Morwen hurried across and put her cool hand on the little girl's hot forehead.

'Yes, 'tis me, my lamb. I'll sit with you and read to you, shall I?'

Cathy shook her head. 'Story 'bout the clay,' she mumbled. 'Tell 'bout the big boots.'

Morwen was startled for a minute, and then she remembered how charmed Cathy had been when Morwen had once told her about the clayworkers' long boots, made especially for each man on his own special last by the local cobbler. Each man could be identified by his own footprint, and Morwen had made up the tale of the clayworker striding over the mist-laden moors and leading a group of children to safety by making them walk in his bootmarks.

She was surprised Cathy could remember it, but it had evidently stayed in her mind, and the child became drowsy as Morwen's soft voice related the same tale once again.

By the time she had finished Cathy was asleep, and Morwen rose stiffly, turning to see Jane in the doorway. Morwen put her finger to her mouth and tip-toed out.

'Morwen, you shame me. You're better with my own child than I am,' Jane said humbly. 'Forgive me for putting on such a show downstairs. I'll try to be calm while I'm here. It all seems too much at times, with no news of Tom, and now Cathy—'

Her voice broke, and Morwen put her arms around her. For once, it didn't seem odd to be comforting Jane Askhew. It seemed natural and right.

'You'll have news soon, I'm sure,' she whispered. 'Be patient a little while longer, Jane. And Cathy will get well, I promise you.'

She had no way of knowing if she spoke the truth, but she offered up a silent prayer that it would be so. A prayer for herself too. She wanted Ben back. And every moment that Jane and Cathy spent here, Morwen knew that he wasn't wholly hers.

She mustn't think like that. If Cathy was her child she would be so grateful for all the help in the Killigrew household… but during the next critical days, Morwen began to wonder if Ben was taking too much on himself, because Tom Askhew was not here to comfort his own wife.

He spent more time at the house, and in Cathy's room, taking a progress report to his father as if the child was his own granddaughter. When Cathy smiled, and through Ben's coaxing began to take some solid food at last, he behaved as though he had personally won a battle.

Morwen held her tongue at such times, but the hurt was all the more real because Cathy's slow recovery was something Ben and Jane seemed to think they shared together. In reality, it was Morwen and Nurse Stevens, Charles Killigrew's nurse, who had done most of the sick-room attending, and it soon became obvious that Nurse Stevens had had enough.

She appeared in the drawing-room one evening, cape around her shoulders, hat speared squarely on her head, her carpet-bag gripped tightly in her hand.

'What the devil are you doing, woman?' Ben jumped up from his chair, annoyed at this intrusion. 'You have your own room—'

'Not any more I don't! I've just informed Mr Charles that I've had enough of this household, Mr Ben,' she declared crisply. 'I'm not employed to be a child nurse, and I ain't putting up with that old man's hollerings and carryings-on for one more minute. I'm going to join up with Miss Nightingale and do my bit for the soldiers, where my services will be more appreciated. I've quite made up my mind, and I'd be pleased if you would give me what's due to me up to this evening, Sir.'

She paused for breath. She looked so incongruous standing there, tall and angular with her ridiculous flowered hat perched on top of her tight little curls, that Morwen felt a sudden urge to laugh. She felt the sofa shake beside her, and realised that Jane, too, found it hard to contain her mirth. They shared a moment of mutual understanding before they each felt forced to glance away from each other. Ben folded his arms, every inch a Killigrew.

'You realise I could turn you out without a penny because of your decision to leave without proper notice?' he said coldly.

'But I know you won't, because you're a gentleman and a Killigrew,' Nurse Stevens said triumphantly, 'and it's more than your reputation's worth to have me spread it about that you were an old skinflint, Sir.'

Ben looked murderous at that, but all three women knew that the nurse was absolutely right. Ben strode across the room, and Nurse Stevens flinched for a moment.

'You will come with me to the study,' he said coldly. 'Your wages will be given to you immediately, and your reference will follow if you will leave a forwarding address.'

The woman's eyes flickered. 'You'll give me a fair one, Sir?' Her voice wavered.

'Nurse Stevens, I'm a gentleman and a Killigrew. You said so yourself. Please come at once. I have guests in the house.'

As the door closed behind them, Morwen heard Jane's admiring tones.

'Ben can be so masterful, Morwen. You must be very proud of him for the way he deals with any situation.'

Morwen had already moved to the small table where coffee was ready to be poured. Her hand shook a little as she handed Jane a cup. Yes, she was proud. Yes, she didn't need to be told that her man was masterful, nor to see the admiration in Jane Askhew's eyes. Jane had the glib tongue of a lady. She would feel no hesitation in telling Ben her opinion, while to working-class folk like the Tremaynes, such praise was usually thought to be vanity-provoking, and best kept quiet.

'What will happen about Mr Killigrew now?' Jane's next words took Morwen by surprise. She gave a small shrug.

'Ben will find another nurse. Or I shall care for him myself. He always preferred my touch to any other—'

'But you cannot sit with him night and day, Morwen! You must have professional help. You're Ben's wife before you're his father's nurse, noble though it sounds—'

'I don't say it to be noble!' Morwen said angrily. 'I care for my father-in-law, and if 'tis me he wants by his bedside, then he shall have me.'

'I'm sorry. I only mean to help,' Jane said delicately, her own cheeks a warm pink compared to Morwen's flushed ones. How beautiful she was, Jane thought. How beautiful and headstrong and impatient. No wonder Ben loved her. She was a perfect match for him…

'I know. I'm sorry too,' Morwen muttered. Jane was a guest. She must remember that.

Heartened by this apparent submission, Jane leaned forward. 'Morwen, I have no-one to talk with about matters concerning women. My mother – she will not listen if I talk about Tom. She never liked him, as you know. And I do miss him so dreadfully. You and Ben are so lucky. Don't spoil it. Ben is the one who needs your time. Mr Killigrew can always get another nurse.'

Morwen's sliver of sympathy as Jane began this hesitant lecture disappeared at once. She didn't want this girl telling her how to conduct her marriage. She had only ever shared womanly secrets with Celia, and they had resulted in disaster. She didn't want Jane Askhew for a confidante.

'I'm sure a nurse will be found,' she said stiffly, ignoring all the rest. 'How is your mother, Jane? And your father? I thought they would have come to visit Cathy while she was ill.'

The Tremaynes would never have stayed away from a sick child. Fine folk evidently acted differently. Jane bit her lip.

'I keep them informed of Cathy's progress daily. It's foolish to risk spreading the infection to another town. But they'll be longing to see her. As soon as Doctor Pender gives the word, I shall take her home, Morwen. I feel guilty at imposing on you all like this.'

Ben came back to the room in time to hear the last words. Having dealt with Nurse Stevens, he was not happily disposed.

'What rubbish. It's no imposition to have you and Cathy here, Jane. As for taking the poor little mite home, you're welcome to remain as long as you wish. You know that.'

'Thank you, Ben,' Jane said softly. 'But I think I would like to go home as soon as possible. Guests, like the measles, begin to irritate after a while.'

There was a small embarrassed silence.

'Ben, I'm worried about your father,' Morwen said quickly. 'I hope Nurse Stevens hasn't upset him unduly. I think I shall go and sit with him awhile if you and Jane will excuse me.'

He gave her a grateful smile, and she left the two of them together. Her heart beat fast as she wondered if it were foolish of her to do so, and knew that the thought was shaming.

She must learn to let go of Ben a little, if only because Ben's world did not revolve around herself alone. For a start it concerned several hundred men in his employ, her own family included. So many depended on him.

For all the freedom of speech and the running wild on the moors of clayfolk like herself, Ben had always been part of a much wider world. Perhaps she should remember that if she wanted to keep his world part of hers.

It was a sobering thought, as she pushed open Charles Killigrew's bedroom door and forced a smile to her lips for the bedridden shell of the once fine old man.

Chapter Fifteen

Charles Killigrew opened his eyes as he heard the light step approach his bed. Of all the people in the world, he would choose to have Morwen beside him, and good riddance to that old snot-bag of a nurse... his hands waved feebly towards his daughter-in-law, and she leaned over him to catch the words.

'Sorry, my love – couldn't stand – the woman – a minute longer. More work for you—'

Morwen wiped his chin gently. 'Stop gabbling,' she said cheerfully, which brought a lop-sided grin to Charles's mouth, for gabbling was an impossibility for him. 'Anyway, what else would I do with my time? I'm glad to care for you, Father. Ben has his own worries with the clay works, and I would far rather be useful up here.'

Even as she said it, Morwen knew it was only partly true. What she would infinitely rather do was to be caring for Ben's children. Hers and Ben's... she blinked back the mist in her eyes as she saw Charles's shrewd old watery ones watching her.

'Ben won't – have it,' he wheezed. 'He'll insist – on a new nurse. You see to it, love. You'll know – the right one.'

He drifted off to sleep again, awakening after a few minutes to request that Morwen read to him. His moods were as changeable as ever, she thought sympathetically. He just didn't have the stamina to control them any more.

But there was no reason why she couldn't care for him. There was a bell beside his bed, the cord placed in his hand every night. One of the maids could sleep in Nurse Stevens's adjoining room and call Morwen the moment Charles needed any assistance. There was no need for a professional nurse.

–

After two weeks, Morwen was forced to revise her ideas. She was utterly exhausted. Jane and Cathy Askhew had long since gone home, escorted by an attentive Ben, and Charles had become irascible since their departure. He alternately moped and ranted, and finally Ben put his foot down, as she sat wearily on the side of their bed late one night.

'You're worn out,' he said angrily. 'I know you think it's for the best, but Father needs more than a loving daughter-in-law to nurse him, Morwen. I'll see Doctor Pender about it tomorrow morning.'

She didn't argue. 'Just one point, Ben. Your father has asked me to choose any new nurse. Please give me that privilege, otherwise I shall feel utterly useless.'

He pulled her into his arms. 'My dearest one, I don't mean to imply such a thing! You've been more than a daughter to my father, and no-one knows it better than I do. But I want a wife, not a drudge.'

His hands combed through her long black hair, and caressed her neck, his fingers warm against her skin. She felt them move across her soft lips to quieten any more discussion, and then his mouth replaced the fingertips, and she was held fast in a sweet embrace. She felt the familiar swift response to Ben's hard demanding body, and swayed against him as they fell together across the bed.

'Are you too tired for me, my Morwen?' he said softly, and she knew that all the aggression in him now was of the man for his woman. The exquisite aggression of love...

'Oh, no,' she breathed. 'I'm not too tired, Ben. It's been so long—'

He undressed her quickly, pausing to kiss each new exposed area of her as he did so, and the need to belong to him completely was as new and elating as ever.

'Too many problems have come between the important things, Morwen,' he murmured against her throat as they lay together for a moment, cocooned in their own world beneath the bedcovers. 'But nothing is more important than my love for you.'

'Nor mine for you, dar.'

She felt the exploring fingers she knew so well, teasing and loving. She followed her own instincts to give Ben the pleasure he gave her, and the love words between them became an erotic accompaniment.

But they were both too impatient for preliminaries, and as he eased himself over her, she felt the small sweet pain as he entered her, and gloried in it. He moved gently, and she moved with him, part of him, as she had always wanted to be. She lost all sense of time as the pleasure engulfed her, winding herself around him, her flesh his flesh, her love his.

When the final moments came, and the love flowed from each of them, she clung to him as he rocked her against him, as close to heaven as any two mortals could be. Ben's skin was damp with exertion, and Morwen pressed her mouth to his smooth muscled shoulder, thinking faintly that she asked little more from life than this. To be with her man… and to have his child…

'You said something very special to me tonight, Morwen,' she heard the throb of his voice against her breasts.

'Did I?' She gave a shaky little smile. 'I don't ever remember what I say, Ben. At such times I fear you have a wanton for a wife—'

He laughed with her. 'Then I wish every man could have such a wanton!' He was reluctant to move away from her, and cupped her flushed face in his hands. 'God, you're so beautiful, Morwen. I love you so much it scares me at times—'

The moment was too emotional for Morwen. Her throat thickened. 'Nothing scares you, Ben,' she said huskily. 'It's one of the things I love about you.'

'Oh?' His mood changed. 'What are all the others then?'

'I'm not telling you,' she teased. 'You'll be swollen-headed. But you still have something to tell me! What was this special thing I said to you?'

His finger circled her cheek. He leaned forward and brushed his mouth intimately against hers, just touching it as he spoke, his breath soft and warm.

'You don't use many endearments, Morwen. You're like your mother in that respect—'

'Clay folk don't waste useless words—' she began in mild defence. He silenced her with firmer pressure on her mouth.

'I know that!' he said, moving his lips against hers once more. 'But you called me dar, your mother's special word for your father, and it was the sweetest sound I ever heard.'

She didn't remember. She only knew it had been the only word to use at the time. The right word, for someone who was more precious to her than life. She didn't have his education to put it into words, but if that one little endearment had said it all, then it was as rich an inheritance as Ben Killigrew's.

-

Ben contacted Doctor Pender the next morning, and a succession of ladies arrived to be considered as Charles Killigrew's new nurse. Morwen interviewed them all, and took the most suitable to Charles's bedside. After three days she began to despair that they would ever find anyone, but at last his eyes sparkled as the small and sprightly Nurse Wilder breezed into his room. The moment their eyes met, Morwen knew that Nurse Wilder was the one.

'Wilder by name, and wilder by nature, if 'tis no nonsense that you want, m'dear,' Doctor Pender had chuckled with his usual addiction to clichés. 'She's a fine little body, and a midwife to boot, so mebbe she can do two jobs in one in due course, if you take my meaning, dear Mrs Killigrew.'

Morwen certainly wouldn't let that influence her! But once Nurse Wilder was installed and Charles seemed more settled, she felt free to visit her mother and find out how Freddie fared.

Bess was a little scratchy at first at not seeing her daughter for several weeks, although she knew of the measles in Killigrew house, and would not have wanted it carried outside. But once Jane Askhew had taken her child home to Truro, Bess had expected Morwen daily.

'Mammie, I'm a married woman now, and I can't come running every minute!' Morwen retorted.

'You're still my daughter, and I'm your mother and deserving of some respect,' Bess came back.

Morwen bit her lip. They had always been more than mother and daughter, and she couldn't bear this prickly reception, especially when she felt it was undeserved. She ran to her mother's side and put her arms around her, leaning her head against Bess's plump shoulder.

'Mammie, I'm sorry, but if you knew what a time we've had with Ben's father! His nurse walked out to join Nurse

Nightingale in the Crimea, and I had to do all the fetching and carrying for un—'

Bess softened at once. 'I thought you had skivvies for all that, my lamb!'

'Not for nursing,' Morwen said feelingly. 'The old man only wanted me – until we found a treasure called Nurse Wilder. Now she's living in the house, and I'm not so tied, so here I am, and dying to know all about my family. I've missed 'ee so, Mammie.'

'We've missed 'ee too, lamb. Sit down while I warm some tea and then we'll talk.'

Morwen watched as Bess bustled about in her little house, as clean as a new penny, and the pride of her mother. The tiny cottage where Morwen had grown up on the moors had been snug and warm, but so cramped with them all, especially when her brothers grew so big and broad.

Sam and his family would have the same problem in the cottage when their children grew... but when Morwen had lived there it had seemed no problem, because the Tremayne house had always spilled over with love, the same as this one did now.

'How's Freddie, Mammie?' Morwen couldn't wait for the tea to brew to ask. She kept her tone casual, but she saw Bess's lips tighten a little.

'He's as contrary as a cat with a mouse. He were all for this posh school in London and now he don't want to go, and all he says is he wants to go a' boat-building wi' our Jack in Truro. I don't know what to think.'

'What does Daddy say to it?'

'He's tired of it all. Sam says we should let the boy go wi' Jack, and 'tis only what he expected wi' our Freddie getting too big for his boots and getting cold feet because of it. What frets me is why he changed his mind so sudden, and if he'll change it again if we let un go wi' Jack.'

Morwen took the cup of tea and kept her eyes down as she stirred it.

'Let him go, Mammie. He said summat about the boat-building to Ben and me, and I think 'tis what he's fitted for. Don't send him to London.'

Bess stared at her. 'Nobody's sending un away! 'Tis what he wanted, and now he says he don't. What did Ben say to it all, since it seems you've already discussed it?' Her voice was ruffled.

'Ben says that a young boy on his own in London can be very unhappy, and he knows what he's talking about, Mammie.'

She dare not say more. How could she describe to this simple countrywoman all the drama of the Peterson affair?

Her mother didn't answer for some minutes, and Morwen felt her heart begin to thud. If she was questioned further, she was so afraid that all her bitterness towards Captain Peterson might overflow. But whether or not Bess sensed that there was something she didn't know, she evidently decided not to pursue it.

'You know that I trust Ben's judgement, Morwen, and I'll pass on his thoughts to your Daddy. 'Tis probably for the best. Our Freddie would only have got above himself at this posh London school, and he and Jack should do well together, if Boskelly's will have un.'

'I'm sure they will, Mammie. Ben will see to it,' Morwen said with relief.

Bess laughed, and handed Morwen a fresh-baked bun that rivalled anything that Fielding's Tea Room could provide.

'Does Ben have a finger in that pie as well? He don't have shares in Boskelly's boat-yard, does he?'

'No, but folk respect his wishes, Mammie. 'Tis useful at times.'

'Oh, ah! 'Tis useful to have a name and a fine house and a reputation for fair treatment. So tell me, what's the news about the rail tracks? Your Daddy keeps tight-lipped on it lately, which means he knows nothing, and won't admit it.'

'You don't think I'm going to betray anything I know, do 'ee?' Morwen teased.

Bess pounced on the hint. 'So you do know summat. Out wi' it, our Morwen, and 'twill be just between ourselves.'

Morwen shook her head sadly. 'Mammie, I never thought you'd suggest such a thing. Ben was summoned to Bodmin yesterday, and was told that Engineer Trent had died from the consumption in Switzerland—'

'The poor man! But wasn't Ben in a fury over the need for more delay? If the rail tracks aren't in use soon, 'twill mean using the old waggons to transport the autumn clay blocks to the port. Your Daddy's been bemoaning the fact for weeks now.'

'Listen, Mammie! A new chief engineer has already been appointed. Knowing the situation here, the business of Killigrew Clay was given priority. He's studied all the information, and was present when Ben went to Bodmin. And since there was no real evidence for subsidence, or of rogue tin mines under the moors, he says the rail tracks can begin full use again. Ben's gone to the works to inform Daddy today, since it was too late when he got home last night.'

Her mother's eyes were shining when she finished speaking.

'Thank the Lord for it! I daresay Ben will get the town excursions going again while this fine hot weather lasts, and after the autumn despatches, the children can go on their annual excursion to the sea. Quite a few on 'em thought their babbies wouldn't get their treat from Killigrew Clay this year.'

She smiled broadly. 'And mebbe my menfolk will show more cheerful faces from today. Dora says that Sam's been a real sore-head these past weeks, and Primmy's teething and screaming is nearly driving her to the kiddleywink.'

Morwen was thankful she had been able to bring good news for once. She changed the subject.

'You'll have heard the news from the war, Mammie?'

Bess looked vague, her thoughts still on more homely affairs. Morwen looked impatient. Ben had been so full of it, and it was surely important to them all.

'There are great hopes that the French soldiers will conquer Sevastopol very soon! They've been bombarding the city for several weeks now. They say it will all be over by the middle of September—'

'Oh, Morwen, lamb, what does it mean to folk like me? 'Tis no more than a name I've heard Ben mention. As long as my family is safe around me, a foreign war means nothing.'

Morwen was shocked, and realised in an instant how effortlessly her own attitudes had changed since being Ben Killigrew's wife. At one time she, too, would have felt nothing for a war across the sea. But now she shared Ben's fervent wish for it to be over. She even shared Jane Askhew's anxiety for her Tom to come home safely, and knew that she meant it sincerely.

'No doubt you'll be joining in the celebrations on the moors, though?' Morwen said coolly. 'When the news comes, they'll light bonfires as usual, and dance around them—'

'Oh, we'll all be there then,' Bess said happily, oblivious to any reproof in her daughter's voice.

-

Ben was so cheerful, it was as if he had been given the moon and stars on a plate. His works were in full production again.

213

There was no more talk of the men not getting their fair dues and bonuses. The rail tracks could begin operations the very next week.

Meanwhile, he had teams of men cleaning the tracks from the mud and grime that had collected on them in their idleness. Others cleaned and polished the little rail trucks, and made them as comfortable as possible for the re-opening of the town excursions to see the porcelain hills glinting in the sunlight, and watch the mysteries of the clay works at first-hand.

Ben had ridden over to Truro and called on the Carricks, receiving a stiff welcome from Jane's mother, and an enthusiastic one from Jane and her father. Cathy remembered him and climbed all over him. And he had never felt so good as when he gave the news about the rail tracks to Lew Tregian for *The Informer.*

Morwen would like to have gone with him, except that she had no wish to meet Mary Carrick again, who had always either snubbed her or ignored her on the few occasions they had met.

'And *The Informer* will announce that the rail excursions are to begin again?' she asked on his return from Truro. 'I hope that folk won't be afraid to risk the journey because of what's happened, Ben.'

'I hope so too,' he commented. 'But since you and I and various others will be taking the first invited tour from St Austell town to the works, I hope it will prove our faith in it, Morwen. I've asked Jane and Cathy and her parents. Mrs Carrick has declined, but Richard is agreeable to bringing his daughter and granddaughter. I'm going to invite thirty or more notables from the town, and have promised to let Lew Tregian know their names when they accept. He'll print them in full for the readers of *The Informer* to read, and has also said he will be on hand to report on the day.'

'So you spent some time with Mr Tregian in Truro too?' she asked with forced innocence.

Ben laughed, twirling her round in his arms until her long hair spun around her head and around Ben's shoulders as he held her close, capturing both of them in its dark tresses.

'Yes, my jealous darling, I spent some time with Lew Tregian. It was not all in Jane Askhew's company. It seems to me that we've had this kind of conversation before!'

But this time it didn't matter. Ben was too elated by his own news to bristle at her words, and Morwen was too sure of his love to waste time on real pique.

Besides, she hadn't expected the first rail journey after its long absence to be such an occasion. Nor to be included in the list of notables. She said as much to Ben.

'Included! Morwen, you and I are the owners of Killigrew Clay!'

She stared at him. 'Don't be silly. I own nothing. I'm just your wife—'

He shook her gently, his eyes teasing. 'And if I were to die…?'

'Don't say such things! 'Tis bad luck!' Quickly she crossed her fingers behind her back. She would have crossed eyes and toes too if he hadn't been laughing down at her. But it was her old Ben, her teasing, laughing, wonderful Ben, and she forgave him everything.

'All I'm saying, you goose, is that if I were to die, then Killigrew Clay would be yours. It would belong to you. How does that sound to you, Morwen Tremayne?'

She was numb. It had never occurred to her. His teasing with her old name told her he guessed at her feelings. Morwen Tremayne, clayworker's daughter, the sole owner of Killigrew

Clay? It seemed as unlikely as suddenly donning a crown. As for what her family would think…

'Ben, I don't want to hear any more of such talk. I never want it to happen, because if it did, it would mean I no longer had you. And I wouldn't want to live without you—'

'Darling, stop it,' he commanded as her voice wavered. 'I was only stating a fact for your own security. We'll forget it was ever mentioned. Instead, help me draw up the list of people you'd like included on our excursion to the porcelain hills.'

'How grand it sounds.' She was forced to smile. 'I know that's what the townsfolk call the clay-tips, but they always seemed no more than cosy places where Celia and I could keep out of sight for a while in our tea-breaks.'

Her smiled slipped a little. How far away it all seemed. With a little shock she realised that for a second she hadn't been able to recall Celia's face clearly, though four years had done nothing to dim her memory of the awful events of that time.

Ben was still holding her, and she felt his lips touch her cheek, and heard the swift sympathy in his voice.

'Come back, Morwen. Does it still pain you to remember?'

She nodded. 'I think it always will,' she said simply. 'I can never forget what your cousin did to her, any more than I can understand how my brother Matt could have gone off to America with him the way he did. It was as if he could charm his way into any person's mind that he chose. If I was old Zillah, I'd say those people were ill-wished to have Jude Pascoe's attentions.'

She shuddered. Celia had found Jude charming and exciting… to Morwen, the very thought of him had been odious.

'Well, there was at least one person's mind he couldn't charm,' Ben said drily. 'I thought we had decided never to mention Jude's name in this house. The less I know of his doings, the better—'

'I would still like to know of our Matt's doings,' Morwen said sadly. She took a deep breath, knowing she was clouding this lovely day, the best day the Killigrews had known for some time. She put a smile on her lips.

'Are we going to begin this list for the excursion? And do I have to go knocking at fine folks' doors to invite them?'

'You do not!' Ben caught her determined gay mood. 'We'll have invitations sent round to their houses, and do it as grandly as my lady wishes.'

—

So there were to be celebrations all round. The next issue of *The Informer* took up half a page in telling people that Killigrew's rail tracks had now been declared safe by the new Chief Engineer of the district, and that therefore the excursions to Killigrew Clay would begin again immediately.

Those wishing to enjoy the benefit of the fresh moorland air, the views of the town and the sea, and the excitements of the clay works, were advised to contact the Killigrew Clay offices in St Austell town, where bookings could be made. The first excursion was by invitation only, and there followed an impressive list of the wealthy and the elegant who wished to be known as Ben Killigrew's guests. Particularly as Morwen had suggested holding a fine tea for them at the house afterwards, an expense to which Ben readily agreed. It was a sound move, he told Morwen. There were plenty of people who considered an invitation to Killigrew House to be a status symbol.

'I know that,' she smiled. 'Why else do you think I suggested it? Invite them to tea, and they'll all want to come on the excursion!'

Ben laughed, delighted to see the lights dancing in her eyes once more. 'Mrs Killigrew, I'd say you have all the makings of a shrewd businesswoman,' he said admiringly.

'Thank you, Sir, but I think I'll leave all that to you. Just so long as you'll agree to joining my family on the moors for the bonfire dancing on Saturday night. You know they're lighting them to celebrate the victory at Sevastopol. Please say we can go, Ben!'

'My lady is so knowledgeable all of a sudden,' he teased. 'Of course we'll go! Do you think I'd deny you the pleasure, my pagan love?'

He smiled back, and she wondered if he understood more of her feelings than he ever revealed.

For it would be so good. So good to dance around a bonfire, one of the glowing orange faces whirling and laughing, with the scent of woodsmoke in their noses and stinging their eyes, and the crackle of bracken underfoot. To smell the wild gorse and the crushed purple clover, and to be a child of the moors once more…

She smothered the thought, reminding herself that she couldn't ever go back…

Only for a little while, just a little while…

Chapter Sixteen

There were no folk like clay folk for knowing how to enjoy themselves, Morwen thought elatedly on Saturday night.

An exuberant clayworker swung her around the bonfire in a wild dance, oblivious of the fact that she was now Mrs Ben Killigrew, and that her husband was somewhere in the crush of merrymakers, clapping his hands to the tune played on an old penny-whistle the same as all the rest – stamping and hollering and laughing on the summer-baked earth beneath a starry sky, while the wood-sparks from the bonfire burst into the air like fire-crackers.

They celebrated the victory at Sevastopol. Half of them had never heard the name. Most never knew the whereabouts of the city. They celebrated the victory all the same. And they celebrated their own fortunes.

The French were apparently the real victors, and the French were allies of the British; the little Queen and Prince Albert had recently been fêted during their timely visit to Paris and the prestige of it all had reached the humblest ears. And Killigrew Clay could hold up its head again.

To the clayworkers, the last was the most important of all, and they danced and sang with even more gusto because of it. Ben Killigrew was their hero once more. And Morwen Tremayne Killigrew was one of them…

She caught sight of Ben's beaming face in the bonfire's glow as Eric Leeman swung her around, hair streaming, skirts flying. It was a joyous night that had begun with dour faces at Killigrew House that morning, and Morwen thought privately these simple folk with their simple ways were probably better off than someone like Ben, who had received his latest batch of London newspapers as he enjoyed his luncheon glass of porter.

Some of the London papers were less cautious in their reports than the country ones, telling of the huge casualties of war on both sides.

'God knows the Russians are our enemies,' Ben had sworn at the grim reports. 'But to think of the poor devils defending their city and losing a thousand men a day is monstrous. The French are clear victors, and pray heaven it will all end soon.'

'Surely it must. Now that Sevastopol is taken—'

Ben spoke tersely. 'It must have been a hell-hole. The city burned for twenty-four hours, and no-one could get near it for the heat. Think how many perished in that time alone, who might have been saved with medical help. Our soldiers are demoralised—'

'How can that be? We and the French have won—'

'There's national pride involved, Morwen. The French have the honour and glory of this particular victory. Our morale is already at its lowest in the Crimea, with our great losses in previous battles and with the Asiatic cholera sweeping through the camps like the plague in the warm summer weather. The raw recruits we keep sending are more of a hindrance than an asset, and the lists of dead or missing are staggering. It's all here, in bold print, or written between the lines for those who care to see it and are not dazzled by the glory of war!'

Morwen had hardly dared to comment as Ben's face grew more stormy. Morwen suddenly felt alarmed. Killigrew Clay needed him here. Their own troubles had resolved for the moment, but the safety of the rail tracks was still to be tested and proven. No-one had taken that into any real consideration in the euphoria of the chief engineer's report. But surely Ben would not think of enlisting for the war even now…

'Ben – dar—' she said timorously.

As if he read her thoughts, he smiled briefly, his voice heavy with sarcasm. She knew it was directed at himself, not at her. She knew his impotence at being an onlooker at anything.

'Don't worry, my love. I would be as raw a recruit as the meanest clayworker if I offered my services now. We must put our own business to rights and think of the importance of putting fine china on society tables.'

Morwen had rarely heard him speak so bitterly. She ignored his inference that clayworkers were of little account.

'Have you not forgotten the importance of the china clay in medicine and in newspaper production?' Morwen said quietly. 'Aren't these things of equal importance to our wounded soldiers and their loved ones at home?'

Ben didn't speak for a few moments, then finally he nodded slowly, the heaviness in his voice lifting a little. 'You have a fine knack of reminding me of my inheritance, Morwen. But so be it. You had best read the more cheerful bits of news to my father, and leave out the gloomy details, for I swear I couldn't trust myself to be so selective.'

He had asked to be left to himself for a while, and Morwen knew it was better so. Ben would wrestle with his own conscience, and eventually see that he could do no more than he did already. His clay works provided far more than pretty china.

Once his frustration lifted, he would see that he played his part in supplying ingredients for medicines that might mean the difference between life and death for the British soldiers and their allies in the Crimean war.

And by the time the festivities high on the moors began, Morwen had sighed with relief that Ben had come to terms with himself again.

-

'Did I ever tell 'ee you dance like an angel, Morwen?' Eric Leeman bellowed in her ear. They twirled madly, making earth and sky spin together for a few wild seconds.

''Tis more than I can say for you, Eric Leeman!' she gasped as he trod on her foot for the tenth time. 'I shall have bruises all over if you don't stop squeezing me so tight—'

''Tis the only chance I'll ever get to hold 'ee, now you've gone up in the world, my pretty. No other maid could ever hold a candle to 'ee, though, Morwen.'

She giggled, revelling in his harmless flirtation. It meant nothing. Eric had had too much ale, and would never dare to be so bold at any other time, especially with the boss's wife. But the night was gay with laughter and merriment, and clayworkers and bosses mingled like currants in a cake.

Ben didn't begrudge her this excitement. He stood easily with her Mammie and Dora, little Primmy cocooned in a warm blanket in Dora's arms. When Morwen finally extricated herself from Eric Leeman's damp clutches, she danced across to join them, and the two younger children began leaping up at her at once.

'Dance wi' us, Auntie Morwen!' Walter begged.

'An' me—' Albert echoed in his piping voice.

Morwen grabbed at both their hands, loving the clamouring of the two small Tremayne boys, their hair as unruly as Freddie's ever was, their blue eyes large and sparkling. One day they would be as handsome as Sam, their daddy. As handsome as Hal, and Jack and Freddie – and Matt.

'I'll dance with you both!' Morwen shouted down at them above the din. 'Where's your Daddy gone? Wouldn't he dance you round the bonfire?'

She wove her way in and out of the cavorting figures, who readily parted to make room for two more little Tremaynes who wanted to join in the fun.

As she spoke, she saw her brother Jack, more handsome every time she saw him. He had his arm around a pretty girl's waist, a girl Morwen didn't recognise, and she felt a small shock that Jack, too, could soon be thinking of courting and marrying.

Since he had been away from the family and the clay works and fulfilling his needs with the boat-building, Morwen hadn't given much thought to how he would have grown and matured. To her, it seemed to have happened overnight.

She glimpsed Freddie too, with his old group of friends, kiddley boys as gangling and tousled as himself. She drew a sigh of relief that they no longer ostracised him for being so posh now he was away at St Austell school, which was as alien to them as a London college; and that Freddie seemed perfectly capable of enjoying himself once more.

'Daddy's gone wi' Granddad to help carry the pies for the feastin',' Walter squealed. 'I'm having two on 'em—'

'An' me,' added Albert.

Morwen laughed, skilfully keeping the two children away from the large boots of the older dancers.

'You'll be ill if you do. What would your Mammie do then, with two sick babbies in the house, and little Primmy to look after as well?'

'I ain't a babby,' Walter said indignantly. 'I'm three!'

'An' me—'

'You're not! You're only two. You're a babby, Albert Tremayne—'

'I'm not! I'm not!' Albert screeched, and Morwen laughingly hauled their enraged little bodies away from the group of dancers before they got trodden underfoot.

'Can I give them back to you, Dora, before we have another war up here?' she grinned. 'I've never known such tempers. They'd do credit to a pit captain!'

Dora took her charges a mite smugly, handing over the baby to Morwen's willing arms. Primmy settled cosily into this new haven. But the little boys instantly tore away from their mother, pulling at Morwen's skirts, wanting her to dance them around the bonfire again.

Above the child's head, Morwen met Ben's eyes, and interpreted his look instantly.

How fulfilled she must look at this moment. How glowing and alive, surrounded by Sam and Dora's children, here on the firelit moors in her own environment.

For a second she felt apart from Ben, alongside her own womenfolk. Yet strangely not with them. It was as though it was just Morwen and the three children, isolated in the soft shadows away from the firelit crowds.

Quickly Morwen went across to where Ben stood, nestling her head against his shoulder as his arm went around her waist. As if they were part of her, the little boys went with her, still clinging to her skirts.

Primmy was held softly between them, and the soft sweet baby scent of her rose poignantly into Morwen's nostrils.

This is how we should be. The thought suffused every pore of her. *Ben and me, and our own little family…*

'Morwen! Come over here, our Morwen!'

She heard her brother Jack's voice calling her, deep and strong, and blinked away the small scalding rush of tears.

These were Dora's children, and Dora was impatiently saying that she must take them home to bed before the boys became too naughty, and Primmy kept them awake all night with all the excitement. Dora took the baby from Morwen's arms. Bess tugged at the boys to help her daughter-in-law, and the spell was broken.

'Our Jack wants 'ee to meet somebody,' Bess murmured in Morwen's ear.

Before Morwen could ask any more, Jack was at her side. Morwen had to look up at him. He must be six feet tall by now, she thought in amazement, as tall and powerfully built as Ben. Jack was the tallest of all her brothers. She had always expected Sam to be, but he was stockier and so it didn't show so much.

'Morwen, this is Annie,' Jack said. The words were simple, but the tone of his voice and the softening in his eyes, and the protective way he held his arm loosely around the girl's slender shoulders said far more. 'Annie, this is my sister. I've told you summat about her.'

'Not too much, I hope,' Morwen said teasingly, feeling this was quite a momentous moment.

Young Jack was clearly enchanted with this pretty girl with the dancing golden ringlets and eyes the colour of warm toffee. And Annie too… looking up at him from beneath her spectacular fringe of eyelashes as though uncaring if she saw anyone else ever again…

For some reason the sight of them both, on the brink of love, brought a lump to her throat. This was herself and Ben… she felt as though she looked into a crystal ball and saw the future…

Jack and Annie with a brood of golden-haired children with blue Tremayne eyes, while she and Ben…

'I'm very happy to meet you, Annie,' she heard herself speak as if in a dream. She was twenty-one years old, and suddenly she felt so old. She felt her life slipping away from her. She felt as futile and frustrated as Celia.

Yet not like Celia. Celia had conceived a child, and had known the feel of it in her belly. For the first time in her life, Morwen felt bitter resentment towards Celia, and a fury that the two of them had wickedly brought that child's life to an end before it had begun.

'Are you all right, our Morwen?' she heard Jack speak as though from a distance. 'You look a bit greenish—'

'Of course I'm all right!'

Ben was joining them, and she forced away the strange fey feelings, and especially the resentment of Celia.

'I've had too much dancing and too much sweet-drink. It always made my head spin.'

She bit her lip, remembering a time long ago when she and Celia had gone to Truro Fair, and Celia had let Jude Pascoe ply her with sweet-drink, and Celia's head had been turned by the attentions of Ben's roughly handsome cousin. From now on, there must be no more sweet-drink for her, Morwen vowed…

'It's Annie Boskelly, isn't it?' Ben said with a smile. 'What are you doing here so far from home? Did your father allow you to come all this way with this young rogue?'

As he spoke playfully, Morwen guessed Annie's identity at once. Boskelly… Jack was an apprentice at Boskelly Boat-builders in Truro. Ben had known the Boskellys and arranged the introduction for his brother-in-law. And this was Annie Boskelly.

The girl hugged Jack's arm. 'Father knows I'm safe with Jack. He's becoming quite an important person in the yard. Father says Jack has more feel for the wood in his little finger than a lot of so-called skilled boat-builders. Father says—'

'Annie, if you go on so, Morwen will begin to wonder if 'tis her brother you're talking about, or some paragon she's never met!' Jack reproved her slightly as Morwen laughed, but it was obvious that they knew each other well enough for the words to make no difference.

Annie clearly idolised him, and Jack was already a different person in the short time since he'd gone to Truro. He had even begun to lose the old dialect, and to improve his speech in line with Annie's. Just as Morwen had done during her marriage to Ben. In a way it saddened her to realise how they were all changing. In another way, she was pleased that Jack had found himself this delightful girl.

Ben spoke again, as a thought occurred to him. 'Your father and uncle are to be invited to the opening of the town excursion next week, Annie. Perhaps you and Jack would care to come too? We're all having tea at Killigrew House afterwards—'

'Oh, it would be such fun! I would love it!'

'We would both be delighted, Ben,' Jack said with such studied formality that Morwen could have wept with a mixture of love and pride. Young Jack, no longer the awkward, most irritating of her brothers, but a young man wanting desperately to impress his love.

'We shall love to see you both there, Annie,' she added her words to Ben's. 'Perhaps you and Jack would care to come to tea some other time too, when we can get to know each other without all the other folk around.'

'Thanks, our Morwen.' Suddenly red around the ears at this sisterly approval, Jack lapsed into his more familiar tones. 'Mammie's asked us to tea at the little house tomorrow for the same purpose.'

–

It was evidently quite serious then, Morwen reflected as she and Ben drove tiredly back to Killigrew House very late that night. Harold Boskelly must approve of Jack as a suitable suitor for his daughter to have let him accompany her to the bonfire celebrations that night, although Jack had taken her home shortly after their introduction. That, too, was a novelty.

Jack hadn't wanted to go drinking with his old friends or stay up until the small hours like the rest of the young bucks undoubtedly would. Bess and Hal must be delighted too. Morwen hadn't had time to speak to them again after the festivities ended, but how exciting it all was…

Another possible wedding for the Tremaynes, and such a feather in Jack's cap to have captured the heart of a pretty and potentially wealthy young lady. Not that that would matter a jot to Jack. Morwen knew him too well. His ambitions were all centred around his craft, and the Boskelly brothers would recognise and rejoice in this particular facet in their young apprentice.

Morwen sighed happily, snuggling up against Ben beneath the rug in the small trap. The September evening was balmy, the night still and glittering with stars, the moon full. It was a night made for lovers…

'I almost hesitate to ask for your thoughts, sweetheart,' Ben said softly. 'You seemed so deep in concentration, I know they must be worth far more than a penny.'

'I suppose I was thinking how lucky we are to have one another,' she said with the simple honesty he had always loved in her. 'I'm so happy for everyone who has someone to love, yet a little sad for those who don't.'

'What a profound statement,' Ben commented, his voice gentle. 'Was it Jack's appearance tonight that brought on this introspection?'

'If you mean, am I thinking more than usual, then yes, it was Jack's happiness that brought it on,' she said lightly, a small bristle in her voice. 'There was a moment back there tonight when I felt – oh, somehow close to God, to nature, to the earth – I don't know – I don't have the words to say it—'

'You don't need the words, dar. Your eyes said it all.'

The horse clattered through the narrow cobbled streets of St Austell town, taking them towards Killigrew House. It was as though they were the only two people awake in the whole town.

It was an unearthly feeling, adding to Morwen's own deep conviction that all of life was only loaned to them.

That they had to give something back and couldn't constantly take… it was her own peculiar kind of religion, and it was something to which she hardly gave conscious thought.

Only very rarely with Ben had she ever shared these most intimate thoughts and feelings. Without him saying a word, she knew he shared them now as he covered her hand with his; as he leaned forward to brush her cheek with his lips; as he whispered that he loved her in a voice as soft as thistledown, and as meaningful as if it soared out in some vast cathedral.

She leaned against Ben's shoulder, safe and warm. 'We're the lucky ones, aren't we? You and me; Mammie and Daddy; Freddie, now he's over his bad time; Jack and Annie; Sam and Dora and the children. There's only our Matt – oh, Ben, if you knew how I crave for news of our Matt at times. 'Tis the only thing missing in our lives, to know how he fares. 'Twould bring the joy back into Mammie's life to know it—'

Her voice thickened, as much from the desperate need to sleep after all the excitement of the night, as for the sudden poignant longing to see all her family together again. The ties were as strong as ever.

The Tremaynes themselves were strong, and they always came back… Morwen and Jack; Freddie who nearly went away; and Sam who had never left… everyone but Matt, her dearest…

'There's no use wishing for the moon, Morwen. I wish it was mine to give you. If it was—'

'I know,' she whispered. 'And I'm so grateful for what I have. I am, Ben, truly I am!'

'Grateful? What kind of word is that to use between husband and wife?' He teased her out of her dark mood.

She gave a tremulous laugh back.

'I told you I was no use with words, didn't I?'

His arm around her shoulders meant more than words. His strength and his love were more dear to her than gold. She wanted to tell him…

'When did you and I need words, dar?' Ben said simply, using the sweet endearment they had now made their own. 'There are better ways of showing love than merely telling it.'

She felt the soft colour steal into her cheeks. Even after four years of marriage to Ben Killigrew, there were still times when it seemed as though she stood apart from herself and watched in amazement at the change of fortunes in Morwen Tremayne's life.

And the best of all, the most glorious of all, was that Ben Killigrew loved her, and had vowed in Penwithick church to go on loving her until death did them part.

Morwen gave a little shiver, as the solemn binding words of the marriage vows swept through her head. They had always seemed so awesome to her. Wonderful, but awesome too.

'Stop laying ghosts or chasing rainbows, or whatever else is going on in that beautiful, busy little head of yours, Morwen,' Ben said. 'We're home.'

She blinked. Killigrew House lay ahead of them in all its gracious moonlit splendour. There was a time when Morwen could never have thought of such a great pile of stone as home. But with Ben at her side, that was exactly what it was.

The incongruous thought of acting the lady of the house next week when all the fine folk gathered for afternoon tea after the rail excursion suddenly tickled her. But she would do it, of course. If she had married the most dashing, eligible man for miles around, then Morwen Killigrew could accomplish anything. But there was a faint sense of alarm in the thought all the same.

–

Morwen dressed in the finest gown her mother had sewn for her. No longer someone else's muslin cast-offs, adorned with ribbons to make it a little different, but a gown of fine bronze silk with a little matching cape, appliquéd with roses of pale lemon, and a bonnet atop her gleaming dark hair, curled for the occasion by an admiring Fanny. On her feet were dainty shoes made especially for her by St Austell's best cobbler. Over her arm was a pretty little drawstring bag in which to keep her toilet water and personal items.

Ben was not allowed to see the finished effect until she walked down the sweeping staircase, where he awaited her.

'You look stunning,' he said simply. 'How could any man fail to fall in love with you?'

Morwen laughed, her blue eyes glowing like blue fire at the compliment. Ben, too, was elegant and handsome, and together they would present a perfect couple.

'I'm not looking for men to fall in love with me! Only one man—'

'And he did so a long time ago,' Ben spoke softly as she reached his side. He kissed her gently on the mouth, so as not to ruffle the fine figure she made, and then squeezed her hand.

'We must leave, dar. It wouldn't be seemly for the boss and his lady to arrive after the guests. Although I would much prefer to stay here with you and undo all the efforts you've made to look so delectable this afternoon.'

His meaning was clear to her, and she laughed up into his face, sure of him, loving him.

'It can wait, Ben, and will be all the sweeter for it,' she murmured back.

They walked out to the waiting carriage hand in hand. The day might have been made especially for them. The sky was a limitless blue, the sun warm but not stifling in the still air, and Killigrew's rail tracks were operational once more. They gleamed like silver, the little engine shone with all the loving care and enthusiasm polished into it.

The trucks that were normally used for clay deliveries had their customary wooden seating replaced in them for the excursions, with cushions included to make the journey more comfortable. Ben Killigrew was no skinflint, one and another remarked. He did them proud.

This was a day for special guests. Morwen smiled happily at Bess and Hal, included in the list since her Daddy was Ben's works manager, a position he had once never dreamed of attaining.

Since Freddie was the only young Tremayne left at home now, he too was spruced up beside them and looking more cheerful than of late.

Morwen waved to her brother Jack and the pretty Annie Boskelly, who might have been on another planet for all the notice they took of anyone but each other. Beside them were the stocky grey-haired Boskelly boat-building brothers.

Jane Askhew arrived with her father and little Cathy, quite recovered from the measles and excited at going on a train for the first time. There were many important folk from St Austell and Truro towns, and Lew Tregian with his ever-busy pencil, recording every moment for *The Informer*.

Before letting the assembled guests alight at the little junction built at the foot of the moorland slope, Ben addressed them all. He spoke simply, wishing them an enjoyable day, and welcoming them all to Killigrew Clay.

Sam was to be their guide for the day. When the little train arrived at the top of the moors, chugging and spitting and billowing smoke, he alighted first, explaining briefly the viewpoints all around.

The guests could see for themselves the distant misty sea; the wide spread of fragrant moorland, green with summer; ahead of them the gougings of the clay pits, the pale milky-green pools, the gleaming clay tips…

'I see now why they call them the porcelain hills! They look so pretty, don't they?' trilled one large, well-bolstered lady in a cultured voice.

To his credit, Sam didn't give a flicker of a smile.

'Yes, Ma'am, and this 'ere's known as the porcelain earth, since one reverend gennulman once gave it the name. O' course, thing have changed a mite since his time—'

When it was time for the guests to alight, they walked enthusiastically over the mercifully dry ground towards Clay One. The afternoon shift was in full production, the clayworkers having been warned in no uncertain terms by Hal Tremayne that their wages would be docked if they dared to make cat-calls or disgraced themselves in any way.

They knew better than to disobey. Besides, they were only too glad that all this railway nonsense had been settled. There wasn't a man there who wished to return to the old method of transporting the clay blocks by heavy waggon down the steep and hazardous streets of St Austell, when the rail trucks did it all so effortlessly.

By the time the shift was over, and the clayworkers' wives were tugging the long heavy clay boots from their menfolks' feet, the guests were safely back at Killigrew House, enjoying the hospitality of the house and the successful young Killigrews, and feeling pleased with themselves that they had been the first to risk the rail tracks again, which would all be reported in the Truro newspaper.

'Who'd ever have thought young Morwen Tremayne 'ould be such a fitting wife for the boss?' more than one shiftworker commented. 'A fine lady she be now, and 'tis to her credit that she don't turn up her nose at we because on it.'

They were all in an expansive mood today, because the resumption of the railway meant prosperity for Killigrew Clay, and that meant prosperity for all of them. Even if it had an entirely different meaning for the poorest clayworker to that of Ben Killigrew.

They had had enough of strikes, and lay-offs and arguments. They wanted full bellies for their children and sound roofs over their heads, and that was what the rail tracks meant to them.

Let the fine Killigrews enjoy their own style of life, just so long as the clayworkers had their own humbler needs satisfied.

And at Killigrew House that afternoon, the fine folk thought enviously that Ben Killigrew was indeed fortunate to have such a vivacious and beautiful wife, who dispensed hospitality as though she had been born to it. As Morwen caught her Mammie's approving glance, she smiled inwardly.

Why, it was easy after all to act the lady, she thought in some surprise. *In the right clothes and the right setting, and with the support of a good man, anyone could do it…*

But it was more than that, and most there were aware of it. Morwen had a natural grace and charm, and once, when she almost swore she caught a little wink from Jane Askhew, she realised how much she was enjoying herself. Killigrew's lady had truly arrived.

Chapter Seventeen

Killigrew Clay was at its busiest at despatching times, in the spring and autumn of the year. The clay blocks, dried and scraped in the sun, were loaded into the little rail trucks, now stripped of their finery used for the excursion rides, and ready for service once more. Hal Tremayne watched the last of them leave Clay One with a feeling of immense relief and satisfaction.

For a while it had seemed inevitable that the old clay waggons would have to be brought back into use, and not since the disaster four years ago had the waggons careered through the town, scattering clay dust and angering the good townsfolk.

To revive the old method of clay transporting would also revive all the memories of that horrific day when poor baker Nott had been crushed, along with the foolhardy clayworkers who went blacklegging in order to feed their families during the strike.

They were bad times, Hal thought. He wanted to see no more of them. But now the last of the autumn clay had been sent to Charlestown port, and the clayworkers had watched it go with rousing cheers. And Ben Killigrew sent word that there would be a few extra pennies in each wage packet that week in celebration of the fact.

'A few extra pennies!' Dora Tremayne echoed, when Sam reported as much at the cottage. 'What good will that do for the likes o' we, when Killigrew and his kind are feasting on red meat every day, and we'm still trapping rabbits when we can—'

Sam gave an impatient sigh. Dora seemed to take delight in finding arguments where there were none. She was not like the true Tremayne women, who dug their heels in grimly when troubles came, and did all they could to help their menfolk survive. Sam was very much afraid that Dora would simply lie down and weep if their lives were ever in any real danger. She was not like his mother, or Morwen...

'I suppose you'm including our Morwen in the Killigrews,' he snorted. 'She were allus good to 'ee, Dora, for all that 'ee never really got on—'

Dora sniffed. 'She allus thought herself too high and mighty for we, and you know it, Sam Tremayne. Your Morwen's a Killigrew now all right. You only had to see her in her new clobber on the train to know that. And then to be entertaining all they posh folks! Your Mammie told me how fine it all were!'

'Well, how do you expect our Morwen to behave, now she's Ben's wife?' Sam was angry at the need to defend his sister to her. His needs were simple. As long as his men did their work, and his children were fed, he wanted his family to get along well together. All too often he'd had to listen to Dora criticising Morwen, and he'd had enough of it.

'Ben Killigrew's wife! She don't know the half of what 'tis like to fend for a parcel o' babbies—'

'That's enough, Dora!' Sam thundered. 'I'll not hear another word about our Morwen in this house. You know she'd give her right arm to have one healthy babby like ours, let alone three—'

'From the looks o' Walter, there's one on 'em who's not too healthy.' Dora's anger evaporated. 'He's looking poorly, and if 'tis the measles, then pray to God that we'll have enough pennies to pay for his doctoring.'

Instantly, Sam was all concern.

'Why didn't you tell me this before, instead of babbling on so? As to doctoring – there's plenty I 'ouldn't ask Ben for, but I'd beg for a doctor for my children, if need be.'

The children had been put to bed long ago, but one look at Walter, flushed and muttering irritably in his sleep, told its own story.

'I'll go to Penwithick for Doctor Growse. 'Tis the nearest, and I'm taking no chances if 'tis the measles—'

'Sam – if 'tis, there's nothing he can do. He'll only tell us to keep un warm and comfortable and give un plenty to drink – 'twill wait till morning. Sam, don't go tonight—'

He looked at her keenly. Poor pretty Dora, looking as harassed as a fishwife already with the strain of worrying over Walter. Heaven help her in a real catastrophe, Sam thought fleetingly. But he knew she was right.

He'd heard other folks tell of how the measles had to run its course. There was no treatment. They could only offer up prayers that Walter would get better.

'All right, lamb,' he touched her soft tangle of hair. 'Anyway, it might not be the measles that ails un at all. It might be no more'n a chill. We'm in for a spell of wet weather by the looks, an' 'twill do no harm to keep un indoors for a while. If he looks any worse tomorrow, then I'll get the doctor.'

For once Dora didn't bother to ask who was going to pay for it. She was weary. Her sister-in-law could have no idea about caring for three children, and Dora thought enviously of Morwen in her big posh house with her servants…

Not that she'd want Ben Killigrew for a husband. She had only ever wanted Sam. Only somehow the wanting and the loving had got pushed to the back of everyday living lately. She looked at the large frame of him, almost filling the small cottage. He looked at her at the same moment, and a spark of the old awareness passed between them.

The children were asleep, and she and Sam were here, cosy and warm… he held out his arms to her, and she went into them, fitting there as snugly as a clayworker's boot on a cobbler's last. For a little while she would forget everything but being Sam's wife…

For the next week it rained heavily, and little Walter Tremayne grew progressively more miserable as he was confined to the cottage with the measles. Doctor Growse had confirmed the disease, and Morwen had sent word to say that the doctor should attend her brother's children as often as needed, and that the medical bills would be dealt with by her husband.

'I understand that ever since a visiting child was ill at her home, your sister was anxious that your young ones shouldn't take ill,' the doctor said. 'Walter is a very mild case, fortunately. On no account must he leave the cottage though, and risk others catching it. If the others show any symptoms, keep them in bed for a few days, then in the house for three weeks.'

Walter howled with rage when he learned he had to stay indoors. The outing to the sea for the clayworkers' children was planned for next week, and he was going to miss it. Dora answered him crossly.

'Well, you'll just have to miss it an' that's that,' she snapped. 'Albert and Primmy can't go neither. I'll have to stay home with 'ee all too. Your Daddy must go, because he's to be the rear guard on the train, but he won't enjoy it without us!'

'I wanted to go!' Walter wept. 'I couldn't go last time 'cos o' Primmy making you feel bad inside. 'Tain't fair!'

'There's nothing I can do about it, Walter, so you'd best be quiet or I shall slap 'ee! Just play wi' your puppets or summat while I see what's making Primmy so fretful.'

But she guessed before she lifted the baby's little nightshirt. Primmy had the tell-tale red spots, and it soon became certain that Albert's show of temper when he heard that none of them was going on the outing, was due to the onset of his measles too. Thank God that none of them ailed too badly, Dora thought fervently, and thank God for the hardy Tremayne stock.

Sam informed his family of the children's illness, and although it was thought wiser for none of them to visit the cottage, Morwen sent up a huge basket of fruit, and some sweets and delicacies to keep them cheerful.

'She means well, I daresay,' Dora said grudgingly. 'It still feels like charity, though.'

'You know Mammie don't like to hear you talk about our Morwen that way,' Sam said edgily.

'Then I shan't say it when she can hear me,' Dora rounded on him. 'But I can't help how I feel, Sam, and your Morwen's grown away from the rest on us.'

–

It continued to rain. Low grey clouds scudded across the sky, and a cold wind whipped into faces and tugged at skirts and jackets. Dora was almost glad they didn't need to venture out in it, although the enforced isolation was making everyone in the cottage irritable.

Once Walter began to recover and to become scratchy with everyone around him, he spent hours at the thick window-glass, bemoaning the fact that the outing was coming nearer, and praying that the rain would continue so that they might postpone it until he could attend.

''Tis wicked to wish for the day to be spoiled for the other children,' Dora said with rough sympathy. 'Besides, the little uns couldn't go now, with the measles, and it 'ouldn't be fair for you to go neither—'

He howled with fury, but the matter was resolved by the weather brightening, and the rain ceasing. It was oozing mud underfoot for a few days, but the wind did much to dry it out, and the day was fair for the children's outing, and the little Tremayne children had no choice but to remain indoors with their mother, while Sam took the packed train to the sea.

'I promise to bring 'ee back some shells to string and some pebbles to paint,' Sam said, as Walter beseeched him to take him along.

He hated to deny his son anything, but the doctor had been adamant. The risk was too great, both to Walter himself and all the other clayworkers' children on the outing. Sam himself had had the measles when very young, and had survived it, so it was considered no risk for him to be with the other families.

Looking at Dora's flushed pretty face, harassed with the children, he prayed that she wouldn't succumb to it too. Three sick children and a sick wife were trouble indeed.

Before he left the cottage, he hugged all his family, one by one, lingering with his arms around Dora, feeling her softness against him, loving her more each day, despite the caustic tongue she had developed of late.

'Be gentle with 'em, dar,' he said softly. 'They'm only little uns, and they'm fair sick wi' disappointment. We'll make it up to 'em. We'll take 'em to the sea ourselves when they'm all well again.'

Dora bit back the retort that such outings hadn't come their way much before, with the long journey down to the sea and no means of getting there excepting their own good feet! This wasn't the time to gripe, when Sam was clearly upset at his family's snivellings. She hugged him back, whispering that she'd have a good hot meal ready for his return, and that they'd all be eager to hear how the day went.

'Don't forget the pebbles and shells,' Walter said miserably. Sam spoke gravely.

'I promise I won't forget. I'll bring back the finest collection 'ee ever saw. Now I must go, or they'll leave without me. Be good for your Mammie.'

He waved to the little group of them, framed in the doorway of the stone cottage, told Dora to take them inside, and turned away quickly. He couldn't bear to see the sad young faces of his sons one second longer.

–

Killigrew Clay was in a high old state of excitement. Work at the pit continued with a skeleton shift, consisting of those clayworkers who had no children or were too old to care for travelling to the sea, or who downright mistrusted the new-fangled rail tracks, pronounced safe or not.

For the vast majority, today was a holiday. Whole families poured down the hillside towards the proud little railway, spruced up and gleaming. The bal maidens wore their brightest garb, their long hair swinging beneath their bonnets; the young men smirked and preened themselves as they caught any pretty girl's eye; the small children chattered like bees, clinging to their parents' hands and jumping up and down for sheer pleasure.

Ostensibly this was an outing for the children, but it had rapidly developed into a day out for anyone who cared to join in. Ben Killigrew had been expansive in his instructions.

All who worked for Killigrew Clay were included in this special day, and long before the engine groaned into life, the train was packed to capacity; ribald tales were being bandied about; the baskets of food the women had packed were in danger of being squashed or eaten long before they ever reached the sea.

Ben and Morwen had decided that they would not take part in the works outing. This was for the families as a gesture of thanks for their long hours of hard work, and the presence of the bosses might well inhibit their enjoyment.

It had been strange for Morwen to think of herself in those terms, but she saw the sense in Ben's words. So too, did Bess and Hal, who had also declined the invitation, thinking this was best left to the younger clayworkers to enjoy themselves. Hal would take charge of the day shift at Clay One, and Bess was meeting Morwen in the town.

–

Morwen imagined the day with an odd little tug of nostalgia, all the same. Ben's rail tracks had once been no more than a distant dream. When she and Celia had been bal maidens for Killigrew Clay, that dream had never seemed remotely possible. How they too would have enjoyed this day, giggling and flirting with all the young men, togged up in their Sunday clothes...

Her breath caught in her throat. Such dreams... Ben was one of the lucky ones. He had his rail tracks. While Celia... Morwen forced herself to think the words that were still so horrific to her... Celia had drowned herself in the clay pool. And Morwen herself... living as Ben's wife was a dream that had seemed even more of an impossibility, which only went to prove to Morwen's logical mind that dreams sometimes did come true. If you wanted them badly enough...

She finished tidying herself and smiled at her mirrored reflection. How fine she looked. Quite the lady now. She should be grateful. She had everything she ever wanted – almost. And today, while the clay folk enjoyed the benefits of Ben Killigrew's fortunes, she and her Mammie were spending their hour at Fielding's Tea Rooms, rubbing shoulders with the refined matrons of St Austell.

And if one secret part of her was away up on the moors, careering down the hillside in the little train that was surely alive with the screams of excitement by now, then she was not going to acknowledge it for one moment.

The hillside was crowded with onlookers and well-wishers giving the clayworkers' outing a good send-off. Sam Tremayne stood outside the last truck, waving his arms like windmills to the front of the train, where any hope of whistling or shouting to the driver was completely drowned by the din.

But at last there was a movement from the engine, and Sam leapt on board the last truck, where he managed to squeeze in between the assortment of baskets and bodies, and reminded himself that he was enjoying it all.

Truth to tell, it wasn't the same without Dora and the children. He wouldn't have admitted it to her, to make her even more depressed, but being among all these other families in an official capacity made him miss his own even more.

They were as close-knit as his own parents' family had been, Sam thought with great satisfaction. It was right and proper, but he thanked God for it all the same. Such closeness wasn't given to all.

The train lurched and rattled, and the children screeched with pretended fear every time they went over a bump. The bal maidens screamed too, clutching on to the young clayworkers when there was no real need, knowing that the swaying train was excuse enough to be held tight in a young man's embrace for a few clandestine moments. Together with the echoing cheers of the crowds left behind on the hilltop, the noise was deafening.

'Why don't we all sing a sea shanty?' Sam tried to make himself heard. 'Seems right, since we'm going to the sea!'

Those in the same truck and the one directly in front agreed at once, and a lusty chorus began, quickly taken up by those who wanted to sing, and shouted down by those who didn't.

'I'll give 'ee a penny for a fishy from the sea –
I'll give 'ee tuppence more for a kiss –
I'll give 'ee a smile to charm an old salt's heart –'

The singing came to an abrupt end as the shouting from the front of the train changed to terror.

The noise of the engine and the excitement of the crowds on and off the train had disguised the sudden ominous rumbling beneath the overloaded trucks. Those at the front realised it first, and even as Sam and the rest of them were still gathering their wits, they saw what seemed like a sudden kaleidoscope of colour as the passengers began throwing themselves off the train in their haste to get away from this steaming monster.

'Keep calm!' Sam shouted. ''Tis nothing. There's nothing to fear. The tracks have been pronounced safe–'

'You try telling that to Ben Killigrew when your babbies be crying wi' fear, Sam Tremayne!' a woman screamed back at him, snatching her child in her arms and running from the train.

All around him, the panic spread. Despite it, the train still chugged forward at its normal pace, reaching the brow of the hill before it began its winding descent. As if the driver was desperate to get the train away from any hint of danger, the engine gave an extra spurt once the brow was reached.

At the same instant it seemed to Sam as though the whole hillside began to cave in. He felt as though he was watching it in slow motion, and yet the truth was spinning through his head; the awful knowledge that the subsidence was there all the time; that the new chief engineer had been careless in his assessment; that although the front of the train was hauling on over the brow, at the rear the ground began to split beneath the tracks as if in the throes of an earthquake...

'God help us, Sam Tremayne!' someone screeched in his ear, clutching at him as if he was personally responsible.

Children screamed; women sobbed loudly; people scrambled over each other, uncaring who they trampled in the process, trying to get out, trying to survive...

''Tis worse if 'ee panic! Get out in a sensible fashion!' he roared, but his voice went unheard.

And then there was a metallic snapping sound. The last three trucks snapped from the rest of the train as the ground opened up fully, and the last truck of all plunged deep into the earth, the other two piling on top of it.

—

The watchers at the top of the hill couldn't really believe what they were seeing. One minute they were waving and cheering, and saying what a fine boss Ben Killigrew was, to make all this possible. The next, they were seeing a nightmare happen in front of their eyes, as the last three trucks of the train seemed to leap up in the air for a second, then buckle and disappear into a great gaping hole.

They rushed forward in a great mass. The ground that had been so sodden with rain until this fair day, clogged their boots or their bare feet, hampering their movements. When they reached the scene, they were met by deranged, bewildered folk, rushing back from the front trucks of the train, thankful to be alive, and desperate to get the others out.

If the earth was heavy above ground, there was a great cloud of dust rising from the huge hole, where the tangled wreckage of the last and second trucks lay far below. The truck that had been the most forward of the broken ones, stuck up into the air at an incongruous angle, but those on board it were able to scramble out with no more than cuts and bruises.

A short way down could be detected the crude tunnellings of an old disused tin mine, its walls intact enough to hold together until the added constant weight of the clay trucks had weakened them. Today they had finally disintegrated.

''Tis a rogue shaft, just as were suspected—'

'Never mind what 'tis! Get 'em out! Get down there and pull 'em out! Get the babbies first—'

The cries went up, and hands clawed at the truck above ground, using it as a means of climbing down to reach the trapped and injured. Each truck had held about twenty people, far more than its capacity, and strewn over the ground was pathetic evidence of what the helpers might find. A child's soft shoe; a broken picnic basket, apples and bread scattered everywhere; a woman's shawl caught on the twisted metal.

'Somebody had best go to the town an' tell Ben Killigrew what's happened. An' go for Hal Tremayne at Clay One—'

'What of Sam's wife? She should be told—'

Gil Dark, pit captain of Clay Two, took charge as no-one seemed fit to do anything but issue instructions that weren't being carried out. Since neither Hal nor Sam Tremayne were available, he spoke sharply.

'Not yet. There's no sense worrying her yet, till we find what's left of un. Pray God he ain't too badly cut about – and somebody fetch a doctor. Go to St Austell and to Penwithick. Get whoever will come. You, Tom Storey, and you, Billy Chard—'

The train had been brought to a stop by now, and the driver had run to join the rest of them. He was white with terror, the stain in his breeches telling how the accident had affected him, and it was proof of his anguish that he didn't even notice it.

He volunteered quickly to go to Killigrew House to tell the boss of the disaster. Anything to get away from the scene on the hill… the shock made him too useless to do anything more, and he was sent off at once.

Gil Dark tried to get some order into the feverish searching for the injured. Women wept openly at the sight of the poor little injured children being brought out one by one. Some had broken limbs. Some were badly gashed on the face or body. Some were so bruised and shocked they didn't really understand what had happened.

What was gradually considered to be something of a miracle, was that none of them, nor the adults with them, had perished. They were still alive. However badly hurt, bones could mend, and cuts could heal.

They waited anxiously for the more intrepid of the helpers to climb down to the deepest truck, which had been badly crushed in the fall. Although those who had been rescued from it had survived, the injuries in the last truck were more serious than the rest.

The ground above resembled the aftermath of a battlefield, with groaning, blood-stained people sprawling about, being tended to as best the clayworkers could until doctors could be reached.

A voice came up from the depths of the hole.

'We've found Sam Tremayne. He don't look too good. We'm trying to get un out, but his legs be trapped, and he's bleedin' from his chest—'

The news spread rapidly among the crowd. It was as though a blanket had been thrown over them all as their own voices became muffled and subdued, waiting for news. Sam Tremayne was well liked. All the Tremaynes were. Sam Tremayne was the brother-in-law of the boss, and as such was to be respected, but that meant less than the fact that Sam was still one of them.

Long before they managed to get him out, Doctor Growse from Penwithick had arrived and was tending to the more superficially wounded, though more anxious every minute for the recovery of Sam Tremayne. The longer the weight of those trucks lay on his chest, the worse for him. Any fool could see that, and privately, the doctor thought that the way these simple clay folk were bolstering themselves up with hope was plain foolishness.

But he was wise enough not to say so, and wished to heaven that the older and more experienced Doctor Pender would arrive to give him some support.

–

The driver of the train had been gone for what seemed like hours. Doctor Pender still hadn't come, and nor had Sam Tremayne been rescued from the wreckage when the anxious clay folk saw the lumbering figure of Hal Tremayne toiling painfully up over the hill.

Bess had used the trap to go into town, and Hal's face was nearly puce with effort as he climbed the steep hill, finding the exertion far greater than even a few months ago. But his haste to be at Sam's side overcame all other considerations – even the sawing pain around his heart that had occurred several times recently, and seemed vastly accentuated now.

'I'll bargain with 'ee, God,' Hal mouthed to the wind. 'Give me breath to see my son safely brought into the daylight, and I'll go wi' a good grace if need be.'

He heard the sound of thundering hoofbeats, and almost gagged with relief as the doctor's trap stopped alongside him.

'Get in, man,' Doctor Pender said abruptly, 'Or I shall have another patient on my hands before the day's out.'

He had nearly said another corpse, but there was no use in anticipating the worst, especially when Hal Tremayne looked near to collapse already. God knew what that family would do if their eldest boy was dead…

–

They brought Sam out lovingly and reverently. By the time they did so, the sky had darkened again, almost as if it too was in mourning for what the majority of the watchers already knew in their hearts. There was only one fatality from the train disaster, and that one was the clayworkers' staunchest supporter and friend, Sam Tremayne.

Chapter Eighteen

Hal cradled the crushed body of his eldest son in his arms. It was funny. Not rib-tickling funny, but queer funny. His son Matt had gone away to America, and the odds were that they would never see him again. Jack had left the clay works and was establishing himself as a boat-builder, and that hadn't hurt as he had once thought it might.

Even the thought of his youngest, Freddie, going away to some posh London school and putting on airs, had been a minor hurdle, compared with this. But then Sam was his first-born, the one who had always followed so doggedly in Hal's footsteps, the echo of himself. Sam was the one he knew in his heart he would always weep for the most…

'Mr Tremayne, there's nothing you can do for him,' he heard the quiet voice of Doctor Pender in his ear. 'Come away, I beg you, and others will see to him. He'll be taken to a decent place until – arrangements can be made, since I know there's no room for him at his cottage.'

Hal felt a brief anger. 'No room for him at his own cottage? Are you mad? Where else would a man go to be cared for and loved?'

'Mr Tremayne, Sam's dead.' The doctor spoke slowly, as though Hal were simple-minded, and needed time to understand. 'I only mean what's best. His poor young wife will need your help, and the children will be frightened—'

They couldn't be frightened of their Daddy…

Hal looked down at Sam, the dearest of all his sons, and felt himself become an old man. This should not be! God had betrayed him. It should be his place to go first, not this virile young man with all of life ahead of him. With a pretty young wife, and the three children...

He choked back the stinging tears, feeling less of a man than he had ever felt at that moment, because death made him so helpless. But he knew the doctor was right. Sam's family would need all the support now. Dora... how would Dora take this terrible news? And who would tell her?

As though Sam, himself, was providing the answer, Hal knew that he must be the one. He couldn't leave it to his womenfolk, and a doctor was too distant. Dora had no family now but the Tremaynes. This was Hal's duty. His shoulders squared.

'You'll see that he's – taken care of, then?' His voice dragged with pain. 'His wife will want to see him.'

Doctor Pender nodded. 'There's a special room set aside for such purposes near Penwithick church. Mrs Tremayne will be at liberty to attend at any time, and there is a watchman always on duty. I know your family will all want to pay their respects.'

He spoke delicately, knowing how grief could put a knife-edge on anyone's nerves, and this one looked as though he was due for some attention himself before very long. He made a mental note to get Hal Tremayne to his consulting-room for an examination soon. Right now, the man would almost certainly reject any such suggestion. All his thoughts were with his son.

Hal bowed his head, knowing he must comply. He couldn't seem to think properly. The rest of the family must be told, but Dora must learn of it from him, and no-one else. At the doctor's persuasion, he allowed other hands to take Sam from him, and watched as they put him gently on to a cart and covered him.

'I'll go to my daughter-in-law,' he said heavily.

'You'll ride with me, man, and Doctor Growse will see to things here for the present. Those too sick to be tended in their own homes must be sent to hospital—'

'I'll walk,' Hal said sharply. He didn't want to be cosseted. Nor did he want to hear about folk who would get well. His own misery was too acute. He needed to share it with Dora. She had a right to it. More right than even he did.

They all watched him leave without a second glance at the dark shape on the cart. To him, it wasn't Sam any more. Sam was the son who always spoke simply of his beloved clay country, and never dressed it up with fancy words like porcelain earth or white hills. Sam was a plain, honest man, like Hal himself.

He walked across the moors as though in a dream, not heeding the fact that behind him Ben had just arrived at the disaster scene, sliding off his lathering horse to hear in horror that Sam Tremayne was dead.

Hal strode past the works that hummed with its own noise, avoiding the main sections before anyone began wondering why Hal Tremayne was going past instead of coming back to the day shift. None of those watchers on the moor had dared leave their posts until they knew the outcome of the accident, and the hillside had muffled the worst of the noise. None would have taken any message to the young widow until they knew for certain, in the peculiar respect the moorland folk had for each other. It was Hal Tremayne's place…

He squared his shoulders when he reached the old cottage that had always held so much love, first with his own family, and now Sam's. It was a continuity that had charmed him. And now it was over. He pushed open the door and met Dora's pleased and surprised eyes, and wished painfully that he could have kept that moment for ever, and never had to tell her...

–

Bess and Morwen laughed happily together over the thought of Jack being head over heels in love with Annie Boskelly.

'You didn't expect our handsome Jack to stay unattached for ever, did 'ee, Mammie?' Morwen teased. 'There's more than one bal maiden who's given him the glad eye—'

'I hardly expected it so soon!' Bess exclaimed. 'Barely a few months gone from home, and already he's changed. He's become a man, with that special look in his eyes that a young man has when he's besotted with a pretty girl.'

Her own eyes softened. It was the way of things. Her children couldn't remain children, but she felt a faint regret that the sweet years couldn't last a little longer.

She felt the soft touch of Morwen's hand covering hers. 'Mammie? Don't be sad about it!'

Bess gave a small sigh. 'I'm not sad for un, lamb. I'm very happy. It's just – I wish we all stopped to savour the young times more than we do. We rush through the days, and suddenly we turn around and our babbies have grown. We all do it. We never learn—'

One of the ladies at a nearby table complained loudly to her companion as a group of youths raced down the cobbled hill. Such a sudden commotion was going on outside, it almost drowned out Bess's last words to her daughter, but Morwen thought with some relief that if it stopped her Mammie's brief feeling of gloom, then it was all to the good.

To the lady customer's annoyance, the door of the Tea Room suddenly burst open, and a passer-by shouted excitedly.

'There's been a cave-in o' Killigrew's rail tracks. There's hundreds on 'em up there, dead or injured, an' they'm saying that Ben Killigrew will be ruined after this!'

The lout ran off, while Bess and Morwen sat rock-still for a few frozen seconds. Morwen's heart pounded so fast she feared she would collapse over the tea table, and thought incongruously that the lady alongside them would be even more outraged if she did. She felt her mother's hand gripping her arm.

'Is it true, do 'ee think?' Bess gasped. 'Or is it some terrible hoax?'

Morwen was already on her feet. Folk didn't invent such stories. Those such as the leering lout at the door of the Tea Room didn't have the gumption. It was true. It had to be true…

Miss Fielding hovered near for the money for her tea and fruit buns.

'I'll pay you next time,' Morwen snapped. 'If the tale is true, my mother and me have more important matters to see to.'

Behind her she heard the muttering of the townsladies to the effect that Morwen Tremayne could sometimes act the real madam since she'd become the wife of Ben Killigrew.

Morwen didn't care. Nothing mattered but finding out about the rail tracks for herself. It was the day of the children's outing. None of her own family would have been on the train except her brother Sam. But they were all families that she knew. They were part of her childhood. She bundled Bess into the Killigrew trap, and screamed at the horse to move.

And if St Austell thought her as mad as old Zillah as they careered through the town and up over the moors, she cared nothing for that either.

Was this old Zillah's earthquake? The crazy thought leapt into her mind. Was this, after all, the end to the mysterious warning the old crone had given to Morwen and Celia all that time ago? The earth collapsing beneath Ben's rail tracks in which he took such a pride? The unwelcome thoughts swam and hammered through her brain.

'Hold on, Mammie,' Morwen said finally between gritted teeth. 'We're almost there.'

She didn't need any more telling that the rumour was true. The scene reminded Morwen instantly of the disaster at poor old Nott's bakery four years ago. And yet it was not the same. Nor was it due to the irresponsibility of drunken clayworkers. The great gaping hole in the ground with the last truck still crazily sticking out of it told her that this was on an even bigger scale.

The whole hillside seemed strewn with weeping women and bewildered men, and crying children with poor broken little bodies lying higgledy-piggledy, awaiting medical attention. Morwen and Bess almost fell from the trap in their haste, their hearts pounding with sick fear.

–

'Morwen! Over here!'

Even as she and Bess stumbled across the sodden earth, and it slowly began to dawn on her that folk were avoiding her eyes, Morwen heard Ben's voice. Ben was here already! For a split second Morwen felt wild relief, for Ben was always capable of taking control and putting everything right.

One look at his face, and she knew something had happened that even he couldn't undo.

'What is it?' she whispered, as his arms went around her. Somehow his arms seemed to enclose Bess as well, and Morwen heard her mother begin to weep hopelessly as Ben told them.

'Not our Sam. Oh, dear God, not our Sam!' Bess wept, her bones seeming to crumble to chaff as she leaned against her son-in-law for support.

'They've taken him to a lying-in room at Penwithick church, and your Daddy's gone to tell Dora,' Ben said, his voice thick at having to tell them.

He, too, was as sick inside as a man could be. He had lost a good brother-in-law and held himself totally responsible for all the pain here today, and God knew what the costs of the day would be.

He took on the knowledge unflinchingly, and although this wasn't the time to be thinking of his own future, the sickness was in his soul all the same. And he would have given the earth to spare his wife these agonising tidings about her brother.

'We must go to the cottage,' Morwen sobbed. 'Dora will need us. She can't be alone with the children. I'll stay with her if she'll let me, Ben. You can send up some of my clothes—'

It was terrible to think about clothes, but being practical took away some of the horror for a moment or two. She still couldn't believe Sam was dead. She wouldn't believe it yet. It was the same when Celia had died. Until she saw Celia lying-out… until she touched her and kissed her, and made her peace with her, she hadn't been able to believe it.

The thought of seeing and touching Sam didn't frighten her. He was still her brother, and she needed to say goodbye.

'You're strong, Morwen,' she heard Ben say raggedly in her ear. 'Be strong for your family.'

She gave a small nod, knowing that she didn't want to be strong. She wanted to scream that this wasn't happening… but Bess needed her daughter's strength. Her mother suddenly seemed so small and frail and dazed.

Dora would need her too. And the children. She and Ben were godparents to Sam's children. They were partly their responsibility now. She put her arm around Bess.

'We'll go to the cottage right away. Will you come with us, Ben?' Her eyes pleaded with him. If so many folk needed her, then how much more did she need him. He shook his head.

'I shan't leave here, dar, until the last person is safely taken home or to hospital, and the wreckage is recovered. And then I shall go immediately to see Daniel Gorran and Richard Carrick, and get in touch with the Bodmin engineers. I shall see you when I can.'

She turned away with her mother, not wanting to add to Ben's troubles by weeping for his company. Their lawyer would have plenty to say on the negligence of the new chief engineer in pronouncing the rail tracks safe.

But in the end it was Ben's railway, and Morwen knew very well that he would shoulder the blame and compensate where he could. For the first time, the snide remark made in Fielding's Tea Room struck home forcefully. Could this really ruin him? It was too awful to think about, and she blotted it out of her mind for the time being. She helped her mother carefully into the trap and took her to Sam's cottage.

–

'She don't want to talk about it,' Hal muttered, when they had put their arms around Dora, and found her to be as cold as a statue. 'She keeps saying Sam'll be home later, and she's not goin' to worry her head about it just now. I'm feared for her. 'Tain't natural. She should weep and clear her soul—'

Bess sat bouncing Primmy on her knee. The child cooed and smiled, and no-one noticed her. The little boys climbed all over Morwen, asking curious questions.

'Why be 'ee all so sad?' Walter demanded to know. 'We didn't know 'ee was coming to visit. Can I come to the big house one day?'

'One day, love,' Morwen murmured. She looked desperately at her father. The children had to be told. Presumably no-one had done so yet. She looked at Dora.

'Shall I take the boys upstairs to play with their puppets, and tell them about today?' she said carefully.

'All right.' Dora seemed distant. She sat aimlessly twisting her hands together, not offering refreshment or hospitality to the family wanting so desperately to help her.

Morwen picked up Albert, still miserable with the measles, and told Walter to follow them. They perked up. Morwen was more fun than their Mammie. Morwen would always play with them and tell them stories…

It was Bess who made them all a hot drink, needing something to do with her hands, while Hal rocked Primmy awkwardly. He felt so useless.

'We'll have to get a message to our Jack,' he said abruptly. 'And we should get Freddie out of school afore somebody else tells un.'

'And Matt,' Bess said, her voice catching in her throat. 'Who's going to tell our Matt?'

Before Hal could think of anything to say to comfort her, there was a loud wailing from upstairs, and Walter and Albert came clattering down the stairs to throw themselves in Dora's arms. Their faces were brilliant with furious colour and disbelief. Morwen came slowly down after them, hating herself for shattering their small world.

''Tain't true, Mammie. Our Daddy's not dead, is he?' Walter sobbed. 'I don't want it to be true—'

'An' me don't,' Albert's echoing voice said chokingly.

Dora gathered them into her skirts, closing out the rest of them.

'They say 'tis true, my babbies. You two are going to be my big men now, and help me wi' Primmy. Will 'ee do that? Your Daddy 'ould want it. We'll go an' see un when he's laid out nice and smart, and 'ee can tell un so.'

Morwen wanted to swoon at the thought, but the little boys eventually nodded tearfully. They didn't really understand what it was all about, but as long as Dora insisted it was what their Daddy would want, then they had some purpose. And Dora herself still didn't seem to take it all in.

'I want to stay here with you for a while, Dora,' Morwen said gently. The other girl's head jerked up.

'What for? We don't need 'ee—'

Morwen forced back her usual impatience.

'I think you do, and I know the doctor will think so too. You'll need time to get used to – the new way of things – and I can help with the children. Please let me stay, Dora. Sam would want that, too, I know it.'

'Stay, Morwen. Stay wi' us!' the boys chanted at once.

'Well – I suppose so,' Dora said grudgingly. 'But I don't know where 'ee'll sleep. There's the corner where 'ee used to have the curtain across—'

'No!' Morwen said quickly.

She still remembered too vividly being in bed when Matt had pulled back the curtain holding the drowned, slime-covered body of her friend Celia.

'I'll sleep in the boys' bed. There's room for three, if they sleep end to end and leave me one side. They're only little uns.'

Poor little waifs, she thought suddenly. And what was going to happen to them now, with no man to bring in money to feed and clothe and house them?

Morwen insisted on the arrangement, and the boys were enchanted by it, their horror at their father's death already diminishing a little in their young minds by this new exciting turn of events, and by their mother's calm acceptance.

Was Dora right after all? Morwen wondered. She knew her own family better than the rest of them. But she wasn't convinced. A woman should cry for her man, just as in other circumstances a man should cry for his woman and feel no shame.

'Daddy, I think you should see about informing Jack and Freddie,' Morwen went on quietly, realising that she was fast taking control at the cottage. She had to, since Dora seemed incapable of coherent thought. She seemed to be carved out of stone, and only when the children needed attention did her arms and her voice respond automatically. Morwen was alarmed by the apathy she showed.

'The doctor will call in on you when he can, Dora. He'll want to give you something to make you sleep tonight—'

'I shan't sleep,' she stated rather than commented. 'I doubt that I shall sleep again without Sam there to warm me.'

'Dora, love, think of the babbies,' Bess said worriedly. 'You must get your rest to care for 'em—'

'Morwen can do that. She'll be here. I'll keep watch for Sam to come home.'

Primmy began to cry, and Hal handed her over thankfully to his wife, saying he'd best get off to St Austell and Truro, and he'd certainly be bringing the boys back to his own house with him. As soon as they could, they would want to see Sam.

'I'll tell un,' Dora said graciously. 'He'll be pleased to have a visit from all his folks.'

'Oh, God, what's happening to her?' Morwen whispered to her mother. 'Doesn't she realise?'

'I don't know, Morwen, but I'm thinking 'tis summat for the doctor to sort out. I'll go wi' your Daddy, and send word for one of the doctors to call as soon as possible. I don't like the look on her at all.'

'Mebbe 'tis the measles coming on,' Morwen said, and even as she said it, she prayed fervently that it was not.

Dora was never very robust, and for her to contract the measles on top of the shock of Sam's death was something Morwen didn't want to contemplate.

Once her parents had gone, Morwen set about preparing a hot meal of soup and bread for the children, and tried to make Dora eat some of it. She merely stirred it about, and then pushed it away, glancing through the window at the darkening sky.

'We must light the oil-lamps. Sam allus does it, but he's late tonight. Will 'ee put the babby to bed while I see to it, Morwen? She's too tired to wait up for her Daddy.'

'Dora! You know Sam won't be coming home tonight,' Morwen said, appalled at this.

'Well, put her to bed anyway. She's tired.' Dora neatly turned away every reference to Sam's death. It began to horrify Morwen. Dora was as flushed now as she had been pale before, and long after all three children had been put to bed, the girl was pacing up and down, peering through the window as though waiting for Sam's homecoming.

Ben had called in to see that they were all right, and promised to be back in the morning. He had looked haunted, and Morwen's heart had wept for him. He had told Dora briefly that he would pay for all Sam's expenses, and that she wasn't to worry over her family's welfare. And Dora had nodded and gave a half-smile.

'Sam will like that,' she'd said approvingly.

'I swear that her mind's turned,' Morwen had told Ben when they were out of earshot. 'I pray that it's only temporary. Please see if a doctor can call, Ben. I know they are terribly busy right now, but Dora needs help too.'

'I'll do what I can,' he promised. 'And what of you? Will you survive, my brave little love?'

Her throat felt thick as she nodded. She had lost a dear brother, but this family's loss was far greater. And Ben would be suffering for every other family whose members had been injured that day, while his own future was at stake. Morwen's own feelings seemed of very little importance at that moment.

'I'm a survivor, remember, dar?' she said huskily. 'Please go home and rest for a little while, and let tomorrow take care of itself.'

'We both know it won't, but I'll take some of your advice, for if I don't rest I shall drop. I shall miss you tonight.' He held her tightly, and kissed her soft mouth. Tonight of all nights, they should be together, to console one another on the tragedy. But even as she thought it, Morwen knew she must stay with Dora, who would never again know the comfort of her own man's arms around her.

–

They buried Sam in Penwithick churchyard a week later. The Tremayne family formed a silent, dignified group, with Ben Killigrew supporting the young widow, and Morwen holding on tightly to the three little children.

Ben had wanted to buy Dora a fine black dress for Sam's burying, but she had flatly refused in that strange unreal voice she had used since Sam's death, saying that he preferred her in light pretty clothes, and she saw no reason to dress any differently, when it was Sam's day.

She seemed to comprehend what was happening, and yet she had put a barrier between herself and any real pain. The doctor said it was delayed shock, and that once she was able to break down and weep for Sam, the barrier would be broken.

She hadn't done so yet. Morwen knew it for a fact. They had hardly been apart since she had moved into the cottage, and there had been no sounds of weeping through the bedroom walls, nor any evidence of swollen eyes. Morwen was desperately worried about it.

When her friend, Celia, had died, she had been told that grief after bereavement was as necessary as breathing. It needed to be expressed, and Morwen had already done her own share of it for Sam. She did it now, quietly, as they laid Sam to rest in his own beloved clay country, and one by one they walked around the grave, throwing in flowers for remembrance. For once, Morwen didn't linger by Celia's corner. Today was just for Sam.

Ben had sent Killigrew carriages for all of them, and once the burying was over, they all went back to Killigrew House for tea, since the children were now pronounced free enough of the measles. After a week at the cottage, it was strange to Morwen to be in her own home again.

The rooms were so big and high after the cramped confines of the cottage. The children loved the space and freedom, and it was good to see Freddie lose his pallor at today's ordeal, and begin playing with them on his hands and knees.

Morwen met Ben's eyes above the small cameo scene. They would survive, all of them. They had to. And Ben had plenty of trouble ahead of his own. She had learned briefly of the daily meetings that Ben was attending, and of how adamant the accountant Daniel Gorran had been against Ben's initial passionate avowal to tear up the entire railway system and sell up Killigrew Clay immediately.

The idea had been called foolish and a total waste, and that Ben must think again. And that Daniel Gorran would fight tooth and nail to exonerate Ben from this mess in the court case that was being brought against him by the indignant townsfolk, instigated so virtuously now by the Honourable Mrs Stanforth.

Morwen had been shocked to hear of a proposed court case, but Ben had seemed to expect it and to take it quite calmly – in a way, as though one anxiety eliminated a little of the pain of all the rest.

Morwen understood that feeling. She, too, had known it, and had shamedly known a faint relief when she'd thought of the disaster as being old Zillah's forecasted earthquake. It had happened, and therefore it couldn't happen again.

And that unworthy thought at such a time had made Morwen feel so guilty she knew she would never ever put it into words for anyone else to hear.

Chapter Nineteen

Bess was thankful for young Freddie's company at home. The school could do without him for a few days, and Jack didn't want to stay away from Truro too long. Bess could understand it. There was the added attraction of Annie Boskelly, as well as the job which Jack was obviously enjoying.

His talk was peppered with little anecdotes about Annie, until his mother asked him tartly if he'd forgotten that they had only recently buried his brother, and that it was hardly the time to be talking of frivolous matters.

Jack sounded strained when he answered.

'I don't ever forget our Sam, Mammie, but I can't live the rest of my life mourning un. Neither should you. Our Sam 'ouldn't want that. He once said that gloomy faces were a slight against God, who gave us our good country living.'

Jack wasn't given to religious utterances, and his face reddened at the frankness. But they had truly been Sam's words, and Bess recognised them at once. Her voice was gentle and sad.

'All the same, a man can never guess how hard 'tis for a woman to lose her sons.'

Jack put his powerful arms around her small frame, thinking as Morwen had done, how frail she had become. All the comfortable weight she had put on in recent years seemed to have disappeared, and she was as fragile as though a puff of wind would blow her away.

'You haven't lost Freddie and me, Mammie. And our Matt will turn up one of these fine days, you see if he don't.'

Bess felt her eyes mist. They all knew what she tried so hard to hide. That it was like losing a limb to have no news of Matt. If they only *knew* that he was well, then she would be content. The brief communication passed on through that odious woman, Hannah Pascoe, was completely unreliable as far as Bess was concerned, coming as it did from her awful son, Jude. Even though the woman had died horribly, Bess could still not think of her with any real compassion.

But she made an effort to be more cheerful for her family's sake. It did no good to wallow in grief once the crying was done, and she had done her crying for Sam. Any more of it would embarrass Freddie, who was at an impressionable age, and hanging on Jack's every word regarding the boat-building.

She would lose Freddie too, Bess thought sadly. But only over to Truro. He and Jack were not out of reach for ever, like the other two. She didn't have Jack's determined faith over Matt's return. He had made his choice.

'When can I come an' work with 'ee, our Jack?' Freddie was saying eagerly. 'I don't need no more schooling—'

'That's not what Ben 'ould say,' Bess reprimanded him. 'He says that schooling's important, and you've got another year yet. You're not at any old village school now, so be thankful for the chance, even if 'tain't that posh London school. If it weren't for Ben and our Morwen, you'd still be a kiddley boy and have no proper learning at all.'

'We've all got a lot to thank Ben Killigrew for,' Jack said half-grudgingly. ''Specially for marryin' our Morwen—'

'He married Morwen for love, not to help the likes of the Tremayne family!' Bess said indignantly, and then began to smile as she realised that Jack had been baiting her.

Jack gave her a hug. 'Thank God. I thought you'd forgotten how to smile, Mammie. That's the first smile I've seen since our Sam died. That's one to mark up.'

'Do 'ee reckon he's up there somewhere noting that Mammie's just been smiling?' Freddie said curiously, glancing at the ceiling. 'I don't reckon he'd mind. He liked a good laugh, our Sam.'

Bess found herself laughing and crying at the same instant at Freddie's words, and it was a good sound. Already the healing process had begun.

–

Morwen found it harder to come to terms with Sam's death, partly because of Dora's strangeness. Ben had come to the cottage several times on his way to and from Bodmin, and while he was visiting there, three days after the funeral, Dora announced she would take the children for a walk while the two of them had private words together.

''Tain't right for 'ee to be parted on my account,' she said prettily. 'Sam keeps saying 'ee should go home, Morwen. Think about it while we'm gone strolling.'

They watched her slender form as she wheeled the baby in the baby carriage, the little boys clinging to her skirts as ever, and Morwen swallowed the lump in her throat. What Dora was expressing wasn't bravery. It was something sinister and frightening, and Morwen didn't know what to do about it.

'What does the doctor say?' Ben asked at once.

'He's as helpless as anyone. He gives her sleeping potions that she doesn't take, and advice that she doesn't heed. He tells me to watch her, as if she's a kettle about to boil over. Sometimes, I think that's exactly what she is, Ben—'

'My sweet darling, don't take all her troubles on yourself!' Ben pulled her into his arms, and the feel of security she felt there was as powerful as any drug. If only she and Ben were together, perhaps she could cope with all this.

'Oh, Ben, I miss you so!'

The words burst out of her before she could stop them. She leaned her face against his cheek, cold from the morning air, and still felt warmed by his presence.

'God knows I miss you too, dar,' he muttered. 'The house is empty without you. Father keeps asking where you are, and only half understands what's happened. He had to be told, of course. Killigrew Clay is part of his life, but we softened it as best we could. I want you back, Morwen.'

His words were like sweet music to her, but even as he said them, and his hands moved down over her shoulders, and caressed the long curving shape of her spine and slid over her rounded hips, she shuddered slightly.

'Ben, we cannot find comfort in one another in this house, at such a time. 'Tis wrong—'

'How can it be wrong? It would be the only thing to keep me sane right now,' Ben said half angrily. 'God knows what will happen to us, Morwen. I didn't want to tell you yet, but we could be ruined over this business.'

He hardly noticed her small gasp as he went on.

'I'm insisting on paying the workers who suffered in the accident, and making good their hospital bills for the women and children. It's the least I can do, and it's a pittance compared with the enormous costs I fear will come from the court case. How do you feel at having the town of St Austell versus Ben Killigrew blazoned all over *The Informer*, dar?'

His voice was harsh with bitterness, and she knew how deeply he felt at this town turning on him, when he had done so much for them.

'Perhaps it won't come to that, Ben' she whispered, and he moved away from her, slumping down in a chair and leaning his head wearily against its hard wooden back.

'You were never one for burying your head in the sand, Morwen. Don't do it now. I don't want any false hopes. We're in a serious position, and we have to face it.'

She was frightened at hearing him speak like this. All her sorrow over Sam was smothered for the moment in her anxiety for Ben and their own future. Ben looked more beaten than she had ever seen him. And she should be by his side. She knew it. She rushed to him, kneeling on the rush matting floor to look into his eyes, her own full of love.

'Ben, darling, please don't look like that. Whatever happens, we will always have each other. We don't need wealth and position and a big house. It's only pride that makes folk want those things. When you look at others – like Dora, for instance – you know as well as I do that we already have all the riches in the world.'

For a second, she thought he wasn't going to respond. She reached up her hand to touch his cheek, and suddenly he caught her hand in his, twisting it to press it to his mouth.

He pulled her towards him, and somehow she was on his lap and his arms were holding her close, and he was crushing the breath out of her and saying against her mouth that she could always put things into perspective for him. Because of where they were, it was in no way a sexual embrace, but the love that flowed between them was as strong and binding as the vows they had once made at Penwithick church.

She wanted to stay in his arms for ever, but she knew that wasn't possible. Ben was on his way to Bodmin, and reluctantly he said that he must be on his way.

'But I have your faith in me, dar, and it's a talisman I cherish,' he said.

'And we shan't always be apart like this, Ben,' she whispered back. 'Dora must come to her senses soon, and then I shall come home.'

'And you and I will make up for lost time,' Ben said softly, knowing that while she still grieved for Sam she wouldn't want to be reminded yet of sleeping in his arms. But reminding her, too, that they were still young and healthy, and must continue to live their own lives.

When he had gone Morwen wandered about the cottage, doing the menial tasks she did for Dora, since the girl seemed incapable of settling to anything for long. She made a pretence at caring for the home and the children, but she spent long hours staring out of the window for Sam, and virtually did nothing.

Morwen was beginning to feel exhausted, but still believed that this situation couldn't last. Sooner or later the dam on Dora's emotions must break, and once her grief was out in the open she would be well again.

She had made them all a mid-day meal by the time Dora brought the children home from their walk. For the first time, the young widow seemed to realise something of Morwen's own strain, as she snapped at Dora for not eating properly.

'Why don't 'ee take a walk later, Morwen?' she said kindly. 'The babbies need a rest, and 'twill do 'ee good to get away from us for a while. There must be folk 'ee can visit hereabouts.'

Her concern was so different from the usual scratchy way she reacted to Morwen, and that in itself was an oddity. But the thought of getting away from the cottage for a short while was suddenly overwhelmingly attractive.

Where would she go? She didn't want to encounter sympathetic old friends who would be embarrassed by her presence. She wouldn't visit Bess, because she didn't want to stay away too long. But why visit anyone? Just to be alone on the moors would be comfort enough…

She nodded. 'You need time to be on your own too, Dora, and the children will only be upstairs. I daresay 'twill do us both more good than becoming each other's shadow.'

Morwen wrapped a woollen shawl around her shoulders, for the late September afternoons could become cool on the moors, and as she stepped away from the cottage, she felt as though she shed a heavy load. Until that moment she hadn't realised how claustrophobic the atmosphere at the cottage had been, and how introverted she, as well as Dora, had become.

It was so good to get well away from the huddle of cottages, skirting the clay works so that she did not have to answer any stilted, polite enquiries about her family, and walking towards the great open space of the moors she had always loved so much.

As she did so, it was as if she breathed new life, and even while she thought instantly of Sam and how he had loved it here too, she could suddenly think of him only with love, and therefore with fractionally less pain.

The scents and sounds of the moors were part of her life, the wild beauty and the sense of freedom an extension of her own emotions. In no other place had she ever felt so much attuned with nature – with some great universal plan that needed no fancy education to explain. To Morwen these things just were.

Who could explain the origins of the gaunt granite Larnie Stone, rearing out of the moorland mist? Around it she and Celia had walked so long ago, solemnly following old Zillah's instructions and hoping to find the face of their true love peering at them through the hole in the stone.

And Morwen had seen Ben, and tasted the first heady beginnings of love. Whatever else had happened that was bad and ugly, as when the hateful Jude Pascoe had raped her friend Celia, nothing could change those moments. The Larnie Stone had been the setting for those first wild sweet moments when Ben Killigrew had held her in his arms.

As she realised she was nearing the Larnie Stone now, Morwen caught her breath. For a second she felt no longer Ben's beloved and self-assured wife, but the uncertain, strikingly beautiful bal maiden, Morwen Tremayne, who dared to imagine that the boss's son could love her.

'Be 'ee dreamin' again, Mrs Killigrew?'

A voice that seemed to come right out of those lovely dreaming days jarred into Morwen's ears. She whipped round to find the weird woman of the moors leering at her. More wizened than ever now, Zillah leaned heavily on a gnarled stick, but her beady eyes were as bright and knowing as ever.

In an instant all Morwen's brief feeling of well-being vanished. This old crone and her evil ways… tempting folk into thinking they, too, could foretell the future by taking potions that could hurt and distort the mind…

''Tis more like a nightmare to be seeing you again,' Morwen snapped. Old Zillah cackled.

'You've not lost that fine old temper since you been wed to yon Killigrew boy, I see,' she wheezed. 'Nor been crushed in spirit like your brother was in body—'

'What do you know of our Sam?' Morwen hissed. 'Was all this some kind of wicked revenge, because Celia took the potion at one gulp and then drowned herself?'

What was she saying? She was becoming as crazy as this old woman. What could the train accident possibly have to do with Celia Penry's foolishness of four years ago? Morwen was angry with herself for appearing so gullible, and Ben would be just as angry if he ever got to hear of it.

'Your friend was a ninny,' Zillah said sharply. 'You were allus the sensible one, for all your wildness. You know full well we can make or break our own destiny, and if your brother hadn't been on the train, he'd be alive now, same as you and me.'

Morwen had never heard her speak so fluently, without the usual patois of the moorland folk. Was she really this articulate, and tempered her speech to suit those who consulted her? If so, Morwen was even more suspicious of her, and agreed fervently now with her mother, who had always forbidden Morwen to visit the old woman's hovel. A demand which had made the secret visits all the more exciting to Morwen and Celia, and occasionally young Freddie too. But it was no longer exciting.

All Morwen wanted now was to get away from this woman who knew Celia's secret too. Zillah knew about the baby that had to be destroyed before it was born because of the disgrace. Zillah knew why Celia had drowned herself when her mind was turned because of the shame…

She turned quickly to go back to Dora and the children. Even Dora's strangeness was more palatable than the obscure mutterings and warnings of Zillah. As if she wouldn't let Morwen get away without one last word, the old crone's mocking, rasping voice followed her.

'Fate's not done with 'ee yet, Morwen Tremayne Killigrew. There's more sorrow before rejoicing, mark me well!'

She wouldn't take any notice, Morwen thought furiously. It was all nonsense, evil, black magic. But it was a damnable truth that being as Cornish as Zillah herself, Morwen was only too inclined to give credence to things mysterious and unseen.

She walked more briskly back to the cottage over the pleasantly spongy turf. Since the rains had stopped, the drying winds and autumn sunshine had given a new burst of vitality to the ground. Sam had always loved times like this.

Autumn and spring were his two favourite times, the spring especially when the earth began to revive again after the long winter months. Morwen found the soft slow tears running down her cheeks in a final farewell of grief for Sam, and resolved that this would be the last time. She was helping no-one, and she had resolved to help Dora in any way she could…

–

She pushed open the cottage door, ready with cheerful words on her lips to tell Dora she was back. The cottage was quiet, and obviously the children were still resting after their walk that morning. Morwen crept inside in case Dora, too, was asleep, and then a noise from the small back scullery made her peer inside. She drew back in silent horror.

Dora was furiously ironing a small pile of Sam's shirts. Whether they had been washed or were still soiled, Morwen couldn't tell. What appalled her was the frantic way Dora worked, as though driven to it. Even as Morwen watched, Dora thrust the iron down and picked up the hot shirt, burying her nose in it and closing her eyes as though in ecstacy.

'What in God's name are you doing?' Morwen whispered.

Dora's eyes flew open. For a second she didn't speak, and then she threw the shirt away from her as quickly as she could. Her face suddenly crumpled, her whole body shook, and she stumbled past Morwen into the main room of the cottage and sank on to the hard settle. Morwen sat beside her, holding Dora's shaking hands in hers.

'Nobody knows how I feel!' Dora gasped out the words as if desperately short of breath. 'I'm not deranged or ill, Morwen. I know Sam's dead. I know I'll never see un again, or hold un again, and I'll never feel un holding me, and filling me with his love, and if it offends the fine lady 'ee've become, then I'm sorry. But I miss my Sam so much, and 'tis me that's dying without un. And I thought – if I iron his shirts, it brings out the smell o' my Sam's body, and I've got un with me a little while longer—'

It was the most she had ever said to Morwen. By the end of it Morwen was filled with anguish for her sister-in-law, and all the tears Dora hadn't been able to shed came spilling out of her like a torrent as Morwen rocked her in her arms.

—

'Cry, Dora. Cry for Sam,' she said, over and over.

It was the start of Dora's healing, she thought thankfully. Once she was able to talk about Sam and accept the truth of what had happened, and once she was able to cry for him, then her life could begin again. Never the same… but without that awful unreality that had plagued it since the accident.

'He allus said we were a matching pair o' turtle-doves,' Dora sobbed against Morwen's shoulder. 'We were so happy in our warm little nest, and when the babbies came along, they were our little fledglings. Sam was mine, see? He weren't just Hal Tremayne's eldest, nor Morwen Killigrew's brother. He were mine, and none of 'ee knew un like I did.'

'Dora, I understand, really I do—'

'Mebbe so. No woman gets to know the heart an' soul of a man until she's married to un. So you'll know what I mean when I say I miss his body next to mine at night, and 'tis more than just the urges of the flesh. 'Tis the belonging that I miss. The words that only Sam ever spoke to me, the feel of Sam's hands on me, the look in Sam's eyes when he was ready for the loving. Oh, God, how am I going to live wi'out my Sam?'

There was nothing Morwen could say to console her. Nothing she was able to say. She just held Dora while the girl sobbed out her bitterness and despair, and knew that she was witnessing a broken heart.

—

'I really thought this was going to be a turning-point, Mammie,' Morwen whispered to her mother when Bess came to the cottage a few days later. 'Instead, she seemed so distressed I asked one of the neighbours to go for Doctor Growse, and now she's struck down with the measles, and I'm so fearful for her. I don't think she has the will to get well.'

'If 'tis God's will that she does, then she'll survive this illness, my love.'

Bess hoped she sounded more comforting than she felt. She was as uneasy as Morwen. If Dora felt that she had nothing to live for, she could simply pine and die. She ate nothing, and only took sips of water and cordial.

The children raised no more than a wan smile from Dora each time Morwen took them to see her, and already the boys were finding Morwen more interesting than their ailing mother, and Primmy at eight months merely attached herself to whoever indulged her at the time.

Morwen began to feel desperate. How much longer was she going to stay away from her own home at the beck and call of Sam's family? It wasn't that she didn't love them, but she began to feel as if she no longer had a life of her own. And that terrible outpouring of Dora's had only made her miss her own man. She needed Ben's love too.

'Tell me the family news, Mammie,' Morwen said, when she had got them each a drink. She had settled Primmy with her bottle, and a neighbour had taken the little boys for a walk. 'Is Daddy all right? He looked so grey at Sam's burying.'

'He's well enough,' Bess said cautiously. 'Doctor Pender wanted to see un, and says he should take things more easily, but no more than that. He's been over-taxing himself at the works, instead of acting the proper overseer like he should.'

'Quite right. Where's the sense in him being Works Manager if he does the work himself? Ben says there's no point in keeping a dog and barking yourself!'

'Ben allus had a clever turn of phrase,' Bess gave a small tight smile, and Morwen knew her mother was more worried about Hal than she admitted. She would get Ben to have a word with the doctor as soon as she could.

Dear God, let Daddy be all right! Morwen offered up a silent prayer. This family had had enough worries for a while, and now that Dora was ill, and with Ben's court case hanging over all their heads…

'Have you heard from Jack lately?'

Bess looked at her quizzically. ''Tis only just over a week since he went back to Truro. He'll be busy wi' his work, and spending his spare time with Annie. She'll be taking his mind off our Sam, I've no doubt.'

Morwen realised how insular she had become at the cottage. She had no idea of time. All the days were the same. The pleasure in caring for these three delightful children was lost in the worry over Dora, and the lingering sorrow over Sam.

'What of Freddie?' Morwen said, determined to get a proper smile from her mother, and this time she succeeded.

'The young can allus get over things. He was a real comfort to me until he went back to school, Morwen. The house was cheerful, despite all. I miss un now.'

'Well, it's not far up here now you've got the trap, and I'm glad of your company. You can take the boys back for tea any time now they're better. They'd like that, Mammie.'

'Perhaps I will sometime,' Bess said vaguely. 'Has Ben heard anything about his court case yet? Your Daddy says the men are bandying rumours about like fishwives, wonderin' what's to become o' the works.'

Morwen felt a great annoyance at this news, and was instantly defensive of her husband.

'Killigrew Clay won't close, Mammie, nor will it be sold off!' she said passionately. 'Ben's father put his whole life into it, and Ben has done the same since he took control. You know it as well as I do, and Daddy should put a stop to it. He and Sam were always a good team when it came to ending rumours.'

She stopped abruptly, and her mother patted her hand as she saw the glint of tears in Morwen's lovely eyes.

'Well, that will give your Daddy summat to live up to, then. He wouldn't want to let our Sam down.'

They all propped one another up, Morwen thought with deep emotion. When one of them was down, another held out his hand and led them out of despair.

That was really what being a family was all about, and the Tremaynes were a family that was stronger than most.

They both heard the thin voice calling from the bedroom above, and Morwen lay Primmy in her baby carriage before following her mother upstairs. One look at Dora, and Morwen felt a stab of alarm. The girl breathed so oddly, as if she could hardly draw in enough air for her needs, and she motioned Morwen to come near.

'Take care o' the babbies if anything happens to me, Morwen,' Dora gasped out. 'I give 'em to 'ee. They'm yours and Ben's, with my love. Sam 'ould want that.'

She lay back exhausted. Morwen said roughly that nothing was going to happen to her, but Dora was already sleeping. She had no strength to fight, and no wish to remain in a world without Sam, and long before the dawn of the following day, she had given up the struggle.

Chapter Twenty

Morwen and Ben took the children home with them to Killigrew House. It had been Dora's wish, and it was the most natural thing to do since they were the children's godparents. The little boys were still bewildered by all that had happened, though mercifully too young to understand fully, while Primmy merely gurgled and clapped every time Morwen went near her.

The cottage had been left with the bits of furniture intact, until Ben found a suitable family to rent it. Right now, he had no heart for it, knowing how Morwen's family and then Sam's had made such a cosy nest of it.

Once Dora's burying was over, she and Ben had come to a decision. The children must have as normal a life as possible. From now on they would be brought up as their own family, with no thought of favour to any child of their own that may eventually arrive.

Only Bess guessed at the guilty delight that caring for Sam and Dora's children brought to Morwen. In her heart Morwen knew it was almost wicked to thank God for giving her this chance of fulfilment. In doing so it seemed that she was thanking Him for Sam and Dora's deaths. But it wasn't meant like that, and Morwen hoped fervently that God would understand.

But now when she went walking in the town she looked every bit the young matron with a small family. Walter and

Albert soon got over their shyness when ladies paused to admire the straight-backed children with their shining dark hair and blue Tremayne eyes, already looking as handsome as their father. And the baby, who could enchant anyone with her tumbling curls like Dora's, and already with the look of a tiny temptress.

And Morwen also held a secret too breath-catching to reveal to anyone yet. Not even to Ben. It was Doctor Pender who looked at her keenly one morning when she took him upstairs for his customary visit to Charles Killigrew.

Nurse Wilder had gone into town to fetch some of his regular medication, and Charles was sleeping, his lopsided mouth slack and pathetic. As always, Morwen gently wiped away the spittle that gathered there, careful not to waken him.

'How long is it since you've given any thought to yourself, Morwen?' the doctor said bluntly. She looked up, startled.

'To myself? I'm fine, save for my natural grief for my brother and his wife. I don't get over that in a day, but I control it—'

'That's not what I mean, girl. I'd like to take a look at you, and have a little talk. I don't want you overdoing it with these three children in the house—'

Her beautiful face seemed to glow as she laughed at his words, leading him dutifully to a small sitting-room near to Charles's bedroom.

'There's no hardship in that for me, Doctor! I didn't think I needed to tell 'ee that! They're little angels. Mammie's taken them off for the day, though, to give them a change.'

'Angels they may be, but I want to talk about you, not them,' he said drily. He looked at her thoughtfully.

'You look a mite pinched in the face, and not quite as robust as you should, even giving due regard to all the unhappiness of late. I've seen you come through bad times before, Morwen, and they've always put new fire in you.'

She gave a grimace. 'Mebbe those other times I wasn't plagued by feelings of nausea every time I think of our poor Sam and Dora. Grief can tie a body up in knots, Doctor—'

'So can pregnancy,' he said calmly.

Morwen's heart leapt at his words. She stared back at him, her face flushed with colour. The doctor went on before she had a chance to speak.

'Hadn't you even considered it, my dear girl? The fact that it has not happened before doesn't exclude the possibility, as I've always told you!'

'No, I hadn't considered it!' Morwen stammered, her thoughts whirling. 'There's been no time to think of it, and if – if anything physical was amiss – then I assumed 'twas due to all the upsets of late.'

'But you're considering it now?' the doctor said kindly, seeing how the thought had truly thrown her into confusion. At the moment it was disbelieving confusion. Later, he was certain, it would be ecstatic.

Morwen's thoughts flew back. She and Ben had had no physical contact of the sort that could result in a baby for some weeks. It hadn't seemed right, after the double tragedies… and the threat of the court case still awaiting Ben was enough to quell any loving notions.

But if Doctor Pender could already suspect that she was pregnant, then it must have happened before the railway accident, and surely some time before that for the signs to be showing to an experienced eye. At least six or eight weeks ago…

A night when she had clung to Ben came instantly to her mind. The memory of her softly wistful voice begging him to say that their own little world was back to normal now. Freddie's trauma was settled, and the despicable Captain Peterson had been banished from their lives forever… Jane and little Cathy Askhew had gone home to Truro and Killigrew House had felt like Morwen's own domain again… They hadn't known then of the disaster still to come.

Ben had turned to her in the intimacy of their bedroom. He had taken her in his arms, and she had felt the powerful strength of him as he held her close.

'This is our world, my Morwen,' he had said gently. 'The two of us here, where nothing else can touch us. Don't think of anything else but that, my sweet one. Shut it all out of your mind. There's only you and me, and the love between us.'

His voice had been almost mesmeric, his hands and lips caressing her in ways that were both new and familiar and infinitely beautiful to her. His eyes had adored her, his body worshipped her, and it was a night when she had truly known the meaning of belonging.

It was a word that Dora had used. In that moment of remembering, Morwen completely understood why Dora had had no more will to live without Sam. When two people complemented one another so well that they were like two halves of a perfect whole, there was no reason for going on alone…

–

'Well, Mrs Killigrew?' She heard the doctor's faintly amused voice as she continued to gaze unseeingly ahead.

Her face suddenly blazed with happiness, as though lit by an inner fire, the hope she had hardly dared consider for so long suddenly a reality.

'I think – I think it may be so! But 'tis early days, and I won't count my chickens yet—'

She smiled shakily, using one of his own fond clichés.

'I'd say there's little doubt, Morwen, but I'll take a proper look at you in a month's time. Meanwhile, if you need any powders for the nausea, just let me know.'

Her brow creased. 'But Dora always said the sickness came in the mornings. It comes on me at any time, so I didn't consider it as anything other than lack of food.' She was shame-faced. 'I must confess that since I've been so busy with the children, and Ben has been occupied away from the house, I haven't always bothered with proper meal-times.'

'Well, if you want to produce a healthy son and heir for Killigrew Clay, you'll start bothering with them now,' the doctor said sternly. 'As to the sickness being only in the morning, that's an old wives' tale. A woman's own body decides what reaction it will take to the welcome invasion of a child.'

Morwen hardly heard anything beyond those first magic words he spoke. A son and heir for Killigrew Clay... it was what she wanted most in the world for Ben; the dream she cherished above all for herself. But still her country-born caution came to the fore.

'Doctor, please say nothing of this to Ben yet. It's too unbelievable, and if 'twere to come to naught, it would be too cruel to dash his hopes.'

'I thought you'd be rushing to tell your husband! How do you expect to keep it a secret with that impetuous nature of yours?' he asked teasingly.

'I don't know. I just know it feels safer with me alone for the present, until it's certain. Just for a few weeks more, that's all. The knowledge is too precious to share. It feels as fragile to me as the porcelain they make from the rough clay. If I'm not careful with it, it will shatter.'

She spoke with quick embarrassment, praying that the doctor wouldn't think her some peculiar specimen of womanhood for not running straight to her husband with this news. But miraculously, he seemed to understand instantly and gave a small murmur of agreement.

'Sometimes the roughest clay makes the most beautiful porcelain, dear lady,' he said gravely, and they both knew he was speaking ambiguously. 'Your secret will be safe with me for now, but don't take too long in denying your husband his right to this most joyful news.'

She nodded, suddenly choked as the momentous realisation really began to take hold of her. She was carrying Ben's child at last. After all these years, these agonising longings were to be answered. There would be a son for Killigrew Clay.

The possibility of a daughter never entered her head. In any case, it didn't matter. That it would be a child of their flesh was glory enough. How beautiful that phrase was... a child of their flesh, unique to them alone, made from their wild sweet loving... but in these ecstatic moments, everything was beautiful to Morwen Killigrew...

'Morwen, I have other patients to attend. I would just like to offer my congratulations, for I know what this means to you.' The doctor prepared to leave the house before he became as maudlin as a young practitioner experiencing his first sight of a woman expecting a much-wanted baby.

'Thank you, Doctor. And you'll remember to keep it our secret?' her eyes misty with tears of happiness.

'I'll remember.' He spoke solemnly, wishing he had the means to bring such joy to everyone he visited. The glow from

Morwen Killigrew was enough to warm him for the rest of the day.

–

When the doctor had gone Morwen was suddenly disorientated. There was so much to think about and, as yet, no-one to share it with. It was partly superstition that stopped her telling Ben immediately. As though to put it into words might mean that it wouldn't happen after all.

She put her hands tentatively on her belly. What miracle was developing there? The thought was both wonderful and poignant. It made her want to cry, where seconds before she had felt like dancing. Was this one of the effects of pregnancy?

Dora had always said a woman was halfway between life and death during childbirth, and went through something similar to a kind of madness while she was carrying – sometimes in a high state of content or excitement – sometimes filled with such tension she was near to tearing the ears off her poor patient husband with her grumbling.

Dora was a country girl, the same as Morwen. She realised she was thinking a lot about Dora lately, and regretted that they never really became like sisters until it was too late. But suddenly Morwen knew what she had to do. It was something Ben might not understand, but Dora would.

Morwen would tell the bees. It was an old country ritual that ensured safety in the telling. Once the bees knew of the new baby growing inside Morwen, it would be safe.

It was no longer high summer, and there were no outdoor hives humming with activity in garden and farm, but there were folk who kept bees up on the moors who wouldn't think it in the least bit odd that Morwen Killigrew was calling on them to spend half an hour in a rickety old shed, while she related whatever troubles she had to the bees.

When she had done, she would collect the children from her mother's house, as she had already arranged. Ben wouldn't be home until evening, and by then Morwen would be perfectly composed and hopefully able to eat her dinner without wondering just how long it was going to stay down.

—

While Morwen was receiving her stupendous news from Doctor Pender, Ben was with Richard Carrick, Jane's father, who was acting for him in the court case. They were in bitter consultation with the surveyors at Bodmin. Engineer Prole, their new man, had carried out his duties to the best of his ability, Silas Newton the surveyor said pompously.

'It wasn't good enough! If he'd done the job properly, and been provided with all the facts, the accident might have been averted—' Ben snapped, ignoring the efforts of Richard Carrick to keep him silent and to lead the discussion himself.

'Are you saying we suppressed certain facts, Mr Killigrew? If so, you'd best watch that you're not in court for libel as well as everything else. Even if we had kept something from Engineer Prole – which we most definitely did not – it would have been only because you were pressing us so badly to re-open the tracks. Such a thought never enters your mind, I daresay!' he spoke with heavy sarcasm.

'I'm saying I'm far from satisfied with the way you conduct your business, and a counter-charge should be brought against the Bodmin surveyor's office for negligence!'

Every discussion between Ben Killigrew and the surveyors ended up as a heated affair, and Richard knew only too well that it didn't do for the boy to antagonise them too much. But it was like telling the sea not to ebb and flow to try to stem Ben's fury and the undoubted feeling of guilt he couldn't suppress.

Ben dismissed the fact that his own loyal supporters said he wasn't to blame for the accident. The rail tracks were his, and in his eyes he was therefore responsible for their safety.

Besides, it was his wife's own brother who had died and that was something for which he could never forgive himself. But he despised, too, these complacent men who sat behind a desk and controlled other people's livelihoods with a stroke of a pen.

'Mr Killigrew!' Silas Newton jumped to his feet, his face red and bristling with indignation. 'We've tried to be patient with 'ee, but you go too far. I suggest your lawyer teaches you to have a cooler head before your appearance in court, or you'll find your business and your reputation ruined. And now good-day to you both. We have other matters to attend to.'

The three men in the surveyors' department stood stiffly, forming a solid band of outraged respectability. Ben might rage all he chose, but he couldn't hope to win the day by a show of temper. Not when he was fighting the entire establishment, as Richard Carrick was quick to point out to him when the two of them sat in a small Bodmin coffee shop a while later.

'You're a fool to yourself, Ben,' Richard said curtly. 'If you want me to advise you, listen to what I say and heed it well. Your case will be heard in a month's time, and you had best prepare yourself for some very close questioning on the safety of the railway, and why you allowed its use to begin again—'

'You know why, damn it! Because this new Engineer Prole gave us the say-so for it! The guilt lies with him, if anyone—'

'Then for God's sake stop acting so guiltily yourself, for anyone hearing you would begin to question whether you're truly blameless. Think on that, Ben.'

'Oh, no, I don't feel guilty!' he said bitterly. 'My brother-in-law is dead, and his wife lost the will to live and died a few weeks after him, leaving three orphaned children. Wouldn't you be guilty if you had that on your conscience?'

'Ben, I beg you not to let emotion take the place of common sense. Go home and sleep on it, boy, and come to my chambers tomorrow, where I'm preparing our brief. We must have a solid defence to offer. You've already come up against Mr Princeton, who's acting for the Honourable Mrs Stanforth. He's a formidable opponent, and with all the public interest aroused in your case, Princeton will be anxious to make a name for himself.'

Ben glared at the lawyer, his feelings of disgust transparent on his face.

'God, this whole thing sickens me. Is it some kind of circus, with you and he fighting for the glory of winning the case, and to hell with who pays the bills in the end?'

Richard's mouth gave a flicker of a smile. 'It's something like that,' he agreed.

'And I'm to be thrown to the lions, am I?'

Richard's smile faded. 'Not if I have my way! Killigrew Clay isn't going under without a fight, and I'm more than ready for it. You may be headstrong, but you're your father's son, and I have a strong allegiance to the pair of you. Trust me, Ben. All I ask is that I don't have to fight you as well as Princeton.'

It made sense and Ben knew it. But he knew that one month from now he would rather be anywhere than sitting in the front of the court at Bodmin Assizes. The eyes of the whole district would be on him, the pen of Lew Tregian for *The Informer* eagerly picking up every word that was said, to be relayed to the rest of the county.

He didn't relish the thought of being so exposed one little bit. Richard Carrick was not a young man – he had years of experience behind him, and the glint in his eyes reassured Ben that he would indeed fight tooth and nail to save the Killigrew fortunes.

'All right, Richard,' he said grudgingly. 'I'll try to curb my temper in future.'

'Then at last you're talking sense.'

–

Bess dandled Primmy on her lap, reluctant to let her go with Morwen after such a delightful day with her grandchildren. The boys were outside, rushing about the garden now, tugging at Morwen's hand and showing her first one thing after another that Hal had planted.

'Grandpa says this be our own garden,' Walter shouted, jumping up and down in his excitement. 'There's cabbages in there, and next spring Grandpa says we can plant carrots and flowers if we like. An' under a bush over there, Grandpa says some primroses will be showing in a few months, an' we can pick 'em for our Primmy—'

'Slow down, Walter!' Morwen laughed. Grandpa was clearly the hero of the moment. Her eyes were soft with love as she tried to calm him.

It took so little to restore the laughter to a child's eyes, she thought. The pity of it was that an adult took so much longer to recover from tragedy. Bess was pleased to have the children here today, but Morwen suspected that half of her pleasure was because she wouldn't have to sit alone with her sewing and brood over Sam and Dora. The children were a panacea as well as a delight. Hadn't she found that out for herself?

For a second, when she'd come down from telling the bees up at a remote moorland cottager's shed, she had been very tempted to tell her mother about the coming baby. It would have given Bess such joy. But she had resisted the temptation because it was Ben's right to know first, and Morwen wasn't ready for the telling yet.

—

Long before the dreaded day for the court case arrived, nerves were strained to breaking-point in the Killigrew household. Ben could barely speak to anyone without flaring up. The children irritated him, and he complained loudly and often at the mess Primmy made, and the way Morwen pampered her.

'Ben, for goodness' sake, she's only a babby—'

'Stop using that ridiculous name for her,' he snapped. 'The word is baby, and it's time you used it. You're not a common bal maiden any longer, so please don't behave like one.'

Morwen's mouth dropped open in disbelieving fury. How dare he speak like that to her! She had been toiling with poor little Primmy all day, who was miserable with teething. The boys were crotchety because the day was wet and they had wanted to be taken for a walk, and the charm of this big new house had palled slightly with familiarity.

Morwen was feeling absolutely wretched with the sickness she had so far managed to hide from Ben, and now he had the nerve to treat her like some kind of skivvy!

'I'm sorry if I displease you, Sir!' She spoke with exaggerated correctness. 'If I'd been born a fine lady like Mrs Askhew, no doubt these appalling mistakes wouldn't slip from my lips so often!'

'You only make yourself sound more foolish by referring to Jane in such disparaging terms—' he snapped.

'What terms are those, Sir? Please speak in words of one syllable so that a poor bal maiden can understand.'

She was treading dangerous ground and she knew it, but his arrogance incensed her. They should be close in times of trouble, but Morwen had begun to realise more and more that Ben was shutting her out of any discussions about the court case.

It seemed as though he wanted to fight this battle without her, and the feeling hurt. And when she was hurt, she hit back any way she could.

'I'm sorry I referred to you in that way—' Ben said stiffly.

'Why?' she whipped back. ''Tis what I was, and I see no reason to be ashamed of it. These hands that you call so pretty and soft were once as red and roughened as any weathered clayworker's. Don't 'ee remember the night I first came here and met Jane Carrick, and how embarrassed I was by the sight of my own hands? Or mebbe such a thought didn't occur to you and your father, so magnanimous in inviting we poor Tremaynes to supper in the midst of the fine folk from St Austell and Truro!'

'Have you quite finished?' he asked at the end of this tirade. 'God, you people are so humble it makes me sick. I thought you'd got over all that by now – and can't you ever forget all that nonsense about Jane?'

'This is not just about Jane,' Morwen said bitterly. 'This is about the two people we are, and there are times when I wonder what on earth Morwen Tremayne is doing in this big house, when her roots are elsewhere.'

Ben was suddenly aware that this was truly more than a mere upset between them. God knew he was temperamental of late, but so was she. And the two of them wrangling together was like setting a match to a tinderbox.

'Morwen, roots are there to grow.' He came across to where she was rocking the snuffling Primmy on her lap. He put his arms around both of them, enveloping them both.

'Grow with me, dar. Don't destroy what we have. We have the beginnings of our own little family tree here, with Sam's children – *our* children. Bend with me, Morwen, for I couldn't bear it if our tree broke.'

She heard the desperation in his voice, and knew that his pride was stretched to the limit in expressing himself so, and as always she responded to it. Her face twisted to meet his, her kiss sweet on his lips, the simple words said from her heart.

'We'll never break, dar,' she said. 'We've come through too much to let this trouble divide us. We love you and we're all behind you, but 'tis not where I want to be. My place is alongside you, Ben. Don't shut me out.'

As if tired of being squashed between her two people, Primmy began to wail and to struggle against Ben's chest. He gave a crooked smile as he took the baby from Morwen.

'It seems this little lady doesn't want to shut me out, either,' he said huskily. 'Let's find some cloves for those nasty teeth of yours, my baby.'

Wordlessly they forgave each other. Morwen and her mother already knew that the children could restore their calm faster than any potions. Ben would discover that too.

Her stomach lurched uncomfortably, and the unpleasant taste of bile rose in her mouth. But it wasn't entirely unwelcome. It meant that their own baby, their flesh and blood, was still growing safely inside her, another precious part of the dynasty they were creating.

Morwen had almost hurled the fact at Ben just now, but it would have been so wrong to tell him in bitterness. She thanked God that her anger hadn't taken complete control of her.

Telling Ben about their coming baby was a moment to be shared with love, as it had begun.

Chapter Twenty-One

The case of the town of St Austell versus Ben Killigrew at Bodmin Assize Court was set for the twentieth day of November, 1855. *The Informer* blazoned the fact as front-page news for several issues before the due date, so that Ben said bitterly that there could hardly be a man, woman or child who didn't see Ben Killigrew for a villain, and would attend to see justice done, seeing it as something of an outing.

'Justice will prove that you were not to blame,' Morwen said calmly, in answer to another angry outburst from Ben. She let him rant and rage and let the tide of it wash over her, having realised that it was the best way to handle the explosive situation at home. Once the trial began, perhaps some of the tension would be released at last.

And when the outcome was known... Morwen's thoughts never got that far. Her imagination drew pictures that were too uncomfortably vivid to contemplate. They couldn't begin to guess at the findings of the court.

The Honourable Mrs Stanforth had plenty of town and county support behind her. The local Member of Parliament had recently taken an interest in the doings of his remote country seat, no doubt thinking the publicity might do him some good at Westminster, Richard Carrick had commented sourly. Nonetheless, it was fast becoming more than a mere wealthy clay-works owner against an indignant townslady.

As for her, she wished to see it proven that she was more than an hysterical woman who had first called Ben Killigrew's rail tracks unsafe. She wanted justice done. If she had her way, she would rid the town for ever of the rough clayworkers who lowered the tone of the district, but while the clay provided a livelihood, she knew that was never likely to happen.

Ben insisted that Morwen didn't attend the hearing, and she insisted just as angrily that she would. It became a battle of wills between them.

'Your place is at home with the children. They need you here, Morwen—'

'The children can spend the day with my mother, and my place is with you. Haven't we agreed on that countless times?'

'I don't want you being upset—'

'I'll be more upset if I don't know what's happening,' she said feelingly. 'Do you really expect me to sit at home twiddling my thumbs while I wonder if some poncy lawyer is wiping the floor with Mr Carrick's evidence?'

Ben grinned at her eloquent phrasing. 'I never know what to expect from you,' he said abruptly. 'You always did do the unexpected—'

'Isn't that what you always called part of my charm, dar?' Morwen could afford to be soft and wheedling now, knowing when she had won. She put her arms around his neck, looking up into his eyes, pressing her warm body against his in a deliberately provocative way.

'Ben, we must be together in this. And afterwards, when 'tis all put to rights, we can start life again.'

She nearly said they could forget the disaster, but that could never be. The disaster had caused Sam's death, and there were still clayworkers with wives and children receiving medical treatment for which Ben was paying generously. Where would it end? Morwen thought with a shiver.

But he was already responding to the soft and pliant woman in his arms. The woman he had always wanted and desired, and loved with a passion that had been sadly neglected of late. If she tantalised him, then he would tease her too, he thought, with a burst of his old masculine arrogance.

He squeezed her waist, and ran his hands over her curving hips, moving upwards until they cupped her breasts. Beneath the warm fabric of her day dress he felt the firm fullness of them, and the peaking of their tips as his fingers gently circled them into awareness of his touch. He laughed tenderly as he felt her squirm slightly at his questing hands.

'You're putting on weight, Mrs Killigrew,' he said softly. 'I like it, though. It suits you, and it more than suits me. A man likes to hold a real woman in his arms, and not a bean-stick.'

'I was never that!' Morwen said breathlessly.

The real reason for her increasing roundness trembled on the tip of her tongue. Would the news of his expected child give Ben more self-confidence at his forthcoming ordeal, or would he be even more beset with anxiety over Morwen's health?

'When all our troubles are over, we'll put the children into your mother's care for a few weeks,' Ben went on. 'If the country of France is good enough for our noble Queen, then perhaps we should take a look at its delights too. Does that appeal to you, Mrs Killigrew?'

He smiled down at her, clearly expecting her to be bowled over by such a thought. And so she was, but not in the way Ben anticipated. Once the trial was over, she intended telling him their own news, and she doubted very much that he'd want to go travelling at such a time.

Nor too, would she want to send Sam's children to her mother's so soon after their own change of circumstances. One major upset in their lives was enough for their small minds to accept, without temporarily losing the two people on whom they had already come to depend and love.

But with an inner wisdom, Morwen said none of this to Ben at that moment. Now was the time for pressing her face close to his, and telling him that the idea sounded wonderful, and that travelling to France was something she had always thought happened to other people…

'And not to the humble Tremaynes?' he said teasingly, and there was no malice in the words, nor in her laughing agreement.

Reluctantly he let her go as Walter and Albert were brought down from the nursery by a huffy red-cheeked maidservant, saying that they wanted their tea and were leading her a right old dance until they got it.

Morwen laughed, her eyes twinkling as she watched poor Fanny blow a stray wisp of hair from her eyes, and guessed at the antics Walter and Albert had been putting her through.

'I'll take over now, Fanny,' she said at once, and the children ran to her side with relief.

'I don't like Fanny, Mammie,' Walter complained with the shrill candour of children. 'She smells o' cabbage water an' she makes me wipe my nose every minute.'

'Well, so you should!' Ben scooped him up in his arms. 'You don't want to end up with dewdrops on the end of it like old Jack Frost, do you?'

The boys shrieked with laughter at that, but Morwen hadn't missed the fact that Walter had called her Mammie naturally and for the first time. She prayed that Ben wouldn't correct him on it, choosing this moment to say that Walter should have said Mamma, and crush his newfound identity in this house.

Thankfully, Ben ignored it, but Morwen knew it must come. She would be Mamma, not Mammie. The children of Killigrew House mustn't use the easy-sounding country mode of address. How grand it sounded to be Mamma… and Morwen suddenly realised how little it mattered after all. The love would still be the same, and that was at the heart of it.

–

The morning of the twentieth of November was grey and colourless. It matched the feelings in Morwen's heart. Ben had been sitting with his father for more than half an hour now, and it was well past the time that they should set out for Bodmin. It wouldn't do for the defendant to be late at his own trial.

The whole affair was still unbelievable to Morwen. For some years Ben had been the town's darling, and now they were hounding him. She had no doubt that there would be plenty of them at the Assize court, jostling to get the best sight of Ben Killigrew getting his come-uppance.

And for what? For building a railway and taking the clay blocks to Charlestown port without offending the townsladies' dignity by throwing up flurries of choking dust through the town and threatening to damage the narrow streets by the heavy out-dated clay waggons!

For giving the townsfolk their excursions and allowing them to exclaim in their superior fashion at the quaint clayworkers' garb and give pretty names to the clay tips and the very country in which the clayworkers lived and breathed. For generously taking the clayworkers' children and their families on outings to the sea that they would never otherwise afford!

Her thoughts veered away from the painful memories of that day. But it was all so unfair. Ben had been their hero, and was now painted as the blackest villain that ever lived.

The Informer had been scrupulously fair in pointing out the fors and againsts of Ben Killigrew's cause, and the articles had provoked a series of letters to the editor that Lew Tregian had undoubtedly delighted in printing. Ben's troubles would have vastly increased the circulation of the Truro newspaper.

Charles Killigrew had already commented on that fact to his son that morning. Charles was not ready yet to be put out to pasture, and had managed to tell his son so in painfully slow terms. He wanted to know all that went on, and Doctor Pender had sighed regretfully and told Ben he may as well tell him everything, or none of them would get any peace.

Charles knew very well that today could change the Killigrew fortunes, and urged his son to keep control of his temper.

'You're a fine one to give such instructions,' Ben grinned. 'If you were in my place, you'd be roaring like a lion, and to hell with the consequences.'

Charles gave a lop-sided grimace. He was going through a fairly lucid patch, his speech more intelligible, and he agreed with Ben whole-heartedly.

'Don't be goaded into saying what you don't mean. Let Richard guide you. Lions stalk their prey before they pounce.'

'I won't let you down, Father,' Ben said quietly.

'I know that. The pity of it is you can't win this day on the throw of the dice, or I might feel a bit happier at the outcome,' Charles retorted.

Ben laughed. 'I don't think my skills with the dice would help much today, especially as I haven't used them for so long!'

Not since the night he had gambled everything he had to win Killigrew Clay from this pathetic old man and enable him to run the clay works single-handed.

Instead of being controlled by Charles Killigrew and his reluctant partner, Richard Carrick, Jane Askhew's father, Killigrew Clay had come into the hands of a young and energetic new owner who had made it prosper. God help him if all that ambition was now going to be its downfall.

He felt Charles's thin hand cover his in a claw-like grip.

'God go with you, Ben. I'll be waiting for the news when you get back.'

'You promise? You won't run away?'

Impulsively, Ben leaned forward and kissed the tired cheek. He swore he saw the glint of a tear in Charles's eyes as he left the room, and shouted to Nurse Wilder that his father was ready for his breakfast.

Time was when Charles would have been shouting for it himself, and Ben could only feel anger at the frustration the old man must feel every single day of his life.

He ran down the stairs to find Morwen hovering near the drawing-room door.

'We should be leaving, Ben. Mr Carrick has been here some little while, and is getting anxious.'

'We're not due to make an appearance until early afternoon, but don't worry. The public will still get their pound of flesh, dar.' He smiled a little to let her know he was joking.

–

Some hours later, Morwen remembered those words. There had been an initial outcry when it was discovered that Engineer Prole was not present in the courtroom, and at first the case was going to be postponed. But the crowd would have none of it,

302

and rather than risk the Assize court being wrecked, the visiting and impartial Judge Manley decreed that a constable should be sent to the Engineer's rooms nearby without delay and bring him to court immediately.

There was more uproar in the Assize court as one and then another gave evidence against Ben Killigrew, and just as many sprang to his defence. When the cat-calls had turned to nothing short of pandemonium, the stern-faced Judge Manley rapped furiously for order and threatened to clear the place if this undignified disgrace continued.

Morwen tried to smile encouragingly towards Ben, completely unsure how it was all going. The lawyers had glib tongues, using words she couldn't always understand, and some of the accusations seemed so damning. They bewildered and shocked her. Surely this wasn't what it was all about?

It had seemed a simple matter, to decide how much compensation Ben Killigrew should pay to those families who had suffered hardship, and Morwen knew for a fact that he was doing more than enough already.

'Do you have any more witnesses for the defence before we hear your client speak for himself, Mr Carrick?' the Judge said finally, after what seemed like hours of arguing and back-biting.

Richard Carrick said that he had not. Richard Carrick had already spoken up for Ben's character and integrity. Clay-workers who wanted to be heard had spoken awkwardly and inarticulately, unnerved by the occasion and the awesome dark surroundings.

Morwen could have wept for them, and also for herself for growing so far away from them. But seeing them here, like fish out of water, she finally realised it, and knew that she had made the choice long ago. And Ben had been right. She was his wife, and should behave accordingly.

She clasped her hands tightly together as she saw Ben take the witness-stand. Her father sat beside her, as grim-faced as anyone there. Jack was there to lend his support. Sam was dead, and there was no helping him, but Ben was their family, and they resented seeing him made a scapegoat.

As Ben cleared his throat, there were a few boos and cheers from the various factions, quickly called to order by the clerks of the court. Ben had elected to give his own evidence, and he spoke clearly and concisely.

'I'm still not sure of exactly what I stand accused.' He paused until the shouting died down. 'I took instruction to re-open my railway from the surveyors' office in Bodmin, and in particular from Chief Engineer Prole, who is conspicuous by his absence today. Wouldn't you take that as some indication of his own guilt in this matter?'

Judge Manley banged for order as the crowd erupted in response, and spoke curtly to Ben.

'Mr Killigrew, you are not to appeal to the court in this way. It is for your lawyer to appeal on your behalf. You are merely required to give a direct account of yourself and your actions and no more. If you do not adhere to these rules, I will have you removed from the witness-stand at once.'

'Perhaps you would prefer it if I stood here mute and let the crowd stick pins in me, since this seems to be little more than a witch-hunt,' Ben said angrily.

'I would prefer you to keep a civil tongue in your head,' Judge Manley said coldly. 'And I would remind you again, Mr Killigrew, that it only takes a nod of my head to have you removed forthwith.'

'He's being grossly unfair to Ben!' Morwen said fiercely from her seat right behind Richard Carrick. The lawyer turned his head and whispered back to where she sat between her father and brother Jack. Freddie had not been allowed to come, despite his complaining.

'My dear girl, Ben is digging a grave for himself, and he should have the sense to know it! Judge Manley is harsh but fair enough, and he won't stand for any arrogance in his courtroom. I warned Ben before we began.'

He signalled to Ben to remain cool, and Morwen could see by the heavy way her husband breathed that it was a tremendous effort for him not to slate these fools who couldn't see that all this was none of his doing.

Once Ben had said what he had to say, Lawyer Princeton's skilful, probing questions began to rile him anew. They went over and over the same things. No, he hadn't known there were rogue tin shafts beneath the moors, since no evidence had been found to prove it. Yes, he had demanded that his railway be re-opened, but God knows he would have built a new one rather than let such a disaster happen!

'God won't help you in this court, Mr Killigrew,' Lawyer Princeton said, smooth as silk.

'Really? Do you set yourself up higher than God then?' Ben said sarcastically.

Judge Manley thumped for order as the laughter rang out.

'Facetiousness won't help your case either, Mr Killigrew,' he snapped.

'I'm beginning to wonder if anything will,' Ben said angrily. 'You've got it cut and dried as far as I can see. I'm guilty as hell, and the Honourable lady and her leeches have decided I'm not good enough for St Austell—'

'That's not true! And anyone who says so should remember what happened four years ago, when Ben Killigrew was your champion!'

There were gasps in the courtroom as Morwen leapt to her feet, her face scarlet with fury.

'Morwen, sit down and don't make a spectacle of yourself.' Hal caught at her arm, but she shook him off as though he were a troublesome fly. Richard Carrick half-rose, but she pushed past him and rushed up to the Judge, her blue eyes wide and blazing, her voice impassioned.

'We all know what happened on the day of the accident, Sir. I know it only too painfully, since it was my own brother who died, but if I and my family don't condemn my husband for wanting to take the children on their outing to the sea, why should these fine townsfolk who can go there any day of the year if they wish? They have no idea of the lives of the clayworkers' families, and how important such an outing was to them. Do you really think a man like Ben Killigrew would knowingly have put those people at risk for the sake of his own prestige?'

'Have you quite finished, Madam?' Judge Manley said icily. Richard Carrick had leapt forward and was trying to restrain Morwen forcibly.

She liked the man well enough, but she was miserable that he was the one Ben had chosen to defend him because Carrick knew the Killigrew family character's history so well, but it was another link with Jane... and to Morwen it seemed their two families were still as close as threads woven into the same weave... However, right now it was her last consideration as she resisted Richard's plea for her to remain silent. Her eyes blazed at him.

'Will you please put me in the witness-stand?'

'Morwen, for God's sake, sit down!' Ben raged at her amid the furore. 'It's not your place to behave like this—'

'Why not? Doesn't a wife know her husband's character better than anyone else?'

'A wife is naturally biased in her husband's favour—' the Judge bellowed out.

'Then put me up as a witness for Sam Tremayne and his family. There are three orphaned children as a result of Ben Killigrew's railway disaster. Let me speak for them, and let Mr Tregian report to his newspaper whether you dared let a woman speak up or not.'

The Judge's eyes narrowed. The court had become little more than a rabble, with the noisy clayworkers demanding that Morwen be heard. He stared into her beautiful, defiant eyes, and knew when he was beaten. But to be beaten by a woman, however resourceful, was something he couldn't forgive.

He gave a short nod to the lawyers to let the woman be brought to the stand, and that Ben Killigrew should be returned to his seat. As they passed one another, Ben muttered despairingly to his wife.

'You shame me, Morwen. This is not how a lady should behave.'

She flinched visibly. Then her chin went high. Perhaps a *lady* wouldn't fight with every weapon she had to save her man's skin, but Morwen Tremayne would, and she had every intention of doing so.

That Judge Manley was extremely irritated with her was never in doubt. That he looked upon this whole case as a pointless exercise between a townslady hoping to make a small stir in the county and a wealthy young clayworks owner, was just as obvious.

Someone was going to pay for this utter waste of time, when cases more deserving of his expertise were kept waiting. He had every intention of cutting this one as short as possible.

He snapped at the lawyers, and threatened that the court would be cleared of spectators if there was any more disturbance while the girl spoke up.

He needn't have bothered. They wanted to hear Morwen. She stood up straight in the dock, thankful for its protection so that none would realise how her knees shook as she looked out on a sea of faces. Thankful, too, that none would guess at her condition, hidden as it was beneath her full skirt and the wooden partition in front of her.

The crowd was hushed as her clear soft tones began, and more than one man wished he had someone as beautiful and fearless as Morwen Killigrew to defend him.

'My family have all worked for Killigrew Clay. We knew the Killigrews long before I became Mrs Ben Killigrew. We knew them for fair bosses, and we were as loyal to them as every other clayworker—'

'What about the strike a few years back? Some on 'em weren't so loyal then!'

The Judge let the man's cat-call pass when Morwen answered it immediately.

'The strike was over pay rises, and I freely admit that Charles Killigrew was at fault in delaying them. But who was it who got your pay rises for you and put an end to that strike? Who believed so deeply in the future of Killigrew Clay that he gambled on his own inheritance to gain control of the business? It was my husband – and one of the first things he did was to put money back in the clayworkers' pockets. Is this the man you accuse of being irresponsible?'

'You're meant to be giving evidence for your brother and his orphaned family, not extolling your husband's virtues, young lady,' Judge Manley sternly interrupted her impassioned speech.

Morwen turned to him, her hands gripping the edge of the dock, her knuckles white as bone.

'The two things are interwoven, Sir. I'm trying to show my husband's integrity. My father was a pit captain at Clay One works for many years, until he became Works Manager. My brother, Sam, succeeded him, as he had always wanted to do. It was Sam's proudest day when he became pit captain of Clay One.'

Her voice wavered a little, but she didn't stop.

'My brother, Sam, was a simple, loving family man, but if he had ever put it into words, I think he'd have said he would die for Killigrew Clay. And that's what he did, taking children for an outing to the sea. Killigrew's railway is still the proudest achievement in the story of Killigrew Clay.'

There were mutterings of agreement from some of the townsfolk as well as from the clayworkers.

'Why should you demean that achievement because of this terrible accident, when those who loved Sam the most don't condemn the man who built that railway? If the people of St Austell want their moment of glory, let them look to their consciences and visit the clay folk and their children still in hospital and give them as much comfort as Ben is trying to do!'

The unrestrained cheers and applause stopped any further words. But Morwen had said enough anyway. She felt utterly drained, and shaken now at what she had dared to do here. Richard Carrick helped her back to her seat, and she felt Ben's hand grip hers before he took her place in the dock.

His face was set, and she couldn't tell his reaction to her words. The clayworkers acclaimed her as their champion, but the accusing lawyer hadn't done with this chit of a girl who threatened his entire brief, and his legal tongue was more than ready to reply.

'Mrs Killigrew has painted a charming picture of the clay-workers' plight, helped by a husband who is apparently an ambitious gambler! Not the most respected of persons, perhaps, but we'll let that pass—'

He went on, glibly undermining all that Morwen had said. And in the end, Judge Manley's own irritation with this case, and the weight of the townsfolk, backed by their Member of Parliament, whose interested letter he had in his pocket, decided him. Ben Killigrew could not be allowed to get away with building a railway that had collapsed into the so-called porcelain earth.

As he was preparing to make his final judgement, there was a flurry of activity at the courtroom door, and a young man rushed in waving a note, too shaken to stand on ceremony.

'If you please, Sir, Engineer Prole's fled the county. This here's a note found in his rooms saying he holds himself responsible for the tragedy, and he can't face the enquiry. By the time you read this, he says he'll either have left the country in disgrace or shot himself in his remorse.'

If there had been uproar before, it was doubled now. Engineer Prole had damned himself and the surveyors' office too, by his actions. Morwen was too weak with relief to feel real sorrow for the man. But once order was restored, it was obvious that Judge Manley did not accept the note as lessening Ben's own responsibility.

'Neither Engineer Prole's cowardly action nor your wife's intervention has tempered my decision, Sir. You will pay due compensation to the town of St Austell. Some of its streets have been badly damaged by your own clay waggons in the past. They will be renewed at your expense. The town is in need of a new administration building. You may have your name set to it when you have provided it. Your present railway will be dismantled immediately. If another is to be built, it must pass the most stringent tests. Apart from that, the injured must have full compensation. You will pay the costs of this court case.'

The voice went on and on, the mounting costs unbelievable to Ben's ears. It was impossible. The future of Killigrew Clay seemed gravely in doubt as he stumbled outside into the grey November day, and wondered just how he was ever going to pay for it all.

Chapter Twenty-Two

Ben insisted that Morwen went straight to her mother's house with Hal and Jack. The children had to be collected, and he and Richard Carrick were to go directly to St Austell for a consultation with the Killigrew accountant, no matter how late the hour when they arrived there.

Daniel Gorran had naturally been in court to hear the proceedings. He was incensed that the surveyors' office in Bodmin hadn't been heavily fined as well, but as Richard Carrick was quick to point out, the case had been the town of St Austell against Ben Killigrew.

At least when Ben had done what the Judge demanded, he would once again be redeemed in the eyes of the town. It was small comfort to any of them, and on hearing the Judge's outrageous demands of Ben, Daniel Gorran had suggested an immediate interview with him and his lawyer back at his chambers.

To Ben, this sounded ominous. If Daniel Gorran was going to say there was simply no money to meet all the court's requirements, then there would be no option but to sell up.

There had been more than a hint lately of a wind of change in the hitherto prosperous clay business. Orders had begun to dwindle a little, and if the current receipts had to be shown to prospective buyers, who would be interested in a declining business that might go the way of the tin-mining?

He tried to push the thought from his mind while he was surrounded by well-wishers and gawping bystanders. They crowded him, when all he wanted was to get away from here... Morwen caught at his arm as he went to push through.

'Ben, are you very angry with me?' She tried to stop the catch in her throat as she asked. It had never been her intention to stand up and defend him so vehemently, but when the moment came, she had been totally unable to resist it. He saw how her mouth trembled, and forgot his anger. It wasn't directed at her any more, anyway. He squeezed her hand tightly.

'I was, but I've such pride in you, Morwen, that it would turn your head to know it,' he said quietly instead.

'And I in you,' she said. 'We'll weather this storm, Ben, as we've weathered so many others.'

And she had something momentous still to tell him that would restore their world to rights... but she couldn't tell him here, with so many folk jostling them about. Many still wanted to shake Ben's hand and wish him luck, and as many others watched every emotion on his face to see how the court's decision would affect the mighty Ben Killigrew. Morwen's news must still wait.

He left her in the care of Hal and Jack, the two Tremayne men as white-faced as Richard Carrick. Later, Hal commented to Bess that Ben and Morwen themselves seemed the most controlled of any of them. Sam's little boys climbed all over him as they told Bess all that had happened.

'If I appeared controlled to 'ee, Daddy, then you don't know your own daughter!' she laughed shakily. 'My knees felt as though they were turning to jelly every second I faced all those prying faces. If it hadn't been for seeing you and Jack behind Ben, I don't know if I could have said all that I did.'

'She was magnificent,' Jack said gruffly. He wasn't given to superlatives, except when describing the charms of Annie Boskelly, and Morwen felt a stinging in her eyes at this compliment from her brother. Matt, of course, would have been wild with his praise, but then, Matt always had a way with words…

Why she should have thought of Matt right then, she didn't know, but her emotions threatened to run away with her. Rather than let the children see her cry, she went into the little scullery to make them all a drink. Bess followed her, and her voice was calm and soft as she closed the door behind her.

'When are you goin' to confide in me, Morwen? I've seen that look in a woman's face before, and you've a certain roundness that you can't hide from me, even if you've hidden it from your husband. Has the miracle happened, my lamb?'

Morwen couldn't reply for a moment, and then she ran into her mother's clasping arms. She hadn't betrayed Ben's right to know first. She should have known that her mother would guess. And there was such relief in the sharing. But she whispered to Bess not to tell anyone else just yet.

'I'll not tell,' Bess said gently. 'But tell that man of yours as soon as possible, love. 'Twill put the life back into un after today. 'Tis too late to take the children home tonight. Let your father take you in the trap, then you and Ben can be alone.'

Morwen knew she was right, and suddenly she couldn't wait to be home, to be alone with Ben after the busy, traumatic day, and to tell him that in the spring there was to be another baby. Their very own child… she caught her breath at the thought, and as quickly she remembered the vow she and Ben had made.

To care for Sam's children like their own… and so they would, but Morwen would have been less than human if she had not welcomed the child she carried beneath her heart with an extra special love.

The entire county would know of Ben Killigrew's self-styled disgrace by the time *The Informer* was next published, Morwen was thinking as her father left her at Killigrew House. By then she hoped their own happy news would have dispelled some of Ben's anguish. Tonight she would take away some of the pain.

It was the early hours of the morning by the time he returned. Morwen had long since retired, and she heard him creep into the bedroom, trying not to disturb her. But what she had to say couldn't wait.

When he slid into bed beside her, her arms went around him, and before she could say a word, he was holding her close. The tension wasn't over yet, and she realised it at once from his bitter words.

'God, Morwen, it's worse than I thought. Our affairs are in a sorry state. We won't see the returns on the autumn clay despatches for several months, and Daniel says we may have to close all but Clay One to keep our heads above water with that bastard Judge Manley's directives. A fine clay boss I've turned out to be. A fine husband for you—'

'Don't say that!' Her voice was vibrant with anger. 'Don't ever say that, Ben Killigrew. You're the only husband I ever wanted—'

'And you're the most beautiful and loyal wife a man could wish for,' he muttered against the softness of her hair. 'But it won't solve my problems. I wish to God that it would. Everything I've worked for seems doomed to failure. I'm not sure it's worth going on at all. Why bother with it all? Why not let the damn clay works fall into decay and forget they ever existed?'

Morwen knew that there would never be a better moment than this. Her voice was low and soft now, her breath a warm caress on his cheek. Her arms held him close as though to shield him from all worry. She spoke slowly, so that he would take in all the sense of her words.

'Because it's your heritage, that's why! Because your father built it up from nothing to give to you, and an inheritance like that is something to be passed down through the generations.'

She took his hand and pressed it gently against her belly. 'I give you your son, Ben, growing here under my heart, and ready to be born with the newness of the next spring. Don't throw away our son's heritage—'

She felt him tense as she finished speaking, suddenly too emotional to go on. She felt his hand press more protectively over her rounded belly, and heard the strangled joy in his voice as he answered. 'Is it true? Are you certain, dar?'

'Certain sure!' She gave a shuddering, heartfelt laugh, because at last they were sharing in this miracle, and Ben's defeatism had vanished, however momentarily. He shook off his tiredness like discarding a heavy cloak, demanding to know how long she had been aware of it, and why she hadn't told him before... demanding and arrogant like the old Ben, his masculine pride and his belief in himself restored more by the second.

'I've only known a month or so – yes, a whole month... no, I made up my mind not to tell you before, until today's business was settled... Doctor Pender says I'm fine, a wonderfully healthy specimen, and there shouldn't be any problems... but I'm thinking there may be if you crush me so...'

She was laughing and crying at the same time, because Ben was wholly here with her again, and it was as wondrous as the night they were wed, when everything was fresh and new, and the only important thing in the world was sharing their love...

'Morwen, God knows I should be exhausted, but right now I feel as though I could conquer mountains. I want – I want

– hell's teeth, but you've turned me into a gibbering idiot by this news! Am I forbidden to touch you from now on? I mean, will it hurt the baby? Then again, are we in danger of Primmy waking up as usual and taking you away from me?'

Morwen felt herself blush. She, too, felt the newness of their relationship. It was a strange and beautiful feeling. She took Ben's hand and covered her breast with it, feeling his palm close over her.

'The children have stayed at my mother's house. Touch me all you want to, my love,' she whispered. 'Lay with me, and be part of me. Your needs are my needs too, and oh, Ben, it's been such a long lonely time without you—'

She got no further as her mouth was covered by his own. Such a tender kiss at first, deepening into one of mounting desire. All the anger of the day, of past weeks, was forgotten in the exquisite joy of belonging.

She felt his first sweet invasion inside her, and gloried in the power of a man's body that could be alternately gentle and thrusting, and bring such pleasure to a woman. In those ecstatic moments, she pitied anyone who had not known the love she knew, and even more, she pitied every woman in the world who was not Ben Killigrew's woman.

Despite his new-found energy, their joy was swiftly over, but as fulfilling to them both as the longest night of love. When his passion was spent, Ben lay with her in his arms, careful that his weight shouldn't crush her.

'Thank you, my love, for keeping this secret until the best moment of all,' he said softly.

'I truly didn't know when the best moment would be. I only knew that I would recognise it when it came,' she answered.

'Your instincts were always uncannily right. I always said you were a little fey, my dar.'

'Not fey. Just Cornish,' she said, and they both knew that for certain people it was one and the same.

He was aching with the need to sleep, but still reluctant to let go of consciousness and the best news a man could have.

'Shall we tell the children they're to have a little brother or sister yet?'

'I've wondered about that, and I think so. It will make them feel part of a real family. Besides, we must tell your father tomorrow, and mine too.'

'Your mother will be thrilled. I'm surprised she hasn't already guessed,' he murmured, no longer able to stay awake, and thankfully, Morwen saw no need to tell him that Bess was already aware of her coming fourth grandchild. Ben finally slept, still holding her, and they were still in one another's arms when daylight awoke them.

–

The Tremaynes and the Killigrews had something to celebrate, and while they did so they could manage to put the other matter out of their minds. But for Ben those other times encroached on him like a cancer. He had to find so much money. His own priority was to help the clay folk who had suffered, but he was already doing that, and it was no hardship to continue.

The Judge's dictum to refurbish the badly broken St Austell roads was an insult, since Killigrew's clay waggons had not been solely responsible for their condition, but Richard Carrick had advised him against an appeal, which would only cost more money in delays and they might very well lose anyway.

The railway was to be torn up, as Ben himself had wanted, and the entire moorland surveyed for a more suitable route. But the new tracks would have to wait until the finances were found. And the town building Judge Manley had so pompously ordered Ben to finance would take a crippling amount of his resources.

For a few mad moments he had been tempted to try his luck at gambling again, but he was older and wiser now, and had a family to support. At that thought, the glow filled him all over again, for not only was it the legacy of Sam's children, but a child that grew from the love he and Morwen shared.

He had something worth fighting for now, and for the first time he understood why Charles had fought to make his son love the clay as much as he had. Charles's reaction to their joyful news was quite pathetic. Tears ran down the old man's cheeks just as his nurse appeared to wash him, and Nurse Wilder tut-tutted and said he wasn't to be upset like this.

'We're not upsetting him!' Ben laughed, and Morwen had nodded quickly at his raised eyebrow. 'We're letting him know he's to have a grandson in the spring, Nurse Wilder, so how do you fancy an extra job as midwife?'

She went pink, and exclaimed with pleasure, though Morwen suspected she, too, had guessed and had wisely said nothing. Her own family had been overjoyed, and the two little boys shouted that they hoped it would be another boy, as they couldn't abide little girls who dribbled and cooed all day long.

'When will it be here?' Walter shouted. 'Will it play with me?'

'An' me,' Albert obligingly added.

Morwen hugged them both. 'Not right away,' she said. 'It will sleep a lot at first, but we'll be able to take it for walks, and you'll be its big brothers, whether it's a boy or a girl, and Primmy will be a big sister too!'

'No, she won't. She's only a babby,' Walter scoffed.

'Baby, darling. But she'll grow up, just like you.' She met Ben's eyes over Walter's head, and smiled into them.

Morwen's pregnancy was an uncomfortable one. The sickness that had plagued her at first now seemed to happen more frequently, but the doctor merely said that some women were unfortunate in that way, and teased that it was a penance they bore for the joy of having a child.

Privately, Morwen thought that for her it was a different penance. When she first knew about the baby, she had thought a lot about Dora. Now she seemed to be thinking constantly about Celia. She couldn't rid herself of the feeling that these wretched months when she should be feeling at her most serene, were being made so miserable as some kind of Divine revenge.

She and Celia had tampered with nature, visiting the old moors woman and taking a potion to kill a child. However much Morwen dressed it up, the stark facts were the same.

Celia had so wanted to have a man to love her and care for her. Instead, she had been defiled by the brutal Jude Pascoe, and been so deranged by it all that she had drowned herself in the clay pool rather than live with the memory.

But Morwen lived with it. She thought it was dead and buried like Celia and the appalling thing they had disposed of in a moorland grave, that Zillah had called 'the waste'.

But there were times when the memory haunted Morwen, and never more so than now. She wanted desperately to confide in Ben, but he was too involved with business meetings and worries of his own for Morwen to add to his worries.

Hers was, after all, a perfectly normal happening in a woman's life. It was something she had longed for, but she hadn't expected Celia's presence to be almost like a visitation.

The children took up much of her time. She adored Sam's little ones, and they looked forward excitedly to having a new baby in the house. They had slipped into the Killigrew household as easily as if they had been born there.

Ben had once suggested changing their names to Killigrew, but Morwen had decided vehemently against it.

'It would be wrong, and my folks wouldn't like it,' she said positively. 'Everything else has been taken from them except their name, and I won't see them deprived of knowing who they are. Sam would turn in his grave to know it.'

'All right, I didn't mean to make an issue of it, love. I just thought it may seem odd to them that their new brother has a different name, that's all.'

'We'll just have to explain it to them then. 'Tis only the grown-ups who take such things seriously. As long as the children have things explained to them, they'll understand.'

'Yes, Ma'am,' Ben said with the ghost of a smile. 'I wonder why we rich folk think we have to send our children away to be educated when my moorland wife is so all-seeing!'

It was a rare moment of teasing in the dark days when Ben thought seriously of selling his heritage. He and Gorran and Carrick had had endless consultations by the time Christmas loomed near, and had finally made a long list of priorities to be done. The rail tracks had already been torn up by a team of clayworkers on Ben's instructions, since he couldn't bear to look at them a minute longer.

Before he could even think of getting new land surveyed for building another railway, if indeed there was still a clay business to warrant it, the town's needs must come next. The narrow broken streets, that had been a trial to townsfolk for years, must now be put in order, and then must come the new administration building the Judge had so unfairly demanded.

Contractors were approached, endless estimates were given and mostly rejected as being catchpenny affairs, and the whole task began to seem impossible for one man to undertake. Most of Ben's assets were tied up in Killigrew Clay, and the thought of finding all the money that was required was a nightmare to him.

He tried not to worry Morwen with the problems, but Morwen had never been one for being shut out, and insisted on knowing all that was going on.

'Oh, Ben, if only I hadn't married a clay boss,' she tried to tease him out of his melancholy. 'We don't need this big house, nor fine carriages, nor to be lord and lady of the manor! We could be just as happy living in a hovel—'

'Well, that's something we're never going to do, so forget it! And if you're really sorry you married me—'

She could always bait him into believing her for a few seconds, and she could just as easily coax him out of the doldrums by proving to their mutual satisfaction that there was no-one else on earth that she could love.

Ben was her whole life, but she was wise enough to know that she had to share him with Killigrew Clay. The clay that was so vital to them was gouged from the earth by simple, hard-working folk, changed beyond recognition and moulded into something of classic grace. For Morwen there was something vastly beautiful and symbolic in the thought.

The children could cheer Ben too, as they did old Charles Killigrew. Charles was ailing fast, but he said stoically that he wasn't giving up this life until he'd seen the Killigrew fortunes revive, and more importantly, until he'd seen his new grand-child.

Morwen loved him all the more for including Sam's children in his affections. They called her own father Grandpa, but they called Charles Pa, which pleased him enormously. He was a man who liked little fuss, and the simple name suited him.

Morwen had little wish now to visit the moors that she had once adored. The thought of seeing the newly filled-in ground where the little trucks had plunged deep into the ground made her nauseous, knowing that it had been Sam's tomb.

She had been there once or twice, needing to sort out Sam's family clothes and possessions at the cottage, but it had been painfully embarrassing to meet the clayworkers she knew, and realise that they hardly knew what to say to her. Once, they would have done…

'I'm not one of them any more,' she had almost wept on Ben's shoulder. 'We couldn't find the words to say to one another, and it pains me, Ben. They're old friends, yet I don't know them any more.'

There was nothing he could say to comfort her until she thought things out for herself, realising once and for all that Ben Killigrew's wife and Morwen Tremayne, bal maiden, could never be one and the same. She couldn't cling to both worlds, and even now, after four years, it was hard to let her old world go.

–

They had intended to let Christmas pass quietly, but in the end, Morwen's entire family came to Killigrew House for a lunch of goose and plum pudding, and despite the anxiety hanging over all their heads, the antics of Freddie and the children lifted their spirits.

There were little gifts for everyone, and if this year wasn't quite in the old Killigrew style, no-one noticed. It was still a house filled with love and subdued laughter, since none of them could quite forget those who were missing. Sam and Dora, and Matt…

Jack was on tenterhooks, wondering when he could decently make his departure during the afternoon, since he'd been invited for afternoon tea with the Boskellys, and Annie Boskelly was clearly more of an attraction than his family, however loved.

And rightly so, in Bess's eyes. A man and woman who found one another out of the whole world and wanted to spend the rest of their lives together, were fortunate indeed, so why should the rest of the world keep them apart?

'I'm sure Ben and Morwen won't mind if you go on back to Truro, Jack,' she said finally, when she could stand his fidgeting no longer. 'Give Annie our love, and say that we'd like 'ee to bring her to tea one Sunday. Do you think her father and uncle would care to come too, or wouldn't we be posh enough for the Boskellys?'

His handsome face lit up as he smiled. He hugged Bess with rough affection.

'You're posh enough for anybody, Mammie, and I'd fight the man who says you ain't!'

'Don't do that, Jack,' Bess laughed. 'Just ask the Boskellys for tea and leave it at that.'

She felt hot even as she spoke. Inviting the Boskellys to tea! What were the Tremaynes coming to, behaving so grand and proper?

She caught Hal smiling at her when Jack had gone, and knew that their thoughts were similar. But they could hold up their heads in any company now. The days were past when the idea of coming to Killigrew House would have thrown the whole family into a tizzy. This was her daughter's home, and it was as warm and loving as the old cottage had ever been.

'Will your father come downstairs this afternoon, Ben?' She turned to him before she began to feel maudlin on this day when they had all decided to put other worries aside.

'I fear not. Nurse Wilder suggested to Doctor Pender that we carry him down in a chair, but he couldn't be bothered with all the noise. I know he'd be pleased to see you if you could spare him half an hour though. I said we'd go up at intervals.'

'Of course I will!' Bess rose at once, her one-time awe of Charles Killigrew completely gone. Who could fear such a poor old man whose roars had dwindled to no more than a whine?

–

By early evening, the children were nearly dropping with sleep. None of them had had their usual daily nap, and they made no protest when Bess and Morwen took them to bed. They left a low light burning safely in the nursery, and stood together in the doorway for a moment.

'Our Sam would have blessed 'ee for caring so much for his babbies, Morwen,' Bess said quietly. 'No children could have wished for a more loving mother.'

'It's easy to love them, Mammie, and Ben and I truly feel we're their parents now. This little one—' she put her hand lightly on her swollen belly – 'This one is the joy that we never expected, but Walter and Albert and Primmy will always hold their own special place in our family.'

The soft darkness seemed to make it easier to speak from her heart, and she felt her mother's quick kiss on her cheek. They were not often a demonstrative family, and Morwen treasured the moment.

–

Such sweet moments seemed less frequent in the difficult days in which they were all concerned. Ben called a meeting of his Works Manager and his pit captains shortly after Christmas, and warned them that it seemed very likely that all but Clay One pit would have to be sold. He prayed that his face didn't betray how desperately he hoped he would find a buyer. If he didn't...

He spent long hours alone in his study, feeling more of a failure than ever. It was a feeling he hated and despised. He had always been able to rise above whatever misfortune life had dealt him, but this time he couldn't see the end of it.

He couldn't take an interest in any of the things he used to find stimulating. It was even an embarrassment for him to go to his own pits. He forced himself to make brief visits to the families who had suffered in the accident, and knew that they avoided any mention of the future.

Newspapers remained unread for days, where before he had immersed himself in them avidly, wanting to know full details of the Crimean war and how the two sides were faring.

The newspapers had said as fatuously as ever that it would all be over by Christmas, but Christmas had come and gone, and the turn of the year was on them already. It was 1856, and there was no real sign of an end to the war, nor to Ben Killigrew's personal problems.

He could do nothing about the war, but several days into the new year Hal Tremayne came hammering on the door of Killigrew House with some news that was to change everything.

Chapter Twenty-Three

'We've had news of our Matt, Morwen!'

Morwen gasped, seeing that Hal could hardly contain himself as he was shown into the drawing-room, and she knew at once that Bess's own sadness over her lost lamb had been as deeply felt by Hal all these years. He had rarely spoken of it, but the pain had been there all the same. But there was nothing but excitement in his eyes now.

Morwen's heart beat so fast she thought she would faint. She clutched at her father's arm, since he looked more than ready to do the same.

'Sit down, Daddy, and tell me what's happened. You look so dazed. Will you take some brandy?'

Hal laughed recklessly. 'Why not? Yes, I'll take some brandy, my love. We should all be taking brandy! Where's that husband of yours? I want him to hear this news too.'

'He's taken the boys for a ride because they were so cross today – oh, Daddy, please tell me. Don't make me wait until Ben comes back—'

Hal drew out several pieces of paper from the inside of his coat. There was also a large packet that he set down on the sofa beside them both. The letter had already been well-thumbed, and Morwen guessed that Bess would have wept over it. Hal handed it to her, his voice jerky with emotion.

'The postal man delivered it to the cottage at first, and the neighbours told un there was no-one living there. He were about to take it away again, when somebody asked who 'twere for, since clay folk don't get many letters sent to 'em. The man said 'twere for Hal Tremayne, so they sent un to the works, and then to the little house. 'Tis a wonder it reached us at all!'

He lapsed with exhaustion as Morwen handed him a glass of brandy from the decanter and sat down with Matt's letter, glad to see he hadn't skimped on it now he had finally got in touch with his family. In fact Matt had enjoyed the spasmodic schooling given to the clayworkers' children, and he had always been the more eloquent of the two older Tremayne boys.

As she began to read quickly it became clear, too, that in the years since he'd been gone, Matt had lost his old country style of speech, and wrote an articulate letter. She wouldn't have cared if he'd said no more than a few sentences. It was as though Matt stood beside her, speaking the words in her ear...

'Dearest Mammie and Daddy and all my family,' Matt wrote.

'This is a hard letter for me to write, yet it's been on my conscience to write to you for a very long time. I know how bad you must have thought me when I ran off to sea with Jude Pascoe, and in the early days I regretted it a hundred times.'

Morwen bit her lip at reading Jude Pascoe's name, but at least Matt appeared to have seen him for what he was.

'When we reached America after the weary weeks at sea, we got work at the docks in New York. America is a land of opportunity for those prepared to work hard, and I soon discovered that Jude and I had different ideas about that.

'Eventually we parted company. He stayed in New York, and I joined what's called a waggon-train, and travelled across the country to California. America is a vast land, and it took several months to arrive here. Most of the waggons contained families, and I was attached to a family called Wainwright, the parents and a small boy, and a girl about our Morwen's age, called Louisa.

'Mr Wainwright was a teacher, and they were travelling to the gold diggings to start a school in the new towns that were springing up. To pass the time when the waggon-train halted each night, he taught small groups of interested people. I joined his classes, and so did Louisa, of course.'

Morwen glanced at her father. The brandy and the excitement had taken their toll, and he leaned his head back against the cushions and closed his eyes. Morwen read on, already with a faint premonition about her brother and Louisa Wainwright.

'I won't bore you with details of the journey, except to say that it was an exhausting time. Many folk gave up halfway across the country, and set up homesteads just where they were.

'The rest of us reached California, and lived as best we could, though most were in little more than shacks at first. The conditions were terrible. Either it poured with rain and was cold and miserable, or it was blisteringly hot and we were bitten half to death by mosquitoes. I wonder any of us survived.

'But we knew there was gold to be found, and Mammie – Daddy – I did find it! I had a big strike, where there was more gold than I ever dreamed existed.

'I didn't even know it was gold at first. I was grovelling in the mud with my shallow pan like everybody else, shaking the dirt and slime out of it in the hope of seeing the little gleaming golden specks. Sometimes somebody found a bigger piece, the size of a little finger or even bigger, and you knew he was going to be rich!

'What I'm trying to tell you, my dearest family that I miss so much, is that I'm now one of those rich men. I have a fine house and men working for me at the gold diggings, and a lovely wife called Louisa, née Wainwright. And in the spring there will be a new Tremayne babby on the other side of the world.'

Morwen felt too choked to go on reading until she had wiped her eyes. Matt was rich and married, and his wife was expecting a baby at about the same time as she was. And for all his grand new status, Matt didn't forget his roots. He, too, would hold a *babby* in his arms...

Hal was watching her now, and she smiled tremulously as she neared the end of the letter.

'I can't quite believe all this,' she said shakily.

'Read to the end, my love,' he told her, his voice as thick as hers.

Dutifully, Morwen did so. 'I never forgot any of you back in Cornwall. I love Louisa more than life, but I still miss my family. I miss the scent of the moors and the little cottage where we all lived. The thought of Mammie's cooking still makes my mouth water, and I miss sparring with Sam and Jack. And I bet our Morwen's the prettiest girl in the county by now, and Freddie's still as troublesome.

'Mammie and Daddy, I hope you can forgive me at last, and that you'll accept what I'm sending you. Not as charity, but because I love you all, and I want to share what I have. It's my dearest wish that one day I can bring my wife and child home to Cornwall to visit you. Until that day, if any of you care to write to us, it will be the happiest day of my life. I long for news of home.

'Your loving son, Matt.'

—

Morwen swallowed back the tears. The last paragraph tore at her heart. Dear, sweet Matt, clearly still homesick for the place of his birth. For the cottage that was no longer theirs; for his family, his sister and brothers… not even knowing that Sam was dead. Nor that she had married Ben Killigrew or that all his family's lives had changed so dramatically since that day he had taken his chance to start a new life across the ocean.

She blew her nose hard, and Hal patted her back. He and Bess would already have shed their tears of happiness that Matt had come back into their lives again.

'I can't express what I feel, Daddy—'

'No more can I, my love.'

She managed to smile through her tears. 'What did Matt send you? Was it a nice gift?'

Hal picked up the packet at his side and handed it to her without saying a word. Mystified, Morwen opened it. There was a letter from a lawyer in California, explaining that the sealed packet enclosed was to be taken immediately to a reputable lawyer of Mr Hal Tremayne's choosing, to be opened and read in the presence of witnesses. Morwen frowned.

'I don't understand—'

'Nor I, but Ben will know what to do. I've had no dealings with lawyers, but I'm mazed with curiosity. Should he be back soon?'

'He's here now,' Morwen said with relief as she heard the noisy chattering of the two little boys. When they came in, she instructed them to run at once to the kitchen for some lemonade, and to ask Fanny to take them to the nursery to play with them.

She ignored all their howls of protest, and after one look at her and Hal, Ben insisted that they did as their mother said. As soon as the three adults were alone, he asked what had happened. Morwen ran to his side, hugging his arms.

'Oh, Ben, 'tis a letter from our Matt. He's married and his wife's having a baby, and he's rich from the gold diggings! Can you believe it all!'

She couldn't stop laughing and crying at the same time, and at his incredulous face, Hal affirmed that what Morwen said was true. He thrust the letter under Ben's nose, who scanned it quickly.

'This is wonderful news,' he said. 'I know how badly you've all ached for news of Matt. I'm so happy for you all, Hal, and Bess must be overjoyed.'

'That she is,' Hal said softly. 'But there's still this other business. Perhaps you'd put me right on it all.'

Ben read the official letter. 'You must get this attended to straight away, Hal—'

'I don't understand lawyers, but I'd prefer it if that Mr Carrick were to see to it for me. At least I don't feel too uneasy in his company.'

'As a matter of fact he's coming here tomorrow,' Ben said, wishing he didn't have to think of his reasons for asking Richard to Killigrew House. The likely closure of three of his pits was not going to be a happy day. But he didn't want to dispel the joy of these two with his own troubles.

'Look, you and Bess come here in the afternoon,' Ben said. 'I know she'll be bursting with curiosity to know what the packet contains, and she can see her grandchildren at the same time. We'll get your business settled before Richard and I get down to mine. Does that suit you, Hal?'

—

Bess and Hal were there promptly the following afternoon. The children were kept strictly out of the way, and the Tremaynes waited anxiously with Morwen and Ben for Richard Carrick to arrive. When he did, he looked surprised to see so many people awaiting him, but readily agreed to deal with the Tremayne business first.

It was like reading a Will, Morwen thought. Not that she had ever attended a formal Will reading, but she'd heard that this was how it happened for grand folk. The lawyer on one side of the desk, the hopeful recipients on the other.

In this case Richard sat in one of their easy arm-chairs; Ben lounged against the piano, while the others sat like a row of peas on the sofa. She heard Richard Carrick give a sudden exclamation and look up sharply at Hal.

'My dear Mr Tremayne, had you any idea of what this packet contained?'

Hal shrugged. 'A gift from my son in America.' Morwen noted how he said the words now with unconscious pride.

Richard smiled slightly. 'Some of my clients would sell their soul to the devil for such a gift! This is an authorisation to pay into a bank the sum of ten thousand dollars for your use, Sir. May I offer you my sincere best wishes and congratulations, Mr Tremayne, and ask that you'll allow me to act as your lawyer and adviser?'

None of the three people on the sofa said a word. They were pleased and stunned. Besides that, the amount of money meant less to them than to those who had dealings with such sums. Neither did they understand the value of dollars.

Ben Killigrew did. He gave a smothered gasp, his mouth dropping open, and Morwen knew by his reaction that this was riches indeed.

'Can you explain what this American money means to my family, Mr Carrick? Is it of use here in Cornwall?' Morwen said hurriedly, as her parents seemed devoid of speech.

She blushed at seeming so stupid before this educated man. Truly, she had no more idea of the value of dollars than Hal and Bess, but it was mainly for their benefit that she asked, since they both looked totally bemused.

'Yes, my dear Morwen, it most certainly is of use. Ten thousand dollars can be converted by any bank into our own currency, and the amount your brother sent would buy you half of Cornwall if you wished!'

Richard spoke jocularly to break the tension this news evoked. The Tremaynes seemed more baffled by their sudden wealth than anyone he had ever seen, and seemingly unaware of what it would mean to them. He spoke more kindly to Hal.

'You'll need time to get used to the idea, Mr Tremayne. If you would like me to come and see you at your home when you've had a few days to think things over, I can advise you on the best ways of investing your money.'

Morwen saw her mother put her hand on Hal's. She whispered quickly in his ear. They looked at one another, and each gave a small nod. Hal's voice was more resolute.

'We don't need time, Mr Carrick. Both Bess and me know where we want the money to go to be put to best use—'

'*No!*' Ben said angrily. 'I know what you're thinking, Hal, and I won't take a cent of it. This is your money. Matt sent it to you with love, and it was never intended to get me out of my difficulties!'

Swiftly Morwen moved across to him, linking her hand through his arm, as though to stand by whatever he said. Richard sat back, while they sorted out the matter among themselves. He couldn't deny that the thought had immediately occurred to him too. He also knew that Ben had far too much pride to accept this money out of hand.

Hal spoke roughly. 'What do we want with all these dollars or cents, whatever they are? Bess and me have everything we want. Your family have been more than generous to ours, so why shouldn't we invest in the clay works instead of any other business that we don't care a damn about?'

'Mr Tremayne has a point, Ben—' Richard said quietly.

'Ben, please don't turn us down without considering it,' Bess put in, her voice shaky. 'You'll be used to handling such big sums, but I tell 'ee it will be more of a worry to Hal and me than a blessing. Take it with our love, and build your new railway and set the town to rights.'

Ben shook his head decisively. 'No. My answer is still the same. Matt sent this for you, not for me.'

'What about our Morwen, then? She'd benefit by the money, and if you don't take it, what's to happen to the clay works?' Hal was on safer ground now. 'You'll be putting a lot o' families to hardship if the clayworkers have no jobs.'

'Don't bring me into it, Daddy,' Morwen said quickly. 'I'm touched that you and Mammie want to help, but it must be Ben's decision, and whatever he says is right by me.'

'You weren't so backward in coming forward when you stood up for un in court!'

That was different. This was Ben's pride at stake. She could see it as clearly as Richard Carrick, if her generous and loving family could not.

Richard cleared his throat. 'May I make a suggestion to you all? Mr Tremayne, you mentioned investing your money in Killigrew Clay. I know that this has been your life for many years, and indeed for all your family, so I think this is by far the best idea, rather than give it as an outright gift to Ben. I could make all the necessary arrangements so that Ben would have access to the money immediately, and you would also reap dividends, of course.'

Hal was ready to agree to anything. The lawyer made it all sound feasible, but the thought of such a large sum of money began to feel like a millstone around his neck, and he was already wondering how rich folk coped with the responsibility of it all.

And if Matt could send them a sum to make Ben and Richard Carrick treat the matter so seriously, then how much was Matt really worth? It was something beyond Hal's imagination.

'I have a better proposition.' Ben spoke before Hal could do more than nod his head. His voice was clear-cut, forcing them all to listen. 'No family has been closer to me over the years than the Tremaynes. You've been my best pit captain, and now my trusted Works Manager. But it's more than that. We're bound together by love and respect. Because of that, there's only one way I would accept your investment in Killigrew Clay, Hal, and that is for you to become my partner.'

Morwen gasped with delight, hugging Ben's arm. The solution was so simple, and so beautifully obvious. Ben's pride would be saved, and Hal would have security for his life-time. He sank back against the sofa while he digested this undreamed-of idea.

'As your legal adviser, I must say it's a fine offer, Mr Tremayne. Whether Ben would want the name of the Works changed or not is another matter—' Richard put in helpfully.
'*No!*'

Hal and Ben spoke simultaneously, but it was Hal who got the words out first.

'I've worked for Killigrew Clay all my life, and God willing, 'twill still be Killigrew Clay when I die! Mr Charles wouldn't have it any other way, and no more would I. As to this partner business – I thank'ee, Ben, but I'm more than happy the way I am—'

The Tremayne women decided spontaneously that it was time to stop these dithering men from walking on tip-toe all around one another, when the way was so clear to them.

'Daddy, if you turn this offer down, you're a fool!' Morwen said explosively, her eyes blazing down at him.

Bess turned to him at the same moment. 'For pity's sake, dar, is the fact that you'm a partner in Killigrew Clay going to stop 'ee being Works Manager? Who's to know of it if we don't tell 'em?'

'That's right!' Morwen stormed on. 'Mr Carrick himself was a silent partner in Killigrew Clay for years, and since this is so important to us all, I hope he'll forgive me for telling 'ee so. Is there any reason why Daddy can't be the same, Ben, and carry on with his Works Managing job, if 'tis what he wants?'

Ben shook his head. 'No reason at all, if that's what you'd prefer, Hal. We haven't heard from you on this yet.'

Hal got to his feet. He was nothing if not his own man, and not his son-in-law nor the educated lawyer, nor his own two womenfolk were going to decide it for him.

'What I say is that we all sleep on it. You may regret this offer tomorrow, Ben, and me and Bess have got to talk it over by ourselves without our Morwen trying to twist me around her finger. I'm happy enough to give 'ee the money and be done with it—'

'And I flatly refuse to take it unless you become my legal partner, and take on whatever job you like to our mutual agreement,' Ben retorted.

Richard cleared his throat again. These clay folk were among the most cantankerous and strong-willed of people, and he most

337

definitely included Ben Killigrew in that description. But he couldn't deny that he had a deep and abiding respect for every one of them in that elegant drawing-room.

'Then may I suggest that we all give it serious thought and meet here again tomorrow, if that suits you, Ben? Does your own business need discussion today, or can that wait as well? This has taken rather longer than I imagined.'

'My business can wait,' Ben said shortly, realising as he said it that his interview with the lawyer now depended on the outcome of Hal Tremayne's decision.

—

Hal and Bess were very quiet on the way home to the little house. As if by mutual agreement, they said nothing about their new status until they were safely indoors and alone.

'Well, dar.' Hal felt suddenly awkward, because they had never had such things to consider before now.

In the early days, they had been as poor as any other large family, when Hal had been the only breadwinner while Bess had the children. Then she, too, had worked for Killigrew Clay as a bal maiden, taking along each child in turn to work for the bosses in St Austell.

If anyone had said then how their fortunes would have changed, they would have laughed in total disbelief. But it was something that had to be faced. Money had come their way, and with it, the offer for Hal to be Ben Killigrew's partner.

Bess's mouth began to twitch. It was all so ridiculous, so impossible, so unbelievable…

Before she could stop herself, her shoulders had begun to shake, and the laughter was churning inside her, as much of a release as the tears of joy she had shed earlier, when she had first seen her beloved Matt's letter.

'Well, dar!' she gasped. 'How do 'ee fancy being a partner, then? Will 'ee swank about the town on Sundays and ride in a fancy carriage, and expect me to call 'ee Sir?'

He looked startled for a moment, then he caught her reckless mood, and swung her into his arms.

'And will 'ee be my lady and dress in fine silk gowns instead of sewing 'em for others, and enjoy hearing other folks call 'ee Madam?'

They laughed in sudden glee like a pair of children, and just as suddenly the laughter died as they faced one another, arms still holding each other tight, chests heaving.

'Is it right for me to do this, Bess? You'm the wise un between us. Tell me what 'ee think truthfully. I'd gladly give Ben the money and be done with all the fuss, but would our Matt want it that way?'

She looked at him with love softening her eyes; he was as dear to her as he had ever been.

'I think our Matt 'ould be mighty proud of 'ee, dar.'

'So you think I should accept this idea?' He still wanted to hear her say it, to boost his own uncertainty.

Bess drew him down beside her on their own modest sofa. At that moment the comfortable piece of furniture seemed to epitomise their position. It was grander than the old wooden settle they had left behind at the cottage; nothing like as grand as that at Killigrew House. They were somewhere between the two, and it was where they belonged.

'Hal, I'm thinking 'tis for the best. 'Twill be of help to Ben, whatever name you give yourself at the Works. But perhaps my reasons are a mite more selfish than that.'

'You never had a selfish bone in your body, dar,' Hal said gruffly.

Bess smiled. 'I never had the means to give my children something that only rich folk can give them, either. Think what it will mean to be Ben's partner, Hal. We'll have an inheritance to leave to our sons, and that's summat we never dreamed possible. That means more to me than being called a lady!'

Hal's arms went around her and held her close. 'You've always been a lady to me, dar.' His voice slowed as he considered her words. ''Tis right what you say. Our Matt has done summat more special for us than he believed. And he being one of our sons, he'll benefit in the end as well!'

'That he will,' Bess said softly. 'The money will go full circle. Some of it, anyway.'

Hal released her, frowning in thought. 'This needs some thinking out, Bess. Yes, I'll agree to Ben's idea of being his partner, though it still makes my stomach lurch to think on it! But we'll see the lawyer privately once all this is settled, and see to making a proper Will for when the time comes.'

He caught sight of her expression and gave her a squeeze. 'There's no sense in shirking it. All rich folks have to make their Wills, dar, to provide for their children!'

She smiled again at that, although she didn't like the thought of making a Will. But it needed sorting out between them, before they put their wishes to the lawyer. And long before they went to bed that night, they had made their decision.

Bess insisted that she wanted no share of the clay inheritance, declining such responsibility, and that all she would want was a decent allowance of money for her to live on comfortably in their adored little house.

How she would even exist without Hal was something she refused to think about, but this had to be a sensible discussion, and she tried to stay as unemotional about it as possible.

They reasoned that since Morwen would naturally inherit Ben's half-share of the Works, they needn't apportion any of it to her either, but would leave a special legacy for her to spend as she wished.

Apart from those sums, the entire half-share of Hal Tremayne's interest in Killigrew Clay was to be divided equally between his three sons.

He had almost said four, and felt a swift sharp grief that Sam could not have lived to see this incredible day.

By the time the Tremaynes went to bed in their snug little house that night, they were quite determined in their minds what had to be done. And they both decided that the contents of Hal's Will should be kept private between the two of them and Richard Carrick.

So much had happened so fast, and Bess was still dazed by it all. It was humbling to know that she and Hal could do what they had never thought possible – provide for their sons after their death.

In due time, Matthew, Jack and Freddie Tremayne would be equal partners in half-ownership of Killigrew Clay.

Even more dear to Bess's heart as she finally drifted off to sleep, snuggled up against Hal's broad back, was the knowledge that Matt had finally stretched out his hand to them from halfway across the world, and in doing so, had opened the gates to a new beginning for them all.

Chapter Twenty-Four

Richard Carrick was experienced enough to show surprise when he learned of Hal Tremayne's wishes. The contents of the Will was known to no-one but the lawyer and the Tremaynes. The partnership between Hal Tremayne and Ben Killigrew was also to be a private one between the parties concerned, but once it was in the form of a legal signed document, the money from Matt was quickly put into Ben's hands to do with as he wished.

Richard's wife, Mary, was buzzing with curiosity as to why Richard should suddenly be acting for those common Tremaynes, who had never had a penny between them, but he was as tight-lipped as a clamshell, and refused to satisfy her probing.

Any mention of the Tremaynes had the effect of making Mary Carrick's blood-pressure rise. She could still not forgive Morwen for taking Ben Killigrew away from her daughter, however much Jane protested in exasperation that she and Ben had never had any intention of marrying.

Although, seeing her daughter's joy on hearing at last that her newspaper reporter husband was safe, Mary was forced to admit that Jane did seem to have found her match.

And that was another thing. That vulgar Yorkshireman, Tom Askhew, with his brash ways and hard flat vowel sounds... no doubt when he returned as something of a hero from the war he would be taking Jane and dear little Cathy back to that miserable northern county of his.

Cold and bitter though Mary Carrick had become, the thought of losing Cathy yet again was something to make her weep. Jane did her best to make her realise that it would certainly not happen at once!

Tom had not returned yet, and until she held him in her arms, she would not quite be able to believe it. And seeing the anxiety in Jane's pretty eyes, Mary held her tongue for once.

–

In St Austell Ben was able to instruct a firm of road engineers to begin the repairs to the town streets. There had already been too much delay while his affairs were being sorted out, but now all the work required by Judge Manley could go ahead as rapidly as possible.

Plans for the new administration hall were submitted and approved, but most importantly to Ben and Killigrew Clay, there was no need now to delay the negotiations for the new railway.

Ben had expected some intervention from the Bodmin surveyors, but after the fiasco in which they guiltily held themselves more than half responsible, they were just as ready to get this whole sorry business behind them, and brought in an impartial engineer to assist them in a proper land survey so that work could begin immediately.

A more satisfactory new route was plotted, skirting the sharp drop of the moors on which the old one had been built, and taking a longer, more winding route, but one where there was no possibility of old tin workings putting the railway at risk.

Ben had a meeting with Lew Tregian, and asked him to insert a piece in *The Informer* about the new plans, and inviting comments or objections forthwith. Coupled with the approval of the surveyors and the engineer, the article carried a lot of weight, and Ben realised that the attitude of the town had changed towards him again.

Folk stopped to pass the time of day when they met him, and he and his young wife were once again acknowledged to be the most handsome pair in the town of St Austell.

Any invitation to Killigrew House was eagerly sought, though few were forthcoming, because of Morwen's condition. Entertaining was mostly confined to the family now.

'I know that I owe all my good fortune to Matt,' Ben said thoughtfully one evening when the two of them had come home from visiting Morwen's parents. 'I just wish your father would let me make it public knowledge that he's now my partner. He deserves the recognition, Morwen.'

She shook her head forcefully. 'It's not his way, Ben. Leave things as they are, I beg you. It's enough for him to know he's done what he could for Killigrew Clay. 'Tis in his blood, Ben.'

She smiled slightly, and he caught the movement. 'What's taken your fancy now, dar?'

'I was remembering when I first saw you at the Works, years ago when you were home from your posh London school,' she said softly. 'I thought you such a snot-nose! You looked as though you never had the slightest intention of ever dirtying your hands with your inheritance! And now 'tis in your blood, the same as in Daddy's.'

Ben laughed. 'Yes, it's in my blood. It's a part of all of us, and that's what makes it special. We're moulded together by the clay, and that's what makes us strong, Morwen.'

She drew a long deep breath. And God willing, there would soon be another Killigrew to carry on the dynasty Charles Killigrew had begun.

'Do you think the rail tracks will be ready for the spring despatches, Ben? There's so little time—'

'I'm hoping so. Now that we need spare no expense, the men will be working all hours to get them ready. Even if we delay the despatches by a month or so, it won't matter. April or May will make little difference, except that the later we despatch, the bigger load we'll have to deliver to the port. Either way, we shan't lose.'

He took her in his arms and held her close, and she felt a sweet tremor run through her. It was always so at his touch… but this time she had a more precious reason for feeling so affected by his words.

April or May… the difference in the two months was very important to Morwen. In May their baby should be a month old… in April the days would be long and tedious, and she would be heavy and clumsy and longing desperately to hold her first-born in her arms… and wondering just how much longer she must wait.

As the first hint of the usual early spring began to make itself felt in the warm south of Cornwall, hopes of an end at last to the Crimean War were finding voice in every local and national newspaper.

A Peace Conference was to be organised, but was beset by frustrations and difficulties, and the main issue was over allowing Prussia to be included in the discussions. Prussia and the German Federation had not supported Britain and her allies in their struggle, and many officials insisted that they should be excluded from any further association.

'What fools they all are!' Ben said in disgust. 'Our soldiers are still being killed daily as the war drags on, and they fuss over nations being present at a conference table!'

'Isn't it more delicate than that?' Morwen asked. 'I believe the Queen herself is in a quandary. Her eldest daughter is betrothed to the King of Prussia's nephew, and the Prince of Prussia is the Queen's and Prince Albert's close friend. Yet politically they are forced to agree that Prussia should not be admitted to the discussions.'

Ben's eyes had widened with pleasure and surprise.

'You constantly amaze me, Morwen! Just where did you glean such information, may I ask?'

She laughed self-consciously. 'I was not even aware that I had absorbed it! But when I read the London newspapers to your father, he does so love to hear about the Queen and the Prince and the devious games these important people play. He says wickedly that it's more fun than playing a real-life game of chess, and I have become just as interested in the moves.'

'Fun is hardly the word I would choose! They are devious and dangerous games, at times,' Ben said seriously. 'But I'm truly delighted to hear you take such an informed view of world affairs, Morwen.'

'You're pleased to discover that I have a brain too?' she said teasingly.

He laughed, and caught her around the waist, thickened and swollen now as the birth of their child became imminent. She was still close to him, in body as well as spirit, and it was where they both wanted to be.

–

It was not until March 30th, 1856, that the formal treaty of peace was signed. The Crimean War was over at last, and because of the electric telegraph, news of it was not slow in reaching the four corners of Britain.

As always, bonfires were lit to celebrate as towns and villages received the joyful news, even though to those not personally involved through soldier sons and husbands, the war had been no more than a distant happening in a remote part of the world. Victory was still something to savour.

The celebrations went on for days or weeks, according to how organised were the communities. On the moors above St Austell, there were additional celebrations.

Through the diligence of Ben Killigrew and the land surveyors, and the enthusiastic and determined team of construction engineers, the new Killigrew railway was ready to transport the clay blocks to Charlestown port by late April, and the clayworkers intended lighting their own bonfires high on the moors when the last of the despatches had gone.

They would celebrate the end of a war together with the hoped-for beginnings of new prosperity for Killigrew Clay, and they would raise their ale jugs to Ben Killigrew for the security of their jobs. The boss could be justly proud of his achievements.

His silent partner and official Works Manager, Hal Tremayne, echoed the sentiments the clayworkers voiced noisily at the end of the day shift when a chain of bonfires was lit right across the top of the moors, proclaiming to the townsfolk of St Austell that Killigrew Clay was in full production once more.

'I'm so happy for Ben, Hal.' Bess hugged his arm in a quiet corner amid the din and excitement of the clayworkers' celebrations.

'And rightly so, dar. I'm proud to call him son-in-law. He'll rise above anything this town can throw at him—'

'With your help. Don't forget that, Hal.'

He put his hand lightly over hers. 'I do forget it, and so should you. Our part in all this is to be kept silent, Bess. Put it out of your mind, and we'll go on as we are, as we've always been. Is it enough for you, dar?'

For the first time since the wonderful news from Matt, he wondered if she wanted more. They had had it in their means to buy their own fine house, and to rise up in the world. Hal had been so certain that what they did with Matt's money was the right solution, but more than four months had passed since that ecstatic day, and now he looked uneasily at his wife for a moment in the bonfire's dancing light.

She spoke simply and he knew that she was sincere. 'I have all I ever need right here, Hal.'

And yet, in Bess's eyes, he suspected it was perhaps not quite all. The family was not quite as complete as it had once been. Still, Hal counted himself as one of the happiest of men. He had a wife he adored, a snug house, and their children.

Jack was as happy as ninepence in Truro, proving himself to be something of a craftsman for Boskelly Boats, and moving closer towards a lasting attachment with Annie Boskelly.

Freddie had recovered from whatever nightmare had haunted him some months back, and when he had finished his time in the school in St Austell, it was all settled that he, too, should be apprenticed to the Boskelly firm. Right now, Freddie was dancing around the bonfire with a group of his old kiddley-boy friends, and a giggling froth of young bal maidens.

The two younger Tremayne boys would be fine and successful boat-builders, Hal thought, with his own insight into their characters. Even though they no longer worked with the clay, it was good for brothers to be together, and that was satisfaction enough for any father.

But at such moments of reflection, he could never ignore the sharp sadness for Sam, and for Dora too. Matt was gone from their lives, and yet had come suddenly close to them all again, and more letters had been exchanged since that glorious day in early January. Hal was the first to admit that he, himself, had never fully been able to accept Sam's death.

He knew that he was more stooped than before, his thick hair greying rapidly, his step slower. Sometimes he felt as though he aged as quickly as old Charles Killigrew, whose days must surely be numbered now.

He kept such morbid thoughts from Bess, who had seemed to glow with new life ever since hearing from Matt. Strictly speaking, they didn't have favourites… but if they did, then Matt was surely hers. Just as Sam, his firstborn, had been his. Though he would always have a special place in his heart for Morwen, his girl…

Morwen was fulfilled at last, Hal thought. She had Sam's three children safely under her wing, and they had settled into their new life at Killigrew House as though they had been born to it. And very soon now there would be another much-wanted child…

The bonfire on the moors sparked and showered, drawing shouts of excitement from the crowd, and loyal toasts to Queen and country. Countryfolk danced and sang as though in some pagan ritual. In St Austell townsfolk continued to echo the same sentiments with less exuberance.

Hal Tremayne was prepared like everyone else to stay out on the moors all night if need be, until the last fire had died out. His heart swelled, knowing he was truly a part of all this. He was among the clay folk that he loved. His wife's hand was tucked tightly in his. He was home.

—

At Killigrew House Morwen was having very different thoughts about feelings of contentment. She was far from comfortable. Her pains had begun early that day, but she had said nothing to anyone until it became clear that it was going to be a long exhausting time before anything happened.

Nurse Wilder looked at her at intervals throughout the day, and said that since the waters had broken early, the birth was almost certainly going to be a dry one.

The thought filled Morwen with apprehension, and by late evening, she was threshing about on the bed, while Ben wiped the beads of perspiration from her face and neck, and muttered that it surely should not be like this, and perhaps the nurse needed assistance... He heard Nurse Wilder say crisply that there was no earthly need for Doctor Pender to be here, and she would be the first to send for him if the need arose. This was a perfectly normal birth, and Morwen was strong and healthy...

Ben gritted his teeth and tried not to flinch when she gripped his hands so tightly he thought she would stop his circulation. The midwife had given Morwen a twisted towel to bite on, but it was Ben's strength that she needed.

'I never thought the pain would be so cruel, Ben!' she gasped out as the next searing contraction subsided.

Each time it came it carried her high to a peak of agony she had never known before. And each time the pain enveloped her, she remembered Celia. It was uncannily as though Celia was there beside her, wanting to share the pain, yet unable to relieve her of one fraction of it.

In a way Morwen could never have put into words, her own pain was a kind of exorcism for what she and Celia had done. They had rid Celia of an innocent, unwanted child...

That faraway time kept flashing in front of her eyes, and yet it was as though she saw it all through a mist. She was still holding Celia, as she had done so tenderly then... but was it now that Celia was supporting her? She was too muddled to know, but now she knew Celia's pain, and was part of it at last.

'Hold on, my brave girl.' Ben's voice was hoarse with his own emotion. 'Nurse Wilder says it can't go on very much longer. The baby will soon be born, and you'll forget the pain once you hold our child in your arms.'

'I don't want to forget!' She mumbled the words through dry lips. 'As long as I remember the pain, it will remind me how much this baby was wanted, dar. I don't expect 'ee to understand what I'm saying—'

He wiped her face with a damp cloth, his hands gentle on her burning flesh. There was a shake in his voice as he spoke.

'Perhaps I do, my Morwen. Ramble as much as you like, as long as you come back to me from wherever it is you've gone.'

God, but he would give anything to spare her this. He could hardly bear to see her in such agony on this bed where they had loved so gloriously. For the first time, Ben was truly afraid of losing her...

Nurse Wilder came into the room, lifted the bedcovers to take a look at Morwen's progress, and shooed Ben out of the room.

''Tis women's work from now on, Mr Killigrew, and 'tis best that the missus and me get on with it alone. You go downstairs and get ready to wet the baby's head when 'tis all over. I promise you it won't be long now, and it's all coming along nicely.'

She spoke as though it was a rabbit stew coming to the boil, Ben thought irritably. Her manner was clearly meant to dispel a troublesome husband's worry, and send him away where he could be more usefully employed.

The strongest men had been known to faint after their insistence on seeing a child born to prove that it wasn't switched at birth, and besides, Nurse Wilder had never been in favour of the idea. The indignity of childbirth was best left to those who could face it.

Ben could hardly wrench himself away from Morwen, yet neither could he bear to stay. Her beautiful black hair was spread about her like rats'-tails on the white pillow, her face was swollen and distorted with pain, yet she was still more dear to him than anything in the world.

He bent swiftly to kiss her, regardless of Nurse Wilder's scolding. As he let her go, Ben felt as though he left most of himself behind in that large lonely bed.

He went downstairs and poured himself a large glass of brandy. He needed it. His hand shook, and he thought grimly that women were the strong ones after all. His thoughts were scrambled. He should go and tell his father that the birth was imminent, but he found the moments too private to share.

Somewhere in the house, he heard the faint sounds of laughter from the other children. He prayed humbly that his own child would be as whole and healthy as those three. He didn't often pray, but suddenly Ben Killigrew found that his eyes were tightly closed, and a plea for his beloved wife's safe deliverance came from somewhere deep inside his soul.

–

The celebration fires still burned brightly as dusk began to enhance the moorland scene. The flames leapt skywards, and townspeople far below stood outside houses and taverns and looked upwards to enjoy the spectacle. And many wished they had been born with the same lack of inhibitions as the clay folk. Peace had made victors of them all.

To the sounds of such rejoicing, Justin James Killigrew was born. He cried lustily as he came into the world, beating his small fists in the air as Nurse Wilder turned him upside down and smacked his bottom.

'You have a fine boy, Mrs Killigrew! He's a fighter already, by the looks of un, and the spit of his Daddy. And with all the cheering all over Cornwall to welcome un, I'd say he was born under a lucky star!'

Morwen turned her head towards the nurse, the exhaustion of the birth miraculously beginning to leave her at the longed-for words. And with it went all the bad memories... for one poignant second she imagined Celia's smile. It was contented at last. And just as suddenly, the image faded and was gone.

Morwen held out her arms for the baby, hers and Ben's, and gazed down on the perfect little face, to make the acquaintance of her son. His eyes were open, and they were deepest blue Tremayne eyes. But his downy hair was lighter than her own, the rich deep brown of his father's.

A smile of pure joy lit Morwen's face as she touched the baby's velvety skin. She put her lips to his cheeks and whispered a soft hello. The moment was enough to send a lump to Nurse Wilder's throat, who had seen it all before.

'Once you're tidied, I'll let your husband bring the other babbies in to see 'ee, Mrs Killigrew,' Nurse Wilder said briskly. 'They've been plaguing to see their new brother or sister, so mebbe now we'll all get some peace! And once all's in order, I'll send someone to let Doctor Pender know the babby's arrived safely. He'll be here to see 'ee now 'tis all over.'

She couldn't resist a small sniff. Doctors! What did they know about birthing, the time when you really got to understand the heart and soul of a woman?

And this one... this brave and beautiful one... had spirit enough for ten men. Nurse Wilder, who thought little of the male species, thought it a shame that they even had to be involved in producing such a picture as this.

When she had got things all tidied-up to her own satisfaction and not before, she gave a small nod, as Morwen sat up in bed with the blanket-wrapped child in her arms, impatiently awaiting Ben and the children.

Nurse Wilder called down the stairs, where Ben was having a difficult time in keeping the children still once they had heard the baby cry.

'Is everything all right?' he asked roughly.

'If a fine and lusty son is what you would call all right, Mr Killigrew—'

She got no further, as Ben rushed past her with Primmy in his arms, taking the stairs two at a time. The boys raced ahead of him, too excited to wait downstairs. Ben reached the bedroom, and Primmy struggled to be out of his arms, trotting across the room towards the bed on her uncertain little legs.

The three of them peered into the face of their new brother, awed into sudden silence. And Ben stood at the bottom of the bed for a moment longer, while they had their fill. His heart was full, knowing that everything he ever wanted was here.

It was a little tableau he wanted to imprint in his memory for ever. Morwen leaning over the baby with her long black hair caressing his tiny cheek; the three children that were Sam's and theirs, flushed with excitement; Morwen's sudden awareness as she looked towards Ben, and the fulfilment in those incredible blue eyes; and the love they shared, as endless as eternity.

Ben wasn't a man to whom tears came easily, but emotion threatened to overcome him at that moment, seeing the five of them so united in love. This was his family… Morwen stretched out her hand towards him, wanting to draw him into the circle.

And to Ben, she had never looked more beautiful.

The Cornish Clay Sagas